THE DAYS OF MIRACLES AND WONDERS

THE DAYS OF MIRACLES AND WONDERS

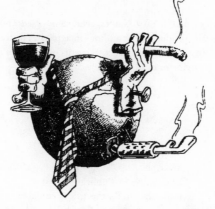

Simon Louvish

CANONGATE

First published in the UK in 1997 by
Canongate Books Ltd, 14 High Street, Edinburgh EH1 1TE

First published in Canada by Somerville House Books,
a division of Somerville House Books Limited,
3080 Yonge Street, Suite 5000, Toronto, Ontario M4N 3N1

Jacket illustration © Chris Brown

Cataloguing-in-Publication Data
A catalogue record for this title is available
upon request from the British Library

ISBN 0 86241 666 3

PRINTED AND BOUND IN CANADA BY FRIESEN PRINTERS

*The publisher acknowledges subsidy from the Scottish Arts Council
towards publication of this volume*

In memoriam—
Tim O'Keeffe,
The Good Publisher

Other books by Simon Louvish

A Moment of Silence

The Therapy of Avram Blok

The Death of Moishe-Ganef

City o f Blok

The Last Trump of Avram Blok

Your Monkey's Shmuck

The Silencer

Resurrections from the Dustbin of History

What's Up God?

Contents

Prologue
God's Little Acre **1**

Book One:
The Asylum: or, Going Mad in the Post-Communist World **17**
ONE   At Drem Station **19**
TWO   Blessed Are the Hungry **38**
THREE   The End of the World or Whatever **53**
FOUR   A Flexible, Nested Set of Fields **74**

Book Two
The Pillars of Society **93**
FIVE   Ragged Edges **95**
SIX   Sandworm Holes **115**
SEVEN   Shut up and Soldier On! **125**
EIGHT   The Loneliness of the Long-Distance Templar **144**
NINE   The Operating Theatre **169**
TEN   The Peristaltic Waves. Just a Short Ride to Victory **189**

Book Three
Waiting For The Apocalypse **213**
ELEVEN   Guilty as Charged **215**
TWELVE   The Mirrors of the I **226**
THIRTEEN   Genetic Deceptions **249**
FOURTEEN   Come on, Angel, Flap Your Wings… **268**
FIFTEEN   Inadequate Fulfilments **283**

Book Four
Asia After The Rain **313**
SIXTEEN   Riders of the Sky **315**
SEVENTEEN   Systemic Delusions **330**
EIGHTEEN   The Annals of Gilgamesh **343**
NINETEEN   Angels Arise! **363**
TWENTY   The Promised Land **382**
TWENTY-ONE   Dead Heat in the Home Stretch **398**
TWENTY-TWO   The Persistence of Memory **416**

A Glossolalia and Timeline **435**

PROLOGUE

God's
Little
Acre

WHEN RICHARD THE LIONHEART DIED, STRUCK BY A CROSSBOW BOLT during a minor siege of the castle of Châlus-Chabrol in the Limousin, his heart was cut out and taken to the cathedral at Rouen; his entrails were removed, preserved in vinegar, in a jar, and taken to the Abbey of Charoux, near Poitiers; and the rest of his body was taken to the Abbey of Fontevraud, near Chinon, for interment. But, after a while, his restless nature asserted itself, and he rose from the vault in which his remains had been placed, to walk about the cloisters, chapel and kitchen of the abbey, dressed in a friar's grey robe, his brow furrowed in thought, his hands clasped behind him, as he struggled, in his mutilated state, to make sense of his life, his battles, his desires and the general apathy of the Creation.

Eventually, he grew tired of the peaceful tranquillity of the cloisters and made his way up the hill, past the midday trippers and the Lazarus Chapel, out the southwest gate of the complex into the rue Saint-Lazare, following its curve into the marketplace, thronged, on a brilliant spring day, with tourists clutching their souvenir booklets, road-maps and Michelin guides. It was a Thursday, and the local townspeople were out in force, besieging the stalls of the cheesemongers, greengrocers, butchers, bakers, fishmongers, potters and postcard salespersons; the housewives and husbands were cramming plastic shopping bags with long sticks of bread, cheeses, cold meats and frozen chickens, tinned bouillabaisse and fresh carp, carrots, cauliflowers, cabbages and corn.

The pungent smell of goat cheese propelled him past the crowded stalls, by the moss-grown walls of the old enclosure, into the Fontevraud shopping mall, the department stores, post office, souvenir shops and cafés almost blocked by the parked tourist cars. He skipped hurriedly to avoid a braking BMW and maneouvred his way into a plastic chair by a table at the Café des Amis, protected from the sun by a bright red-and-white-striped awning. The café was crowded with the visitors who had come from the four corners of the earth to marvel at the ancient abbey's Royal Tombs. The father, Henry II Plantagenet. The mother, Eleanor of Aquitaine. The son, minus some vital organs. And also stocked, in gold urns in the crypt, were the hearts of Richard's brother John "Magna Carta" Lackland; of John's third wife, Isabelle of Angoulême; and of their son, Henry III, who reigned from the age of nine for more than half a century.

Tourist jabber wafted and waved. At the next table, to his left, a white-shirted young man with golden hair, golden beard and two enormous gold earrings purred softly at two healthy young girls in yellow and blue T-shirts balancing cigarettes between their fingertips. To his right, a heavy-thighed German couple held two golden children in a vice-like grip of large brown palms. The waiter, a cheerful black-haired young lad in a striped apron, sauntered up.

"Alors, m'sieu?"

Richard chose the Sandwich Jambon and Tomato Salad and settled down to watch the cruisers dragging Main. Germans, English, Japanese, Dutch, Swedes, and French families from the urban north, the world's *petite bourgeoisie* tripping along the Châteaux trail. Châtillon, Loches, Tours, Chinon, Saumur, Fontevraud L'Abbaye. Relics of fallen empires, ploughed battlefields and remaindered wars. Bleached bones, dried-out and disappeared tendons and sinews of old warriors and youths who never became old warriors. Sacked villages, ashes of peasant huts burned with their inhabitants inside; the dead echoes of the cries of men, women, children, the bleating of farm animals driven off by maces, crossbows, lances; smoke rising to the blue sky, the crackle of flames; the tolling of church bells, the massed chiming of chain-mail, the clank of mounted knights, the metal charge, the flash of swords in the sun, the splintering of skulls,

2

the severing of arms. The blood, seeping into the soil. The captives, led off in chains for ransom and profit, mere assets in the knightly game of human supply and demand.

And once he has entered the fray let each man of high birth think of nothing but the breaking of heads and arms; for it is better to die than to be vanquished and live . . .

"Medic! Medic!"

The army sawbones swoop, splatter. Gangrenous limbs litter the field. Wine poured in open wounds. Invocations of God, the Father, the Mother. Priests intone what comfort they can. Saints stand and scratch on pillars, which grow higher and higher, till the shouts below are not heard.

A flight of military Mirages, training, cuts through the Angevin sky. The king's jaws work methodically through the fresh bread, butter and ham. The teeth bite, the tongue propels morsels down the gullet, to the emptied maw. To his right, a dark, moustached man of wiry build and a thoughtful if mischievous look, and a petite, lightly freckled red-headed woman, both appearing to be in their mid-thirties, approach and sit at an available table. The man's eyes meet the king's gaze briefly before he turns to hold, with a transitory air, his companion's hand, on the table top, as if unsure whether their moment of rest in the sun will endure.

Dust to dust. The earth moves, a gentle rocking. King Richard's eyes close, the last morsels of ham sinking, the eyelids heavy with old dreams. Memories and hopes. Unrequited desires and passions. Failed ambitions and vanities curtailed. Home is the sailor, home from the sea, and the hunter . . . ? So much fatigue. The old warrior, eviscerated. No heart, no guts. No more glory.

And nevertheless . . .

The deep-blue sea, the deep-blue sky. A ship moves upon calm waters. The morning mist scatters, revealing the battlements and towers of a fortified port, and a vessel, flying the flag of the King of France, closing in on the harbour. The King of England's ship approaches, his master mariner hailing the French vessel. Bales of hay, herds of sheep and goats, casks of grain, the odour of round cheeses and the unmistakable contours of siege machines. A Saracen supply ship sailing under false colours. The King orders the galleys into action. The sailors grapple and board. Hand to hand with sword and axe among the bleating sheep, the squeaking pigs, put aboard to fool the blockading Franks. The Crusaders, fresh to their first battle, prevail. The Arab captain scuttles his ship to prevent his supplies falling into enemy hands. First blood for the Lionheart, at the walls of Acre, the city taken by the sultan Saladin four years before, A.D. 1187, as a prelude to the defeat and capture of Christian Jerusalem . . .

The Cross, the Crescent. Monks stamped the village squares of England, France, the Holy Roman Empire and beyond, carrying garish painted images of the Messiah struck down by a mailed Saracen fist. A mounted Saracen knight standing over Golgotha, his horse urinating on the Saviour's tomb. The call to arms. The battle for the abrogation of the Judaeo-Islamic plot. At the grand Cathedral of Tours, the King of England took the cross, below the unblinking gaze of Apostles and Saints and the Nazarene in person, and pledged to liberate the Holy Land. But on the way, at Messina, he was overcome one day by the unexpected weight of his sins. Secular slaughter, venality, fornication. He scourged his skin with sheaves of thorns. But the burden would not lift. In Sicily, still wracked by the guilt, he summoned the eminent hermit Joachim of Fiore, who walked, across the sea, from Calabria, to explain to the King, at the mouth of a cave by Mount Etna, the true revealed pattern of History: There were three ages — the Age of the Father; the Age of the Son, and of the Spirit; the Third Age, the apex of History, to which all events were leading. An Age of Love, Freedom and Hope in which God would be revealed to every human heart. But for this to be achieved, the persecutors of the church would have to be driven from God's city, Jerusalem. "It is God's will," the hermit said, "that all this be brought about by your actions. God has chosen you as His Hand of Glory."

The heart, the entrails, the right arm. The tools of manifest destiny. And thus Richard joined the Frankish besiegers of Acre, who had been bombarding the port for eighteen months. In Sicily he had constructed a great siege machine, "Mategrifon," which, stored in sections aboard ship, was rebuilt facing Acre. The French king, Philip, the Templars and the Hospitallers had their own machines in place: "Malvoisin," the Malicious Neighbour, and the towering height of "God's Own Sling."

The King of England was tall and powerfully built, with flaming red hair and deep-blue eyes. He had been at war since early adolescence. The Arabs watched his coming with fear, as the Frankish knights cheered, lit fires into the night, sang hymns and war songs. *Malik al Inkitar.* The Sultan, Salah ad-Din Yusuf, Saladin, wept bitter tears, in his camp outside the city, as he saw the mangonels and weaponry brought ashore, and realised the city of Acre could not withstand this power. The Arab garrison within was doomed. But still they fought on bravely, hurling by catapults, from within the walls, the pots of deadly "Greek fire," an early napalm, which burned on impact and could not be doused. Only hides soaked in urine and vinegar could protect the wooden siege towers. But Richard's engineers burrowed deep below the city walls, sinking shafts which they then filled with brushwood and set alight to weaken the supports above. Section after section, the walls fell. The moats between filled with rubbish, stones and the piled bodies of the dead, over which the invaders crossed. "God's Own Sling" hurled fire back into the fort. On 11 July, A.D. 1191, the port of Acre fell to the Crusade.

The Arabs mourned, and the Crusaders celebrated, that night. But already, in the midst of the battles, the King of England had begun negotiations, through intermediaries, with the Sultan, Saladin, which he continued throughout his campaign. Messengers were sent to the Sultan's brother, al-Adil, probing for terms of settlement. The Sultan sent back gifts of fruits and of snow from Mount Hermon, to cool the King's parched summer. Grace and chivalry prevailed while the foot-soldiers clashed and died. Blood, blood, blood. The Franks' demands were the release of all their prisoners in Arab hands, the return of the True Cross captured at the Horns of Hittin four years earlier, and the surrender of Jerusalem. The terms finally agreed upon, on the surrender of the garrison, but without the Sultan's permission, were: the ceding of the fortress, all its weapons and equipment, 200,000 dinars, all the Frankish prisoners in Saladin's hands, and the True Cross, in return for the lives of the 3,000 defenders. The Frankish banners were unfurled over the mosques and minarets.

The red-haired king had triumphed. Yet Saladin delayed fulfilling the terms he had not authorised. Money was not paid, the True Cross held back. Richard fretted, anxious to press his advantage. The army was poised to march south, to Jaffa, on its advance towards the Holy City. On the afternoon of the 20th of August, 1191, 27 Rajab 586, the 3,000 Moslem prisoners were marched out of the port into the plain between Tel Keisan and Tel al-Adiyyah. There the Christian knights, swordsmen and foot-soldiers fell upon them and butchered them where they stood, with swords, axes and lances, until not one remained alive. Men, women and children were slaughtered that day, their cries piercing the hot summer sky.

"What choice did I have?" Richard cried aloud in his anger, pounding the café table. The waiter, who was laying his tray of coffees and *croque-monsieur* sandwiches down for the couple beside him, was startled but managed to balance his burden, while the other tourists looked round in alarm.

What could I do? War is War, not a bloody picnic, and those of faint hearts and weak livers should stay home, tending their gardens. I had to move on, on, on! The Saracen king had broken his word! And he had no cause to complain. Had he not, at the Horns of Hittin, when his armies routed Guy of Lusignan, Raymond of Tripoli and Reynald of Châtillon, capturing all three with the cream of the Frankish knighthood, ordered the massacre of all the captured Knights of the Temple and the Hospital? The flower of Christendom in Outremer, put to the sword, not a single one was spared.

"I was a man of my time," Richard said, aloud. The customers of the Café des Amis nodded, soberly. So are we all. Richard smiled apologetically at the waiter, motioning him with his finger. "Un double."

The smoke of the cooking-pots rose from the valleys. The sprawling camps of the contending forces, spread over miles of plain and beach scrub. The massive Saracen city of tents, at Shafr'amr, housed more than a hundred thousand souls. Foot-soldiers, wives, children, cooks, fletchers, blacksmiths, engineers, not to speak of the Turcoman archers and their steeds. In the Crusader camp, an almost equal number, swollen by the loose women of Tyre and Sidon coming down to entertain the expeditionary troops. Painted women, with bangles and jewels in their navels and hair, eager to do business and accumulate valuable foreign specie. But the rutting could only be short-lived. Men must fulfill their duty to God.

Life is onerous, brutish and short, but magnificent! Who could say other-wise, as one watched the troops, now unencumbered by prisoners, march on towards Jaffa . . .

Some comments on military strategy: It is imperative, when marching one's army in hostile territory, to deploy the proper defensive configura-tion. I arranged the troops in three main divisions, the entire host hugging the coastline, with the sea and our fleet protecting that right flank. One part of the foot-soldiers marched between our mounted knights and the sea, keeping them fresh to reinforce the second section, marching between ourselves and the hinterland, which was swarming with the Saracen horse-men. The essential strategy to keep close order and avoid provocative assaults by the Moslems from breaking up our phalanx. The Turcoman horsemen, lightly clad and mobile, harassed us, charge after charge, shoot-ing off their bows at close quarters, though our soldiers' chain-mail pre-vented casualties, so that we often remarked on the somewhat humorous look of our foot-soldiers bristling with arrows like so many hedgehogs, but still keeping the discipline of the march. Nevertheless, the ferocity of the attacks forced us to peel off sections both of foot and of horse to press the Turcomans back to their camps. At the end of the day we had to stop and fight them, at Arsuf, where Saladin deployed a vast army on the plain coming out of the pine and cypress forest. I knew this battle would be decisive, so placed the Templars and Hospitallers, our most seasoned knights, in the vanguard and the rear. In the main force, the knights of King Guy of Lusignan, and my own men of Breton and Anjou, bearing the dragon standard. The Turcomans charged towards us, their banners and flags flying, but we held firm, revealing the iron determination of our knights to overcome impetuousness and impulse. Then, as stout hearts and rising blood decreed, two knights of the Hospital broke forth, and I, seizing the time, hastened to call up the charge. The Frankish knights, armoured upon their fortified steeds, the banners, the pennons, the crash of our onslaught, the turf flying beneath the horses' hooves, the massed lances. Our cavalry charge, calculated and withdrawn until the right moment, sweeping all opposition before us, on that day of glory.

Dust, ashes and burnt earth. Only memory survives. We took Jaffa, whose walls Saladin had destroyed in his retreat, lingering there, among the orchards and gardens, pomegranates and persimmons, as the summer heat gave way to autumn. I had decreed, as I had since setting out on this mission, that the only female personnel to accompany the expedition would be the washerwomen and cooks. But men's appetites are ever eager. Down from Acre and Tyre came the women, a ravening horde of harlotry and lasciviousness, sapping the men's strength and will. I, too, could not make my lizard rest. It darted and played, in the enchanted caves. I was enraptured, and enticed, too, by the miracles and wonders of the Orient, the gateways of Faith, the seven pillars of Wisdom, the visions and revelations of the Saints: The Holy Lance in the dreams of Peter Bartholomew, the sacred places of the prophets and seers, the holy footsteps of Christ, the divinity and the numenon, which resound far beyond the limited canons of the Church. The foundations of mystery, the gnosis that awaits the pure in blood and heart.

Now my heart is in a jar in Rouen and my entrails, too, gone, so that the café food and beverage sloshes uselessly about my empty stomach. Jaffa. The town in which Saint Peter had his vision of tolerance of the uncircumcized: *And I saw a certain vessel descend, as it had been a great sheet, let down from heaven by four corners, upon the which, when I had fastened mine eyes, I saw four-footed beasts of the earth, and wild beasts, and creeping things, and fowl of the air.* And God commanded Peter to slay and eat these creatures, which were forbidden by the Hebrew Law, for God said: *What God hath cleansed, thou canst not call unclean.* For it is God, and not Man, who is the true Law, and those to whom He speaks are true.

And from Jaffa, Jonah took ship, to flee from the presence of the Lord. But the Lord would not release Jonah from the embrace of His commands.

I sent away the impure women. I ceased my banter with the infidel Sultan, my offers of cease-fires and alliances, my pleas of the impoverishment of the country by the pestilence of wars. Peasants dispossessed, women widowed, children orphaned, fields laid waste. Inflation, devaluation and ruin. One weeps, but one cannot abandon the True Path. The mystery and glory of Jerusalem, a Lady of the Lake that could not be ignored. I marched on, from Jaffa towards the Holy City. Choirs of angels led me on my way. Rays of sun, beaming from the heavens through the scudding dark clouds, bathed our heads in balls of light. But a premature winter bogged us down, slowing our advance, so that we seemed to move sluggishly through an ocean of mud. The Turcomans continued to harass us, but I sallied forth on my patrols, never failing to bring back at least two or three heads to show our enemies were bleeding. Nevertheless, the army council decided to withdraw, before the storms of hail, sleet and torrential rain that slowed our advance to a crawl. I turned back, the angels shrieking in my head, whether lamenting or laughing I could not make up my mind.

Jaffa, Ascalon, Acre . . . Our quest bogged down in petty, mundane cares and squabbles . . . Provisioning, defence against disease, politics. I ached again to speak with my opponent. Saladin, Sultan of Egypt and the Levant, the warrior of another fearsome God. Who were these people, who laid down their lives as nobly and joyfully as any warrior of the Cross for their faith and their commander? I had the burden of our own "nobili-ty," the squabbling Lords of Outremer: A choice to be made between two kings — Guy of Lusignan or Conrad of Montferrat, the gallant loser or the fickle success. As men do, we chose the latter, only to find him struck down by assassins ten days later. Two men, in monks' habits, fell on him as he rode to dinner. They stabbed him and he escaped into a church, where they stabbed him again. Immediately they were caught and questioned, confessing that they were servants of the Old Man of the Mountain, Sheikh Sinan, sent from his far northern fortress at Masyaf.

No end to intrigue, in that country. We tore those men's skins from their bones. But they confessed happily, for they were assured of Paradise by their sinister lord. Imbibing a potent brew, they were shown images of enchanted gardens in which they would spend Eternity when they fell in the service of their master. They were feared by everyone in the East, for they regarded Saladin himself as an infidel, and he slept for years in a wooden cage guarded by his most trusted lieutenants, and even they, some tales told later, could not be vouched for in the end.

I was enmeshed in rumours. Since I had favoured Guy, some dared accuse me behind my back of Conrad's murder. I had to dispel the mists of confusion decisively and quickly. We gave the crown to Henry of Champagne, marrying him to Conrad's widow, Isabella, a lady happy to be shot of her grim spouse. Councils, politicians, monks' poisonous whispers. Throughout the world, they foul the air. But, in May, I was on the march again, taking the war south, to Darum. Nevertheless, there were messages from Europe, telling of the treacherous antics of my brother John. Now who would want a king's crown?

I had just one more chance to execute my holy oath. Up we marched in the June sunshine, from Ascalon towards the Holy Grail. Again, the choirs of angels. We reached Beit Nuba in five days. But I could wait no longer. I rode, with my best lieutenants, William of Barres and Mercadier, to the top of the hill of Montjoie, which looked out across the Valley of Aijalon, through the parting of the trees, over the brown, parched hills, to the walls and turrets which shone and glinted on the horizon.

Jerusalem! I thrust my shield up before my face, for I did not wish to look upon the City of my dreams unconquered. But the light burned, through my shield, and I cried out, as fire seared through my skull, and my companions had to support me as I dropped to my knees. I had seen, in that moment, the glowing, incandescent spark of what might otherwise have been. The numenon, flaring in a world beyond our fears and desires. The burning bush that cannot be consumed. But, like Moses, I was not to be allowed into my Promised Land. I would return, across the mountains and oceans, to a life of ordinary tribulations and travails. Captivity in my own exile, my purgatory, released after a year to the grind of small battles in my own lush, gentle lands. The mundane birthright, until Châlus-Chabrol, the crossbowman's dart.

No heart, no guts, no staying power.

The slow trudge back to Acre, in parched summer to the coast. The merciless sun of that country that gives no quarter to the weak. The troops, laden down with their baggage, armaments and disappointment at this second withdrawal from the goal. A convoy of sighs and frowns. In Jaffa, to perk us up, one final battle, as the Sultan conceived one last spurt to try to dislodge us from our gains. The cleaving of heads, the rending of limbs, the despatching of souls. Deeds of courage and nobility, carnage and desperation. Immediately after the battle I fell ill with a familiar distemper of campaigns. My hair and fingernails and toenails began to fall out. My mouth was full of boils. I sent to the Sultan for his snow and fruits but was told he, too, had been struck down. This country had exhausted us both, he, after a lifetime of struggle and strife, me, after a mere two years. We lay, in our separate beds, our deliriums comingling in an opiate sphere of hashasheen-like dreams:

We rode, together, alone, without our satraps, lieutenants or flag-bearers, up the melting, molten coastline. The sea, the dunes and beach scrub. Thorns tore the ankles of our steeds. Sweat poured down our necks into our chain-mail. The sun was at its merciless August peak. We reined in our beasts on a small hill overlooking the curve of the coast leading south. There, coming up from Gaza, we espied a mass, hazy as a Fata Morgana at first, but then hardening into a still shimmering army of men-at-arms marching north, dressed and appointed with apparel and weaponry that seemed to us wondrously strange. They marched in close order, sweating like pigs in thick woollen blue jackets, trouser suits and cloth hats, although without armour or mail. More than ten thousand strong, with a thousand more men at horse, they dragged after them forty massive metal tubes, borne on great wheeled carts. Camel trains of baggage and boxes followed in their wake, and each man appeared to carry, apart from the vast pack on his back, a thin, long tubular weapon, with a knife fixed at its end. Ahead of them rode an odd, impressive figure, a stumpy, bullet-headed man whose eagle gaze shone out from under a black, bicornered hat. His squat torso wrapped in a thick black cape under the sun, rather like those desert Arabs who absorb the intense rays in their clothes. We looked back towards Jaffa. A pall of smoke rose from the city, and the Sultan, whose gaze was more piercing than mine, pointed out to me the mounds of corpses the blue-clad army had left behind. "Another slaughter of prisoners," he said in his soft, sad voice. "The West, with its poisoned gifts again."

A strange bounty, indeed, hung on the saddlebags of the squat general's armies: astrolabes, compasses and measures and other instruments of science, with scribes on horseback scribbling on parchments, noting the progress of the horde. Camels bearing boxes of various plants, cages with the Levant's fauna — jackals and porcupines and hyenas, wild foxes and deer, even a brace of leopards, and smaller cages of birds: hoopoe and owls and griffons, hooded crows and sullen, trapped eagles. But one species they need not and could not cage — the vultures travelling over the host.

11

Onwards they marched, around the Carmel, to Acre. But the city stood unbreached before them, in the majesty of its walls. The Sultan nudged me with his arm, pointing out the Saracen flag and banners over the minarets and turrets behind the buttresses and embrasures. Clearly, command of these fortresses ebbed and flowed with fortune's tides. The pull and push of combat and politics, the constant recapture of old, blood-soaked ground. One would think the earth would be fertilised by so much human manure, but no, it remains parched as ever.

The city is surrounded on three sides by the sea. On its fourth, a massive ditch, running the entire land-length of the wall, protects the inner fort. The invading force bivouacked below this rampart and deployed its cannonades, firing large metal balls into the city by means of an explosive mixture. As a substitute for "Greek fire," they appeared to induce less terror and panic among the defenders, though they were heavy enough to crack the stone bulwarks. The French troops, for I could now hear their cries in the familiar, though somewhat degraded tongue, poured bravely into the breaches, and closed in hand-to-hand fighting with the Turks. Saladin and I, overlooking the affray, could hardly restrain ourselves from joining in. Our chargers pawed the earth, but their kings were too weary, the distemper still wracking our flesh. The little caped commander, spurring his horse, galloped ferociously up and down the line, urging his troops on and cursing his captains with all the verve of a born field general. A man after my own heart. Even Saladin, I could see, was impressed by that boundless energy. And valour, for the Turks were firing their own explosive charges at the invaders from the ramparts. Soldiers at the front of the assault were cut off and sur-rounded by the defenders, who decapitated them with their swords, dis-playing the severed heads on their lances, or flinging them by catapults into the midst of the invader's ranks.

Meanwhile, a miasmic wind was drifting up from the south: conta-gion of the plague, born in the rotting entrails of the dead the little general had left piled on the coastal plain. A foul breeze of mutilation and death, covering the contending armies like a shroud and striking down attacker and defender alike. Vast tent cities of the sick sprang up in the invading camp, and the putrid air reverbrated to the groans of the diseased and the dying, only partly drowned by the martial airs played by military musicians to lift their spirits, as doctors moved among the sick, distributing opium and hasheesh.

In vain the little general raved and roared. The Turks waved and laughed at him from the battlements, and blew, with vast cloth fans, the contagion of their own sick back into the attackers' camp. The lament of mourners nevertheless sounded from the cemeteries, mosques and minarets. The air of suffering and affliction was like a thick, dripping phlegm. The little general could not withstand it. He pulled and pushed at his drooping troops: "Cunts! Ladies in uniform! When did you last see your balls?!" Defeat does not bring out the best in men. Nor victory, often, for that matter. A character is tested in extremes. The entrails burn, but the heart, does that beat true?

The little general could not prevail. He gathered his troops, his sick, his wounded, his dejected horde, and marched back south, abandoning the walls. On foot, ceding his horse to an injured adjutant, he trudged away from his Zion. The remnants of his men of science, his botanists, his philologers and philosophers, his musicians and his scribes, dragging their bleeding feet through the midsummer sands. The burning wind slapped and scraped at their faces. The gathering dead shrouded and pushed out to sea. The Turkish banners drooping but unstruck on the walls of Acre.

The tentative couple had risen from their café table and wandered off in the direction of the abbey. The T-shirted girls had deserted the golden-haired young man, but he remained, his white shirt dimming in the lengthening afternoon shadow. The German family had been replaced by a short, stocky man of Mediterranean appearance, dressed in an expensive-looking suit and tie, accompanied by two tall, casually dressed men, in dark glasses. The stocky man eyed me strangely. Exhaust fumes from the arriving and departing cars were taking their toll on my lungs. I called the waiter and settled my little slips of bills, using the small purse of notes and coins I had taken from the abbey exhibition's cash desk. I rose and walked back up the Fontevraud high street, against the flow of the returning tourists, but the short man and his tall companions also rose and followed at a distance.

Home, home! Remembering that endless post-Crusade journey, the long trek through the enemy zone of Germany, incognito, with none but my most trusted lieutenants, disguised as pilgrims, with our tattered scrip, our faded staffs of poverty. But a king cannot be hidden under rags. Discovery, capture, imprisonment in the dark castle overlooking the Danube. Hostagedom and the long bargaining and raising of ransom. Ironic to know one's price: 100,000 marks. (And what might that be in current coinage, dollars, ecus, francs?) While throughout the kingdoms and dukedoms of Europe, armies moved on like pawns on chessboards.

One year, six weeks and three days. And then, the old war games again — England, Normandy, Anjou and Aquitaine . . . the criss-cross paths of intrigue. Castles besieged, walls breached, the crushing of heads and arms, the courage of yeomen, the cowardice of kings, a brother's perfidy. One tries so hard, one gallops so far, rushing from point to point, shoring up the weak elements, hardening the crumbling foundations, lifting dejected spirits, striking fear in the unworthy, blessing one's friends, damning one's enemies. When will it ever end?

Châlus-Chabrol: The crossbowman's arrow. The sawbones came, and busied about my shoulder. Hack hack hack, cut cut cut. Pain. I wished I had kept with me some of that potion the hashasheen used to glimpse Paradise. Instead I just lay there, dying. I forgave the crossbowman who shot me, and commended him on his initiative and marksmanship. I tried my luck with some of the lusty Limousin wenches. My doctors cried that I was only hastening the end. I said: Better a sweet end than a dry. The wound turned rotten, suppurating. I smelled the stench of my decay. My mother came and sat by my deathbed. She brought me priests, to whom I confessed my sins. That seemed to go on for ever. Enough of all that. I closed my eyes. I saw my coronation, felt the anointing oil on my bare breast. *Not all the water from the rough rude sea can wash the balm from an anointed king.*

The three strange men were still following. I paused, at the top of the hill. The sprawling bulk of the old abbey complex. The restored monasteries, the great church's apse and belfry, the cloisters, quadrangles and chapter house, the rebuilt Romanesque kitchen, its pungent memories and echoes. Six hundred years of Tradition, Faith and Power. In 1561, the Huguenots attacked and desecrated the abbey, but it was not until Anno

Domini 1792 that the chain was snapped when the Revolution suppressed the Order, scattering the monks and transforming the entire edifice into a prison for *les malheureux de ressource*. The Convent of Saint Madeleine become a smoke-belching factory and a workshop, where the inmates toiled to pay for the New Order killing and ravaging to survive outside its walls. One can read all about it in a brochure one picks up at the abbey entrance, a neat package of recycled tumult, discord and disarray.

Death, the old man on the clapped-out nag. The seer hermit of Calabria. The three ages — the Father, the Son, the Spirit. The Age of Love and Freedom, when God will be revealed to every human heart. They cut out my heart, and my entrails, and put them in jars, and scattered them about France. They hoped I would never be whole again. God's Will, the severed Hand of Glory.

Ebb and flow. Sturm und Drang. The light and the dark. They could have at least told me the future, but instead I have to read about it in *Le Monde*. Fontevraud remained a prison for almost two hundred years, until 1963 — one year after Algerian Independence, the country exhausted from a decade of colonial wars, incipient military rebellion, terrorism and dissension. New voices and images. A new/old spectre haunting Europe, crowds marching up and down the great grid of Paris, filling its alleyways, armed with its cobblestones. New Holy Grails, just out of reach.

"CE N'EST QU'UN DÉBUT, CONTINUONS LE COMBAT!"

But all this, too, will pass.

I stepped back into the main church transept, but the three men still followed me inside. I paced along its hundred-foot length towards the glassed-off crypt, where a dozen archaeology students crouched, in their youthful vigour, busy scraping the gravel floor with trowels. I stopped before the glass cases holding the Plantagenet Tombs, which, alas, merit only one star in *Michelin*. The recumbent effigy of my father, Henry II, clutching his rod of office. My mother, Eleanor, Queen of France and England, Duchess of Aquitaine, and Countess of Poitou and many other properties, holding, as if she had just fallen asleep under a bedside lamp, an open book made of stone. And my own tomb, the rod of office pointing from the stone beard to the groin. I read my epitaph:

Châroux, in Poitiers, her Duke's entrails guards,

His body, Fontevraud in marble shrines.
The Normans boast the King's unconquered heart.
Three countries thus the glorious ashes share
Of a King too great to rest in one alone.

Ashes are only ashes, after all. Bones are only bones. Blood only blood. Intestines and sinews dry and fade, even if preserved in vinegar. Memories, too, fail and warp and bend and malform down the faltering, twisting, misread, falsifying and forgotten paths of history.

The short, stocky man stood at my side, his two obvious bodyguards holding back about twenty feet behind us, out of earshot. He had a thin, carefully clipped moustache and dark brown eyes, the long-lashed lids continuously blinking. We both stood and looked into my grave.

"Richard the Lionheart?" he said, in French. "My name is Aziz Khamash, of Lebanon. I think we have a great deal to discuss."

BOOK ONE:

The Asylum;

or,

Going Mad

in the Post-Communist

World

ONE

At

Drem

Station

GOING MAD IN THE POST-COMMUNIST WORLD. IT'S MORE COMMON THAN you think, Doctor. I read this article in *The Sunday Crimes*, telling me there are two million dust mites living in the average British bed. At least, I thought, we are not alone. I took some comfort, I can tell you, in that fact. An entire small nation living underneath my arse. What am I saying? There are countries with just a fraction of that population which are represented at the United Nations. The Seychelles have a mere sixty-four thousand inhabitants, and they can throw their vote about with the worst. So my bed deserves at least a permanent seat at the Security Council. Little beasts beavering away at their mysterious dreams while I toss and turn. Building their homelands and their armies, sending out colonial expeditions to the farthest reaches of my limbs. Importing coal from my toenails, bitumen from my eyelids, sulphur from my nostrils and mouth. In the dead of night they call my name, murmuring their incomprehensible propaganda in my ears: Awake, Daniel Hohenlohe, failed scribe and mental patient, they mumble; time to climb out of the den.

The other night I, Daniel, had a singular dream. I was travelling along a narrow potholed road in Romania, between Tirgoviște and Ploești, in a clapped-out East German Trabant. The landscape was flat and bleak, blotched with vast piles of old tin cans and torn rubber tyres. Dead rabbits lay squashed on the verges. Suddenly there was a clatter in the sky, and a drab khaki-coloured chopper descended in a field just ahead of my dirt-encrusted windshield. The deposed President of the Socialist Republic, Nicolae Ceauşescu, and his wife, Elena, dressed in tattered furs, burst out of it, surrounded by a platoon of leather-coated thugs. Waving machine-pistols with silencers, they stopped my car with their steel-padded kneecaps and bundled the President of the Republic and his wife into the seat beside me. Three of the bodyguards then crowded into the back seat, pushed their weapons up against my neckbone, and spat: "Drive on, bastard!"

I drove on, in the direction of Ploeşti. This used to be prime oil-producing country, in the Second World War. I was not around at the time but the world was. Or so they say. There were five-hundred-bomber raids on the Ploesti oilfields, the entire sky darkened by khaki Lancasters, filled with Royal Air Force pilots and bombardiers, dressed in their sheep-skin Biggles jackets, waggling their ginger moustaches, and falling from the sky like so many burnt moths. What ho, cripes and whizzo prang! Ex-president Ceauşescu turned on my car radio and listened to the broadcasts from Bucharest. The rebels had taken over the radio station and were transmitting ecstatic accounts of the tyrant's overthrow and details of his profligate life: "He had seven hundred inscribed gold dinner-plate ser-vices! His Frigidaire was stocked with prime meat sausages! His wife bathed in Bourbon whiskey! They ate an aborted foetus every Sabbath!" The ex-president's head slumped on the dashboard, but his wife yanked him upright by the shock of his hair. She thrust a silver-plated Luger up my right nostril and placed her foot on mine, depressing the accelerator pedal. My Trabant droned on.

"We shall go up into the mountains!" said the ex-dictator, perking up, stabbing the air with a well-manicured finger." We will organise the peo-ple's resistance! The masses will once again flock to our flag! Partisans, we shall march to the drum beat of the people's hearts! Liberty, fraternity, and egality! Long live the Communist Party of Romania and its Great Archi-tect, my Exalted Self. Are you with us?" he asked, jabbing me in the shoul-der.

Luckily the Trabant chose that moment to run out of gasoline. "I know a petrol pump just up the road," I told the dictator. "Just wait here, I'll fill a jerrycan."

I trudged on, with an empty, but heavy, rusted old petrol can, leaving the ex-Benefactors and their goons to flag down a bewildered passing cyclist and pile aboard his back saddle. But to get back to the dust mites, Doctor. According to the newspaper they would inspire absolute terror if they were anywhere near our size, but luckily they are so small an entire convocation of them could hold a Nuremberg rally on the point of a pin. These are fellows who would obviously have no problem getting into the gates of heaven. They are, it appears, harmless, mindless and blind, borne every which way by the wind. Man is nothing but a parasite and a carrier, bearing his invisible universes with him wherever he goes. So how do I get to leave them behind, eh, Doctor? Answer me that, for God's sake!

I am not a doctor, he said, blinking at me through his dusty trifocals. His vision was split into the close, the middle and the far distance. It was not clear where I was positioned in the languid sweep of his gaze. His sparse greying hairs drooped towards his forehead and strained to escape from his ears. The coastal sea fog drifted between and around us, maroon-ing us in billows and wisps. There was an inevitable chill in the air, although spring was, as it were, at the door. I could see, faintly appearing and disappearing in the middle distance, the gangling figures of Glasgow trippers, refugees from the nearby caravan site, carrying folded deck-chairs as their bare feet slid and slipped on the rocks and pebbles towards the invisible beach.

Unclean! Unclean! Tinkling my leper's bell. I am supposed to be on an outing in the fresh air, getting away from the musky odour of The Retreat at Drem. Brightly painted little rooms, with melamine bookshelves, pos-ture chairs, daisy-chains of get-well cards and old honest landscapes of Scotland, with a quartet of daubs by the local artist, Bellany, on the walls of Andrew Mackenzie's office, huge bright-coloured things of staring eyes and crucified fish, just to make you feel you're not the only one around who is completely out of his or her box. There is a great, garish portrait of Mackenzie himself, just above his desk, his bearded jovial features wearing the inner contours of a tormented demon, with a hint of horns, sweating in some dilapidated ante-room of hell, hung with anatomical posters, the ubiquitous fish, tridents, nets, and an old, pinch-faced couple, all-purpose patriarchal avatars. Mackenzie had spurned an offer of thirty thousand pounds from the Tate Gallery in London to have the thing taken off his hands.

"Truth will out," he stated. "Ye can run, but ye canna hide."

Sweat pours down Ex-president Ceaușescu's chin. I know exactly how he feels. One moment the world's your oyster, the next you're tipped into despair. The globe rolls on, turning its face away from you, revealing the shaggy hairs of its arse. If you can tell the difference. Failure has many fathers, success is an orphan. Or is it the other way around?

From the subliminal to the ridiculous. The ex-dictator twists and turns. Outside the crowd fills the streets, having ripped the central Socialist symbol out of the national flag, marching down the previously empty boulevards, bellowing the national songs. From tunnels beneath the city, the maggots of the President's secret police crawl out, firing their automatic weapons at the rebellious armed forces. Battles erupt. Young and old, students and workers, climb aboard the army's tanks, bursting through the iron gates of power and privilege. Scenes from the iconography of our mutinous youth: the vengeance of the masses against *anciens régimes*. Only now it is the old revolutionaries who are being overthrown. I sit with my lifetime wife, Elena, on rickety wooden chairs facing a tribunal of my subordinates and underlings. They lambast me with imaginary crimes against the people. Horrific massacres and murders, grand larceny, treachery and betrayal. All their crimes are projected onto me. There is no point in arguing my case. I thump my fist, in vain. They pronounce sentence. I spread my palms. My wife just shrugs.

The firing squad. What else can we expect, for the arrogance, the hubris, of pretending to exist? Of trying to make one's mark. Look at this man facing me. The Doctor who is not a doctor. A lay healer. Mackenzie's assistant. This Doktor Blok, the trifocal man. I understand he was a lunatic himself, many years ago. The ultimate qualification for his task. Sitting on his plastic folding chair in front of me, twiddling with his clipboard, appearing and disappearing in the Lothian mist.

"The trick in carrying the past with us," he says, "is like the old child's question: What's heavier, a ton of feathers or a ton of lead? It's all a question of tension, of pressure, stress, strain and torque. Think of Salonican porters, who carry pianos on their backs up seven flights of stairs. You and

I can hardly lift the thing one inch. It's the old balance. Mind and matter. Body and soul. Light and dark."

Luckily, it's my mother who is paying for this. In the distance, a dog barks. It looms into view, chasing some metaphorical stick. Finding only us, it sniffs our ankles and returns, bounding, to its silent master or mistress, hidden out there in the fog.

Life and death. War and peace. Truth and lies. Love and carrots. Moussaka and beans. I once saw a sign on a pub blackboard: GOD AND CHIPS, £1.65. A volley of bullets, and the ex-dictator and his wife fall to the parade ground, lifeless. *Sic semper tyrannis.* But all my aches and pains are still here.

"Let's go back home," says Doktor Blok, lifting me by the elbow. Home! He is speaking of the Drem Retreat, of course. Haggis supper or meatballs Mackenzie, courtesy of the Bejam deep-freeze. The old nursing home, connected by its gravel umbilical to the rural heart of nowhere. Drem, of course, is Dream without the A. No aardvarks, abacuses, anchovies, adzes, aetiologies, aesthetics or acknowledgments, no agape or allegories, alligators or alternates. Only the dust mites, thriving in the follicles, pores, oxters and skin of the few lugubrious inhabitants in their small bundle of somnambulant houses, nestled up against the Scotrail station (schedules to Dunbar, North Berwick, Edinburgh) and practically nothing else. And down the road, in tepid isolation, we baker's dozen of apostles or inmates of Andrew and Rhona Mackenzie's convalescent home for the Depressed. No five-hundred-Biggles-bomber raids would shift us from our perch, as we shuffle down the corridors, nodding at each other, with the desperate air of survivors in the same lifeboat in the middle of the Atlantic Ocean. Which one of us is the Nazi spy? Pictures of God, snipped out of fashion magazines, float by on the oily waters, and now and again an old chair, a cuckoo clock, or a chipped plastic skeleton rocks queasily upon the waves. A smell of dried-up mincemeat sticks to the newly painted walls. And what is that whiff? Rice pudding? A couple of the older inmates are without teeth, or intestines for that matter. They clink dryly as they pass. "Top o' the mornin', cock!" I should not like to see its bottom then.

Twenty-five times a day, the Intercity Express clatters by, this way and that, its startled passengers looking out upon our fleeting dot. Mackenzie, who grew up in the area, on the coast, told me they used to paraphrase the Lord's Prayer, in his childhood: instead of Lead Us Not Into Temptation– Leave Us Not at Drem Station. It was a perverse reason to accept the post of director of this newly refurbished private sanctuary, out of sight and mind of local councils, whose machinations and cutbacks had forced the closure of his beloved hospital training school for the mentally handi- capped at Craddock, the patients wheeled away towards far and scattered destinations, the building itself sold off to the Department of Nuclear Energy to train asbestos-clad stooges for the post-Chernobyl age. The middle of nowhere, but with some viable escape. Colditz, handy for the Tube. Ruins of old minor castles. Churches of the Late Pointed Period gutted by the English, who, I am told, carried off the organs and bells. (Thanks God they left the Teachers.) Volcanic plugs holding down the muddy dank fields, as if gravity were not quite enough. An ancient earth- house, of prehistoric man: A mossy bump in the ground, into which one crawled to commune with the worms and the ghosts of ancient Celtic sto- ics. No graven images upon those walls. No totems, plenty of taboos.

" 'In the lonely glens or over the bare hill-tops of the Lammermuirs may be heard the cries of the curlew and the golden plover. Ring-ouzels haunt the burns, peregrine falcons prey on the grouse and rabbits, the pestilent rough-legged bustards reign over the moors till they fall victim to the gamekeeper. Merlins also are not unknown, and dunlins are known to nest. Herons are common all over the county and king-fishers haunt the reaches of the Tyne.'

"But that was a long time ago, laddie, and now we are left with noth- ing but the pestilent rough-legged bastards, bashing along on their motor- cycles, with nary a gamekeeper in sight."

Mackenzie, slapping down the old guidebook, lovingly caressing the Auchentoshan before decanting small doses into thimble-sized glasses.

"Slainte!"

The common-room, in the gloaming. Sharp returns of meatballs ris- ing from the oesophagus, escaping the lips in trills and burps, dancing round the drooping pates of the ingathered, night staff and clients unwise enough to have picked up the news of Drem isolation in an advertisement in the colour supplements of *The Observer* or *The Sunday Crimes*:

Mackenzie, in his best James Robertson Justice mode of mellow bonhomie and roll-top sweater; his wife, Rhona, deputy, partner and senior head-banger; Avram Blok, the world's most taciturn therapist, amanuensis and part-time insomniac. Matuszek, all-purpose bouncer and long-order cook, ex-Hearts-of-Midlothian goalie and now stuck between the goalposts of life. Emma Prideux, night nurse and keeper of the tablets. Mackenzie's cure prefers positive thinking, slaps on the back, dank Lothian air, after-dinner repartee with occasional drams and a complete withdrawal from television. We are to be bored back into association with the miracles and wonders of the outside world. And then the inmates, to whom one turns with a sinking heart: Lucy Mongolfier, cracked-up social worker, paralysed by the inability to decide; Mansur Darwish, multiply failed entrepreneur; Jimmy Gold, ice-cream-van man traumatised by occupational violence; Alois Crumb, ex-vivisectionist, drummed out of his career by animal-lib-erationists; old Maggie Mann, last surviving silent-film pianist in Scot-land, who has, at the age of eighty-six, developed delusions concerning the designs of Rudolph Valentino on her person. Finally, *ipso facto*, yours truly, Danny Hohenlohe, progenitor's name Pick, world's worst-selling author and confirmed manic-depressive. Absent, as usual, the three Watson brothers of Doncaster, who had booked in to cure their allergy to each other's company by common confinement, but who are too terrified of the rest of the world to show their dullards' faces downstairs. Shadowy figures moaning in the background of our narrative, like beggars vainly stretching out their empty, calloused palms in underlit underpasses.

"Your health!" Mackenzie greets one and all. "Did ye know, ship-mates, that even this forsaken backwater once echoed to the kettledrums of war? Cromwell, the bastard, beat the Scots at Doon Hill, just down the road. The Scots, with their usual foresight, had backed King Charles the Second. However, at Prestonpans, in 1745, the Jacobites . . . "

Saved by the front-door bell chimes. Enter Kathleen, Avram Blok's better half, a strong lass with short-cropped brown hair and an excellent pair of pins, who roams the coastline picking up lumber and flotsam and fashioning it into strange shapes which she exhibits in art galleries in Edin-burgh and Glasgow. I believe she has sold her junk to American, German and Japanese buyers, thus enabling her to keep up the mortgage on a crumbling seaside house on the outskirts of Craddock, a small town of eight videocassette shops and nine Protestant churches a few miles down-mist. There they live, she and the reticent therapist, in bucolic frugality, with the incoming tide lapping at their window, threatening to swamp their conjunctive repose. Once, Mackenzie apocryphally related, they were swept out to sea on their orthopaedic mattress, and had to be rescued by a shrimping trawler, whose crew, having heard their cries for help in the fog, wrestled them aboard with grappling hooks.

"Found the secret of life on the beach yet, hen?" asked Mackenzie.

"Not tonight, Andrew."

"Come and sit by the fire." Rhona pulls up another chair. The log fire is an illusion sustained by Scottish Gas. The Desolation, thought Hohenlohe, looking round at the gathering, each soul wrapped in its seclusion. Mackenzie eagerly proceeded to outline his latest intellectual fad, morphic resonance. He had picked this up from a book by a Cambridge professor of biochemistry, one Rupert Sheldrake, who had specialised in the physiology of tropical legumes in India. Having watched these legumes closely, the professor had developed a theory of "formative causation," whereby all nature consists of "morphic fields," which constitute a collective memory that determines, together with genetic coding, the shape and behaviour of all things, alive or inanimate. The persistence of memory, the squishy droop of Dalí's dripping watches. Does this reassure us? or return us to past despairs?

Excusing himself from Doctor Mackenzie's imminent exegesis, Danny Hohenlohe left the common-room and climbed the flight of pale-banistered stairs to his cubbyhole. He looked at his bed but could not bear to lie on it, imagining the two million dust mites bickering and feuding. Or worse, they might have built a harmonious society, of mutual aid and self-determination, a microscopic utopia: from each according to his ability, to each according to his, her, or its needs. Or did they prey upon each other, on invisible battlefields, in indiscernible Sommes and Verduns? Were there a million cries of unheard pain, under the bed linen?

He sat down at the bedside desk and opened the Document Wallet containing the unfinished manuscript so rudely rejected by his ex-editor, Gordon McTeague, of Hammer & Stern Publishers. The morphic resonance of abject failure. On either side of the walls, he could hear the filio-phobic Watsons tramping about like so many splintered Ahabs. He closed the Wallet and rose from his chair. Clasping his boots to his chest, he padded back down the stairs, tiptoeing through the kitchen, opening the back door. The windswept chill of Drem gusted in. Putting on the boots and choosing from the coat-pegs a tattered fur thing belonging to Alois Crumb, he stepped out, closing the door softly behind him, heading down the gravel pathway towards the distant lights of the neighbouring village of New Mains, with its single tavern, the Sheep's Head, three-quarters of a mile distant. No amenities at Drem apart from the post-office branch and Scotrail.) Trudging onto the deserted main road, the silence broken by an increasing drone, the echoes of the five-hundred-bomber raid, and the first ginger handlebar-moustached Englishman, in Biggles parka, falling burning from the sky, one brushes the burning corpse aside with one's foot. A lone motorcycle rushes by, one of the ragged-trousered bastards of Mackenzie's ire, heading from nowhere to nowhere.

Remembered days of glory: Publication week, millennia ago (or was it only two years?). Eager interviewers at local radio stations: "So tell me, where do you get your ideas?" "Uhh . . . " "Excuse me, we have to inter-rupt this interview for a newsflash: A naked man has broken into the Pet-O-Pamper in Widdlesham High Street and stolen several bags of birdseed at knife point. Residents are warned not to approach the man as he is armed and dangerous. And now back to our guest, Danny Hohenlohe."

"My ideas? I used to get them in an old Chinese hock shop on Orchard Street, Lower East Side New York. The proprietor was a very old man who had been an aide-de-camp to Chiang Kai-shek. He had been held by the Communist Red Army for thirty years in a cell, chained to a rabbi who had taken a wrong turning at Kasrielivke when fleeing from Denikin's White Hordes. Now he sold notions to novelists and short-story writers in little bottles and flasks. His name was Soong Yah Ong. His were the cheapest ideas in the city. If you wanted quality, you had to go Uptown, to Central Park West, to see a wizened old Wasp, Cornelius Van-derflopt the Third, who after sniffing your elbows, would decant you, pre-cious drops of nectar into little packets of gauze. Pulitzer Prize, National Book Award. But, from my man, you got all the more modest dross, stuff pawned by hacks who couldn't pay the rent, dusty old anecdotes, clapped-out notions, moss-grown narratives, *bobeh-mayses*. For a short-story concept you would pay between five and seventy-five cents, for the embryo of a novel anything between a dollar and five bucks. Ugly, seedy, squalid things they were too, squirming behind filthy smoked glass. When you uncorked the stoppers, you had to handle them with care, or you would lose them down cracks in the floorboards, skirting boards, mouseholes, ventilation ducts and drains."

Thank you very much, Danny Hohenlohe. And now, a man who juggles eels on his toes. Or, a Conservative politician. Or, the man whose new sound is beating at the eardrums of England. Butter them on toast, they all melt just the same. But, for a brief and vanished moment, the upturn: My short-story collection, *City of Schmucks*, in the stores. My editor, McTeague, brushing up his Kraut for his descent to the Frankfurt Bookfest, to reveal my wares, among the glut, to the world.

"Don't let 'em vomit on your tie, Gordon!"

"I shall keep beyond drooling range."

My friend Gurdun Pasha, off to save Khartoum from the pagans. But it is I who later got the spear in my back, coupled with the barbs of McTeaguean defiance: "All this self-pity, it's unattractive, Danny. Mental body odour, very pungent."

So how's that for a "morphic field," Doc? I can hear Mackenzie now, quoting Albert Einstein among the tropical legumes: *The individual feels the futility of human desires and aims and the sublimity and marvellous order which reveal themselves both in nature and in the world of thought. Individual experience impresses him as a kind of prison and he wants to experience the universe as a single magnificent whole . . ."* Speak for yourself, Albert. Morphic resonance returns us, claims Mackenzie's legume-sleuth, to the idea of a world with constantly evolving laws, rather than a Cartesian machine with eternally set rules. It's all of a piece with ecological fashions. Gaia, the living world, Walt Disney, anthropomorphic frogs et al. The burden of guilt, on aerosol sprays.

How do birds know how to fly south for the winter? How does new behaviour spread through a species? How do rabbits learn to say "What's Up, Doc?" Evolution, it's all around us. There are no more immutable atoms or even quarks. No certainty, just the dim roar of creation. In colossal cyclotrons, under the earth in deepest Switzerland, new particles that have not even been named by scientists appear out of nowhere, zapping back and forwards in time, confounding all traditional faiths.

Perhaps I should have joined Nicolae and Elena Ceauşescu in the Carpathian Mountains. Sitting with them in the freezing night, over a stealthy Primus fire, as she cooks up nettle roots and fungi in a small rusty pot. One bite of the poisoned apple, heh heh, and there is no cure for the SLEEPING DEATH! heh heh heh. The last three members of the Romanian Communist Party plot their return to total power. I coulda been a contender, I told Mackenzie, and whadid I get? A one-way ticket to Palookaville. And I have already been to Palookaville.

"You see — you found your way back," he said.

Go argue with a lapsed Presbyterian.

"So tell us about yourself, how did you get started? Why did you choose the name 'Hohenlohe'?" I always understood that everyone is famous for fifteen minutes. What I didn't understand then, in Widdle, Widdleshire, with the naked pet-shop thief gaining on me fast, was that that was it:

"Well, love, nobody could spell my original name, 'Pick'. Of course, the missing 'r' —— raccoons, roustabouts, riddles, ragamuffins, rigatoni. I was a sensitive Hebrew lad of North Wembley. Between Harrow-on-the-Hill and Church End. Ah, the thrill of it all! The kosher butchers, impaling each other on meat hooks in their vicious clan wars! But I lie. Nothing happened in my childhood. I was destined for a life of crashing mediocrity, but its achievement was fraught with peril. My mother wanted to marry the local mohel, but married Pick of Pick, Steradent and Fleisch instead. It was my first lucky break. The second was when, on return from the United States and total failure to place my work with the literary establishment, I was referred by an old schoolmate who had made good in the business to Gordon McTeague, at Hammer & Stern Publishers. An entrée to one of the prestigious houses of the land. McTeague professed delight in my book of short tales, and Shazzam! I sit before you now, the phoenix risen from its own ashes!"

Âllo! Âllo! Anybody there? Merely the whisper of the wind, the echo of the bomber-jacket raids, the jingle of the cosmos. It is difficult enough to figure out who one is, let alone anybody else. In one of my short stories, "Where Have All the Powers Gone?", a deceased science-fiction writer, publishing true tales from the beyond after his death, reveals that many world leaders were, throughout history, and continue to be, clones, put in place by the alien inhabitants of Procyon, in the constellation of Canis Minor, replacing the original human leaders, who were still alive, imprisoned together in an artificially maintained time-warp facility on Jupiter's moon Antaeus. Thus, Idi Amin Dada, Joseph Stalin, Lyndon Johnson, Adolf Hitler, Napoleon, Robespierre, Attila the Hun, Caligula, Tamerlane, and so on, all perfectly harmless and fun-loving specimens, were eking their lives out in a galactic bubble, playing Parcheesi and discussing Kierkegaard, while their clones kept the Earth in a state of perpetual fear and tension, so it could not unite in a World Government which would threaten the hegemony of the Procyonic Empire.

There should always be someone else to blame. Who is this infamous Architect, this Blind Watchmaker who fiddles with biological fate and providence? I am not the first or the last to ponder this question. Who is in charge? Or is there free will, after all? For I, too, cheered and wiped my tears with Kleenex when, on the television screens, the vital images of the collapse of tyranny strobed across the globe: The falling Berlin Wall, the massed keyrings of Prague, the budding of Budapest and Bulgaria, the bloody blooming of Bucharest, all the straw spilling out of the hollow men of old. And let the voice of Freedom roar!

McTeague encouraged me to go ahead and write my first novel. It would be called *Adult Single*, and take place entirely on an underground Tube journey between Hammersmith and Turnpike Lane. The book would be based on the most extensive research, for which I purchased a month's unrestricted Travelcard, going troglodyte beneath the city, observing the minutiae of the passengers, speculating about their lives, loves, hates, fears, dreams, nightmares. Their imagined perceptions of each other. Was it not R.D. Laing who said that my experience cannot be directly experienced by another, and vice versa. I cannot experience your experience. We are both invisible men (or women). But only experience is evident. Everything except experience is illusory. R.D. Laing's ideas went out of fashion, and they say he wandered about Glasgow, loaded and baying at the moon. So much for gurus. But can one truly tap into that great morphic field in which we troubled toil, or is everyone in the carriage an alien from outer space, or Belgium, delete the inappropriate.

Banalities, banalities. It's too far to the pub, thought Daniel. Another motorcyclist zips by, almost throwing him in the ditch, raising the spectre of a convention of ragged-trousered bastards in the Sheep's Dread tonight. Some resonances must be avoided. Danny turned back, bypassing the gravel driveway towards The Retreat and walking on towards the station. Clouds totally obscuring the moon. From the direction of the deserted station house he thought he heard tentative chords of music, or could it be the wail of the wind in the electric-railway wires? As he approached the low buildings, the sharp-angled new-built walkway, the sound resolved definitely into a wistful mouth-organ whine:

He stumbled past the empty car park, pressing himself against the wall of the station house, brushing past the peeling poster (SCOTRAIL PUTS SMILES IN YOUR JOURNEY). The lilting tune appeared to be coming from the far end of the railway platform. Daniel padded cautiously forward and moved his head carefully round the corner. In the shifting moonlight he glimpsed three men, two standing and one sitting on the bench, away down the platform's end. The embers of a cigarette glowed from one of the standing men, while from the lips of the man seated on the bench the doleful chords emerged. The digital platform clock silently flipped another minute past the hour. The cigarette smoke wreathed in the gloom, the embers lighting a dark, moustached, Middle Eastern face. The low guttural syllables of an unknown language floated and dipped from his lips. The other man looked at his watch. The mouth-organ continued its anthem. Then it merged with the humming of the rails.

The train approached, from the direction of Edinburgh. A local Sprinter, its three carriages came to a stop, the cheerful warm light of their windows casting a glow on the platform. Danny pressed himself against the exit. But no one appeared to alight. The automatic doors opened, and shut. The train moved on, into the night. The three men on the platform seemed to have vanished into thin air, leaving only the echoes of their dirge to flip away in the wind.

Daniel walked away, towards the nursing home. But halfway down the road he turned, to the clip-clop of feet behind him. A man, wearing a red plastic cape and carrying a baggy valise pocked with labels of foreign towns and cities, came up to him out of the dark.

"Do you have a light?"

The accent was foreign, a combined twang of Yankee and Mediterranean. A Gauloise drooped from his lips, under a massive, coal-black moustache, which gave him the appearance of a Mexican bandit. He wore a leather peaked cap, pushed back over a shock of untidy hair.

"I'm looking for a Doctor Mackenzie. A place called The Retreat. Do you know it?"

"Doctor Angel! Petros Angelopoulos!"

"Andrew! Good to see you, man."

"Thought you were due tomorrow. What'll ye have? It's a toss-up between the Auchentoshan, the Inchgower or the Glendronach."

"Any firewater will do. I became bored with London. Got on the Intercity and the last wagon out of town."

"Well, meet the troops. Rhona you already know. Kathleen is our non-resident artist. She keeps us in line with the Force. Avram Blok, my right arm. He listens our patients back to life. I think we're supposed to call them 'customers' now, but we're stuck in our old ways. Mansur Darwish, Jimmy Gold. Daniel you already met, our scribe from south of the border. A talent unrecognised by the world, but it is only a matter of time." (Only Time?? Why not add Space as well? Every day, millions of dead cells fall from my corpus, to be carried off by the microcosmic hordes.) "The rest have retired. You'll have noticed there's not much of a night life around here, away from the ragged-trousered bastards."

"It looks a cosy berth, Andrew."

"Any port in a storm. It's a quiet life, after the kids. Rationalisation. But we got attached to the area. I succumbed to the age, Petros. Not like you, the wandering practitioner. What are you practising on now?"

"Just wandering. Making my slow way east. I got back pay, for my stint in Lebanon. No hurry to get anywhere, for a change."

"The Terrorist Doctor of Beirut!" Mackenzie flourishes the malt. "I remember you showed me the cuttings. Our Avram Blok is from that part of the world, a little south of you. Opposite sides, perhaps, of the same coin."

"My sympathies," says Blok, warily.

"We made the pilgrimage once," says Mackenzie. "Was it '75, Rhona? Or '76? Jerusalem. Tiberias. Capernaum. The Jordan River. Holy sepulchres, churches, mosques, tombs. Old roots. I have to say, I found them very dry."

"Memories, hopes, disappointments," responds the newcomer. "We supply them all, in bulk purchase."

But Kathleen moves in with glittering eyes. Tantalised by the mention of iconic place-names. Fountainheads of the wretched of the earth. "When were you there?"

"I was there from 1984 to '86. But I had to leave. Too many people wanted my head on a pole. It's difficult to help targeted people, when you're the first on the list of targets."

"Too many people wanted to kill me," Jimmy Gold chips in unasked. "Mainly it was the Francocitti Family. They owned the Mister Breezy franchise. I was working for Stromboli Ices. They put a land-mine under my van. Eight different flavours blown sky high."

"Where was this?"

"Kilwinning."

"Our friend Jimmy was caught in the crossfire of a gang war over ice-cream futures. The infection spreads farther than you might think, Petros. But at least here we have enclaves of sanity."

"No, we had no truck with those. I worked in a suburb of Beirut, basically a refugee camp of the Palestinians. We were besieged for a year by Shi'a militias which were backed by the Syrian Army. It was a classic case of the poor killing the poor. I organised the hospital in the camp."

All ears rapt, as he relates his tale of woe and oppression, but my mind had already wandered away from all this into my own nooks and crannies. I had thought of a new title for my magnum opus: *Jewish Ninjas from Mars.* I would abandon Underground minimalism and attack McTeague on several fronts. Besieging him in his office with a bombardment of manuscripts, and, if manuscripts alone could not achieve this, drastic measures might be called for. One recalls the rejected comic in Martin Scorsese's movie, who has to kidnap the talk-show host he admires to get himself on the show. But if I kidnapped McTeague, no doubt Hammer & Stern would simply abandon him to his fate, opening a cupboard and releasing another Corporation clone, ready to do their bidding. Arbiters of culture and success. Heads I win, tails you lose.

"Eh, Danny boy, it's hard for me to tell you this, but I'm afraid we can't go ahead the way we'd have liked to. . . . The figures, Danny, the figures! You can take water to the horse, but you canna pour it in his mouth. He spits it back out of the trough. It's a hard business in a hard world in hard times. . . . The Returns, Danny boy, the Returns . . ."

My manuscript, Returning from the depths of McTeague's desk. Mackenzie's meatballs, returning from the kishkas. Petros Angelopoulos's voice, returning from the drone:

"I would love to go back, Kathleen, but I can't. . . . The last time I left, the Hizbollah had to smuggle me out, past Syrian lines. I was disguised, as is often the ploy, as a woman, covered up in a black *abaya.* They would rather let you through than violate the proprieties and search a woman. Haram! That was how we used to get medicines through, and ammunition, in the cease-fires. The men could not get in or out, but the women, with their fat stomachs, bulging with bullets and phials. . . . Then the next thing you would know, they were shooting at them, when the cease-fire ended, and they tried to get back out. You can't imagine it, Kathleen."

Dewy-eyed, she sits at the feet of the healer. Avram Blok, at the farther end of the sofa, emitting small grunts and coughs. Rhona Mackenzie enquiring pertly after technical details, operative procedures under fire.

Perhaps she wishes to be prepared for a siege by the biker militias of the Sheepish Dead. I find this intrusion of the world into The Retreat hard to take, and pad away upstairs, back to the dust mites. They at least have my measure. They know my limits. They are the status quo. I lie awake, and hear them singing their mournful dirges, underneath, as crack columns labour mightily to remove a piece of dried snot that dropped off my nose. Heave ho! All together lads! As, jabbering in their inaudible patois, they carry my congealed detritus far in the unknown depths of my Slumbereezee mattress, there to set it up on a pedestal far above the multitude, who converge, waving their antennae and pincers, worshipping the manna from heaven, reciting psalms and offering thanks to their benefactor, the mighty giant who slumbers above the earth. . . . I strain my ears, but still cannot make out their jargon, drowned as it is by the continuing patter of the prodigal guest downstairs, his voice booming out like a foghorn:

". . . remember when we first met, Andrew, in that television studio in London, it was early '83. . . . I'd come to talk about the continuing impact of the war in Lebanon on the Palestinian Camps, and you were booked to talk about lack of funding for handicapped children in Scotland. We introduced ourselves and began to chat in the waiting-room, with half an eye on the item they were recording before us — remember? The hockey players who had survived an airplane crash in the Himalayas by cannibalising their dead comrades. The interviewer asked: 'So what does it feel like to eat your best friend?'. . ."

I would have had no compunctions. Into the microwave and Bob's-your-uncle. One should not give these things a second thought. McTeague! There would have been a succulent morsel, rotating and reddening in the stove. AUTHOR CONSUMES EDITOR. Did not the Lord consume His enemies? But Angelopoulos is clearly one of nature's healers, like our Mackenzie. Life ruptures, they repair, with needle and thread and thumb and lip, stitch, stitch, stitch at the torn skin, stapling the shattered bones.

McTeague, McTeague! Why hast thou forsaken me? He climbs over my prone, remaindered body, reaching for the mahogany door with his name chiselled on the plaque. The massive curved desk. The key to the executive washroom. The Masonic handshake. The triple-locked door, the blindfold, the tingling fires. Naked authors and authoresses chained to blood-soaked lecterns, their skin inscribed with Kabbalistic symbols. The black-suited men of Sales and Marketing, poised with their dripping tomahawks. In a recess at the far end of the initiation chamber, the Chairman of the Board, Brent Browbeat, the infamous North American homunculus, with his ram's head and foaming nostrils.

Gunpowder, treason and plot. In the mountains, Nicolae and Elena share with me their last baked potato. We are all three in tattered rags, our bones sticking through our flesh. The barking of the dogs getting closer and closer. There is nothing for it but to join our skeletal hands together and sing the Party's National Anthem:

> God, Strike the Masses Blind,
> God, Save Me from Humankind,
> God Save My Skin.
> Make Me Victorious,
> Save Me from My Tsores,
> O Tempora, O Mores,
> Go-od Save My Skin . . .

Two million dust mites, who cannot see. Five billion humans, who cannot hear. The injudicious spectre of the lean, the marching tackle of the skeletal legs, the calloused feet dragging the desert paths and alleyways of history. My own pettifogging little problems are quite enough to drive me to earth-shattering despair. Taunt me not with the heaving struggles of the global throng, the forgotten men and women. What is the point of their being forgotten if we keep remembering their plight? The dribbling illogic of our guilt. (All major credit cards accepted.) What are the dispossessed to me? The shirtless, the pantless, the shoeless, the dwellers in want and misery. It's the sixties all over again. The dead echoes of far-gone battle-cries, the delusions of moral grandeur, the deification of defeat. I supped it with my mother's milk, *glatt kosher*. I already gave, at the womb, the forced entry into my unpromised land. Wembley, Middlesex. The black dawns, the grey mornings, the drizzle and drooping socks, shimmering banalities of swinging ideals and hung desires, the long haul, towards obloquy and betrayal.

Perhaps one should be content after all with zero. I had a girlfriend once who was a "vegan." Anita. She claimed to eat virtually nothing, as a matter of choice, but roots and dandelions, and nevertheless she grew fatter and fatter as each day passed, incomprehensibly, until I discovered her secret addiction to meat pies, which she confessed to tearfully prior to leaving and booking in at a voluntary prison camp in Wiltshire for victims of "nutriment abuse." Later she joined a group of animal-liberationists, living in damp country cottages, dedicated to the freeing of cats, dogs and monkeys from the evil clutches of modern science. They refused to use insecticides, and called the beetles creeping about their homes by pet names, such as Sadie, Mickey, Slim and Hilda, leaving them regular plates of lettuce and Ribena.

Aye, the skies are full of portents of wonders, unknown poisons spreading through the air. The hand of death extends over the landscape, scattering its invisible seeds. We can exchange an invisible for a visible destruction. It's merely a throw of the dice. Nietzsche, Beyond Good or Evil. The "discipline" and "ennobling" of great suffering. Perhaps one should sell this to the third world. Or do they already have it, in the form of Islam? Is the death of God the same as His fossilisation? This is not my cup of tea. I shall have to leave this to Doctor Angelopoulos, the Angel of Beirut and points east. . . . He and Avram Blok and Kathleen and Andrew Mackenzie can hammer out a new philosophy for the post-historical world.

Sanctuary! Sanctuary! But what is that faint echo just outside the house? The shuffle of feet? A cleared throat in the ferns? Old, dead Iron Age Britons shifting in peat bogs? Stirring consciences? The creak of forgotten legends, crusades, expeditions? The morphic resonance of far-away dreams?

TWO

Blessed

Are the

Hungry

A GREY PRE-SPRING SUNDAY MORNING. THE EAST LOTHIAN SEA LAPPING gently at the pitted, weed-grown rocks and gullies, the receding tide revealing the barnacled sewage pipes thrusting out into the Firth. The massive chimneys of the Prestonpans power station looming over the small towns. Palls of black smoke belying the briskness of the air, hanging over the gulls perched on chimneys and aerials, the fishing boats in the harbour. A floppy black dog bounds over the sand, scattering the squatting birds.

"Hey, Alistair! Here, boy. Heel, Fido!"

The dog momentarily considered Avram Blok's call, then ignored it, leaping over the slippery rocks. Blok followed a slight distance behind Kathleen and Angelopoulos, as the doctor waved his arms to encompass the widest possible domain —

"The West worships the God of stability, while all around us the pot seethes and boils. No more cold war. No more mighty monoliths facing each other across an ideological abyss. Will their nuclear weapons find another target? In a multipolar world, entire countries can be consigned to the dustbin of the 'new dispensations.' The Global Village — yes, television, the information explosion, computers jabbering to each other across the globe. I can get on a flight and be in Zambia or South Yemen in a few hours, plunged into the sights and smells of another world, not to speak of the other galaxy of Beirut. But the gap, despite technology, is not closing. It's getting wider all the time . . . Who wants to fight over control of Chad, or inherit the misery of Mali? Half of Africa is being ravaged by AIDS. Millions will die. Tens of millions will be simply written off. At most you will see them on posters of charities and global pop concerts. The ghosts in the machine of progress. The moment the great powers stop seeing them as subjects for manipulation, they will stop seeing them altogether. If they have no purchasing power, in the brave new global supermarket, they will simply not exist."

They reached the green outside the derelict Craddock swimming pool, with its stopped clock at half-past two, a brace of motorcycles buzzing round each other on the perimeter path like mating flies. The caravan trucks of the spring carnival shows parked idly on the gravel seafront. Washing lines strung between the caravans, and wizened fairground folk dangling their legs over the breakwater, fishing rods poised for the high tide. A lone hot-dog stand dispensed stale buns to three pale boys, who ran off, taunting the bikers from a distance. The bright signs beckoning on closed stalls: TRY YOUR LUCK. SPEAK YOUR FATE. LONESOME GHOSTS. From the doorway of the nearest house, next to the VideoShop, a plump man in a red sweater and woollen cap emerged, lifting an old battered megaphone to his mouth:

"Blessed are ye that hunger now, for ye shall be filled! Blessed are ye that weep now, for ye shall laugh. Blessed are ye, when men shall hate you, and when they shall separate you from their company, and shall reproach you, and cast out your name as evil, for the Son of Man's sake . . . for behold, your reward is great in heaven! But woe unto you that are rich, for ye have received your consolation. Woe unto you who are full, for ye shall hunger. Woe unto you that laugh now, for ye shall mourn and weep . . ."

"You can't win," said Doctor Angel. Dark clouds swept up from the south, bringing drops of rain. The amblers hurried back down the green, towards a low greystone house standing isolated between the road and the sea. The big black mongrel, Alistair, leading the way, settling rapidly inside on his scuffed wicker mat and taking no further part in the day. Angelopoulos manoeuvring professionally round and through the flotsam of Kathleen's beachcombing odysseys on the covered patio and in the hall, her putative *objets d'art*, cast-up logs; shreds of old fishing nets; waterlogged old shoes, trousers and jackets; indeterminate bits of torn rubber and rags; the rotted ribs of a shipwrecked fishing vessel; mounds of pebbles and shells.

"Sit where you can." Blok waved nonchalantly. "There are still some chairs around that haven't yet been pledged to the Hokamoto Gallery in Tokyo. You get a cash prize if you can tell the difference between the raw material and the ready-for-sale."

"Just brain him with a mallet, Petros, while I get the booze." But the doctor just moved about the large room, gazing at the sculptures lined against the walls, on shelves and cases. Faces moulded with old bits of wood and netting, figures in motion made of old rags and lumber, shapes evocative of sailing and the sea, half person, half boat, iron ribs patched with shards of posters, pebble spirals reaching for the sky. "This is impressive," he called out to the kitchen. "It's amazing what can pay the rent," Blok agreed. "I just pretend I'm Jonah, living in the whale's belly. The Walt Disney version. Kathleen plays Gepetto. The Pinocchios, as you can see, are still dormant."

She returned with Glenfiddich. The Angel reunited with an old friend. Blok waved the bottle away. "My stomach's my enemy. Like Hitler, it plans the final solution; it's only looking for an excuse."

If one lacks immediate external enemies, they can be replaced by the enemy within. Blok sipped at a Marks and Spencer's Real Orange Juice while the gossip from the exotic East resumed. The Angel's trawl of alien flotsam for Kathleen's intellectual storehouse, tales of faraway traumas brought to these bleak humdrum shores:

"When the militias besieged us," twanged the Angel, "we were reduced to an area of about two hundred and fifty by two hundred yards. Two thousand four hundred people had to be fed, clothed and kept alive, under constant bombardment and the fire from snipers night and day. I was treating casualties with major trauma daily. Our clinic was in an old apartment house whose upper storeys had already been blown away by the shelling. We had to operate on the kitchen table of this family which had fled to Europe. Our pharmacy was in the children's bedroom, our main equipment was in the basement, with a generator to keep us going after the electricity was cut off. And on top of all this we still had all the pressures of internal Palestinian politics, the Popular Front against the Popular

Democratic Front, the Fatah and the Communist Party and the Lebanese National Movement, the Shi'a Amal and the Syrians and Hizbollah, the Lebanese Army, the Christian Phalange, the Druze, the Kurds, Armenians, Assyrians, Chaldeans. Feuds going on that had their roots in millennia of foreign invasions and crusades. Not to mention, of course, the Israelis always poised to attack in the south . . .'"

Hostilities that had stood the test of time. The Angel's history lessons: How Greater Lebanon was gouged by the French out of Syria. The Palestinian influx of 1948 in the establishment of the State of Israel. U.S. Marines' landing of 1958. The Civil War of 1975–76. The 1982 Israeli invasion. Kathleen wished to understand it all, but the gap was too narrow for the flood. Dried by the telling, the Angel paused for liquid refreshment.

"Avram doesn't talk to me much about the Middle East now," Kathleen said. "He used to tell me his tall Israeli tales. Now there's just the old volumes of the scrapbooks he's been adding to for years, ever since the Six-Day War. The Blokbook."

"I got two good items this weekend, you have to admit," Blok murmured; "the Poll Tax riots in London, and the finding of the name of Allah in aubergines in Leicester. Muslims are flocking from throughout the country to set eyes on this modern miracle."

"You can't beat Faith," said Doctor Angel. "Not when you've seen it move mountains, not to speak of creating mounds of corpses."

"Some of the aubergines have been preserved in vinegar," said Blok, "though some, it appears, have been eaten."

"Eating God is an old practice," said Angelopoulos; "the body and blood of Christ. The cavemen who worshipped wolves and bears used to eat their Gods regularly. But it's a bland dish for atheists."

"Are you going back there?" Kathleen asked; "to the Middle East?"

"Well, I will head back eventually," said Angel, "not to Lebanon, but probably to Amman. I wanted to go to a hospital in the Occupied Areas, the West Bank or Gaza, but the Israelis made it clear I'm not welcome. I was in Israel only briefly, in '82. The army had taken me prisoner in Beirut, but I was released after Red Cross pressure. I spent three weeks in Tel Aviv and Jerusalem."

"Avram's home city, Jerusalem. We're overdue for a visit, but it's like

41

trying to drag a horse to the knacker's yard."

"It's a beautiful city," said Angelopoulos.

"Ah yes, beauty," said Blok. "I've heard of that. Blessed are ye that hunger. But I don't hunger any more, not in that way."

"I think I know what you mean," said Doctor Angel. "You tend to look for the small things that make life worthwhile. Or even just bearable."

"Avram believes in reinventing himself," said Kathleen, "but he hasn't come up yet with a workable patent. You can't cut off your roots entirely —"

"Vegetables need roots, but human beings . . . "

"Even the jokes are recycled. Doing Your Own Thing. I Did It My Way." Kathleen was not impressed. "It's like those Marks and Spencer's half-cooked meals you put in the oven for twenty minutes, gas mark six, for a full and richer flavour. At the end of the day you stick with some random choice and call it destiny, or ideology, or Faith, so as not to realise quite what a chump you are. But I believe you have to keep on trying . . ."

"Keep right on tae the end of the road . . ."

"You have to make some choice," said Doctor Angel, "even in the supermarket of precooked concepts. Self-definition, it's the only way to travel . . ."

"First you have to have a self to begin with. You shouldn't take that for granted. Not if you know our customers. The personality subsumed in illusion. Or simply mothballed for the duration of some Great Escape of the psyche. Like our client Danny Hohenlohe. Pen name. Birth name: Daniel Pick. Published one book and was turned down the next one. Enters into melancholia. Delusions of persecution, probably faked. They used to call it Munchausen's syndrome. Malingering. Took a break, to stop annoying his mother. He'll be okay, enjoys winding us up. You know he came to me yesterday claiming three Middle Eastern types are following you. He saw them first at the station when you came and the next day, skulking in the bushes in a white Volkswagen van."

"This doesn't sound like a delusion to me," said Doctor Angel, unperturbed, "just good eyesight."

"Why should anyone follow you here?" A puzzled query by Kathleen, watching the other two exchange knowing glances like veterans remembering an old shipwreck.

"I never worry about such things," said the Doctor. "If you live with paranoia all your life, you just do what has to be done and fuck the rest. I have so many enemies, they tend to cancel each other out. How often does your Daniel see such things?"

"Fairly regularly," Blok admitted. "He drives poor Jimmy Gold to despair, every time an ice-cream van passes. The cornettos are always laced with arsenic, the flakes are explosive fuses."

"Well, I'm a light sleeper," said the Angel, "and I only have one suitcase, so I'm always quick off the mark. I seldom have to linger."

"The wandering Greek," said Blok.

"Bearing no gifts . . ."

"Fill the man's glass for God's sake, Avram . . ."

"Now, Kathleen, tell me about your work here. Is it all things washed up on the beach?"

"The Wave Cycle, yes, whatever comes at random. Most of these are works in progress. I have a few on exhibit at a gallery in the city. We can do a guided tour, tomorrow, if you want, no obligation to buy."

"It'll be a change from what gets washed up on the beach at Beirut, I can tell you. Now this one here, that's quite evocative. I like the ragged edges. That's a pretty fearsome nail you found there . . ."

The pitter-patter of conviviality on a lazy Lothian Sunday. The snores of the dog, the grey waves growling into the shingle, lapping over smooth rocks and weeds. And is anyone watching, from the verges of the adjacent main road to Dunbar, or from the cover of the caravan site just off the Craddock high street? Or behind the frosted glass of Macdonald's Fresh Fish? Prying eyes, over foreign moustaches? Well, at least, Danny Hohenlohe would infer, it shows somebody cares; it would be some indication, if not proof, that we are not alone, in a cruel and callous world . . .

AUBERGINES REVEAL TRUE FAITH TO MUSLIMS

The curious phenomenon of God's name appearing in Arabic inside aubergines has spread from Nottingham to Leicester, where three cases have been reported by devout Muslims in the past week. As many as 5,000 pilgrims from all over the Midlands are reported to have visited the remarkable vegetables.

T.M., of K. Street, Leicester, told *The Independent* yesterday that her mother found two significant aubergines on Friday night when she sliced them open. One, sliced twice, shows the Arabic characters for Allah repeated three times. The other, she said, appeared to contain a verse from the Koran, though this has not yet been deciphered.

"It's quite clear," she said. "You don't even have to have a magnifier. Everyone who has been round to see it and pay their respects has said it's a message that it's going to be the end of the world or whatever. It is a message to tell all the Muslims, and all the other faiths, that this is the true faith. No other religions have had this happen to them. A human being could have written the name in a frame. To have this written in a fruit or a vegetable is a miracle."

The aubergines are displayed in a bowl in her parent's living-room. "Anyone who hears about them comes and prays and has a good look and leaves to pass the message on. People are coming at all times. They just want to sit there and gaze at it." Miss M— said.

Manzoor Moghal, vice-chairman of the Leicester County Council Race Relations Board, said: "As far as Muslims are concerned, they can find Allah in all the objects on this earth, because Allah is everywhere. The fact that certain configurations can appear to read as the word Allah should not surprise anyone because Allah's ways are very mysterious."

The Independent, March 28, 1990

POLL TAX BATTLE OF TRAFALGAR SQUARE
Buildings Ablaze and Shops Looted as over 100 Protesters and Police Are Injured

Riot and arson swept central London last night as hundreds of left-wing agitators broke away from a mass rally against the poll tax and engaged in a brutal battle against the police.

Shocked eyewitnesses compared the scenes of devastation with Belfast riots as Central London exploded into the worst civil disorder ever seen there.

44

By late last night, bystanders said that many shops from Trafalgar Square a mile northwards through Oxford Street had been smashed and looted. More than 300 people were arrested and damage is likely to run into millions of pounds.

One eyewitness said: "This was class war. Expensive cars were attacked and set alight, and anyone smartly dressed was abused or attacked."

A Downing Street spokesman said Mrs Thatcher, at Chequers, was being kept informed about the situation in Trafalgar Square. She travelled to Chequers after addressing the Conservative Conference in Cheltenham earlier in the day.

The Sunday Telegraph, April 1, 1990

HITLER'S PIANO STOLEN

A guillotine from the French Revolution and a piano that had belonged to Adolf Hitler were stolen from a Hamburg warehouse by thieves using a forklift truck, police said . . .

The Guardian, August 8, 1989

PERON'S AVENGERS RAISE THE DEAD

Buenos Aires police are puzzling over the latest outbreak of that most Argentine of crimes — political grave-robbery.

Two years ago, former president Juan Peron's hands went missing. Now, claiming to avenge that theft, a group calling itself the Organisation of Upright Argentines has stolen some bones belonging to the grandfather of a former economy minister.

The Upright Argentines chose to dismantle the skeleton of Miguel Alfredo Martinez de Hoz, they said, because his grandson was "the ultimate symbol of a nationless sepoy." (The Indian sepoys of the British Raj symbolise grovelling weaklings for Argentine nationalists.) The Upright Argentines left Miguel Alfredo's wrists in an envelope on the doorstep of the sensationalist tabloid *Cronica*, and dumped his skull in the Economy Ministry's car park. Attacking a politician by disturbing his bones makes sense only in a country where death and its symbols hold powerful sway, and a strong streak of necrophilia does permeate Argentine society . . .

The Independent, March 13, 1989

Blok turned and turned the pages of his random news-clip history of a warped age. And when is the age unwarped? Is there a linear saga of progress achieved, visions fulfilled? Ye can run, but ye canna hide. The past catches up with you, even as an ebullient whisky surgeon, bringing the whiff of charcoaled corpses into one's hiding-place. Can one subsume one's identity in a place, in an adopted, foster home?

An end to wandering. The still centre. Genetic restlessness damped down, exiled to the id, where it flutters, beating its wings against the rock-candy bars. Sparks from the feet of *Adam Kadmon,* shadows of the stone walls of his childhood, Jerusalem of the 1950s, bent alleyways and red-roofed houses, cracked steps leading under low stone arches to tiny court-yards, the Hebrew signs warning against defilment of the Sabbath, television, secular literature. The light of the annual *Lag Ba'Omer* bonfire on its bearded, black-garbed celebrants, hands linked, slowly and deliberately circumnavigating the flames, intoning, over and over:

"THIS IS THE GATEWAY TO THE LORD, THE RIGHTEOUS WILL PASS THROUGH IT . . ."

The Mediterranean light, the deep-blue waves of the Tel Aviv beach, the tarred and rubbished sand, the massed loud-radioed sunbathers. Hair-chested young men seek bare-chested women. The odour of rancid hot dogs and hamburgers. Old timers bouncing their flab on cold winter mornings. In the distance, the white pillar of the Jaffa lighthouse, the minaret of the mosque. Difficult to superimpose on the pallid grey of the Firth of Forth, the melancholy hoot of ship's horns, the hint of Fife behind the mist, the Glasgow trippers' splayed deck-chairs, crushed cans of McE-wan's and empty bottles of Beck's with no ships or genies inside. Dead sar-dine and corned-beef tins, the *prima materia* of Kathleen's creations. Who can predict the twists and turns of fate? When he had first met Kathleen he had assumed she was penniless, another floating lost soul. And who would have thought her dreams had cash value? Now Japanese and German buy-ers flocked to the Bridge Gallery in Edinburgh to bargain for her work with the gallery's director, Kathleen's old friend Sophia Salvadori, trustee of twentieth-century art. The destiny of inertia and mass.

The year before the Angel's invasion, Kathleen had led him on a reluc-tant museum tour of New York's collections and heritages. A tourist-cum-business trip on behalf of Sophia in advance of a planned series of exhibits at the Bridge of the surrealists and their ilk. She took him to see Marcel Duchamp's bicycle wheel in the Metropolitan Museum of Modern Art.

The moving object, nailed motionless to its perch, with a uniformed guard watching eagle-eyed for any felonious touch. The irresistible urge to twirl the wheel, versus the certainty of alarm bells, drawn pistols, public opprobrium and prison cells. He dragged his feet around the other exemplars of surreal wit, the strange stoppered bottles of Cornell's *Egypt de Mlle Cleo*, Oppenheim's furry cup, the extravagances of Max Ernst, Magritte, Dalí's *Persistence of Memory*, whose small size sent him into terminal shock. There was no relief in the great space of Rothkos and Jackson Pollocks, before whose majesty Kathleen stood, entranced, as at the portals of the Enchanted Castle. But Van Gogh's *Starry Night* blazed at him off the wall. That "immanent power behind the natural world," the twists and whorls of intangibles caught by the brush and frozen. Blok expected it to come alive at any moment, dancing its brazen nocturnal dance as soon as his back was turned.

Art and Life. New York City struck him as it had on his first visit, twenty years before, as a place where multitudes ate incessantly and ravenously as if every meal was their last, while in the streets, below the tall indifferent towers, the tattered homeless threaded through the crowds like sweating ghosts, thrusting out paper cups, which they were now obliged to buy for fifty cents at the junk-food stores. Even destitution requires its investment. They stayed in an apartment block on 95th Street, in a flat belonging to a Manhattan painter whom Kathleen had met at an Edinburgh Festival some years before, and who had decamped for the summer to the West Coast in search of balmier air. Every night, they had to make their way up Broadway, past the army of the dispossessed bedding down for the night by doorways and shop windows with their supermarket trolleys bearing all their worldly goods. Some spread out for sale on the pavement a pathetic array of old shoes, shirts and jackets clearly salvaged from garbage. Or if they still had a few dimes to their name they could sit in McDonald's or Dunkin' Donuts for an hour or two over a yoghurt or a coffee, pretending, briefly, to be normal citizens.

What has this all got to do with us, wondered Blok. In an adjacent bookshop, we can pick up a volume telling us about "50 Things You Can Do to Save the Earth" for only fourteen dollars ninety-five. Just consume less, to save those who'd rather consume more.

A stifling New York heatwave left him riveted to the grinding air-conditioning in the apartment while Kathleen sallied out to talk proxy business with gallery owners, leaving him to consume *Awakenings* by Oliver Sacks: "*A neurologist's account of his experience with a so-called miracle drug which temporarily brought back to life the zombie-like sufferers from the epidemic of sleeping-sickness which swept the world in the 1920s.*" Blok took it down off the shelf now as he idled about the Craddock house, waiting to depart for the afternoon shift at Drem, Kathleen away in the city . . . "*Dr Sacks writes beautifully and with exceptional subtlety and penetration into the state of mind of his patients and the nature of illness in general . . .*" But are there not certain minds that are best left to sleep, Blok thought, considering the simmering neuroses of The Retreat. The exhaustive paranoias of Daniel Pick/Hohenlohe, the elaborate subterfuges of the Watson brothers, who manoeuvred deftly about the house, avoiding each other as if equipped with bat's radar; Mansur Darwish's loss of faith in money that prevented him from conducting the simplest transaction, such as paying a bus fare or buying a Yorkie bar at the New Mains corner shop, all acts which had to be carried out for him by a chaperone or innocent passers-by; Lucy Mongolfier's compulsive indecision as to which tap to turn or which towel to use, to have or not to have toast at breakfast, which exit to take to the garden; Alois Crumb's clinging to his fur coat as perverse evidence of his guilt by association for the mass murder of small cuddly animals; Jimmy Gold's ice-cream-war traumas; and poor old Maggie Mann's refusal to come out of her room unless convinced that Rudolph Valentino was not lurking in the corridor, exposing his rampant sexual organ.

The impossibility of healing minds versus the cut and stitch of Doctor Angel. The charlatanry of the one versus the messy effectiveness of the other. But what do we mean by a diseased mind? Visions, delusions, false perceptions? One man's truth is another man's treason. Freud analysed himself and was so terrified by what he found he projected it on all mankind, or at least on middle-class Vienna. Blok had not tried to analyse himself, preferring not to meddle with and perhaps awaken the sea of serpents writhing, Goya-like, under the skin, the ghosts of the past, the unfettered demons and angels slithering along the maze of choices, queueing for bread and circuses at so many false exits.

"I feel more comfortable with the so-called sick," he told Angelopoulos. "It's the healthy ones that scare me out of my skull."

"I insist on health," said Doctor Angel. "I won't allow sickness through my door. I know, it's a losing battle, but I'm a Greek. We never give up." Nevertheless, for all his hair-raising tales of battlefield surgery, Mackenzie's guest appeared in no hurry to leave the languid comforts of East Lothian, for he had been introduced, in the course of Kathleen's guided tour of Edinburgh, to Sophia Salvadori of the Bridge Gallery, her childhood friend and artistic collaborator, with whom he decamped, after a Tandoori threesome in Queensferry Street, to a cold stone apartment in Marchmont, lit by the spark of mutual fires, while Kathleen returned alone to Craddock.

"I think I lit a fuse there, Avram," she told Blok.

"You should never introduce a Greek to a redhead." But he was relieved, that the wanderer's fiery eye had moved off Kathleen, the hero finding a new audience. "Yes," said Kathleen admiringly, "that man wastes no time." Indeed. In his notes to *Awakenings*, Blok recalled, Doctor Sacks described a patient who suffered from a condition in which she could not stop or change her direction of motion: Once started she had no control over her trajectories. Heroically, she managed to lead a life outside institutions by calculating the precise paths of any required moves in her home. She might launch herself through sets of open doors, across several rooms, to reach her desired destination, or, if the doors were closed, calculate her course by bouncing off doors or walls at such an angle that she would hit her target, a chair, the kitchen, or her bed. Sacks commented about the concept of "behaviour algorithms," calculated substitutes for the intuitive movements destroyed by disease.

Nations, too, could fall prone to this grotesque malady, which might be more common to societies than individuals. The difference between them and Sacks's patient, Lillian T. being that, more often than not, they miscalculated, splitting their skulls, breaking their limbs.

Blok returned to the balm of his scrapbook —

CONDOM BOMBS:
Sulphuric acid, potassium chlorate and granulated sugar, are the ingredients of "condom bombs," as found, in vast quantities, in a flat in Londonderry yesterday. The acid, placed in the

prophylactic, erupts in a huge ball of fire when it finally eats through the rubber . . .

THRILL SEEKERS RISK DEATH TO LICK TOADS . . .

Certain species of toads excrete a mind-altering chemical called bufotinine that has been on the US Federal Drug Enforcement Agency's list of contraband substances since 1970. Although not on the verge of becoming a national drug rage, toad licking is reportedly practiced in South America, Australia, and certain parts of the United States . . .

The San Francisco Examiner, May 29, 1989

HANGING — A VERY BRITISH AFFAIR:

. . . By 1864 central London was no longer scattered with gallows at the approximate frequency of modern tube stations; the mob no longer gathered at Tyburn to join the condemned man in the 51st Psalm: "Against thee, thee only, have I sinned, and done this evil in thy sight." The bloody code of the 18th century which permitted the execution of "malicious" eight-year-olds had gone and with it the death penalty for stealing turnips, impersonating a Chelsea Pensioner and associating with gypsies...

The Guardian, August 12, 1989

PEACE HAVEN HOME — FOR HORSES AND DONKEYS

Please can you help us save the lives of Horses and Donkeys, to send them to the Peace Haven Home for Horses and Donkeys . . . You can help us send these animals to the Peace Haven Home after a life of work to a well earned retirement by giving us your castoff clothing, cookers, carpets, bicycles, sewing machines, old pictures, china, old clocks, old mirrors, fridges, musical instruments, old jewellery, car batteries, brass, copper, lead, furniture, and anything else you think may help us . . .

OUR COLLECTORS WILL CALL TOMORROW.

If you cannot help us please leave bag outside . . .

One must do what one can in this world, Blok thought, leaving out some unsalvageable laundry (the difficulty of distinguishing dross from Kathleen's *prima materia* . . .). Perhaps the poor beasts would have some succour staggering about in his torn old pants or moth-eaten sweaters. Outside, the clouds continued to darken the sea. The grey waves growling into the shingle, lapping over rubbish and weeds. While, at Marchmont Road, the other side of the castle and the extinct volcano, Petros Angelopoulos and Sophia Salvadori rampaged through each other's bodies, exploring orifices and epidermis, pumping up their cardiovascular systems, plunging along their tactile trajectories, surrendering to no behavioural algorithms, enacting the oldest clichés. Doctor Angel having produced his own condom bombs the night before, triple-strength, triple-thinness, specially manufactured by Turks in German *fabriks*. "You don't have to worry about safe sex. I'm a doctor."

Let us fly, starless nights! Let us fly, straight into the moon, and hide away on its dark side. Let us not bother with time, space and the universe!

"I have to tell you something about me, Sophia. I am the most inconstant man alive. Medicine and hygiene apart, I'm a complete monster. I am absolutely not to be trusted."

"I'd never dream of trusting you, Angel."

"But I am very good at major trauma."

"I'll bear that in mind, when the time comes. Can you do that again?"

"It might require the memory of ancient perversions."

"Go ahead. Let me give you a hand . . ."

"Aaaaaaahhhhhhh . . . !"

But the shadows gather, none the less.

"Angel?"

"Yes?"

"You're not asleep."

"I lost the habit. I have some pills, but I left them at Drem."

"Tell me about it."

"Tell me about yourself, Sophia. What's your genealogy? How did you get your name?"

"The usual way. My grandparents were immigrants from Genoa. They didn't have the money for the Atlantic crossing, so they ended up in a Glasgow sweatshop. My father worked with the British Army in the War, near Mackenzie's place there, at Haddington. There was an airfield near Athelstaneford. He helped them plan air raids on his father's country. Later he never wanted to visit the old country, but I went there, on an art binge, when I was seventeen. It was an eye-opener. Kathleen was with me on that trip. There were three of us, at school together in Craddock. Kathleen, Janet and me. Janet's father is a Polish ex-airman. Kathleen's mother was a German-Jewish refugee. We were known as the 'Wee Threes' at school. We had our own weird religion. We worshipped the sun, but never got there till quite late in life . . ."

"Only the sun, or any other planets?"

"The Sun and Karl Marx, in that order. Always the village troublemakers. At university we were the vanguard of the Vietnam movement. We marched for Ho Chin Minh down Princes Street."

"Uncle Ho. They don't make 'em like that any more."

"Don't they?"

"They broke the mould."

"Tell me about it."

"God, it's fucking cold in this town."

"I'll turn the heating back on."

Wrapped in an outsize T-shirt, she exits the room in the gloaming.

Outside, the swish of passing cars.

Where are the broken shards of plaster? The shattered vessel, to be glued anew. Where are your instruments, repairman? Your scalpels and knives, tweezers and sewing needles? Where is the flesh that yesterday was whole? The bedsheets give off a fresh, sweet flavour. Or is it slightly burnt? The repeat of repressed smells. The voices, hammering, yelling, shrieking. The pain, the anger, the drum-calls to arms. The End of Time! Blood of the Martyrs! An eye for an eye! A spleen for a spleen! Who said vengeance is the Lord's? Expropriate the son of a bitch! What's ours is ours! What's yours is neither here nor there!

"Fuck off!"

"What is it, Angel? I've turned the heat back on. Man, you're freezing, I'm sorry."

"Not your fault. Nothing to do with you."

"It's okay, Angel, it's okay I'm here."

"The bastards!"

But even in the morning, in the pale grey light, the shadows still linger, moaning and muttering, echoing and droning on.

THREE

The End
of the World
or Whatever

A RAVAGED SQUARE, IN A RUINED CITY. SOME TIME AGO:

"THE END OF TIME!" The Cleric swept his eyes over his audience, the rapt faces, the bristling forest of gun barrels, the backdrop of blood-red banners and portraits of the deceased Imam. *"When you see that truth has died, and the people of truth have gone underground, when you see that injustice rules and the Koran is despised, and when you see the masters of error prevailing over the masters of truth, and when you see evil done in the open without shame, and moral depravity, men going with men and women with women, and adultery rife, and usury, The Book and its Laws flouted, and people living together like animals. When you see false testimony, immorality, crime, the equality of women, repression by the imperialist and the transgressor, the hegemony of lies and the suppression of the truth are rampant, then you will know that we have entered upon the times of which the wise have spoken, the preliminary days which the Imams have forecast.*

"The Imams and their followers have foreseen our predicament: That, when the flag of the Q'aim, the Lord of the Age, is raised, it will be cursed by the peoples of both East and West. For the believers will be besieged on all sides. The atheists of the East and the polytheists of the West will join hands against The Book and its people. And we have seen the signs, and the people are ready.

"We know that, in each generation, the martyrdom of the beloved Imam Husayn is re-enacted in the political sphere. There is no 'progress,' no Marxist 'dialectic of history,' no materialism which determines man's fate. There are

only eternal spiritual truths, articulated in the Koran, and re-enacted in our lives, if we so choose. For we can choose the light or the darkness.

"Imam Ali invites us to 'enjoin good and prohibit evil.' That is the foundation of our faith. To walk in the path of God and not of Satan. What is the path of God? Husayn reveals it. To defend your faith by jihad, and when jihad is impossible — shahadat — the joyful embrace of martyrdom. When you are weak, when all the forces of the world are against you, when massed armies and battleships and warplanes and nuclear weapons can all be wielded to defeat you, when living means surrender and shame and dishonour and apostasy — then Husayn teaches us we can choose death as the white shroud signifying an eternal life. We can throw our death in the face of our oppressor with a power no nuclear bomb can equal.

"Then, when the call itself reverberates from heaven, and the great war will come upon Syria and Baghdad, when the sun will rise in the West and the star appear in the East, and the Muslims will throw off the yoke of all foreigners, when the Q'aim returns, and the Imam Husayn rides before him, with the seventy-two martyrs of Kerbala, and the three hundred and thirteen knights who fought with the Prophet, Peace and Blessings Be Upon Him, at the battle of Badr, and the other Prophets, Moses, Adam, Ibrahim and Jesus will ride at his side, you too, the shahid, the martyr of these days, will be there, your robe pure as snow, your lance glinting in the sun of the new world of peace, justice and the final judgement . . ."

How does one describe the indescribable? Let's talk about man's inhumanity to man. And woman. And child. No. Let's talk about bricks and stones, about concrete things, about places and measurements, length and breadth, height and depth, about size and weight and mass, proportions and dimensions: The Jaffa Camp, Beirut, autumn of 1986 (Moharram 1406, by the Moslem date). Reduced, at its present extent, to about 250 metres by 250 metres. No, exactly 243 by 264 metres, according to Mad Latif, our idiot-savant, who has even brought it within 10 centimetres, give or take some rubble or loose stones. There is a precisely delineated no man's land between us and the enemy's closest positions. Mad Latif calculates the nearest gun at 118.5 metres, going by the condition of spent bullets ricocheting off barricades and walls. At barely sixteen years old, he is a living ballistic expert, mathematician and human computer, but he cannot tie his own shoelaces and dribbles food onto his clothes. There he goes now, loping down the alleyway, alone, at a time when even the armed comrades creep from wall to wall like shadows. The untouchability of the insane. Though even that, in this country which is no longer a country, has been confounded and disproved. The rubble of the asylum, on the outer perimeter of what was once the fruit market, testifies to that. Our Latif is far from being the only madman or -woman thrown naked into our world.

How do we tell them from the sane? The Amal militiamen, crouching behind sandbags to shoot children bearing sacks of flour. The Syrian artillerymen, behind them, in the stadium, training 150mm cannons, with armour-piercing shells, on our battered piles of old bricks, fortified with corrugated iron and sacks of earth and stones. The politicians and army commanders, who sit in marble palaces and move the pieces of their human chessboards about their fields of dreams. Our own comrades, fighting shoulder to shoulder by day, separating at night into their basements, whispering and wondering whether their rivals are stooges and spies of the other side. All of us, hunched in our cellars, swatting off the sounds of the constant bombardment like light sleepers plagued by mutant flies.

Mad Latif sees nothing of this. He just sees numbers, shapes, quantities, volumes, abstract relations between things. What is a man to him? A human being? A voice is a travelling wave of sound. The Cause is an agglomeration of data, things overheard without comprehension: Dates of the Palestine National Council meetings, names of representatives, delegates, spokesmen, leaders of the twisting maze of sects and parties. Dates and procedures of armed operations. The number and composition of our enemies' troops, as read out to him from files and journals, by Limping Nabil, the commander, who thought up the trick of entrusting information to the mad boy's brain in case of destruction or loss. The cardboard boxes piled in the Movement's office, now doubling as Umm Bathir's kitchen, amid the smell of what little cooking can be done, the blend of corn and sour cream, and herbs to spice starvation diets, flavouring the tattered pages of old reports and academic treatises by distant professors in the safety of their universities and colleges, in other lands, in other worlds.

We are an object of study. This we can't escape or deny. Like five-legged horses, or two-headed sheep, we are strange subjects of fascination for people sitting in the calm of their homes, throughout the "civilised" world, drinking their beers, watching their televisions, while we scurry in our enclosures, killing and being killed, like scorpions sealed in a jar. Exotic throwbacks to some age of cave dwellers. The kaleidoscope of our desperate diversity dissected on the desks of journalists and politicians: Amal, Hizbollah, Fatah, Popular and Democratic Popular Fronts, Liberation Fronts, National Liberation Fronts, Popular Struggles, Kataebs, Communist Parties, Rejection Fronts, Steadfastness Fronts, Lightnings, Ba'athists (Iraqi or Syrian), Nasserists, neo-Nasserists, Shehabists, Joumblatis, Yazbekis, Social Nationalists, "Phoenicians," *ad nauseam.*

But to Latif, and God, one presumes, we are all bags of bones and sacks of sinews, musculature, flesh, gristle, blood. A glutinous mass of molecules. Is that all we have of a common humanity?

We are returned to primal fears: Fear of Death. Of Isolation. Of Loss. A sniper's bullet whistles past the idiot. It has left the barrel of its gun at a velocity of 850 metres per second, he would no doubt inform us, cutting through the resistance of the air, which is, at the best of times, minimal. It misses, and ricochets off a naked girder. Someone shouts out to the fool, who takes cover behind a pile of sandbags, looking impassively around. At least he has a sense of self-preservation. I am alive; therefore, I am alive. We cannot go farther than that.

Loss. Of course, when one has lost everything. Country, home, family, friends. Paradoxically, we now have them all, in the most concentrated form. A country of a few thousand square metres. A home of a mattress, when lucky, and a knapsack of salvaged personal belongings — a dwindling stash of cigarettes, matches, sewing kit, soap — no, the Angel requisitioned the last bars two months ago — three ballpoint pens, three soggy notebooks. A map of the city, showing when it was possible to simply walk from street to street, without passing five dozen checkpoints, or being shot for one wrong step. A dozen homelands, now, where previously there was one corner of a subdistrict of a precinct . . .

I had a family, once. Mother, father, aunts, uncles, cousins, grandparents. Wife. Children. But I cannot speak of that now. That was yesterday. This is just me, now: Tewfiq Abd-el-Khalil. A Palestinian. That is, no one, as recognised by the world. I was a journalist, too, once. Now I have nothing to report. I exist neither in space nor in time. I am a fragment, torn off history, tumbling over and over in a vacuum. I am a moving target, trapped in a frame like those electronic dots on video games randomly darting to escape the player. The player, who is God, or the CIA, or the clever, desperate men in Tel Aviv, or the clever, ruthless wolf in Damascus, or God knows who or what.

Volition, will and self-determination. I peek out through a hole in the wall. "Latif!" The call again. I read somewhere, about idiot-savants, that these prodigies who seem to articulate only in numbers live in a profound harmonic field — that they perceive the world around them as a symphony of shapes and sizes and resonances. What mad symphony might our Latif be secretly constructing of our tiny, caged world, in the sharp crashes and thuds of bombardment, in the twisting, wailing piles of flesh cut down by gunpowder and steel? The blood, seeping into the ground, staining our clothes, hands, souls, as we rush the wounded and the almost dead to Doctor Angel's clinic.

A stomach, spilled on a carpet. Intestines glistening in dark red flow. It was a second-hand carpet. I remember the shop we bought it in on Hamra, in 1979. We had just rented the apartment and decided to refurbish it completely. It was an old, Turkish design. The shopkeeper, Abu-Fakri, gave us a special discount because, he said, he saw the light of a new life in our eyes. It cost us ninety-five Lebanese pounds. We couldn't afford anything more lavish. The bathroom had to be completely refitted, as its wall had taken an indirect hit in the Civil War, three years earlier. But it was close to the newspaper's office. Beggars can't be choosers. I remember, it was an optimistic phase, despite the usual political betrayals which we expect like winter chills.

"Latif!"

It's Benjamin calling, our Israeli hostage. He has adopted the crazy adolescent as a sort of mascot. A sense of guilt? Who knows. We did not intend to keep a hostage, in this mess, but we were trapped with him, as he was transferred to the camp, as part of a succession of "safe" houses, which turned out safe neither for him nor for us. A Skyhawk pilot, he fell into our hands during a reconnaissance flight above the city. For several months he was kept locked in rooms and cellars, but now, paradoxically, we give him the freedom to roam with us about the cage. Doctor Angel convinced us there was no point in guarding him, wasting human resources. "Will he defect to Amal? Or to Hizbollah?" Angelopoulos had his own reasons. Benjamin, trained as a medic, was a piece of gold dust for our Angel. "He can't run and he can't hide," said Angel. "To guard him here you tie up at least two men. Give him to me."

We gave him to Angel. We give Angel everything. Our electricity, our rations, our trust, our hopes, our fears. Most of all, our bodies, shattered and mangled and broken, which only he can repair. Crushed, fractured, lacerated, limbs practically severed, insides thrusting through shreds of flesh, only Doctor Angel can save us. The last resort, the only bulwark between ourselves and God.

So how does one describe the indescribable? The Cabinet of Doctor Angelopoulos. In the basement of our makeshift hospital, formerly a three-storey apartment block belonging to a family who managed to escape to Europe just before the siege began — late in '85 — Doctor Angel stands, in his white gown (ah, the saga of the laundry!) arms poised, hands in rubber gloves (the short supply endlessly rewashed), over the operating table, formerly the family's kitchen table, its wooden top gashed by a thousand cuts of knives that chopped tomatoes, onions, parsley, herbs, spices, now swabbed clean and prepared for the slab of humanity laid out for his scissors, scalpels, stapling guns and sutures, sacs of intravenous fluids and phials of drugs on the shelves which previously held the jars of sugar, flour, salt, pepper, oregano, basil, chives. An ordinary anglepoise side-lamp fixed at the head of the table, by the anaesthesia machine plugged into the basement generator, grinding away in a niche, aside from the cylinders of oxygen and anaesthetic gas, the diathermy coagulator and the suction machine. The nurses, readying the patient, who has been rushed in, fresh from the killing-ground, laid upon the chopping table, almost single-handedly, by Anneka, the blonde Norwegian giant who is Angel's head nurse. In her country, cold seas and rivers cut into mountains, people earn their living, shop, watch game shows on television. They are members of the European Community. We are members of the community of the damned. Climbing down from her mountain, she has joined our shrunken nation of troglodytes, out of the dictates of her conscience and the greatness of her heart. Or is it merely chance that drives such people across the oceans of indifference? At any rate, she has been with us from the moment the Syrians and Amal sealed off the last exits from the camp and stopped all movement in or out. Although they offered safe passage to "trapped foreigners," Anneka and the two West Germans, Klaus and Heinz, her assistants, all three decided to remain.

The prognosis is not rosy. Angel moves forward to the table, masked and capped, eyes glinting, the fatigue of eighteen-hour shifts gashed in his forehead, the sweat wiped away by nurse Nabiha, who was a schoolgirl only the other day, the last time I blinked — several months or several years ago? Impossible to tell. The patient, Anis, the old ironmonger's son, his calves and thighs shattered by the shrapnel of a 105 shell. An amputation. This boy will leave this room a half-man. A heroic stump. I was once a whole man myself, with ambitions, hopes, even expectations. I was going to procreate, build a future, wielding the weapon of fertility and the word. Now I am just a body with a gun, shooting at phantoms in armour. Angel stands, poised over the table, the surgical mask hiding his thick moustache, the cheeks which were once chubby, I dimly remember, from our first meeting, in a different Beirut, a decade ago, but none of us needs mirrors now; we see our emaciation in each other's faces. Reduced to bags of bones, rattling as we walk, like empty gourds with a spoonful of dried-up peas. Our legs no longer bend, our limbs creak like ancient furniture that's always just about to break, but somehow never quite does. Blood seeps, spurts, stains the white smock and gloves. Soon enough, on a busy shift, our Angel will resemble a butcher in a malfunctioning abattoir, blood-spattered like Doctor Frankenstein, pieces of bone, tissue, viscera, sticking to his hands, eyebrows, nose, hair.

All of us, including the hostage, Benjamin, totally merged with his enemies, living on thin gruel and yoghurt, looking like cadavers on amphetamines. At the end of the shift, we all collapse together, in Doctor Angel's little "private" room — the only private room in our entire kingdom, two metres by two, as it may be, to unravel our fatigue in all night debates which often take the place of sleep, on nights when none of us can close an eye, and Doctor Angel has the camp's only supply of booze, *arak* or even whisky in bottles of lemon or orange pop, or even labelled surgical supplies, a necessary item smuggled in to keep him topped up, his own vital anaesthetic for the overloaded mind. We no longer notice Benjamin among us, sitting there as if he naturally belongs, with Faisal, Rashid, Abu Daoud, Nabil, Kamal, myself and whoever else drops in to Angel's cell.

"So tell us about yourself, winged stranger! What are you doing here, you fucking Greek Yankee! You're not a Palestinian, not even a fucking Israeli, like Benny. What's your excuse? You Goddamn fucking masochist! Haven't you a home to go to?"

"A home? What in the name of God is that?"

"Pass us some more of that embalming fluid . . ."

"A home? Yes, I suppose I did have a home, once. Come to think of it I had it twice, if you count the brief passage with my wife . . . She was a doctor, too, you know. A saint. She worked in hospitals in Harlem. She stood with her finger in the dyke of poverty, racism, violence. I never saw her, from our honeymoon onwards, except asleep, in the bed. We communicated by phone, in sound bites, like American politicians. I cheated on her, and she severed all relations. I couldn't notice the difference, so I left. She had this huge dog, which never left the house, and was fed on hamburger meat by her brother, who lived on the ground floor. It began as a small, cuddly puppy, and grew up into a colossal monster, about five feet high at the shoulder. I woke up one day to find that I had married the Hound of the Baskervilles, instead of my wife . . ."

"Begin at the beginning, Angelopoulos! None of these shaggy-dog stories . . ."

"I was born into an immigrant family in Queens. It was like being in a big, noisy bear-pit. There were a thousand relatives, who refused to leave. My mother had been an acrobat, in the Yugoslav Circus. My father was the last Greek Trotskyist to come down from the mountains after the Greek Civil War. He crossed the border, after Stalin betrayed the guerrillas to the British and abandoned them to their fate. He bummed about

Yugoslavia, and was taken on as a rigger in a Serbian circus. My mother was living with the strongman at the time, a man named Popov. My father challenged him to a fist fight, to win my mother's heart. He was beaten to a pulp sixteen times. In the end, to save him from annihilation, my mother ran off with him to Italy, where they were married in Milan. She had relatives there, who also had relatives in the United States. She travelled pregnant, in steerage, across the Atlantic, holding me in for three extra weeks so she could give birth to an American baby. My father, who had sustained abdominal damage from his encounters with Popov, developed various ailments and I had to visit him constantly in hospital. I became fascinated by the doctors, who could do nothing for my father except relieve his pains and prescribe pills. I wandered about the corridors and wards, numbed by the mysteries of illness and pain, watching the chaos of the emergency rooms, where poor people waited in endless patience to be paid attention to. I made friends with some of the interns, who showed me textbooks and charts. Then my father died, and I was enraged that nothing could be done to save his life. My mother withdrew into her own shell from then on. But I became, like my father, a political animal, and I became involved with a group of Puerto Rican militants who taught me the life of the streets. I became the only Greek Puerto Rican. My uncle, a clever man, who dealt in scrap iron, offered to pay my way through medical school. He swept me off the streets. But I found my way to the third world, Latin America, Africa, Asia, the Middle East."

"Fuck the Middle East! Tell us about New York women."

"No, give us another Japanese menu. The different kinds of sushi —"

"Ike, Ogake, Ikenaki, Idami, Tatami, Ikebaku, Okedi . . ."

"He's making it all up . . ."

"Otaki, Mitsudami, Hokaiddo, Giderah, Zakebani . . ."

The silence outside is deafening. Sometimes the Amal mortarmen let us get through the night. Sometimes not. The Syrians prefer a nine-to-five bombardment, with three meal breaks. Evenings their officers sit and play backgammon and dream about the whores out of reach in the East Beirut brothels. There is some action in the western sector, by the ruins of the big hotels, but those girls risk the dangers of interruption by the zealots of one or other of the Hizbollah groups which has not been paid sufficient hush money to cancel out the Wrath of Allah. Even masturbation is an offence against God, of course. Oh, how much defiance of the Almighty takes place in the stealthy, slow small hours! Myself, fatigue has practically drained me of lustful thoughts, let alone practice . . . Whatever memory has not already dulled. Though Angelopoulos thrives on the complicated schemes and stratagems he devises to navigate Norwegian Anneka's fiords. We may be, after all, in our absurd statelet, a normal taboo-ridden Arab country, but we have learned to turn blind eyes and ears to the loud moaning of our senior medical personnel on their inspection tours of blind alleys, temporarily vacated rooms and cellars, and even roofs, braving the lethal metal ejaculations of the enemy's war machine. We even managed to stop the admiring cries of Jamil the kebab-vendor, who used to thrust his huge head from his bunker every time that husky breath ensued from some hidden corner, and yell out: "Allahu akbar! akbar!"

Human foibles. The young men and women of our Lilliputian entity have found a different solution to their needs. Amazingly, in all this carnage, we perform marriages, at least two or three times a week. We lost our *kadi*, early in the siege, to a stray bullet, and never had a priest, so Angelopoulos, as the senior figure of authority, performs the ceremonies and records the deeds, not to speak of burying the dead. (He has convinced the devout that circumcisions can be put off for the duration. Everyone knows that the barber, Hakim, is available, though the poor man's trembling, shell-shocked hands keep even the unshaved away from his door.) More often than not, the young man dashes off, before he can even kiss the bride, let alone carry out his obligations, to confront the latest shelling, only to be brought back to the clinic an hour later, bleeding from a dozen places or minus a hand or a leg. We have invented new, terrifying conjunctions. A wedding and burial of the same person in one day. The manufacture of instant widows. And other innovative social forms.

Night dread. Eventually fatigue takes over, dropping us where we sit like rag dolls. The morning waking us, occasionally, to an eerie silence. We crawl out warily to examine the latest town planning carried out by the enemy's firepower. Ruined houses reduced by another few feet, a new arrangement of iron-girder latticework framing the dull, hazy sky. An alley, passable yesterday, rubble-choked today. The corrugated-iron barri-

cades, dented and twisted by shells and bullets into a kind of modern art-
work, screaming against the ills of war. The electric wires, rigged and
rerigged every day to hook over the main cables to steal the city's electricity, were down, and Jamil Kebab already clambering dangerously on a shattered rooftop, with rubber gloves, to rehook the live wires. A Beirut
custom antedating the siege, one of the city's favourite forms of Russian
Roulette. Cursing, the huge man, with his pot belly and massive, sweating
arms, lifts up the fallen wires and begins throwing them over the mains.
From below, Abu Daoud, the Fatah commander, waves and shouts at him:
"Get down, you fucking lunatic!" But the kebab-vendor just spits, spraying saliva towards the enemy, shouting back: "Let them shoot! I'll skewer
their balls!"

Abu Daoud, a scarred, white-haired man with one eye, one and a half
ears, eight toes and, amazingly, nine fingers, shrugs and gives up, limping
agilely over the rubble towards the front line, followed by his entourage of
armed teenagers. People's heads warily pop out from window spaces,
cracks in walls, holes in the ground. From behind a heap of rubble, old
Umm Mahmud comes into view, wielding an old broomstick to sweep the
mess away. Stones, gravel, pulverised concrete, metal shards, spent shells,
splinters of wood and lumps of asphalt, driven across Abu Daoud's path.
He restrains her gently. Umm Mahmud suffers from senile dementia, and
she performs this task come rain of bullets or calm, until dragged physically to safety, in the belief that she is keeping order in the courtyard of her
Jaffa home, in 1946, or 1935, or 1926, whatever. Her dead parents, her
absent or missing or dead brothers, sisters, uncles, aunts, sons, daughters
and grandchildren, nephews and nieces have all merged into a salad of
interchangeable personalities, surrounding her as she labours on, an endless jabber of memories trickling from her toothless mouth. And then suddenly she might freeze, like a bent stick, lifting a bony hand at the sky,
screeching vitriolic curses at the Turks, the British, the French, the Americans and the Jews.

"God strike them blind! Cut off their legs! Shrivel their penises! Burn
the seed in their wombs! God strike down Winston Churchill!" In her
most coherent moments she imagined it was the British who were besieging the camp. Field Marshal "Ukhinlek" was orchestrating the shelling

from the top of the stadium. Umm Mahmud's first husband had been hanged by the British in Acre prison in 1937, for his part in ambushing and wiping out a British patrol in the Arab Revolt. Later she became a member of the Women's Committee of the Trade Unions of Palestine. She spoke at forums, agitated, went to prison, travelled all over the Arab world. Now, a shrivelled hulk, she shouts abuse at the sky. In his eyrie, Field Marshal "Ukhinlek" looked down, unpityingly, at the fruits of his enterprise, and winked.

"God strike them blind!"

"Benjamin!" The Israeli hostage came forward to relieve Abu Daoud of the old woman, coaxing her back down to safety in the cellars. For some reason she is calmed by his soft voice in Hebrew. She jabbers at him about the Jews, he sings her lullabies in German. They are a sight to see, he, Mad Latif and the old woman, scavenging together in the alleys for scrap to fill the sandbag barricades.

The morning lull cannot last long. A burst of machine-gun fire, from the forward positions. Mortars, plopping from the stadium. That terrible incoming whistle. The fighters crouch behind the piles of stones and crumbled walls. I hold tight to my own M16 carbine, well bought from a mercenary Phalange source, crawl over debris and detritus to reach Abu Daoud's side.

"Another day, another dollar," he shouts wryly in the pandemonium. He once ran a falafel store, in New York. Then, one day, two skullcapped youths from the Jewish Defence League, assuming he was someone else, brought a poster calling for the expulsion of all Arabs from "the Land of Israel" and asked him if they could put it up on his wall. He pulled out a gun and asked if they wanted to expel one right now. They told him coolly that he didn't bother them, as he had already expelled himself. The next day he sold his store to an Armenian colleague and bought a one-way ticket to Amman. This was back in '69. And much blood flowed under the dry-wadi bridges from then, and in the running rivers, and the streets . . .

"Ah! They're playing our tune!"

A hit, on the building behind us, showered dust and fragments onto our hair. We had, at Angelopoulos's suggestion, constructed a multi-layered system of barriers, rooms within rooms, divided by iron sheets.

Even armour-piercing shells would eventually slow down and be stopped short of the inhabited inner layers. We spread metal sheets and nets over the alleyways, so the bombs would spring off and ricochet harmlessly into the neutral zones. This provided defence for the families, but in the front lines it was luck, or fate. A boy on Abu Daoud's right scrambled boldly up the parapet of stones, hefting his Kalashnikov AK47, which was twice his size. Tiny Ali, the carpenter's son. He let fly, emptying his magazine at nothing. Abu Daoud's deputy, Abu Salim, scrabbled forward to pull the boy down. But the replying burst struck them both, tearing out a piece of the boy's shoulder and clipping Abu Salim's head. They fell at our feet. "Casualty!" I cried out. A group of four women appeared from nowhere, spreading out two big white sheets. We laid Tiny Ali on one, Abu Salim on the other. Running, kicking stones out of the way, leaping from wall to wall, bursting through to the inner sanctum of the clinic and the emergency room, where Anneka and Klaus are gowned and ready, to deal with Tiny Ali and prepare Abu Salim for Doctor Angel's operating table. The harsh breath, the gasping oxygen machines, the shining spotlights of the battery-driven lights, the drips, the clamps, the gloved hands. The kingdom of the healing knives.

Love is splattered with blood and viscera, razor-edged, cutting deep.

"It's a craniotomy, my friends."

The first head case of the day . . .

Cutting deep. The first incision. The patient's head has been shaved. Cut out the osteoplastic flap, clamp the bleeding blood vessels. Begin sucking up the fragments of bone, blood and brain tissue oozing out. With the bone-nibbling forceps, down into the meninges. Through the scalp, deep into the area of pulped brain. Another excavation into the unknown, irrigating, injecting saline, debriding the devitalised tissue, coasting down the cranial veins. Here we go! Manoeuvring among the torn fragments of personality and experience — the man, creeping along the blocked-in alleyways, carrying the load of his life with him, the armed gunman, the political animal, the committee member, the drinking partner, the loving father, the bereaved parent, the faithful brother, the implacable zealot, the tireless concocter of conspiracy theories in endless café clutches, the smell of roast coffee (the nasal route to the sphenoidal air sinus and the pituitary gland), the taste buds salivating to the spread of mezzehs on small plates (the humus, the t'hinas, the tabouleh, labani, kaftas, the pickled aubergines, basturma, kibbeh, foul medames, falafels, vine leaves, moutabal, lamb's brain salad, man's brain salad), the sweetness of baklava and spring mornings, the conversation of friends (the aural route: magnus, posterior, auriculo-temporal, the vibrating membrana tympani), the sight of almost-naked flesh on the beach, (the occulomotor connected to the levator palpebrae superioris), the teaming streets of Beirut and other cities, the solid mass of Cairo, the sinuous flow of Algiers, the stormy tides of PNC congresses, the faces contorted in excitement, passion, anger, the choking fumes of Gauloise chatter, the endless litany of affirmation —The Cause, The Movement, The Land, The Party, The Arab Nation, The Brotherhood, The Faith, The Return. The ebb and flow of massed dreams. Cut, cut, irrigate, debride, cauterise the bleeding point with the diathermic current, sizzle and coagulate those vessels, dredge up the rubble of childhood — the babe in arms, jolted down the road to exile, the stench and squalour of the refugee camps, running with the gangs, bare feet on gravel, rubbish, excrement, broken glass and dropped cargoes, drawing the Enemy with coloured UNRWA crayons, the unseen demon with his planes and guns, the glottal echoes of humiliation, the empty promises of radio revenge. Dreams! Behind one's eyelids, shut out the dust and dither of the world, the visions, the fine cornfields, olive groves and pomegranates and plums, lazy pathways curving on to unseen horizons, the rustle of an ear of corn, the buzz of bees and wasps, the richness of the earth, life, from seeds that bud, burst, eyelashes fluttering over green eyes, the depths of the pool into which one dives, straining for the fountain of life, the tree dripping with pearls, the enchanted bird's trilling, the rivers of milk, the petals of honey. A man need only float, effortlessly, to achieve, regain, paradise. And then the storm clouds, bursting in cluster of pellets, fire, sulphur, phosphorous, exploding metal and steel. The beloved bursts open, raw meat struck by the butcher's axe. Heart, entrails, kidneys, uterus, womb, erupt in red slime. Compound fractures of the soul. Splinters of bone everywhere.

"Forceps! Clamp! Needle! Thread! Scissors! Sellotape! Band-Aids! Cement! Putty! Glue! Blu-tack!"

Dreams cannot be restitched. Life unsticks everything, hope, desire, aspiration, memory. Even history becomes unhinged. Ah, yes! *Field Marshal Ukhinlek!* The old lady totters down the road, carrying, under her dress, the necessary ammunition to supply the rebels fighting in the Upper Galilee: 7.65mm bullets, Mills grenades, sticks of dynamite, Lee-Enfield rifles, Thompson submachine-guns, mortars, bombs, plastique, Semtex, nuclear triggers, aircraft, tanks. Around the night campfires, the *fidayin* comrades squat, chewing horse meat, cracking open eggs and crunching their way through a consignment of matsohs taken from an ambushed Jewish van. Crumbs of unleavened bread falling upon the holy soil, reverberating to the profane tramp of British jackboots, straps unwinding from ill-fitting puttees.

Revenge! Revenge! Under the surface, the women and children and old men gather in the cramped basements and cellars, immured underground, several hundred people in spaces barely twenty-five by twenty metres, makeshift oil-lamps from soda-pop bottles lighting the piles of pots, pans, plastic baskets of salvaged household utensils, quilts and blankets spread on concrete floors.

DOWN WITH IMPERIALISM! REPEL THE INVADER!

"So what are the prospects for Abu Salim, Doctor?"

"A good chance. Two centimetres more and pffft!"

"Well, you did it again."

"Just pass the bottle."

"Do you want it intravenous, Fallen Angel?"

"Oral will do."

"How long has it been now?"

"Three months, two weeks, five days, eighteen hours and fifty-three minutes."

"And how much longer?"

"Allahu akbar."

Could we have done otherwise? Were there paths we were too blind to walk? The pit is blasted open under your feet, you are kindly invited to step in. Perhaps that bastard Gadaffi was right, back in '82 —— we should have all stayed in the city and committed suicide en masse, like the Jews at Masada. Stoking the legend of our return. So what's two thousand years? A drop in the ocean, compared to twenty-four hours in this hole. Should we have embraced our own disappearance, to shuck the flesh and become a burning bush, a symbol, a set of desolate badges to be sold in souvenir and antique shops?

"Whadayathink, Angelopoulos, are we real or phantoms?"

"Does it have to be one or the other, Tewfiq?"

No route of escape should be shunned. Where do we go, after our death? Is it straight to heaven or hell, or are there more delays on the way? Knowing us, I would not be surprised to find a displaced dead person's camp standing there, in all its filth and putridity, at the foot of the gates of heaven, a final obstacle for stateless bastards whose documents are not in order.

"We are only real to the extent that we struggle. If we stop struggling we cease to exist."

The words of Kamal Abd-el-Rahman, "cultural" officer of the Popular Front. To Kamal, we are all mere jigsaw pieces of the Imperialist-Zionist World Plan, shaken and scattered by the unseen hand, up there, in the White House, of the Old Elder of Zion in the Oval Office, scanning his secret monitor screens with his spidery eyes, tapping out his orders for the subjection of the Wretched of the Earth. It is absolutely necessary for Kamal to be the object of attention by the powerful and the supreme. Glory cannot come from opposition to mere humans who sweat and belch and bleed like us, but to an all-embracing conspiracy. It is a part of our political vocabulary, the symptoms of our underdevelopment: The Plot. Because if it is so, our own mistakes, miscalculations and misdeeds are marginal. And when victory comes! Ah, that is true glory, the triumph of Good over Absolute Evil, a cosmic victory. We are only real to Kamal if we represent a principle, an eternal truth. The leaders, Abu Ammar among them, are all small politicians who have lost their way. He argues passion-ately against Geneva Conferences, a separate Palestinian State in two sliv-ers of the usurped homeland, and all other CIA-Israel plots, manoeuvres and ploys. All or nothing. Victory or death.

Nevertheless, we all need each other. Kamal needs us traitors and CIA dupes for our firepower, which keeps him and his rump unit alive. We need him for his contacts with Hizbollah, the Party of God, who harass their fellow Shi'as of Amal from the outside, picking off stragglers, arranging for a friendly guard to close an eye for some minutes while ammunition or food is smuggled through. They believe in God, Kamal believes in Karl Marx, and both detest the Syrians, who are, in fact, the patrons of Kamal's own commanders outside the camp. Kamal is being shot at by his own sponsors. It's the familiar mess.

"A bound man struggles against his bonds, Kamal, but if he can't get free he has to pause and think out some sort of strategy . . ."

"The Struggle. The Struggle is our strategy."

"No," says Abu Daoud, "I agree with Petros. We have always been reacting and responding. We should be initiating. I think we'll find the whole South Lebanon episode was a blunder from which the Israelis rescued us. We lost a geographical foothold that was in fact a trap . . ."

Kamal: "We should have fought on to the end, in sight of the world, instead of dying here forgotten."

"Should our situation be judged by the presence of television?"

Unbroadcast, we exist even less. Those outside want to kill us all, whatever our political shades. In Tel el-Zaatar in '76, the Maronites (mortal enemies of the Shi'as who are bombarding us now) were so proud of their accomplishment they brought in the world's press to film the mutilated bodies, squashed flat on the roads by the cars of their followers given special chits to loot the conquered camp. In Shatila, too, we were reduced to photographic objects of the pornography of war. Enterprising Lebanese packaging images to export to global networks of necrophiliacs.

The booze, for God's sake, the booze!

One by one, the fighters crawl off to their holes. The night rolls on, quiet again. Just the scuttering sounds of the camp's fitful slumber, the muffled hospital groans. The creaking of the broken houses, scabs falling off their scars and shellholes. There used to be a wailing of cats, till we ate 'em. The hum and cough of the basement generator, always on the point of seizing up. The Angel and I propped against the wall, eyeing the empty whisky bottle, like two Mexican revolutionaries in a Sergio Leone movie, caught by the *Federales* and about to be taken out and shot at dawn. Where are our last rites, Padre? Do your duty, *muchachos!* Blindfolds? No, we've had enough of those . . .

"Tell me about your wife, Tewfiq."

"Oh no, Angel, that's not possible."

"Talk, Tewfiq. Let it out. You can't keep it in for ever."

"What can I say? It's just a drop in the ocean."

"Don't talk tough with me Tewfiq. Let it all hang out."

"Fuck you, Angel."

"Fuck you too, Tewfiq."

He fixes me with his large wet eyes, like a seal, blinking on an ice floe, waiting for the culling crew.

"Tell me more about your wife, Angel. The one with the Hound of the Baskervilles in New York. Tell me about your life in Sin City. What is it like to fuck other angels? Do the feathers get in the way?"

"The angels have exquisite moves, Tewfiq. When they're not binding themselves to rocks and singing. Their vaginas are made of milk and honey. But they live outside New York, my friend. In Westchester County. Some as far afield as New Hampshire. Vermont. I spent a winter once locked in a cabin in the snow with a poetess at an art colony. You know what an art colony is, Tewfiq? The artists descend and rape the pristine landscape, dispossessing the ants, the squirrels, the bears, taking over their habitat and mooning on about the beauties of nature. This woman had pure white pubic hair and wrote in iambic pentameter about the Fall of Mankind. She said we were living in the Last Generation. I suggested we should use the little time left. We fucked like demented rabbits. There was nothing else to do. If she had been a novelist, I would have gone mad, they have so much empty paper to fill. But her poems were never more than ten lines. Menials from the art colony brought us groceries and left them in baskets outside the door. By the end of a month, my hair was falling out, not to speak of my cock. It was a most glorious moment."

"So what happened to her, Fallen Angel?"

"She became a marketing consultant, for a health-food conglomerate. Now she owns a farm in Colorado. I have no desire to see Colorado. But I would like to see those pubic hairs again . . ."

"Exquisite fields . . ."

"Those were the days."

He sighed and fell asleep. I crawled out, in what should have been the

first light of dawn, if such a thing were possible. Scrabbling along the sheltered, rubble-strewn passageways on my hands and knees, like the missing
link. Not between man and the apes, but between the apes and something
more primitive. And not even a moon to howl at. Let it all hang out.
Putrid visions. Idyllic pasts that never happened. Her name was Adela. I
was a Moslem, she was a Greek Orthodox Christian. Thus she ended up
living in the wrong street at the wrong time. The people who came for her
were Christians. The real wolves in lamb's clothing. They shot her in the
stomach and then, with knives, disembowelled her on the bedroom carpet.
The one we had bought second-hand, from Abu Fakri. Friends came to
take me home from work to view the job the Lambs of Bethlehem had performed. They had shot my two children too, by the way: Fawaz, who was
four years old; Adina, who was three. But they did not mutilate their bodies. Everyone draws a line, somewhere. They shot my wife because they did
not like the articles I was writing about their field commander, Aziz
Khamash. The man who commmited the murder in person was a teenage
thug named Rashid Zagour. He was blown up, I was informed, three
months later, in a car bomb set by a rival Maronite militia. The right hand
blows up the left, the left, the right, until we are all mutilated. But Aziz
Khamash still walks the earth, surrounded, in his mountain village, by a
poisoned ring of guards. And I, I crawl the rubbish-strewn fields of Jaffa
Camp, just another maggot in the carcass of what was once a city, now neither of God nor of man. A jumble of warped recollections, not only in
Umm Mahmud's muddled mind. Come on, idiot-savant, give us those
measurements again — 243 metres east to west, 264 metres north to south.
The average size of each building, exclusive of rubble: 8 by 6.3 metres and
declining. The calculated weight of all the stone and concrete debris in the
camp: 61,137 tons. The total length of the underground labyrinth, cellars,
tunnels, shafts (including defunct sewage pipes): 38 kilometres and 635
metres. Population in the camp: 2,076 and declining. Excess of deaths over
births: 300 per cent. The statistical probability of being struck by a projec-
tile (excluding shrapnel), over a period of one month (30 calendar days):
38.6 per cent. The probability of a fatal wound: 18.3.

The Struggle, the Struggle is our strategy.

Over the rubble, from the Shi'a positions, the minaret of a rebuilt mosque emits the call to prayer. In the name of God, the Compassionate, the Merciful . . . Guide us to the straight path . . . At the End of Days, we shall all be judged. There is no shortage of executioners.

The knife, Angel, the knife! Scalpel! Forceps! Sickles! Scythes! Scimitars and broadswords!

Chop off our heads. Our hearts will simply have to get on on their own. There seems so little connection, anyway. Sew up the seams of the neck and let those torsos walk. Or legless, handless, lie twitching in the mud. Let there be an end to this endless cycle. Don't bother with the Resurrection.

I lie there, too drunk and weary in the faint light of the day. My tongue hanging out towards broken glass and rubble, glimmering with fading visions, the echoes of so many bold sermons, lies, diatribes, tales of woe and hindsights. The past, the future, the impossible present, where Field Marshal Ukhinlek and Winston Churchill metamorphose into Ariel Sharon, Menachem Begin, Hafez al-Asad, Bashir Gemayel and Nabih Berri, yesterday's ally. Aziz Khamash, alive on his mountain. The murderers hoarding their spoils. The Struggle —— Al-Thawrah — rebellion, insurrection, revolution. The metaphysical concept, snapping at our innards, the soul's vengeance against ancient wrongs. The Shi'a clerics say it is the primal revenge of Abel against his brother, Cain. We can elect whoever we wish as these protagonists. I am Abel, he is Cain. The Other. The Unbeliever. The Crusader. First there was Adam, the first human. Then he splits, into good and evil. I am Abel. He is Cain. There can be no compromise between the two. The Struggle. Timeless, eternal, never-ending. The battlefield in which all clocks have lost their hands. Where even the dead grow tired. And fallen angels cut and stitch and fix and heal in vain.

> *With earth's first clay they did the last man knead,*
> *And there of the last harvest sowed the seed,*
> *And the first morning of creation wrote*
> *What the last dawn of reckoning shall read.*

Paracletes, with blazing swords. Saviours into sinners, and vice versa. I see, in the blur of alcohol fumes, an armoured knight riding through the broken alleys of the refugee camp, his breastplate and limbs a dull grey, spattered with mud and excrement, his steed a massive, slow-moving water buffalo, scalps and hacked-off hands hanging about his saddlebag, his pennant a bloody skull and crossbones, his helmet's crest a crown of thorns, an ancient, chipped Roman spear held in his right gauntlet, his visor's slit sealed shut, his rusted metal joints creaking in a shrill, steady cadence. He advances till his steed stands over my prone body, its nostrils exhaling fetid breath in my face. A muffled rumble ensuing from the sealed visor:

"Which way to Jerusalem, varlet?"

I point south. The massive load passes over me, one hoof treading on my groin. I cry out with the pain, but he passes on, the Syrian sniper bullets clanging off his cuirass, backplate, pauldrons, as he creaks off into the distance, emitting a steady stream of dry stools, around which squadrons of flies and legions of rats, pushing their way up from the sewers, gather, in a joyful chorus of buzzing, squealing hymns.

"HOSANNAH! HOSANNAH!"

Shahids never listen to advice . . .

FOUR

A Flexible, Nested Set of Fields

"IT'S A HYPOTHESIS, SON," MacKENZIE EXPLAINED SOFTLY. "HOW ARE things created, how do they evolve? Where does the pattern come from? Are things just copies of immutable ideas, latent from the Big Bang and only waiting to come into being? Or are we looking for a concept which allows its own organic development, a flexible, nested set of fields which incorporate all that happened in the past? An endless web, woven with everything that was and, possibly, everything that will be? Picture you this: Each field with a built-in memory derived from self-resonance with its own past. An accumulation, a matter of habit, the more patterns are repeated, the more habitual they become. You are what we all were. But these are probability structures. We are constantly changing and adapting. Its a hard slog, but we can twist it like clay in the potter's hand. The upshot is, you are not alone, laddie. You're part of a harmonious whole. We're finally free of the mechanistic universe. Everything is up for grabs."

Mackenzie believed that stimulating his patients' sluggish minds would pay dividends, but bending Danny Hohenlohe/Pick's ear with "morphic resonance" may not have been so fine a notion. Avram Blok and Kathleen had to bear the brunt of this strategy, as Hohenlohe unearthed an old voltmeter from The Retreat's attic and insisted on dragging them along, down towards Gullane, testing the beaches, the rocks, the gorse-strewn hills.

"The Harmonious Hole. Where do you think it is?" Poking about in caves and rabbit burrows, lifting up the golf-course flags. In the old days it might have served him as a good title for a short story, but now the boundaries between fact and fiction were blurred. This made it difficult for Blok or Mackenzie to place credence in Hohenlohe's tale of three Middle Easterners spying on The Retreat, after their mouth-organ performance at Drem station. Despite Angelopoulos's claim that he had alighted alone, Hohenlohe dragged Blok to the empty Scotrail station, onto the platform, under the sign saying KEEP BACK FROM THE EDGE. PASSING TRAINS CAUSE AIR TURBULENCE, pressing him to the station wall as the London Intercity from Edinburgh whooshed past, almost sweeping them up like Dorothy of Kansas on a tornado to Oz. But the only possible clue was an old cigarette butt, lying under the poster urging them to HAVE A SUPER SPRINTING SHOPPING DAY OUT WITH THE DIMPLIES, which Daniel flourished triumphantly under Blok's nose.

"It was probably the morphic resonance of one of your old stories," said Blok, as they sauntered with Kathleen across the Gullane Links, "a message from the id, saying, get back to work and write. What was that tune you said they were playing? The theme from Once Upon a Time in the West?"

"Believe It or Not," said Hohenlohe, still bent to the ground, "Oysters Growing on Trees Can Catch Rats. Buffalo Bill Never Shot a Buffalo. The Famous Hindu Yogi, Pratapa Hathanoga, Buried His Head in the Ground for Nine Hours. Abraham Was Not a Jew."

"I used to know that stuff," Blok responded warmly, "The Chimpanzee Who Was Convicted of Smoking a Cigar in Public in Indiana. The Roman Poet, Virgil, Spent One Hundred Thousand Dollars on the Burial of His Pet Fly."

"Two Scandinavians Who Rowed Across the Atlantic Ocean in a Bucket."

"Methuselah, the Oldest Man in the Bible, Died Before His Father."

"The King Who Was Crowned Before He Was Born."

Staff and patients, who can tell them apart? Kathleen left Blok to coax his charge back to sanctuary, while she drove her battered Fiat into Edinburgh, rendezvousing for a pub lunch at the Claymore with Angelopoulos and Sophia. The balming burr of small talk, the antediluvian bond between the Scots and their drink, uncomfortable seats and dim lights. Doctor Angel and Sophia chose the jumbo sausage and chips, while Kathleen opted for the carrot and bean salad. Angelopoulos ebullient, about his delight in the city's rugged landscapes, the cold volcano, the castle, the houses of dark stone, the light hearts. "Where's all those dour Scots I've been hearing about, Kathleen? I think you must all be secret Greeks."

"Well," said Sophia, "that was the theory of an old local journalist, Comyns Beaumont, back in the thirties. He wrote two books, proving that Ben Nevis was Mount Olympus and Edinburgh is the true biblical Jerusalem, the castle being the Temple Mount, and so on."

"It makes sense," said Angel. "The bagpipes, the kilts, the Celtic Gods. The love of fucking. But you got the short straw on the climate."

"You're pining for the Levantine sun?" Kathleen asked him.

"Always," said Angel. "The kiss of the heat. The *cafard*. Too much sanity and reason makes me restless."

"So what's holding you here?" said Sophia.

He winked at her over his disappearing sausage. She looked at Kathleen and shrugged. "You live with a Levantine, explain it to me."

"I've given up a long time ago."

"It's the unpredictability," the Angel grunted; "you never know what might come next."

"Not with Avram," said Kathleen. "He came here to escape all that. He wants tomorrow to be exactly like today."

"I can understand that," said Doctor Angel, "but if I had two days exactly alike, I would die. Apart from R and R of course. Rest and Recreation. Sometimes you just have to lie low and recharge the batteries. You can't do that in the Middle East. That's plugging direct into the current. I've seen people burn like that too often."

"Rubber gloves, that's the ticket," said Sophia. A certain buzz between these two. Kathleen eyed them warily. It was characteristic of Sophia that her affairs were transient and tumultuous. "It's the Italian blood, you know," she would claim, taking refuge in self-stereotyping. The trail of confessions in long late-night confidences stretching back to schooldaze and the inseparable Wee Threes, Sophia, Kathleen and Janet of Craddock, amid memories of long socks and freezing fifties winters, dreams of escape to sun-kissed vineyards and phantasies of mysterious assignations in distant cafés. A bond cemented by the partly foreign origin of each: Janet's Polish father; Kathleen's mother, Ruth, who had been a budding sculptress in 1930s Berlin. In 1934 she met a Scots metallurgist on a business trip who whisked her away in the nick of time from Germany and soon abandoned metallurgy to open a garage in Craddock. She taught German in the local school. He died young, when Kathleen was five, and her mother never sculpted again, but lived long enough to meet Avram Blok. "After the first one, anything's an improvement," she commented generously. Kathleen's first husband, Alistair, had been an indigent artist who wanted to live every sixties cliché. Freedom from responsibility and order. Cleanliness is as bad as Leninness. She had named her dog after him, as a dreadful reminder of the pitfalls of gullibility. Janet had given her fair warning, on the second round, having herself endured an Israeli first spouse: "You may think you're getting this self-confident warrior and you end up with a psychotic three-year-old." Janet had since opted for a native news cameraman, and spent most of her current life in London, producing BBC children's programs. So now there were just Kathleen and Sophia, no more Wee Threes, only Too Twos.

"I'm just a sucker for sad, silent types, Sophie . . ." Those confessional nights, before the sputtering gas fire, BCH (Before Central Heating), the cold rain against the windows, the Glenmorangie. Kathleen musing: "After Alistair, it's a boon. At least he doesn't drink, though that's a pain in the ass sometimes . . ."

"You're well shot of that one, *cara mia*. At least you were adamant on contraception. One large adult child is enough."

Nevertheless, the old ridiculous dreams, of the post-nuclear, neo-hippy family, which would scour the world in a psychedelic van. Bob Dylan, winds of change, CND, Vietnam, and Alistair painting strange murals of Mao Tse Tung in a kilt on horseback, slaying the dragon of U.S. Imperialism. After their divorce, Alistair had gone into the brewery business, with his father, as his father had, with his father before him.

"You can plead insanity, Kathy. What do you expect, after all those drafty corridors, Calvinism and reheated mince. We survived . . ."

Aye. Sophia passed to Angelopoulos the last half of her jumbo sausage. "This is far too jumbo for me." The Terrorist Doctor wolfed it down. The pub filling up after working hours, punters small talking along the tables. Football, art and politics. Sophia had not long ago returned from Prague, a pilgrimage deriving from the miracle of the Velvet Revolution, a celebration of the Communist Fall. Further ghosts of times gone by, angry marches to protest Russian tanks crushing spring. But she had returned in a sad mood.

"People are waking up from the dream. It's morning and nobody's collected the rubbish. No one's sure which way to go, after that great, fiery glow of unity. People are still waiting for someone to tell them what to do. But that someone is just another struggling artist, trundling round the presidential palace on a toy scooter, rattling locked doors and looking for the keys."

"No one believed it would all collapse so quickly," said Angelopoulos, "like a house of cards. It shows our thinking about the world is still bound by old concepts. However much we believe ourselves to be independent, self-determining beings, we're still following given patterns. We needed someone like Gorbachev to take us by the scruff of the neck and shake all that dead wood out. And now the genie is out of the bottle, anything can happen."

"Except, of course, in Maggie's farm."

"You never know, you never know. Here, let me get the next round. Who gets what?" He swam off towards the bar, cutting a way through the human surf. Kathleen eyeing her friend solicitously.

"Are you all right, Sophie?"

"I can handle it. I'm too busy to be thrown off balance. I have exhibitions to organise up to here. The Grosz and the Ernst. Endless hassle. Anything new from the sea?"

"I'm just scratching. Something has to turn up on the beach, but I'm not quite sure what. I'll know it when I see it."

"I got another letter from that woman in Australia. The Woolloomooloo Gallery in Sydney. She might come for the Festival. We should always have a bolt-hole in reserve. Eh, what do you think, *cara mia*?"

"You never know."

"How's Avram and the lunatics?"

"Like a house on fire. He went off with that writer. Remember I told you, the one who wants to kill his editor."

"Good luck to the poor bugger."

"He thinks three Middle Eastern types are following our Petros. Shadowing his every move."

"What was that?" The Doctor returned, bearing medication. Two double Bell's and an Export for Kathleen.

"Danny Pick's Three Arab Bears."

"They're probably Saudi surveyors," said Angelopoulos, "hoping to buy the coast for an oil well. Its just the old story. ADPG — Angst, Depression, Paranoia and Guilt. One runs into it all the time."

"Avram's worried because this ex-editor of Danny's is coming to visit him in a couple of weeks. It's another of Mackenzie's weird cures. Shock therapy."

"Yes, he consulted me about poisons," said Angelopoulos. "I gave him some advice, but no prescriptions. Those who talk don't act. It's just working out your aggressions. I saw it in the camps all the time. Better to encourage the mouth than the trigger finger. Well, here's to auld Edinburrrah!"

"Cheers."

"Le'chayim."

The pub swirl. The cosy cocoon. Familiarity. One's hearth and home. Kith and kin. Native abode. Domicile. Motherland. Fatherland. Haven. Shelter. Sanctuary. Asylum. But one can't hide in the crowd forever. Kathleen downed her drink and exited, leaving Sophia and Petros Angelopoulos to their mutual exploration. The peaks and valleys, caves and undergrowth. She marched down Lothian Road in a developing drizzle, turning at the rotunda of the Usher Hall towards Castle Terrace and the car park, the ugly concrete tiers challenging the spotlit grandeur of the Castle, its shining rock crumbling and held in place by massive ramparts of scaffolding. Collecting her car and driving into the rush hour of Princes Street. The bright lights of Marks and Spencer's. Round the Calton, down the London Road towards Portobello. The Joppa of Comyns Beaumont's fantasy. The transposed Promised Land. A fantasy that Avram Blok had embraced as a perverse enticement. "I can fulfil my genetic heritage with-out all of the usual complications," he declared. "No frontier posts, no killing-grounds." A tailor-made delusion. Having followed Janet in years gone by to Craddock, wooed by Mackenzie's siren call to service: "A wor-thy job on lousy pay, laddie." But a fulfilled refuge?

"I'm a retired Citizen of the World, Kathleen. I sent my medals back long ago. Call me a dissident from dissidence. Call me what you want. Call me Ishmael . . .

The one who got away from Moby Dick. She remembered the night they were swept out to sea, a few weeks after he had come to live with her in the beach house. The tide rose, like the Flood, on an unbelievably hot and close summer night, when they had camped out on the sliver of sand in front of the patio. It swept in and carried them off on their inflated rubber mattress, away from the breakwater. The non-swimmer Avram Blok. She had jumped into the water and pulled him towards the shore. But they were spotted and picked up by one of the Craddock fishing boats. He didn't speak to her for two days, but walked off alone, day and night, along the beach, only returning to normal after a brief encounter at the Cockenzie harbour, at three A.M., with a cruising seal, which swam up and down the shoreline, waiting for him to throw in fish. Finally it swam back into the Firth.

And Ishmael clung to passing wreckage . . . The flotsam to be picked up on the beach and moulded into something worthwhile. Not that she had dreamed it would become so bankable with Japanese and German buy-ers. Unlike Avram's Blokbook, which remained a purely private collection of paper jetsam: old postcards, bus and cinema tickets, pamphlets and junk mail, menus for restaurants in Monterey, Greyhound bus schedules, ads for retirement homes in Florida, freeze-dried Astronaut ice cream, plugs for "Madame Olga — Gifted Lady Has Powers to Cure You of All Troubles," classified ads from pornographic news-sheets, and all the mad world's head-lines: "Japanese Yuppies Prepare for Death," "Freedom or Rubbish," "Wel-come Back to Auschwitz," "Bishops Oppose Condoms, Favour Palestinian Homeland," among the yellowing and brittle classics — *Freedom in Papa Dop's Athens: The pro-government newspaper Nea Politia boasted yesterday that the escape of a political prisoner serving an 18-year sentence was proof that there was freedom in Greece — 'this shows the untruth of claims by foreign ene-*

mies *of Greece that prisoners are under continuous surveillance and live under* inhuman conditions. *If that were so, it would have been impossible for any prisoner not only to escape but even to think of escaping.*'"

And in between the bits, the scribbled jottings of mad thoughts and outpourings, disjointed reflections about the world, the universe, the inner flutterings of heart and brain. Should one dress to the right or to the left? Of the necessity of the assault on God. On "cybernetic Jews." On False Systems of Thought. On finding mothballs in one's hair. On Thoughtcrime. On strange legends and conspiracy theories, cults and arcane archaeologies. On Jerusalem, the centripetal, centrifugal city. Even on art and philosophy. "Hah!" she told him, "I caught you out — you are a thinking being!" "Not at all," he demurred; "it's just genetic dribbling." Despite that, he ended up in her bed. Wonders may never cease. What was I looking for, Sophia? Certainly no dream lover. Perhaps a certain comfortable strangeness. Someone to shield me from immersion? How the hell can one know? You just let that hidden tide carry you. ADPG. Why tie yourself up in knots, Kathy? You found a comfortable berth. Neither of you expects too much from the other. That's something to cherish. So he's crazy. It's the normal ones you have to watch. I should know, Kathleen. Indeed. Sophia had contracted an even earlier marriage than her friends', at eighteen, to a Canadian lawyer: "I envisioned him as Perry Mason, dragging his ideals through murky courts, but he ended up in conveyancing. Stick to the maladjusted, my love." And the love child, Sophia's invisible son, Kenneth, now living with his father in Vancouver. Morphic resonances and nested fields.

Kathleen drove on, past Joppa, down the coast road, avoiding the new motorway bypass, through Musselburgh and Prestonpans, past the power station, as dull grey shades into night, the small towns of Cockenzie, Port Seton, Craddock, the darkening waves and rocky beach, at least, a constant, in the ebb and flow of rise and fall, desires and disappointments, expectations and frustrations. While, back in the centrifugal city of stone, the lovers pick up their trail.

". . . Everything that changed, Angel. It's hard to believe it . . ."
"*Plus ça change, plus ça la même chose*, Sophia . . ."

"At Wenceslas Square I sat down and wept, Petros. Can you understand that? I simply put on my sunglasses and bawled my heart out . . . Remembering my visit of '69 . . . The Russian soldiers were still in the streets then, blonde kids in huge khaki greatcoats, wandering about with a glazed look, because people were just walking by them as if they could be wished away like phantoms. I was just nineteen, I'd been invited by the Prague University students to a 'World Symposium on Student Art.' They'd thought up all sorts of tricks to get Western students into the country, to keep up a bridge with the world. But it was already way past spring. February. The whole city was grey and icy cold. People took us into their flats, past prying concierges, and fed us dreadful dumplings and stew and talked in low tones about the Occupation. The buildings were still marked with graffiti of 'Dubček' and 'Svoboda.' Scrawled arrows pointing towards 'Moskva.' Mostly our friends drank, serious boozing. We sat up into the night and talked endlessly, art and politics. There was no dividing line, in a place where culture was subversion. In daytime we climbed down into cellars, and looked at semi-clandestine art exhibitions. Now I found exactly the same exhibitions, above ground, in open galleries, twenty-one years later. As if everyone had marched into a black hole, and come out, blinking in unexpected sunlight. Expecting change, you found the streets, the buildings, looking the same . . . Frozen in time, like the Twilight Zone. But the people I'd met then had aged, the same faces, but grey and wrinkled, trying to pick up where they left off. Do you understand what I'm saying, Angel?"

"You lit a candle for progress, *cara mia . . .*"

"I thought of those heady days, just three months before, watching the whole structure tumbling down on TV. Solidarnosc resurrected. Imre Nagy reburied. The border opened. All those East Germans flooding through. And then the miracle of the Berlin Wall . . . All those people dancing and spraying each other with champagne, that man hammering it with his pick. The masses crossing over. The sheepish border guards. The daisy-chain round the Brandenburg Gate. And then Bulgaria, and then Prague. Who could believe it? All those people, rattling keychains in the snow. And there was that little pudding, Havel, in his baggy sweater, rushing away from journalists to hide in an art gallery's toilet — I recognised that toilet door — I was at that gallery in '69. The dead faces of the Central Committee of the Party, realising their time had come. Then that sight that we'd never thought we'd see, Alexander Dubček, the man from beyond time, embracing the crowd from the balcony. Can you imagine weeping in front of the television?"

"I do it whenever I have a chance, Sophia."

"No, but seriously — all our old icons, Petros . . . Romania, and the masses on the tanks — all those iconic images of the left turned against itself. The Revolution coming, not to install the Communist utopia, but to abolish it. Not to end history, but to resume it, to go back to all the messy uncertainties of life."

"Absolutely, Sophia. But there are societies which have been frozen and there are those that are constantly boiling, helplessly failing to reduce the heat. You have to look at the difference between the cult of the future and the cult of the past. Stalinism wanted to reduce everything that gave a people its history into a marginal, artificial folklore, in the name of a bright future they couldn't define. The machinery of obedience becomes an end in itself, if you have no concrete idea of the sort of society you are heading for. Some Middle Eastern countries reached a similar system by a completely different route. Countries like Syria, or Iraq, under the Ba'ath Party, or Iran, under the Ayatollahs, are looking back, in different ways, to a pristine past, to a kind of Islamic or Arab utopia which is to be recast in our time. All it takes, for them, is the will to burn out all the corrupting, i.e. foreign, ideas. To the Fundamentalists, the Better Man, the True Moslem, is concretely defined by the Koran. There is no need to invent anything. The future lies only in the past. To the Pan-Arabist, both are an undefined abstract, a racial myth, yes, but one that ordinary people can grasp within their own undefined but deeply felt cultural identity. It can unite rich and poor. It precedes and supersedes classes. But at the end of the day, it's not actually there. That messiness of real life, the hum and bustle of the real bazaar of ideas, experiences, desires, examples flooding in from every side. The Western deluge. To shut that out takes an iron act of will. So if ordinary men and women are weak, the government steps in, imposing that discipline for everyone's own good, making sure, by the policeman, the prison warder, the torturer, that the true Faith is upheld."

"So how does one break out of that, Angel?"

"People have to redefine themselves. That's the horrific challenge. How to find the magic equilibrium. To be true to your origins, your culture, your roots, but also to a non-conformist rationality. The mind and the heart. How to connect them. The nerves, the arteries, the veins. I've done the physical route, cutting and repairing. Like reasphalting the roads. But beyond that? It's a job for poets and writers, but who has any time for them? There are too many powerful people who hear Voices, and then hire enforcers to make sure those Voices don't fade away. They mould and sculpt the Voices into convenient forms, ironing away the ragged edges, leaving an efficient tool. It's the abuse of the creative urge, that's all. The superego gone wrong. And, speaking of tools — this one's been far too idle . . ."

"Well, let's iron away its ragged edges . . ."

"Oooohhh . . . Ouch! *Cara mia*, take pity on a decrepit old man . . ."

So what does one expect, in a world in which Bugs Bunny is fifty? asks Daniel, wandering from his den. All one's dreams, hobbling on canes.

Ah, the horror! The horror!

It was not until several weeks after he had decided to murder his editor that Danny Hohenlohe took any active steps in the matter . . .

My life has become a mess of quotes and allusions, quoth Daniel, bits and bobs snatched out of memory's sieve. Every day I find more slivers on the carpet. By night they have been licked up by the cat.

The Mad Surgeon of Beirut was not much help either. True, he stood me a tumblerful of Auchentoshan at the Sleeping Dead, as he pumped me about the men in the bushes. I gave him the fullest possible description. Swarthy features. Zapata moustaches. Filthy raincoats. The limp. The scars. The wooden leg. The flies buzzing around the sombreros. The curled lips. The mouth-organ. "Who are they, His Bollah or Hers Bollah?" I asked him.

"Well, nobody knows I'm here," he said, "but if you want a good subject for a story . . ."

Politics, always politics. The follies of the mass. *Mens Insana in Corpore.*

But he was noncommittal about toxins. "The Iraqis use thalium, for assassinations," he said. "It's tasteless and odourless. They put it in the victim's coffee, or in a soft drink, such as orange squash. Within minutes he staggers, drools and dies."

"Do you have some on you?" I asked. He laughed. I knew he was holding out on me. Some people are just never serious. But I would have wanted something slower working. "I want McTeague to know, in the drawn-out last moments of agony, that I have had my revenge," I explained. "I want the glass to fall from his ashen lips as I sit there, buffing my fingernails. I want the realisation of his perfidy to sink in, as I walk away, tossing my Jezail bullet."

RACHE! RACHE! *A Study in Scarlet. The Sign of Four*, or, if not the four, at least the one. We have found McTeague in rigor, Watson, clutching a pair of puttees on which the word *Smorgasbord* has been inscribed. What do you deduce from that? The murderer is a Swedish pastry chef who has done a stint in the Indian Army, Holmes. By jove, Watson, you never cease to amaze me.

Doctor Mackenzie thought it would do me good to see him. "Recognise your shared humanity, Danny boy," he said, wagging his beard at me in his most James Robertson Justicey mode. "Hath he not eyes, hands, organs, senses, affections, passions? Fed with the same slops, warmed with the same pale sun? If you prick him, does he not bleed?" I should hope so. "He is a publisher," I told Mackenzie. "He is evil, he must be destroyed."

"You have to have a sense of proportion. You told me yourself you got on well in London."

Ah, but that was a long time ago, and besides, the wench is dead. The platinum muse, face down in the waving fields of alfalfa, with a snicker-snee in her back. Yes, those drunken late afternoons in the office of Hammer & Stern, hacking into the mainframe computer of the parent company, Browbeat International, to try to figure out what dastardly plans the Chairman of the Board, Brent Browbeat, had in mind for us all. "Look at this, Danny. The bastard exported five hundred tons of freeze-dried cashew nuts from Basra to Vladivostok in the last fiscal year. What is he getting in return?"

Hands Across the Sea, stretching forth to wring our necks. The aura of power. "As long as the current is going our way, Danny, just relax and enjoy the ride. I'll let you know when we get near the rapids." Treacherous sans culotte. There he was, waving to me from the shore, as I, alone in my leaking barrel, swung over Niagara Falls.

And yet here he is, sitting in front of me over a table at the Creeping Dread, warming a pint of export with his palms, wagging that grey-white head and that bulbous, red W.C. Fields nose.

"Ah, these are difficult times, Danny. It's a shark-ridden world out there. None of us is safe. Publishers are bought and sold like *shmutters*. Mona and I got away from it for a while, at Christmas, with the kids. We went to Grand Bahama Island. It was an idyll. But it never lasts." He passed to me from his briefcase some Kodakolor prints of the clan McTeague *en vacance*: Gordon, Mona, Jack and Geegee, poking away with shovels and spades. White sands. Coconut palms. Black flunkeys in white uniforms. The jolly hotel minibus. Café Lallo, with lobster. McTeague, holding a dead fish.

"I didna catch the bastard maself," he admitted, "but it looked good." Miserable faker. The wife, the weens, looked radiant. Even the lobster looked smug. I sympathised with the fish's dull stare.

"I had to do it, Danny my friend," he said. "Natural wastage. They have hemmed me in in that place. The joy has gone out of it. We are thinking of relocating, the whole family, back to the hame. London is fine, for those who want a big third-world metropolis. But in my old age it's a bit hectic for me. I can't breathe the air any more. It's like swallowing ashes. There are mitey things in the water that are visible to the naked eye. That's if you allow your eye to go naked. Eh, it's peaceful out here, Danny lad. I'd come and live in this area maself, if it weren't for the nuclear-power stations."

Another thought: Radiation poisoning. Remember that film? — Man staggers into police station. There's been a murder! Oh yeah? Who's the victim? Me. A slow-acting, lethal dose, with no hope of remission. But where does one get a phial of liquid radium on a late afternoon at Drem or New Mains? One can't even get a carton of milk. The post office closes at twelve-thirty. They have to import crisps, by wagon train.

"Ah, but we made good music together for a while, Danny. You have to look on the bright side. I have a suggestion you may want to think about. I know you've never wanted to deal with agents. But there's a good woman who is operating out of her home in Beaconsfield. She is specialising in certain light entertainment. Zany science fiction, feminist thrillers. She wants to keep out of the razzle-dazzle of big time, the knife fights, the Booker rumbles. I showed her some of your short stories, and the sections, remember those you left with me? I took the liberty. She said she would be willing to have a go, if you were game. But I think she wants to see you in person. She is frankly worried about your present situation. She wants to know if you're the sort of person who will phone her up and scream after midnight. But she's sympathetic. She spent two years in Jungian therapy. She is a nut case, frankly, but she gets results. Whadayasay?"

Just as I thought, it's absolution he's after. The sinner wishes to redeem his soul. Having stabbed me in the back, he offers iodine, and a year's free ticket to the shows. Trying to buy me with trumpery jewellery. Jung, New Age, touchie-feelie. "She also does TV." Having shot his bolt, he sits there, nursing the last bag of Froot Loops in East Lothian.

"I'll think about it," I said. "You have your people talk to my people. We'll set up lunch some time, say around Easter '92?"

"Danny, you'll never change."

I fumed, as, allowing him to go scot free, I walked out of the Weeping Head. Elbowing my way through the morphic fields of the elegiac clientele, a gentleman farmer with padded elbows, an accountant clutching his boney fides, two comatose ragged-trousered bastards. Brrr! Walking him back up the road past The Retreat to the station, as he continues warbling about nature. Waving at me as he ascends the platform, by the sign WARNING: FRAGILE ROOF. FOR YOUR SAFETY USE PERMANENT WALKING WAYS, DUCK OR ROOF LADDERS, KNEE OR CRAWLING BOARDS. Nothing happens. The devil's luck. My forlorn hope that he would be sucked by turbulence into the path of the Intercity Express is dashed by the early arrival of the North Berwick Sprinter, wafting him off to safety.

But I shall prevail! Creeping up on the headquarters of Hammer & Stern, in the dead of night, hefting, in my old army rucksack, two hundred grams of grade-A Semtex, fuses, timers, alarm clocks, sticks of dynamite, limpet mines, wire cutters and Superglue. Tricking the night guard into opening the door by imitating the call of a female tarantula I slug him with my Punjabi *khitmutgar*, punch for the lift and go straight to the seventh floor: Executive Suites. But as I exit into the dimly lit corridor I hear a strange rustling and snuffling from behind the door whose plaque reads CHAIRMAN OF THE BOARD. I move forward stealthily, now aware of a putrid smell of decay from within the office, filling my throat, choking my nostrils. Tying a bandanna round my face, I crawl slowly along the floor, pushing the door open a smidge. The sight that greeted my eyes, Watson, was not one that could be countenanced by a sane human being. The plush carpeting was covered with a blanket of bones, torn flesh and offal. Bleeding chunks of meat were everywhere, on the executive couches, the nested tables, the shelves, the polished mahogany desk, the reclining-chairs, the banks of monitor screens. There were several kinds of animal remains: a severed sheep's head, a crocodile's skin, a monkey's bloodied paws, torn-out ox tongues, a horse's penis. But this was nothing to the horror of the mutilated, half-devoured cadavers of unmistakably human origin: a woman's leg, a man's hairy arm, half-gnawed breasts, a neck with a bloody string of pearls still attached, fur coats twisted round gory lumps. And in the centre of it all, crouching, naked and covered in blood and slime, the figure of a man, whose face, teeth gnawing on the neckbone of a head I recognised clearly as Hilda the husky receptionist, were the indubitable features, familiar from so many TV interviews and newspaper photographs, of the Chief Executive, Brent Browbeat himself.

"Bad timing, Danny boy." That familiar voice. I raised my head and there, standing behind the blood-soaked entrepreneur, painted in woad and carrying a Thompson submachine-gun, was McTeague. I grabbed the nearest object, which happened to be a woman's painted leg, which I threw with all my might at the villain, deflecting his aim, so that he sprayed the room, a burst of bullets splattering the Chief Executive's brains upon the office walls, staining the framed testimonials and portraits of himself with assorted world figures: Margaret Thatcher, Gorbachev, George Bush, the Pope, Deng Xiao Ping, Madonna. I ran, stumbling to the lift, McTeague slipping and wallowing in the corpse-strewn room. Down to the lobby, signing myself out in the visitors' book, running into the night, just in time to avoid the detonation of my charges, probably struck by one of McTeague's bullets, which turned the entire building of Hammer & Stern into a nightmare glow of fireballs and black spumes of smoke.

Deng Xiao Ping, now there's a name to conjure with. The time is surely coming when I should join Nicolae and Elena Ceausescu in the Moldavian Mountains, marching bravely with our axes, singing the Party Anthem, fighting for the return of a safe world, in which we all knew what was what, the peasants kept firmly in their place, and keep that chopper's motor running . . .

No return to the Sheepish Dread. The *maîtresse* there, one Mrs Whittaker, is a woman about whose night life I have phantasized a great deal lately. I have come to believe she copulates with wolves. Well, it would be a darn-sight more interesting than the real life of this dismal turf. The rolling gorse down to the tourist trap of the Gullane Sands and Craddock, the Beach, the Links, with tam-o'-shantered golfers heaving their little white balls over the rocks into the sea. "Hoots mon, there goes ma richt testacle!" "Never mind, Jamie, ye won't be needin' it onyway the noo."

Taking the opposite direction from the Weeping Shed, I crossed the railway line in the direction of the disused Second World War airfield. A long strip of empty concrete, on which curly-horned sheep graze among the weed-grown cracks. Rhona Mackenzie told me once they were Jacob's Sheep, but I believe nothing from a medical practitioner. Before me the bourgeois desolation of Lothian surged to the horizon, a range of low green hillocks, at whose right flank the phallic tower of the Hopetoun Monument rises to mock the living dead. West Fortune, Dingleton and Needless. The remains of old minor castles, where the sleazy lairds masturbated over their phorlorn phantasies. I walked for about a mile, stopping in an empty field and listening for the drone of dead planes. The morphic resonance of long-dead pilots, the click-clack of Douglas Bader's wooden pegs on the tarmac. Today you can fly even without a brain. But the machines can get us every time. Where is the *Nautilus* now that I need her? The Chinese, burrowing under the earth. They're coming! You're next! But it is only the morphic fields of pipe-sucking moles. And may the wind in the willows never be your own.

I have disturbed an anthill. The little blighters scurry to and fro. I remember an abortive project, a truly epic saga, tentatively titled "Moogli — The Trotskyite Ant." It was the tale of a disgruntled worker in this nest who was developing antisocial tendencies. He dreamed, as he tottered about in the column, staggering under the burden of ears of corn and eyes of potatoes several times heavier than his own tiny bulk, of a world in which this Stalinist grind and bondage would be replaced by a community of insects, each a self-determining individual who would be able to improve his/her life by means of good books, thought-provoking theatre, uplifting art and other New Ant ventures. He dreamed of the overthrow of the dictatorship of the Queen of the Nest, Hatsheptshula, who did nothing but lie about in her protected den, her immense bulk fed constantly by hordes of neutered serfs. But how to spread the doctrine of Liberation and Freedom? All around him Moogli was surrounded by dolts and zombies who had no thought in their tiny heads but absolute obedience to the Queen and the unchanging, age-old traditions. The only thing that could excite them was the occasional infiltration of an ant from a rival nest, the thrill of war, the whiff of ant blood and evisceration. Moogli was in complete despair. His antisocial vibrations had been noted and he had received a summons to appear before the Anti-Anterican Committee, the outcome of which was a foregone conclusion.

Packing his little reed-bag of possessions, Moogli, choosing the heat of the day when all the little ants were snoring, stole away for ever from the nest. He now faced a life of inconceivable danger, of hazards and perils in the unknown terrain which stretched infinitely ahead. He would have to brave exposure to the English weather, the rain-drenched oceans of mud, innumerable predators, spiders, earwigs, beetles, legions of praying mantises evangelising the countryside, pools of pariah dogs' piss, birds of prey and the mysterious bipedal giants who roamed the world spreading death and destruction. His only companion, in this heroic voyage, would be a mongrel dog, a Scotch terrier on the run, called Archibald, who picked him up along the way, and in whose fur he fought ferocious battles against the armies of the flea-king, Zor.

Och aye. What can't be cured must be endured. So many tiny vibrating fields, the actual infinity of Life. Der Great Mystery. But the buzzing in my ears turned out to be something else, a small plane circling the abandoned airfield, Believe It or Not. First it was a dot, then a shape, but I couldn't identify the aircraft. I was never any good at these technical details, which I had to either make up ("He gunned the engine of his Tofoola six-seater") or look up in a book I purchased at the same seedy dive in Manhattan where I got my ideas — *The Writer's Ladder* to *Vehicular and Allied Things*. Why was I not born in the seventeenth century, when all you needed to know was Latin, French, German and Greek and a few katekisms of the kirk?

At any rate, the plane, a twin-engined affair, was definitely coming in to land. As I scrambled forward, out of the anthill, crushing potential Mooglis in my path, I saw, on the road leading to the airfield, a few hundred yards farther on, an unmarked off-white van, very similar to the one I had seen several times, carrying the visiting doctor's shadows, at Craddock and near The Retreat. In fact, it was the same van, without a doubt. I hurried forward towards the road.

The airfield was half a mile farther. The plane dipped, disappearing from my sight. I had no doubt it had landed. But I was too winded to go all the way. The sort of slop dished out at Stalag Mackenzie, combined with stale rolls at the Shlepper's Drek, had ruined my metabolism, never shipshape at the best of times. McDonald's. Burger King. Wendy's. Wimpy's. Colonel Sander's Glop. It's a miracle I am still here. I sat down at the side of the road and mopped my face with my handkerchief. A couple of motorcyclists skimmed by. A cloud passed, peeked and floated on. Then the white van, racing back. I jumped out of the way, as it whizzed past me, catching only the briefest glance at the dark, sunglassed faces of the two men in the front. No doubt at all. The Watchers. Leaving me choking in a cloud of dust. And no passing old man to say: "That's straynge. That plane is dustin' where they ain't no crops." But the plane itself rose, suddenly appearing over the horizon, rushing its twin propellers towards me and then pulling up into the sky. It banked and flew off, in the direction of the Firth of Forth, over Gullane.

I walked back, a longer slog than I'd expected, to Drem, arriving at The Retreat well into dusk, to find Blok, Kathleen and Andrew Mackenzie greeting me with some relief. "Well, here's at least one that's turned up." It appeared they had mislaid the good Doctor Angelopoulos, who had left

Sophia in Edinburgh that morning to spend the day with Mackenzie, but never arrived. "He must have found some drinking partner on the way," said Mackenzie. "Ye canna change human nature, let alone the Angelic." But I knew exactly what had happened, and told them: "He has been kidnapped by the men in the white van and put aboard a plane, which took off this afternoon from the abandoned airfield to a destination unknown."

"That's okay Danny. You look exhausted. How did your session with your editor go? Never mind, you can tell us tomorrow. Why don't you just grab a couple of sandwiches and hit the sack? Fancy a nightcap of the Inchgower? I was holding it for our missing guest. It has that unique peat flavour."

"He'll never taste it." I went upstairs, to commune with the dust mites, the morphic resonance of my own private hordes. But in the morning, Avram Blok, Kathleen and the gorgeous Sophia were at my door, yanking me awake and demanding to hear my story. For the Greek fallen angel had indeed gone missing, truant, AWOL, flown the coop, strayed, gone out the window, skipped, skedaddled, skived off, eloped, evaporated, been spirited away, hijacked, Shanghaied, Beiruted, docnapped, to wit: definitely vanished, leaving behind, may we presume, only his amorphous field, resonating, in the Lothian smog, with all the criss-cross fields it had entangled, backwards and forwards in time . . .

BOOK TWO

The Pillars of Society

FIVE

Ragged
Edges

I WISH TO MAKE ONE THING PERFECTLY CLEAR: I, AND I ALONE, AM THE ONE and only genuine, authentic and authorised Saint Simon known as "the Stylite." No imitations will be tolerated. No Daniel the Stylite, no Simon the Younger, nor Simon the Smaller, nor Simon the Fifth Cousin Thrice Removed. Stylite, there is only one original. It's always the same when you have something new. Fakers, charlatans, impostors, liars, phonies, pharisees and phinks crowd forward, scrabbling for the crumbs of glory. They build counterfeit pillars, all over the landscape, pustulent protuberances that disfigure the desert and disturb its phragile balance. Even in my sleep, I can still hear their cacophonous cackle, their heretical babbles and squabbles, their claims to a thousand clashing truths.

The Nature of the Divine *Logos!* Everyone wants in on the act. So-called Gnostics, Marcionites, Sethians, Manichaeans (Zoroastrians in disguise), Montanists, Adoptionists, Pneumatics, Messalians, with their disgusting slobbering habits (expelling demons through saliva and snot, sweet Jesus!) — the dualists who declared all matter was evil, and that Christ did not die on the cross. Not that the powers-that-be in Rome were one jot better. The Council of Chalcedon, in 451, concocted the most absurd dictum: Two natures, two wills and two energies in Christ, one human and one divine. This they attempted, on pain of anathema, to foist on the Christians West and East. Their message boy, one Bishop Theodoros of Cyprus, came to try to turn me around. I wouldn't even let down my ladder, but shouted to him so everyone could hear:

"One nature! One person! One divine-human energy!" Then I emptied my bucket of slops over his head. In the East, one can't afford to be subtle.

From the top of my pillar, I could keep my eyes on the affairs of men and nations. On my first pillar, which was a mere thirty foot high, my horizons were limited, but on the new Mark II extended model, my vision was altogether enhanced. I could see far and wide, from Constantinople and Rome, to Armenia and the Indus Valley. All the quarrelling little people were spread out naked to my gaze. I could see into the future and the past, though often it was difficult to distinguish between the two. The depredations of men, their folly, mendacity, shadiness, heresy and corruption, are timeless, spanning the ages. Everywhere I see women widowed, children orphaned, men trying to hide their falsehood from the eyes of God, under rocks, in deep caverns, in chambers sealed against the outside world. Treachery and deceit abound in the halls and palaces of the mighty. The armies of night ravage the world. I see the Huns, burning the plains, I see the Vandals, sacking Carthage and Hippo, mocking the deathbed of sainted Augustine. I see the heathen fire-worshippers of Persia persecuting and seducing the stoic Armenians, devastating Mesopotamia, betraying the Ephthalites of Transoxiana, spreading the communistic and ascetic doctrines of the Dualist High Priest Mazdak. This was already several decades after my death, but you can't keep a good Stylite down. I saw them all, with my rotted empty eyeballs, the wars with Rome and the sack of Antioch, and the destruction of Jerusalem by the fire devils, and the razing of her churches. I saw the Emperor Heraclius regain the city, but then I became aware of another, newer, more dangerous threat arising: The insidious ambitions of the savage tribes of Arabia, with their bongo drums and their heretical Prophet, with his satanic verses and his Philistine schemes. Up they came, from their caves and caravans, laying waste the Levant and taking advantage of the confusion, anarchy and chaos which the dualists had wrought throughout the land. No wonder we had to rise up and sort them out. There is never a moment's rest for the righteous. Vigilance, vigilance above all.

But what do the supposedly devout Christians do amid all this turmoil? They drag out to my monastery, moaning and groaning about their own trivial feuds, one set of monks accusing another of slaughtering their innocent pilgrims. Denouncing each other, while the world burns, in pompous letters to the Pope:

Dear Holiness,
While on our way to the pagum figulorum, the Potter's Village adjacent to your cloister, minding our own business and singing our happy hymns of praise, we were set upon by a convoy of ruffians, heretics and Jews, who fell upon us in ambush with cudgels, stones and diverse other weapons, killing 350 (three hundred and fifty) of our number, and injuring countless others. These brigands, we know, were sent against us by none other than the Patriarch Severus of Antioch and the Bishop Peter of Apamea, who have been incensed at our refusal to repudiate the holy decrees of your Council of Chalcedon. They also brought a caravan of harlots into the Monastery of Dorotheus and copulated with them for three days and nights, before they were evicted by the guards.

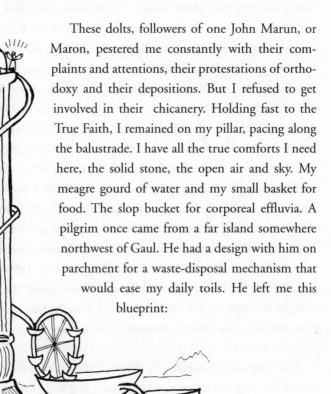

These dolts, followers of one John Marun, or Maron, pestered me constantly with their complaints and attentions, their protestations of orthodoxy and their depositions. But I refused to get involved in their chicanery. Holding fast to the True Faith, I remained on my pillar, pacing along the balustrade. I have all the true comforts I need here, the solid stone, the open air and sky. My meagre gourd of water and my small basket for food. The slop bucket for corporeal effluvia. A pilgrim once came from a far island somewhere northwest of Gaul. He had a design with him on parchment for a waste-disposal mechanism that would ease my daily toils. He left me this blueprint:

I gave him my blessing, but no deal. I have no need for innovations. One's bodily functions are set by God, not to be tampered with by engineers. When I sit upon my bucket and contemplate the pungent fluid and the floating, or subsiding stools, I am brought face to faece with the true wonders and miracles of God's plan. What God ordained cannot be disdained. Therefore I rejoice at my excreta, and mourn their daily passing as I lower the pail. Often I saw the most significant visions in that oozing pool: I saw my father, tending his sheep in the Cilician Plain; my mother, humbly baking bread in her village; my younger self, content to be at one with Nature. But then the Voice, the clear command. Oppose the devil and all his works. Speak to the sick and the afflicted. Do not be swayed by honeyed words. Bless the just and scourge the Ungodly. And so I wandered, across the land blighted by war and lies, until I arrived at this barren place and chained myself to the most desolate rock I could find. And then the people, drifting towards me, asking questions, first singly, then in twos and threes and finally in great multitudes, so that the monks of the plain took pity on me and built my column, raising me higher and higher, away from the grabbing hands and spit-flecked mouths . . .

But to return to the Maronites: When Justin the First became Emperor, their hated enemy Severus, Patriarch of Antioch, knew his days were numbered. Justin, a Chalcedonian, sent his general Vitalian to cut the bishop's dissenting tongue out. Severus had to flee to Egypt, though his authority was still recognised by most pious Christians. It was obvious why the Emperors clung to the Chalcedonian formula, which validates their right to rule in the name of the human Christ *logos*, whereas the divine is God's alone. A Christ both human and divine in one energy leaves no room for their authority. The Maronites first opposed, then supported the Romish view. But when the tables were turned, and Emperor Justinian the Second adopted the monothelite faith they had repudiated, John Maron and his followers had to flee in turn, south, into the mountains of Lebanon. But then Justinian's general Leo overthrew his master, cut off his nose and reinstated Chalcedon. Never a dull moment.

All this occurred long after my death, but although they took down and interred my body, my spirit remained undimmed on my column. Even after they cut off my field of sight by erecting a cathedral round the pillar, and later demolished it to a stump, carting the stones off to be worshipped by dolts all over the Fertile Crescent. On the font they carved a circle of four stalks of wheat on a spinning wheel, which later became a symbol of the Syrian Socialist National Party, an expansionist fascist Ba'athist group. One is helpless against usurpation, the substitution of garbage for ideas. The *dawrat al-hayat*, the Cycle of Life. What enters as food exits as shit. In fact, we were all monothelites, in this region, and the Maronites, like everybody else, invented their own history to suit themselves. But in spite of their twists and turns the truth will out: Our Lord has but one person, one will, one nature and one energy. There is no private Judgement and no original sin! No reward and no punishment before the Final Judgement! The Holy Ghost proceeds from the Father alone! There is no purgatory! Christ suffered in His divinity as well as His humanity on the cross. No questions will be taken.

The Maronites repudiated all these "errors," as they embraced the orthodoxy of Rome. And so they took their self-betrayal with them down the ages, echoing from their mountain retreats. Soon they were joined by the zealots of the Antichrist, the Sunnites, the Shi'ites with their Hidden Messiah, and the Druze, who believed that the mad Caliph of Egypt, Al-Hack'em, was Incarnate God (the "Indefinable One"). Thus the mountains of Lebanon became the sanctuary for all manner of reprobates, aspostates and scoundrels, through the Holy Crusades, and the Antichrist's triumphs, and the long Turkish night, to the atheistic chimeras of Voltaire, Rousseau, George Washington and other Freemasons and Jews. A sorry sight indeed to see from the top of a Telanissan pillar. Oh, the folly, the knavery, the shamelessness, vice, the graft and self-genocide of the Gadarene swine! Ah, in what gleeful anticipation one drags one's self on towards the inevitable Apocalypse and the millennial days of the beast.

How often we have had false hopes and alarms, falling stars and two-headed sheep, plagues and eclipses, visions of fire and brimstone and wagging fingers, not to speak of mysterious resurrections and endurances far past the grave. In fact, is there not a prime sample abuzzing in my ears, entering my field of sight centre left, a somewhat bewildered and reoriented figure wriggling in the passenger seat of a bright red Mercedes-Benz, climbing up the slopes of the Mont Liban, Mount Lebanon, a battle-worn Plantagenet, no less, hurled by a stocky black-moustached driver recklessly round the hairpin bends, and without an armoured escort even, can you imagine, in this day and age?

"You see, Dick — may I call you Dick?" Aziz Khamash, politician, warlord, community leader, public servant, family man, devoted son, husband and father, adulterer, lover, mass murderer, conspirator, sentimentalist, amateur historian and sleuth, took a hand off the steering-wheel and placed it lightly on Richard the Lionheart's knee. "This modern world of ours is one you must find terribly strange, on the one hand, but, on the other, nothing has changed. It's the same human animal, fighting for survival, territory, sex, power, faith. When your predecessor Raymond of Toulouse marched from Arqa to Tripoli, our elders hurried to greet him and he was amazed to find there were still Christians in this part of the world. That was at Easter, 1099. From that moment on we worked with the Franks. At Acre, we supplied you the maps of the fortress. I'm not sure if you remember. Just look at this incredible scenery — have you ever seen anything like it?"

But Richard was still feeling the impact of his first flight, by Olympic Airways, from Paris Orly to Nicosia. Swaddled in the unusual tightness of an ill-fitting business suit, he had allowed Khamash and his bodyguards to shepherd him through check-in and passport control (a fake document, for Monsieur Richard Dupont) and the ordeal of encasement in a metal tube crammed with groaning adults and weeping children. "Can one not walk on deck?" "Non." And then the staggering realization that one was hurtling far above the clouds. It was the first time he was glad he had left his intestines behind. And then the chaos of Nicosia airport, the deeply suspicious customs officer, unimpressed by the red-haired giant's gaze, the bustle of the Levantine city, the sudden whack of nostalgia for that long-lost Mediterranean light. Nicosia-Larnaca-Joûnié, and the motor drive up the spiral road to Daraoun and up the Mountain: The terraces crammed on top of each other, the evergreen pines, the sheer gorges of the Jrid, with ancient unconquered monasteries and hermitages hewn into the solid rock.

"The land of Gods and visions, Monsieur Plantagenet. Our fortress for fifteen hundred years. If you want to survive all the invaders you have to make yourself impregnable in so many ways. Geographical, spiritual, psychological. You have to be a porcupine with steel spikes. Your enemies must believe in your boundless cruelty. But you have to preserve your own morality, you have to know your own worth. You understand this, of course. You who were accused of so many things in your time."

"I did what had to be done."

"Exactly."

They drove past streams and rivulets flowing from the rocks. A goatherd gazed down at them from a narrow ledge on which his flock perched precariously. A family of farmers looked up from the shade of a small grove of fruit trees. An armed youth, his chest criss-crossed with ammunition belts, waved them on. The sun dappled and disappeared teasingly through the branches of the roadside trees.

"An enchanted country," Richard marvelled.

"This is the land of Adonis," explained Khamash. "Here the beautiful young God came when he was wounded by the boar which the jealous Mars sent to kill him. But Venus-Aphrodite came and found him in these very mountains and tried to nurse him back to life. He died in her arms, about ten kilometres up this road, at Afqa, where the red anemones grow. In the winter the river runs red with his spilled blood, and people make offerings to their love. It is a tradition we dedicate to the Holy Virgin. Even the Moslems still come here to adore their holy lady, Zahra. We are a strange people, the Lebanese. We kill each other but often adore the same things. We just call them different names. They are all the same Gods. Adonis-Tamuz-Dionysus-Jesus. Venus-Aphrodite-Mary. There are still wild boars in these mountains. But Aphrodites, that's another matter . . ."

The road climbed on. Khamash turned off onto a freshly tarred side road, stopping after a hundred metres at a roadblock manned by more armed youths who, recognising the car and its driver, moved their barricade of metal spikes aside. The road now rose, ever steeper, wrapping round the contours of the mountain, past men with guns sitting on boulders, until suddenly, around a sharp bend, a village, hooked onto the mountainside, appeared as if in a puff of smoke out of a genie's bottle.

Each house rose above the other, two-storeyed, red-roofed and pretty, with arched windows and stone terraces and balconies hung with washing. Above them all, a tall church, with a white stone Virgin, dominated the location. The Mercedes screeched to a halt at the steps of the largest house, nested in a grove of pines. An immense Dalmatian dog bounded up to lick Aziz's hand, then, taking a brief sniff at the dead ex-king's trousers, howled and hurtled up the steps.

"Don't worry about Franjieh. He'll get used to you." Khamash greeted the villagers who materialised to embrace him. Well-dressed men in suits, T-shirted youngsters, two black-cowled priests and a woman and two adolescent girls, in Western dress, who stood for a moment behind the men, before stepping forward. "My sister, Rose; my daughter, May; my very special daughter, Mouna. My brother, Amin. My cousin Sami. My other cousin Elie. Father Tanur. Father Khamash, my uncle. This is my English friend from Paris, Richard Dupont."

It was already late afternoon, and a table of *mezzehs* was set on the terrace, overlooking the valley. The entire family grouped itself along the two long sides of the table, Aziz Khamash at one end, Richard at his right, Father Tanur at his left, the other end vacant, with an empty chair. The delicacies were comprehensive: moutabal, labanis, lamb and chicken livers, prawns, lamb's brains, quails, arayess, foul medames, et cetera, with an assortment of grills. The armed young men shuttled more laden trays from the house. Khamash conducted a whispering conversation with them, one after the other, as they bent their ears towards his lips. Then, soon after they had begun to feast, a slight, wispy figure emerged from the open French windows of the house, a white-faced, black-garbed woman, whom life and cosmetic science appeared to have frozen at an indeterminate middle age. Khamash rose to greet her, but she waved him down and sat at the vacant table's end.

"My mother, Madame Adele," said Khamash. The ex-king bowed towards her, but she made no response, plucking with thin bony fingers at a bowl of lettuce that one of the young men placed before her.

"I have to explain to you our position," Khamash told Richard, as the others picked at their food. "I had to wait until you could see us in our place, so you could appreciate the heart of the matter. Despite all this peace and tranquillity, we are, of course, at war. You asked me about the muffled explosions, the smoke we saw from the sea. That is Beirut, the capital. In your days, it was a minor bastion. Today it is the ruined shell of what was once a great city. Our country is partitioned between foreign states. To our east, Syria, a Moslem tyranny, has grabbed two-thirds of our land. To the south, Israel, the Jewish State, holds a substantial slice."

"I am aware of some of that," Richard said softly. "I followed the story in *Le Monde*."

"So you know our plight. The Shi'as, the Palestinians, and our own accursed disunity. In Beirut the usurping general, Michel Aoun, has declared a premature war against the Syrians. He foolishly thinks he can chase them from the country by force, allying himself with our Palestinian enemies, and with another Moslem state, Iraq. Meanwhile, as you should know, the Christian countries, Britain, France, the United States, could not care less if we all got our throats cut. It is an impossible situation. But we have lived with the impossible for so long. We have two governments and five states and several dozen armies. There is no order and no law. But we, the Christians, have been here, on this mountain, since before the Moslems were invented, since before Mohammad was a gleam in his mother's eyes. We are not immigrants, like the Jews. We are what we are. You yourself, if you will forgive me, who came here almost one thousand years ago, are a newcomer to me. But we have a common interest. We fight for what we know is right."

"My days of fighting are long over," said Richard, fingering a stuffed vine leaf.

"We'll talk about this later." The wispy woman rose and glided back to the house. Khamash excused himself and hurried after her, leaving Richard at the table, to be addressed by the cousin, Elie, a silvery-haired gentleman smelling of some fragrant oil. "Are you in heavy goods or personal weaponry?"

"I am a retired traveller," said Richard. The young Khamash daughters giggled softly. But beyond them, Khamash's sister, Rose, glanced at him sphinx-like from beneath her dark shawl. She appeared to be in her mid-thirties, with a handsome, unlined face which had learned to keep its secrets. He met her gaze, until the priest, across the table, tapped him on

103

the arm to ask him to pass the tabouleh. The dog, Franjieh, watched with unrelenting scepticism from behind a cherry tree.

Twilight was brief. People drifted away from the table, as the young men cleared the dishes away. Richard was soon left alone with the priest, Father Tanur, as the day faded into a blue-black gloaming, and the lights came on in the house. The guards were replaced by another set of armed young men, patrolling among the trees. The crickets' screak. The stars in clear night sky. Father Tanur silently picking through a bowl of black olives, the pips laid out before him in the shape of the inverted cross of Saint Peter. Then soft footsteps heralded the return of Khamash, who came and took his guest by the arm.

"Come, let's go and see my father."

He led him into the house, through a spacious hallway with walls lined with heraldic trophies. Coats of arms, hauberks, helmets, crossed spears, shields and two complete suits of armour to which the dead king was irresistibly drawn. Khamash stood silently, with folded arms, until Richard turned reluctantly away, began to speak but then thought better of it, and followed his host up the stairs, down a dimly lit corridor to a door guarded by a middle-aged man cradling an automatic rifle. The guard opened the door to an even dimmer room, lit only by an art deco lamp in one corner. A crumpled bed took up much of the room, but beside it was a wheelchair, apparently unoccupied, facing a window, which, curtains open, drew the blackness of the night into the bedroom. The wheelchair turned suddenly, with a creak of wheels, revealing a shrunken and cadaverous old man, whose goitered eyes swung like dirty Ping-Pong balls towards his visitors.

"Papa." Khamash kissed the apparition. "I have brought our guest. Monsieur Plantagenet, this is my father, Michel Khamash."

"Come closer," said the old man, his voice barely above a chicken's croak. "As you can see, I am an ancient monument. I am eighty-five years old. Aziz is my youngest son. I had him when I was forty-four years old. I was Minister of Works. Today the only work in this country is killing. Do you understand me? So we became experts in this work too. I had three other sons, two of them murdered by Christians, not by Moslems or Jews. In 1939 I founded a political party to unite the country. We called for freedom, liberty and socialism. We believed in the Lebanese mission, to preserve our civilisation. But these modern caliphs, these heirs of Byzantine and Sassanian Caesaropapism, will not rest until they have driven us all out and drowned us in the sea like rats. We offered to create a state in partnership with all sects, that would be above all divisions. Now we know this was a delusion. We looked to France, to Britain, to the United States, but they want to make their deals with Comrade Gorbachev, and Hafez the Bloody, and with the Persian Ayat-Allahs. So we have to find our own way forward. My son tells me a strange thing about you, M'sieu. He says you are Richard the Lionheart, come back to life. Is this the truth? Come forward."

The old man wheeled his chair up with one hand and grabbed Richard's suit with the other. The withered claw felt inside the guest's shirt, groping up and down his chest. Then the other hand grabbed his wrist, probing for his pulse. The old man dropped the hand and wheeled himself back, breathing harshly, the popping eyes rolling from side to side. Khamash moved forward, but his father waved him away.

"This man is dead," he said. "What sort of trick is this? There is no heartbeat. There is no pulse. He is a cadaver."

"Don't excite yourself, Papa. Do you want a pill?"

"I don't want a pill. I don't want anything."

"You didn't believe me, Papa, so I had to bring him. His heart was taken in a jar to Rouen. His entrails are at another abbey. But here he is, history in the flesh."

"You want me to negotiate with a corpse? We were counting on metempsychosis, not the living dead."

"This is no Druze or Cathar flim-flam, Papa. It's the real thing."

"I don't want to talk now. Take him away. Go away, M'sieu. We will talk in the morning. Pierre! Pierre!"

The middle-aged guard came running, Galil rifle at the ready.

"Put me to bed, Pierre. I want this room locked until morning. No one comes in. No one! Lock the safety on the window. Double the guards."

Khamash ushered the dead ex-king out of the patriarch's bedroom, twirling his moustache with wry amusement.

"Don't mind Papa. I think he is jealous. I have a room prepared for you in the annex. Tomorrow we'll talk business. He'll be better when the sun shines." He led Richard back through the armorial hall, out beneath the stars, down a quiet passage, to a small one-storey house with a porch partly hidden behind jacaranda trees. "The bed's made. Toiletries in the bathroom. Night clothes in the closet. There is an intercom, dial zero if you need anything, the guardhouse is operative round the clock."

Richard lay, naked, over the covers, as the starlight slid in the window. The dim glitter of the Virgin on the wall. He was grateful for the barren bivouac. His mind wandering, down the ages, back to the truth of dreams. The parched trudge along the road to Acre. The silent arrows felling valiant men. The jackals of the Holy Land. The plump vultures, picking the surfeit of bones. Saladin's gifts of cold fruits and Hermon snow. The Saracen's offers of truce, urged by the destitution of war: and lo, the land is despoiled, starving soldiers and peasants foraging for scraps, the rotting corpses of horses and cattle. Burned fields and abandoned villages. Widows and orphaned children. Blood and rotting entrails. Fevered nights and days. The bicornered general at Acre's walls, with his soldiers' decapitated heads catapulted out of the fort . . .

Jerusalem, the unachieved, the unattainable. Now, it appears, it was in the hands of the Jews. The ironic twists of history. But they, too, were embattled. No one rests easy here. But I, like Moses, was forbidden to enter my promised land. Or is this a second chance? Is there a life beckoning, not just a mechanical compulsion, a conditioned, ambulating trance?

An unusual, feminine perfume seemed to fill the air. At least the olfactory faculties! The door to the room softly opened. She stood, hesitant for a moment, at the door, then cast off her thin silk nightslip and sat beside him naked on the bed. Rose, Khamash's sister, fixing him again with her steady gaze. She leaned forward, took his hand, and placed it on her left breast. He felt the life stirring in his loins. The first erection in seven hundred and ninety years. He gazed at it with amazement. She took his penis in her hand, running her finger up and down the base, the body and the glans. He moved his unpractised fingers along the contours of her belly, hips, thighs. She lay down beside him, still holding his organ. He pushed her hand gently away, taking hold of her shoulders. She allowed him to turn her on her stomach, caressing his hand as it felt her buttocks, thrusting his forefinger into the red shrub of her anus, pushing against the tightness of her sphincter muscles. She gently pulled his hand away, then reached for and guided his organ to penetrate her from behind. He felt the tight muscles closing. She moaned, and clawed the bedclothes in frenzy, ripping the upper sheet in two. He thrust away fiercely. A bubbling cry escaped her lips. He cried out, releasing the pent-up passions of centuries. Then there was a choked-off yelping bark, a flurry of movement at the door, a looming bulk, a sinuous canine shape leaping and snarling, the sudden glare of a pocket torch, slithering over the protagonists. A sharp cry of "Down, Franjieh!" Richard's prick came away from the woman's arse with a curious sucking sound.

"So," said the amused voice of Aziz Khamash behind him. "You can fuck without a heart. I wish I could. But what am I going to do with you now . . . ?"

"More New York stories, Angelopoulos!"

"Tell us about those one-night stands!"

"Everything that goes up must come down . . ."

"What was your most spectacular fuck?"

"You won't believe this, but it was an Iranian woman. She was like fire encased in ice. No matter how steamed up you got, she wouldn't melt. She was a translator at the U.N."

"They are the worst, I agree with you Angel. They are like Fort Knox. Especially the Russians."

"The Russians are easy. But did I tell you about my encounter with the Albanian niece of Enver Hoxha . . ."

"The Iranian, Angelopoulos —"

"It was at a World Health conference at the U.N. I was in a group of doctors sent to lobby the Assembly. The Iranians were just beginning to flex their muscles on Lebanon. This woman came from Tehran in full regalia, sealed and locked in her chador. When she walked through the crowded streets of Manhattan it was like a battleship cutting through the ocean. I knew it was my greatest challenge. Religious faith, tradition, culture, feminist will, everything was there. But there was something in her eyes, when I managed to catch her gaze, just for a moment. But how could I build a bridge?"

"You have to lay it down in sections."

"Exactly. First I had to separate her from her Iranian male comrades. They were as eager as I was to get behind the veil, I could see, but they all had that air of dogs who hadn't got the bone. Are you sure you don't want to hear about the Albanian?"

"Everything in its proper time, Angel . . ."

We all needed this vicarious conquest, at the end of another endless day under siege — (The Jaffa Camp, doctor's log, 11.9.1986, Tewfiq Abd-el-Khalil recording) — three amputations, two abdominal resections, two craniotomies and seven minor operations in one eighteen-hour shift. And they were not combatant casualties. Some of the children had found a breach in the besieging ring round the camp leading to a sewer pipe whose other end lay behind enemy lines. Only the smallest ten- to twelve-year-olds could squeeze through. We forbade them to do it, but they snuck their way anyway and came back with food and ammunition. Unfortunately they had to cross an open space of about five metres between the near end of the pipe and our defences. The Amal militiamen became more and more adept at potting the boys and girls as they rushed by. Eventually they discovered the pipe and closed it, trapping one of the boys, Khalid, inside. Then they detonated a grenade in the duct. That was one body we couldn't bury. So talk on, Fallen Angel —

". . . Try as I could, I couldn't get past that veil. They all stayed at the Iranian legation, an impenetrable fortress on the seventeenth floor of a Park Avenue building, with security guards and alarms. I stayed at the Pilgrim Arms, on East 51st Street, in a tiny room on the second floor, next to the noise of the central-heating ducts. I couldn't sleep, and ended up talking to the roaches who trekked across the walls. Yes, even in the richest metropolis in the world . . . I phantasised about being trapped in the lift with her, on Park Avenue, just the two of us, stuck between floors. But the chaperones were attached to her like limpet mines. I dug out a Farsi tract, about village surgery, and asked her to translate some passages for me, in the U.N. cafeteria, but her consorts watched us from a nearby table like hawks. Nevertheless, I managed to move one foot under the table, touching hers. She didn't blink an eye, but continued explaining about rural immunization procedures . . ."

"You're stretching this out, Angel, get to the climax!"

The bombardment was now without let-up, day and night. The Syrians had become aware of the role of Angel's stronghold in keeping the camp alive. They began shelling directly onto the hospital, which was fortified by our system of wire nets and sandbags and corrugated-iron walls. The shells didn't penetrate down to the basement, but the explosions shook the whole building, vibrating the operating theatre. We rigged up a cover made of plastic bags fixed to the ceiling to stop dust falling onto the patients. But the continual pounding dulled our ears, deadening our concentration. To protect the generator we had to bring it into the operating room itself, its harsh grind adding to the misery, till we could shut it down at night and talk in the dark —

"It's all a lie. He never got under the chador."

"Where the hell is that cigarette . . . ?"

"How much do you pay us, not to tell this story to Hizbollah?"

"Two Albanian leki."

"Come on, Angel, grant dying men this glimpse of paradise!"

"Oh, she'll be there, I have no doubt. Ah, bless you, Khalil . . ."

"The pay-off, Angel!"

"The bang!"

"The score!"

"It came completely without warning. You have to remember this was September. The General Assembly was in session, debating the situation in Afghanistan. A Russo-American duel. Everybody was watching, but it was not my sort of show. I was on my way to the WHO offices when a hand plucked at me from the corridor. She put her finger to her lips and pulled me by the arm up the stairs towards the women's toilet. There was a private shower-room for delegates. It was three in the afternoon. No one saw us. She stripped off and turned the shower full on. I couldn't believe my eyes, my senses. The rest follows, Inshallah. The ice burned away. At the end she turned the shower off, dried herself, transmutated back into her robe and headscarf, and without looking back, left me sprawled there. There was no need. I was the one turned into a pillar of salt.

"The next day she was back in her place, in the translators' booth. I saw her several more times, with her escorts. They greeted me as if nothing had happened. She was just amicable. She told me if I needed more Farsi translations her companions would help, as she was returning to Tehran. I never saw her again. Over and out."

Ah, those Angelic lullabies. It is a bizarre experience, to fall asleep amid a constant, or inconstant shelling, the whump of near and far explosions, the buzz and zing of sniper fire. You can become used to anything. But it vibrates in your sleep, like a giant drum beating on your inner ear, your eyelids, stomach and brain. You wake disoriented, totally exhausted, your limbs like sacks of leaking straw. As much as there was a world outside our besieged Lilliput, it was an agglomeration of Brobdingnagian enemies who all wanted us dead. The entire universe seemed to be out there, lobbing high explosives at us. And to cap it all God Himself and the Elements joined in, and it began to rain. Almost without our noticing, summer had passed into autumn, then winter, October into November. The rains came, flooding the basements and bomb shelters, clogging the alleyways, now covered in mud and stagnant pools. We couldn't burn the rubbish, which was scattered by the exploding shells and lay everywhere in soaked messes. The dangers of disease as, inevitably, from the shattered, leaking sewers, the rats came.

The rats! The more we decayed, the more they flourished. In our office, at the newspaper (prehistoric times) we used to have a poster someone brought from Paris, showing three laughing rats, in a rubbish dump, reading Albert Camus's *The Plague*. Clutching their bellies in amusement. *La Peste, roman* . . . A lingering narrative: In French Algeria, the rats, stricken by the plague, emerge in their thousands into the streets of the city to die, and to spread their contagion. Our rats, Angelopoulos determined, were healthy as horses, but almost as large. They were certainly bigger than the extinct cats, and often faster than a machine-gun bullet. They attacked babies and small children, gnawed through the generator cables and grabbed whatever food they could find. We had to mount special patrols, deflecting armed men from confronting Amal and the Syrians to vermin duties. To conserve ammunition, our men used sticks and axes, sliding and slithering in the mud. An impossible task. We had to accept a *modus vivendi,* of sorts. The rats lived with us in an awful symbiosis, side by side, cheek by jowl. In our delirium and exhaustion we began to recognise individuals, and even name them: Nabih Berri, the sneaky bastard with the grey stripe who kept darting at one's ankles. Sharon, the huge, bloated specimen who stood and leered on the tops of buildings. Hafez al-Asad, the old, grey villain with the grey whiskers and the shrewd, evil gleam, his head cocked as if planning grand strategy, vanishing into holes whenever we came near. Ali, deputy commander of the Popular Democratic Front in the camp, swore he would get Hafez's skin. But Ali crept about the alleys, knee-deep in mud, with his pistol ready, in vain.

Literary memories. In the first few months of our siege it didn't occur to me to mourn the passing of intellectual life. Books, art, aesthetics, culture. Since my own disaster it all had slipped away from me anyhow. But Camus.

Ancient memories from the cerebral sludge. If one could set one's pain in an abstract literary setting, perhaps one could understand. Those metaphors of exile, despair and resistance. The cordoned and sealed-off city. The Plague, striking without discrimination rich and poor, young and old. Camus knew, forty years ago, what we were going through here, despite the ironic fact that, to him, as an Algerian Frenchman, we, the Arabs, were invisible. Moors, natives, we were mute carriers of fate, like The Plague itself. Reading Camus was to become an accomplice in my own annihilation. As an Arab, I was nothing to him. But as a human being, he spoke directly to me. He was unable to connect the two. No hint, as I can recall, in *La Peste,* that Arabs, too, are dying in that city of Oran, Algeria, A.D. 1940. Unlike even the rats, they fail to come up from their holes into the writer's field of sight. And yet he understood the depths of my soul. How can I explain this paradox? There is something fundamentally deficient in the way we view the world.

But I am seeking to crack open the metaphor. Perhaps it has no real meaning. Literary insight and the real world, separate universes. We only imagine a connection. The rats were right to laugh. Camus wrote elsewhere that Sisyphus was happy, accepting the challenge of his rock. He had no idea what he was talking about. Sisyphus was bone-weary, and dreamt only of a good night's sleep.

So much for Nobel Prize winners. But we were immersed in our own universe, as the weather turned colder and the winter rains flooded down the hillsides to the coast, gurgling down our broken tunnels. We worked like miners shoring up collapsing shafts, breaking up every remaining stick of furniture in the camp to bolster the shelters, burning what was left to keep warm. The only electric light and heating was now at Angel's hospital, and as many of our troglodyte citizens as could crammed its cellars and corridors, a seething mass huddling up against each other to keep alive. Private conversations and lewd post-midnight tales became impossible, as everything concentrated on politics. A non-stop revolutionary caucus, with no power to achieve anything, except keep each other going. To answer Camus — there can be no thought of suicide when everyone is watching out for everyone else, and when so many forces outside are doing their level best to kill you. There is no limit to the absurdity you can embrace in these conditions.

From where I sit, or lie, jammed between Umm Zeinab of the Popular Democratic Front and Mrs Khateeb of the Children's Welfare Fund, with the machine-gun of Limping Nabil, the Fatah's Operations Officer, shoved up against my spine, I can see and sense them all, settling and churning like figures from Dante's *Inferno*, or like an Egyptian crowd queuing for Umm Kulcum. Mad Latif perched on a walled-off window-sill, his brow furrowed as his eyes count the heads. Our Israeli hostage, Benny Potamkin, leads Umm Mahmud through the press towards a mattress, while she holds back, cackling and waving right and left like a demented queen. Angel's patients, whom we have completely overwhelmed, can't complain of lack of visits. A packed mass of madly cheerful casualties. Perhaps Camus was right after all. We are defeating The Plague by embracing it.

Mental withdrawal becomes the vital discipline. Close your eyes and go inward for escape. Since the siege began I had shunned this. The truth, I now had to admit, was that I welcomed the communal horror as a sponge to wipe my private pain. I took a morbid delight in the constant danger, the routine fear of death. Angel was right to try to tear that out of me, but I could only confess this to myself. If my murdered wife and children were cyphers, a handful out of thousands, then perhaps the pain would dissipate. But it always returns. Adela, the face at the bottom of the pool . . . Ironic, to hear of Angel's conquests around the world. For she was my childhood sweetheart, and, some clumsy adventures apart, the only woman I knew. The sort of secret a man had to keep, in the hard-bitten world of Lebanese journalism, but who had secrets in Beirut? I was known as Tewfiq the Monogamous, hurrying home at the end of each day to the delights of domesticity. We should have been living in Switzerland, or Holland, or anywhere not liable to catastrophe every fifteen minutes.

In fact, our marriage was an elopement. Her parents less than keen on her marrying a Moslem, particularly not a Palestinian refugee who wasn't worth a bent piastre. They were Communists, but that makes no difference in family stakes. They didn't mind her running about as a little girl with that kid from down the road, but they had other plans for her future. They could see what was coming in this country and planned to pull out and emigrate to France as soon as their finances allowed. But I was a Levantine patriot. I was determined to stay close to my land. Palestine cannot be liberated from Paris. We talked about it a great deal, earnestly, as teenagers do, as we sat in the cafés, or on the beach, or in the corridors of the American University, where all currents mingled, or walking in the hills overlooking the city. The great, brash, Westernised metropolis, the pounding heart of the Levant, its tall buildings, its glutted traffic, its buzz of a million loose tongues. A cosmopolitan staging-post for our return. Yes, there would be war, we argued in the coffee shops, the fashion shops, the public squares. No one would give us our homeland on a plate. We had to be prepared to die. For this reason I urged her to listen to her parents and leave with them overseas. I am a man with no future, I told her, even if I were not a *fiday*, we were all expendable in the war for liberation. But she would have none of it. I know now that, putting it that way, I ensured her destruction. She had no option but to stay. Her parents set the date, sold their home and bought the tickets. On the morning of their departure, she had left. We had gone to hide with a Palestinian family in Sidon. A cruel act of youth. They cancelled their departure, and her father used every ounce of his influence and mercantile contacts to pluck her back. He spoke to Yasir Arafat, who promised to speak to me in person. I was summoned and told off. The Old Man, in his iconic keffiyah, sitting there blinking his big wet eyes at me, pursing his lips and wagging his head, as if he didn't have enough problems. But it was all to no avail. Eventually there was a big reconciliation. My family, her family, *mezzehs* and tears. They emigrated to Paris without her. She remained with me and got killed.

The children I cannot even think about. Their faces are, thank God, a blur. All that remains is the face of the murderer, Aziz Khamash, looking out from billboards and pillboxes and walls, from newspaper front pages. But at least I am spared that now, here in this rat trap, arse deep in muddy water, underneath the ground.

"Incoming!"

The enemy resumes his bombardment. I have to rush, rifle in hand, to the front — one hundred metres away (102 metres and 30 centimetres, Mad Latif worked it out). Sprawling in mud, in the trenches. Shadows of the First World War. One cannot tell where the rain stops and shrapnel begins, until that tell-tale sting or cry. A man's arm erupts in red beside me. I am momentarily blinded by the spray. A figure pulls the wounded man, Farid, off me. I look up into the face of the white-armbanded medic who helps lay him on the sacks. It is Benny Potamkin. The combination of fire and rain has fused us into one mass. He shouts in English in my ear:

"Are you all right? Are you hit?"

It's not my blood on me. Or is it? Is there a difference any more?

"I'm okay! I'm okay!"

He rushes off, two black-garbed women helping him carry the wounded man towards Doctor Angel's scalpels, breasting through the mud, the sediment, the quagmire of unforeseen destinies.

SIX

Sandworm
Holes

THE FACTS, SUCH AS THEY WERE, WERE UNARGUABLE: DOCTOR ANGEL HAD disappeared. The gentle slopes of East Lothian were totally denuded of his presence. A new irritability at large, ripples spreading from the lost stone. Andrew Mackenzie's missing-person report at Craddock police station was not expected to draw much attention but resulted, in fact, three days later, in a visit by one Inspector Druitt, from Glasgow, a thickset, bald, middle-aged man with droop-lidded falcon eyes, accompanied by a young stripe-shirted beanpole who inpoked data on a personal organiser. Settling into an armchair at The Retreat, the Inspector accepted, to Andrew Macken-zie's delight at the transgression of clichés, a wee dram of the Auchen-toshan, drumming his fingers together while Mackenzie rambled through his memories of the vanished surgeon.

"Aye, he was a man who took risks, but out here . . ."

The realisation of Daniel Pick's paranoias. The plane illicitly landing and taking off, the white van, the mysterious strangers, all corroborated by independent witnesses: Mrs Eastwood, who ran the Craddock newspaper shop. Mr and Mrs MacDowell of Drem. Old Mo Finniston, the sheep farmer of Beanston Mains; and Doug and Elvis Macdonald, two ragged-trousered bikers who drove their Hondas up and down the B1377 sixty-five times a day. None, however, had seen the disappearing man himself, nor the moment of his occultation. Inspector Druitt sympathetically interviewed Sophia, whose bed the good Doctor had departed at seven-thirty in the morning, leaving her sprawled across it, nose to the carpet, waving a dozy goodbye, as he called out he was on his way to see Mackenzie.

Subsequent to that there was only one further sighting, by Mrs MacDowell, of the Angel alighting from the Scotrail Sprinter at Drem. This was the key viewing, probed, checked and scrutinised by Inspector Druitt at the price of downing endless cups of weak tea. Unfortunately, Mrs MacDowell could not recognise Doctor Angel from the only photograph Mackenzie could produce, an old *Newsweek* magazine shot taken on the day the siege of Jaffa Camp in Beirut had been lifted, in March '87, depicting an emaciated grinning imp surrounded by equally emaciated grinning children.

"Och, the man I saw was a sort of plump fellah, nothing like this puir puny devil . . ."

She did concede, eventually, a vague resemblance. The clothes she described matched those the Doctor had left in. He was carrying a faded blue sidebag. Or could there have been a deliberate deception? Inspector Druitt obviously thought the scrutiny worth his time. He was, he admitted to Mackenzie and Avram Blok, a specialist of sorts on Middle Eastern troublemakers, belying his homely provincial features. "There could be a political dimension," he confided to Mackenzie and Avram Blok. "Your Doctor Angelopoulos maintained contacts with Palestinian political organisations in Britain and elsewhere. We would wish to eliminate that possibility, as a matter of routine. On the other hand, I understand he was not a man to stay long in one place. We are trying to contact family members, in the United States, to gain a clearer picture. The only 'evidence' I have of any untoward incident is, as you know, hardly reliable."

Tick tick tick, pock pock pock, typed the beanpole. Inspector Druitt was referring, of course, to his unsatisfactory interview with Daniel Pick, alias Hohenlohe, who had voiced his suspicion that Druitt had come as an emissary of his ex-editor at Hammer & Stern Publishers, Gordon McTeague, who had somehow sensed his, Pick's, drive for revenge.

"I intend to kill McTeague," he had told Druitt coolly. "Naturally you don't believe me because I am a mental patient. It'll be the perfect murder."

"Murder is against the law and morally wrong," Druitt had said, nursing a pint of heavy. "And, of course, you'll get caught."

"Nevertheless," said Hohenlohe, "shouldn't you be supplying the man with adequate security? Placing him in a safe house, like Salman Rushdie, with round-the-clock guards, tennis shoes, quadruple locks, moving him in a potato sack every forty-eight hours to a new destination?"

"That won't be necessary," said Druitt. "I'll just rely on your good sense." The outraged author was left unassuaged.

Later, Druitt walked with Blok on the beach, at Craddock, while the beanpole walked behind, trouser bottoms rolled but harried by the mongrel Alistair. "So what's with your Mister Daniel Pick?" The Inspector used a bent twig to lure the dog from his scribe.

"He's obsessed with words," said Blok. "He thinks they can shield him from reality. It's a common malady. Almost all politicians suffer it. But you're a policeman. Which came first, the word or the act?"

"I'm a Calvinist," said Druitt. "I believe in the intention. But the law can only begin with the act. The rest is extenuating or aggravating circumstances."

"Danny Pick won't act. His problem is he can't define the value of his words. So he just drifts, and can be blown off course, by bad luck or ordinary pressures. I've been there myself. What do you think happened to Angelopoulos?"

"I did a course once," the Inspector said, "on Middle Eastern politics. An Iraqi, a Palestinian and an Israeli lectured us. The political sects, parties and rivalries. The Iraqi and Syrian Ba'aths. Nasserism. Zionism. I'm afraid it was over my head. I'm just a glorified customs officer. Whatever they do to each other over there, I have to stop them exporting it over here. You can stop guns maybe, but ideas? That's not the way we see policing, whatever may be true elsewhere. I leave it up to you shrinks to poke into people's heads. Your man has an international file. He had enemies, by the bucketful. He annoyed the Syrians in Lebanon. And the militias, both Moslem and Christian. And the Israelis. And maybe even some Palestinians. Not to speak of irate husbands and brothers. He cut a merry swathe, your friend, medicine and politics apart. How do some people have the energy? It's a mystery to me. Do you know where he was heading after his Scottish tour?"

"He seemed to be on his way back to the Middle East, but he didn't seem to be in a hurry."

"Did he mention Paris?"

"Um, vaguely."

"I don't want to press this with Miss Salvadori. It's neither here nor there to me. Did you know there was an Israeli girlfriend?"

Blok stopped a pebble in mid-throw to the sea. "You don't say?"

"Her name is Naomi Potamkin. Her brother was a hostage in the camp in Beirut your Doctor spent a year stuck in. The brother was exchanged for Palestinian prisoners in Israel in 1988. Miss Potamkin, according to information received, met the Doctor annually, since then, in Paris. Last year they toured the Loire together. I'd love to do that, but Mrs Druitt prefers the Dordogne."

"Do you know my shirt size?" Blok asked.

"Information accumulates, by nature. Sifting the wheat from the chaff, that's the problem. If you have any grains for me, here's my card."

Druitt and his amanuensis departed, leaving Blok and Alistair to wander the beach. Past the harbour, hoping for a glimpse of the elusive seal. But it was broad daylight, and the fishermen were repairing their boats, small children scrabbling over the rocks with little buckets. The tide was out, and the exposed rocks covered with barnacles and flattened seaweed, the sand littered with bits of sticks, bottlecaps, torn shoes and half-bricks etched with the letters EDIN. Tracks of shoes and dog prints led in all directions. The pitted sandworm holes. Blok noted that, in the two and a half years he had been on this shore, he had never actually seen a sandworm. Just the numberless coils of wet sand thrown up in tiny turd-like piles. Where did they go? What was their aim in life? What music did they listen to? Impasse. The word cannot imagine the naked act. Just being. There is, despite it all, always becoming, or silence. Blok retraced his steps, heading back home.

Paris. Naomi Potamkin. Well, whadayaknow.

Ripples spreading on from the lost stone. The bread cast upon grey waters.

THE SANDWORM'S TALE

I watched him go, trailing his apprehensions, his anxieties and reluctance to face who he is, who he was. He wants to be like me, but can't face the monotony and flatness of affect. Life, after all, is dreary. One burrows deeper in the sand, trying to escape the attentions of vermicologists or snot-nosed small boys. It has become worse since the power station, as some researchers from Edinburgh U. have got a government grant to study the effects of toxic emissions on the coastal fauna. They dig us out and subject us to horrendous experiments in their Frankensteinian laboratories, cutting us into segments and sticking electrodes up our arse. Having an anus at either end is no fun, I can tell you. But I digress. The main issue here is concealment, the ability, or instinct, or natural disposition to hunker down amid the cosy ooze and just lie there, kicking one's heels, as it were. The true worm never turns. Unlike the ostrich, the worm is not content to stick its head in the sand but sinks its entire body in among the clammy grains. What do we care if history, experience, events, cultures, pass us by? We have been here, give or take a few dozen million years, since the Palaeozoic Age. We are not some Johnny-come-lately who rushes about all over the place, changing everything, rearranging the furniture every five minutes, and moaning about the meaning of life. We've seen it all. From the first crawling reptiles, through the dinosaur hubris, the scurrying furry mammals, homo sapiens, city-states, empires and Gods. The entire shtik. From Vishnu to Vietnam. But it was all the same to our blind eyes. We just squirmed our way through the sand, and let the sea's flux nourish us as it always had, give or take some effluents and tar. We are adaptable and eternal.

Oh aye. If you want to do something right, you have to be rigorously consistent. No use beating about the bush and complaining that life is hard, the unjust flourish, the good are dumped upon, the proud have hid a snare for me, the wicked persecuteth my soul and no one lets a man just lead a quiet life and mind his own business. You can run but you canna hide, blood's thicker than water, there's nowt as queer as folk. The best-laid plans of mice and men gang aft agley. The only way out is not to lay plans at all, but simply to follow established tradition. Helas, if your established tradition is restlessness, fuss and tumult, hustle and bustle, Heckle and Jeckle, noise, chaos and braggadocio, there's nothing that I can do for you, son. You made your bed, now lie in it. A man's a man, for a' that. What is he doing here anyway? This semi-mute refugee, conceived in the sack of Europe, spat out illegally to a region torn by the

push-me-pull-you of opposites. Now living as another piece in his partner's flotsam, in the clutter of foreign creations. Aye, there he goes, wandering off again down the coastline, gazing off into the sea, yearning for a
repeat encounter with those big brown wet marine eyes gazing out of
fathomless depths, communicating across the impossible breach. The
incomprehensible gulf.

Kathleen was commiserating with Sophia in the cafeteria of the Bridge
Gallery. Cleaning away the afterbirth of Sophia's hard-won George Grosz
exhibition, the endgame of interminable long-distance phone calls, endless cajoling, frustration, panic and hysteria over air-freight and misplaced
cargos, the festering horrors of insurance. But here they are, surrounded
by 1920s Berlin toilet graffiti, beer-swilling Weimar boozers looking down
on the cappuccinos from stick-like drawings on the walls, men with
striped trousers and stretched waistcoats, women with colossal nipples,
whores, devils, square-headed Prussian capitalists and priests shooting
bombs out of their mouths. The bourgeoisie's mask stripped away and
another put in its place. A banner with the exhibition's title: YES, IT'S
GROSZ! hanging over the staircase. And below all this, the itch of a loss suffered before the benefit of a gain.

"It sounds so mean, but I'm annoyed at the bastard." Sophia waved a
mean teaspoon. "I mean, this is not a way to lose a man. He either cuts
and runs, or is shown the door. Clarity is the essence of control, don't you
think, Kathy? You need to know where you are. I mean, I'm left with this
responsibility I can't take on. What am I supposed to do, form a hostage
support group and start lobbying MPs? We don't even have a clue. Just the
meanderings of lunatics and an old bat who can't even recognise a photo.
Or is it just a practical joke? Did I misjudge the man completely? Am I
misjudging him now? It's not what I need, at this time of life, for God's
sake, Kathy. Am I sounding callous to you?"

"No, you can't be expected to carry the can, after all we only met him
two weeks ago. But it is our problem now, we've inherited it from whatever battle zone it came from. What's your instinct, Sophie, what do you
think happened?"

Memories of a last drowsy exchange:

"So what's your next move, Petros? Who's bed are you bound for after mine?"

"Sophia, there is no competition. I don't have a girl in every port. Well, not in every port . . ."

"You're welcome to them all, Angel. Why should I care?"

"I am what I am, *cara mia*. When I'm here, I'm here, what can I say? In Paris I have a friend, Ali. He's an Egyptian journalist I know from Beirut. We sit together and cry over the world. You're not the only one who weeps in public squares. Have I asked about that grinning cherub whose photograph's on the mantelpiece?"

"He's with his father in Vancouver. We communicate by paranormal waves."

"Why worry about the past? The future's bad enough."

"I take things as they come, Angel. My work is the only constant. You have to decide what really matters."

"Exactly, Sophia."

"See you tonight."

"Tonight."

Tonight *nada*. And the next night, and the next again. After a week, Angelopoulos's brother, Paul, climbed off a Boston-Glasgow airliner. He was a garage owner from Queens, New York, a small tubby figure with the same moustache but a sadder, slower demeanour. "My brother wanders all over and I've stayed in one place all my life," he told Mackenzie. But he could offer no new clue, no supposition, and returned home, to his machines, four days later. A strange young man named Farid came north from a Palestinian Medical Aid office in London, and spent a day combing over the cold weeds in the asphalt cracks of the abandoned airfield. But he left just as empty-handed.

And do the waters close over the dead? Sophia, returning to George Grosz. Kathleen, returning to her unshaped flotsam; Avram Blok, leaving the sandworms behind, returning to wrestle with the shadows of the afflicted at Drem. The ghosts, gibbering on post-midnight pillows of The Retreat, clamouring for attention: Rudolph Valentino, trailing translucent sheikhly robes, rapping with his giant penis on old Maggie Mann's door, barricaded inside with a chest of drawers. Ice-cream assassins, oozing up the steps like pistachio to devour poor Jimmy Gold. Multitudes of small furry animals, squealing for the blood of Alois Crumb. All the morphic resonances of two million dust mites, tingling Daniel Pick's skin, pulling him into the depths, down, down, through the mattress, into the microscopic ooze, the netherworld, where strange and ephemeral giants dance, swinging on gossamer threads.

It's not my responsibility!

Avram Blok, pasting in his randomly spotted press cuttings into his old tattered scrapbooks —

POLITICS AND THE BOMBERS OF PARIS

"Son of a pig! First you let me speak, then you tell me to be quiet!"

"Stop insulting the court!"

"But you yourself recognise that you are the son of a pig. 'Man is descended from the animals.' It's not me who says that, but your own books!"

This dialogue is from this week's hearing in the 10th Criminal Court in Paris where ten Islamic fundamentalists are charged with plotting the bombing campaign which killed 13 and wounded 255 people in this city . . .

Fouad Ali Saleh, leader of the alleged terrorists, opened proceedings in court this week by denying that was his name. "I am called Death to the West!" he explained. Mr Saleh has not so far denied his responsibility, indeed he boasts about it. Faced with many of his victims, passers-by and shoppers mutilated by his explosions, Mr Saleh returns to the offensive. "I am a terrorist. The Koran says, 'Terrorise the enemies of God.' Our children are dying of hunger while you eat caviare. Muslims arise! Strike at the nuclear power stations and the chemical weapons factories!"

To the examining magistrate who prepared the prosecution case, Mr Saleh said: "Your questions don't interest me. What interests me are the crimes of the West for which you will be punished without pity right up to the extermination of the last white man from the planet. Judeo-Christians, Greco-Romans, whites and Westerners . . . You will find no refuge!" Asked to show more respect to the court, Mr Saleh said: "This isn't a court. It's a Masonic lodge."

The Independent, 1990

Nada.

Just relax, and concentrate on breathing. At least the nostrils are still free. An acrid smell, not identifiable. Air does rush in, and is expelled. I can't move. I will move. I do move, very slightly. Into the lungs, and out again. The heart pumps, the blood circulates. The kidneys sift whatever there is to sift. Bile and mucus is secreted. Sympathetic fibres stand by to sympathise. The body performs its minimal functions. Everything depends now on stimuli. If not from outside, then from within. Down memory lane. Hi ho, hi ho. Just follow the yellow brick road, with the tin man, the cowardly lion and the brainless scarecrow. Behind, the tornado whips up the road, the houses break up into splinters, the furniture smashes into black holes, torn spectres keen on the wind . . .

Medic! Medic!

Aircraft swoop, laying napalm on the dream. The clinging black jelly that burns through. Humans are not very difficult to destroy, once you set your mind on it. Entire universes of experience can be rubbed out by chemical means. The usual purifying operation. Cleaning out enemy nests. Nevertheless, while the cells still function —

Let the old hacks mount the stage . . .

Ear-splitting, the tight formation of Mirages flashed over the Arc de Triomphe trailing plumes of red, white and blue smoke upon the cheering crowds. Below, the Foreign Legionnaires marched in phalanx down the Champs Élysées, their beards and butcher's aprons swinging to the brass-band blare. The paratroopers, Air Force ground crews, Navy in immaculate white. The tramp of disciplined feet in buffed boots. Then the tanks, churning the asphalt, the armoured cars, the heavy artillery, the mobile nuclear missiles of the Force de Frappé. Above, squadrons of troop-carrying helicopters skimmed the rooftops, on whose every loft, gable, cupola and chimney-pot an armed sharpshooter perched, scanning balconies and windows opposite for the glint of an assassin's rifle. Not that a good professional or even a lucky amateur might have had much trouble potting the Head of State as he passed that Bicentennial day, standing bolt upright in his jeep, the road in front of him cleared by a small three-wheeled municipal garbage truck hosing off the dung pats left by the cavalry escort which preceded him down the avenue.

"Can you see? Can you see?" Petros Angelopoulos turned to Naomi as she stared at the back of a leather-jacketed youth with a tall orange-red Mohican haircut, as he craned behind a solid barrier of enthused citizens waving tiny tricolours, balloons, bottles of pop and cans of beer. Naomi, though only five foot two inches, shook off Angelopoulos's offer to hoist her aloft like a child. His five foot eight hardly gave him an edge, but, beside them, the six-foot-three elevation of Ali Amar kept them informed:

"Now the President's horses are shitting on the road again. Now the little machine is cleaning off the shit. The President and the Chief of Staff are looking straight ahead. No deviations. Very serious. Now more shitting horses."

Ali Amar worked for Agence France Presse, a far cry from journalism in Beirut, the days of guns and roses . . . Having obtained through cultural and personal contacts three much-prized laissez passes for the Great Revolutionary Bicentennial Celebrations of July 1989, he and his guests enjoyed free movement in the half-closed city, the urban arena for the festive weekend. From the Tuilleries to l'Étoile, from l'Étoile to the river, all major roads were shut off by forty thousand gendarmes, each with his personal whistle, and ten thousand CRS Special Police, black-clad and armed to the jowls, securing the motorcades of twenty-three heads of state attending the parallel summit of world leaders. Police helicopters in the sky eclipsed the gleam of a golden zeppelin, floating above the Eiffel Tower.

The crowd began to disperse, a congealed mass crumbling into its parts. Ali, Angel and Naomi drifting with the multitudes down the rue de Marignan to the avenue Montaigne, blocked off, however, before the river, to keep the throng as far as possible from the Place de la Concorde, the bullet-proofed podium from which the heads of state received the parade. Drifting farther over, crossing at the Pont de Bir Hakeim, the celebration of France's victory over the Arabs, the statues of angels and heroes freshly gilded for the occasion. Left, to gawk under the light-festooned Eiffel Tower, its iron feet buzzing with balloon- , saucisson- and crêpe-vendors, proceeding down the rue de l'Université and past Invalides towards the mundane summer of the Left Bank. A welcome rest from power and glory. Couples dawdling in the sun, a blonde girl with legs up to her neck float-

"I just can't stay at home, watching television," said Angelopoulos. "Kill me, hang me, I'm too old to be changed."

"Don't look at me," said Naomi. "I'm not a missionary. You want to play with fire, I'll pass you the matches."

"A typical Israeli," said Angel, "a nation of pyromaniacs in asbestos."

Ali raised his hands in neutrality. In love, one never interferes. The combatants must choose their own battlefields. Memory, reality, distance. This had been from the start an unexpected affair, its roots in the tangle of the Jaffa Camp, and Angel's evacuation, in the summer of '87, from the relieved siege, bivouacking in Geneva, Red Cross headquarters, filling up the barbed-wire gauntness of semi-starvation with massive infusions of megavursts, gigagoulashes, giantburgers, mounds of pasta, bonfires of curry. Resting and recuperating, he was brought a message from one Major Keinan, Israeli-hostage liaison officer, who asked for a meeting on humanitarian grounds, to discuss the subject of one Benjamin Potamkin, Israeli prisoner of war still held in Lebanon.

They met at the Hotel du P., on rue Calvin, the Major, a small balding cheerful man with sideburns, accompanied by a diminutive but deter- mined red-headed woman of about thirty, introduced to the Angel as Ben- jamin's sister, Naomi. Combative and suspicious:

"You were with Benny in the camp? How close?"

"We were all one mass. There was no room for separation."

"Why did you leave him there?"

"It was not my decision. He was taken away by the Movement, to Sidon. He'll be safer there than in Beirut. With the camp wide open, Hizbollah could have taken him. They offered to buy him from us any- way."

"Why did you turn them down?"

"How much did they offer?" Major Keinan asked curiously.

"I think it was fifty thousand dollars. But the Movement wanted him for their own prisoner exchange. I am sure they will honour a deal."

"Will you be the broker?" asked the Major.

Later the wily Major left him alone with Naomi, having discovered another urgent appointment. The waiter brought the dessert course.

"I liked Benny," the Angel told Naomi. "He changed a lot, in the camp. He worked as my medical assistant. There was no need to guard him, he had nowhere to go. When you're in that kind of situation, everyone's equal. He shared the risks with us. After a few weeks, people forgot he was a hostage. They just called him 'our Jew.' I'll do what I can to get him released, but there will have to be a lot of wheeling-and-dealing that's totally out of my control."

She opened up a little to him, less aggressive after feeding time. "They told me about you," she revealed; "the 'Terrorist Doctor.' A paid official of the PLO. You hate Jews, they said. They told me you're a homosexual. They said I shouldn't meet you alone."

"That's a contradiction. Was that Keinan who told you this?"

"Keinan's okay. It was a creep from the security services. I told him I would do what I could for my brother, but I wasn't going to play their games. It's not what you think, Israel."

"I know. I was there for three weeks."

"They told me. After the Lebanon War."

"While it was still going on. They took me prisoner, at Ein el-Hilwe. I was working at the Palestinian clinic. It was an ugly time."

"I know. I was demonstrating, every day, in Tel Aviv. My teenage brother, Benny, thought I was naïve. He was going through a patriotic phase."

"Well, all cats are black in the dark. What else did the secret services tell you about me?"

"You worked with radicals in New York City. You were married to a black woman. You have a fancy for Arab boys."

"The sins mount up. But they forgot the girls."

"If I'd believed them, I wouldn't have come. I asked Keinan, and he said it was bullshit. He said you had a high reputation. He said you had performed incredible breakthrough operations under fire. He said you were the new Albert Schweitzer."

"He must be joking. Look, hands that never touched a piano . . ."

"Can you get Benny out?"

"I'll do my best. I owe it to him."

They walked out into the clear Geneva night. A full moon. She kept her distance, walking a little way ahead of him. The pretty quayside buildings rippling in the lake.

hear the beat of your wings?
Yours,
Junior Angel No. 453,
Naomi Potamkin

Angelopoulos wrote back the next day to the address supplied:
Dear Junior Angel,

I was glad to get your letter. I did get the first one but the timing
was not right. What can I say? I am a creature of impulse. At the
moment I am impulsing in New York City. I've been working at a
clinic in the Bronx. Perhaps I'm just drawn to disasters. I find that
people are at their most beautiful when coping with impossible
conditions. Though that might be a romantic fallacy. In fact I am
surrounded by ugliness and despair. The area I am working in
looks like the aftermath of World War Three. Even Arnold
Schwarzenegger wouldn't dare to walk the streets at night, not to
speak of the day. The buildings look like huge stone giants with
their countless eyes poked out. Heroin and crack rule the streets.
Violence is normal. And yet there is a community spirit, a real
heart beating underneath the rusty armour plating. There are days
I almost feel back in the camp, back in Beirut, minus the shelling,
of course. I have to deal with the ravages of ordinary disease, poverty and neglect, rather than stumps and metal fragments. At least
that's some relief.

What I'm saying is, I suppose, the human condition, Naomi.
The fucked-up fate of our species. There is an imbalance in the
brain. Maybe the pituitary body has been placed in the wrong
position, I don't know, but there is definitely a flaw in the design.
You take it apart and put it together again, but you can't mend
that original fault. Of course, you can try a prefrontal lobotomy,
if you're willing to destroy the personality, and reduce us all to
robots. Maybe that would be the kindest way. But who would
lobotomise the lobotomisers? I'm afraid we have to deal with
what is.

I think the events of the Palestinian *intifada* are enormously
encouraging. I know, the deaths, the maiming, the pain and agony
of so many people, but something had to give. Israelis have often
asked why their enemies refuse to recognise reality and "talk
peace." But you can only securely negotiate if you feel you are in
some way on an equal footing. When people have nothing in a

material sense, they hang on to their pride. This rebellion is pro-
viding that to the Palestinians. So out of this, I hope, hope will
come. I've lived with this conflict for enough time to want as much
as anybody in the world to be rid of it. It's a cancer eating away at
me too. People deserve a rest, so they can get back to fighting
among themselves, inside their families, knocking themselves
about with frying pans, bickering, loving, hating, scrabbling for
meaning with at least some option for a decent life. Enough lecturing. Yes, I'd like to see you too. You didn't write about your work, I
don't know what personal situation you're in. I am, as usual, a loose
cannon. I need to get back to the Middle East, but not just yet, and
Lebanon is not an option. I've been told in no uncertain terms that
I could enter, but not exit again. At least I feel I have the right enemies. It's a consolation of sorts.

I do have to travel in your direction at some stage this spring. I
have friends in Paris I have to see this year. I'm not sure about the
exact date yet. How about going mad and joining me? Can you
afford it? Can you afford not to? Let me know. I'll be at this address
for at least two months. What the hell. You only live once, and
this, for better or worse, is it.

Yours,

They met in Paris four months later, in May. A glorious birth of summer, perfect sunshine. They stayed at Ali Amar's apartment in the rue Serpente for the first week, Naomi in the guest-room, Angelopoulos initially
bedded on the spare couch, Ali then generously remembered a professional engagement which took him to Lyon for three days. The first two days
alone together they kept apart, Naomi hurrying at her usual brisk pace, a
little ahead of the dawdling Angel, glorying in the Big City, its glow, its
permanent hustle. He took her to his favourite bistros, introducing her to
Chartier, the old workers' eatery, where waiters in long aprons barged
through crowded tables carrying piled trays at breakneck speed, scribbling
orders on the paper tablecloths and then growling: C'est finis. What is
known in Jerusalem parlance, Naomi told him, as a Swallow-Don't-Chew

but by now her companion was becoming restless, dragging his feet and murmuring about overdue meetings in Paris with certain shadows of his own ornate past. "I have to see some people you don't want to know about," he told Naomi, as they lunched in a café along the promenade, "Old friends who are your old enemies. I'll have to split for a day or two."

Are you bored, Angel? Have you achieved your conquest? An oasis in the desert. One passes through, but one cannot stay. She waited while a loudspeaker van announcing the imminent arrival of the "Reptiles Vivant" passed and allowed her to be heard.

"Where do you think we might be going, Petros, you and me?"

"Destinations always frighten me, Naomi."

"It's not easy for me to just take things as they come."

"The way I live I have no choice."

"I can't live in chaos, Petros. There has to be something solid, some-where."

"Am I a ghost?"

She paused. "There is a man in Israel, Petros."

"Yes, I would expect so."

"He's divorced, he has two children. He's a reserve officer. A lawyer."

"A solid citizen, by all accounts."

"People are not stereotypes. He works with the peace movement. His life's been threatened. Lunatics make obscene phone calls at night. Other kids throw mud at his kids at school."

"But he's there and you're here."

"There are always doubts, contradictions. Impulses."

"I love impulses."

"You're an asshole, Petros."

"I am a host of orifices. What can I do? I'm a hungry man. Feed me and I swallow."

They drove back to Paris together, rejoining the motorway, dodging the vast container juggernauts slashing the freeways at 130 kph. Twilight into darkness, lights strobing in the night. Neon road signs, freeway junctions, stock iconic blurs. The blaring tangle of the city. When they arrived at the rue Serpente, Ali was waiting for them in his dressing-gown with coffee and bread in the kitchen, as if he had scented their approach.

Angel resumed his berth on the couch while she reigned alone in the guest room. In the morning he went off to his private assignation while she wandered off alone among the stalls and sights of the Seine. In the evening they rendezvoused back at Ali's apartment and she informed him she had confirmed her return journey for the night flight of the next day.

Quit while you're ahead? They went out to a parting dinner at a small nearby bistro which was unexpectedly invaded by a Spanish-garbed guitarist playing fifties country-and-western medleys. *"Stand by your ma-an . . ."* They looked into each other's eyes, over flickering candles. A laughing jag was unavoidable. "All right," said Angelopoulos, "I'll make you an offer. Next year, same time, same place. Let's make this an annual insanity. I'll do what I can to clear the date. God knows where I'll be, but I'll make time to get here. You can't get any crazier than that. Is it a deal?"

"I'll think about it."

She may have been determined to do no such thing, yet here she was, one year and three months later, sipping ice-cold beer with The Angel and Ali Amar at the Place Saint-André des Arts. Why? What brought her back? What possessed her? Was it the common attraction-repulsion of the Levantine trauma, the fear of implosion or explosion, the need to build bridges, the fear of crossing the bridges, the need to recall the forgotten despite the impact of memory, the alien need to resurrect?

"And what happened to the noble and abused lawyer, Naomi?"

"We're still haggling over the contract."

"You have to foreclose quickly these days. The market is fickle."

Can one simply reconnect the ends of a severed thread? Ali's guest-room, ready and waiting, with a small fridge added, stocked for self-containment. But little time yet for privacy in the Bicentennial zing, as Ali whisked them off in the evening for a bâteau-mouche ride up the Seine with his Press Corps cronies, bow-tied waiters serving drinks upon the gentle ripples, floating past the multibulbed Eiffel Tower, the gilded monuments, the presidential fireworks show. Angelopoulos pointed out to Naomi the angry placards of the Seine's permanent boat-dwellers, protesting their poverty in the midst of festive glee:

LA POLITIQUE FLUVIALE!

decisive words into the king's ear . . . And one hundred years before that, Naomi, the true linkage between East and West — here, in this very tower of Coudray, at Chinon, the Grand Master of the Templars, Jacques de Molay, was imprisoned, accused, with all the members of his Order, of fearful heresies and moral crimes. Life is ever precarious, isn't it? No matter where you go, there's always someone to cause maximum trouble. Philippe, back in 1307, accused the Templars of the following crimes:

That they denied Christ, God, and the Holy Virgin, and all the Saints.
That they told their followers Jesus was a false God.
That they denied the Incarnation and the Resurrection.
That they made their followers spit on the cross, trample it underfoot,
*   and that they urinated on the cross or ordered others to urinate upon it.*
That they adored a demonic cat at their ceremonies.
That they enjoined their followers to commit unnatural acts, which they
*   committed in secret and neglected to inform Holy Mother Church.*

The Templar leaders were finally burned in Paris, a far cry from their days of glory in the Kingdom of Jerusalem . . . But now, as everywhere else, the cries for Pepsi-Cola rose to defile the sky. Naomi and Petros pressed on, beyond Chinon, tooling along the hilly side-roads leading to the Abbey of Fontevraud, where they parked their car by the Café des Amis and stopped for a brief coffee and croissant. They gazed curiously at the tall, ginger-haired man dressed in a friar's grey robe, eating a ham sandwich, lost in his own thoughts, at the adjacent table. Then they rose up, walked along the crowded main street, into the rue Saint-Lazare, leading to the main gate of the massive abbey complex, with its restored monasteries, cloisters, quadrangles, chapter houses and Romanesque kitchen. They pressed in a flow of Japanese trippers into the transept of the great church, up against the plate glass behind which archaeology students scraped away at the gravel back of the Plantagenet tombs. There was a sudden disturbance, behind the glass, a flurry of excitement, and fingers pointing at one of the stone effigies, and a babble of officials, priests and abbey guides, pushing back the crowd, calling out "It's nothing! It's only a crack in the stone!" And muffled cries behind the glass as a young girl with a trowel threw herself on one of the recumbent statues and cried out: "Behold! He has risen! The stone is rolled back from the tomb!" And police whistles, gendarmes forcing the tourists back, and the distraught girl ushered out from behind the glass, a bag over her head, and the buzz of rumour from mouth to mouth: Did you hear? It's Richard the Lion-heart, the old Crusader, the gravestone's broken, from within! Nonsense, what will they think of next? No, its true, they usually cover up the hole! And the soothing gull of the guides: There's nothing to see! Everything is under control! But an old Belgian woman, with a shock of grey hair and an immense silver crucifix dragging her down at the neck, pushed past Naomi and Petros and all the other lovers, pilgrims, oglers and strays and fell on her knees, spilling the contents of her handbag on the floor, a compact, car keys, notes and coins of different countries and an unfolding concertina of picture postcards, and she flung her hands out to the crypt and cried out in a loud, commanding voice:

"And it came to pass, as they were much perplexed thereabout, behold, two men stood by them in shining garments. And as they were afraid, and bowed down their faces to the earth, they said unto them: Why seek ye the living among the dead?"

Nevertheless, je ne regrette rien. After my death, I dabbled for a while in the esoteric arts, abandoning my column to hang about the studios of such alchemical masters as Raymond Lully of Aragon, T. Bombastus von Hohenheim (Paracelsus, to the unwashed) of Basel, and Nicholas Melchior of Harmannstädt. They sought to free God from His imprisonment in matter, always, I thought, a presumptuous enterprise. I followed their trail as they hawked their secrets about the courts of Princes, Emperors and Kings, pleading for corporate subsidies. Today they call it R and D. Scratch the skin, it's all the same conceit.

Defiance, presumption, vanity. Even when one strives to eliminate it all from one's own self, it returns, parading up the anal cavity and eating away at one's entrails. The enemy within. As my spirit wandered, away from the root, I could see and smell the follies of the species at close quarters, hair to hair. The stench of conquest, mass slaughter, inquisitions. When will they ever learn?

Aggrieved, I return to the source, hover above the barren, dusty ruins. Once again, palls of smoke rise up from the coastline. Balls of fire ravaging the whipped city. Apartment blocks, already shattered by cannon fire, crumble, floor after floor. Another general, pledged to sacrifice and devotion, struggling to evict the infidels. I give him my blessing and throw him my last grape, which has already turned into a raisin. Victory or death. Marvel not, my brethren, if the world hates you. For he that committeth sin is of the devil, but whosoever is born of God doth not commit sin, for his seed remaineth in him, and he cannot sin, because he is born of God.

You can't have it both ways . . .

"And yet," the Moslem cleric addressed his rapt audience, cradling their automatic weapons, foreheads cooling against the icy steel barrels, *"in the midst of the deepest darkness, a spark appears and bursts into flame! From the abyss of despair and corruption, a figure of hope appears, climbing up determinedly, filled with anger and rebellion against the palaces of the cruel and the mighty. He is the heir of Adam, who has come to teach mankind how to die. He has come to teach us life's greatest lesson, the refusal to bow down to evil. He has come to show us how to avoid the Black Death of cowardice and shame, by*

embracing the Red Death of choice. He is the shahid, *the witness, the observer, the example, the conscience, the model of Mankind. He has come to show us that death need not be imposed on a helpless victim, but that it can be desired, chosen with certainty and awareness. Only thus can honour, faith and the future be ensured. This decision,* shahadat, *is a call sent out in all generations to the believer: If you cannot kill your oppressor, then die! Only thus can the unchanging nature, the anti-human, anti-divine attributes of the usurper be exposed. And thus the martyr, the* shahid, *gathers his small band of the faithful about him, and marches off against the masters of darkness. East and West, he knows that all is eternal, the same fundamental, unending struggle. There is nothing new under the sun."*

Nevertheless, reflected Avram Blok timidly, the world has definitely changed. Entire nations have been freed, people who eked out their days in bondage have cast off their chains and staggered out into the brave new world of Capital Triumphant, though you still can't get a proper newspaper delivery from Mrs Pertwee's Craddock Corner Shop. One day the paper boy is down with the staggers, another the van from Edinburgh breaks down at Blindwells, a third the stupid dog, Alistair, chases the reserve delivery boy down the beach. Not to speak of the days when the tide rises, plucks the morning's *Guardian* off the stoop and calmly wafts it into the Firth of Forth. Even when it arrives the Good News Of Revolutionary Democracy is overlaid with shadows of gloom:

VIOLENCE MARS ROMANIAN ELECTIONS . . .
RENEWED INDIA-PAKISTAN TENSION IN KASHMIR . . .
40 REPORTED DEAD IN SOVIET ARMENIA . . .
CEAUȘESCU STOLE $5 BILLIONS . . .
MAGGIE STANDS FIRM ON ERM . . .

Six weeks have passed since Petros Angelopoulos was spirited away from East Lothian. Its sea, its sand, its rocks, hedges, fences and green fields almost untouched by the brief pat of the Levant's hairy paw on its skin. The volcanic plugs still keep the earth bottled down. The fishing boats still put-

became July, the sun began to shine, and out-of-sight was almost, but not quite, out of mind when, in mid-July, Mackenzie's third reading of *A Brief History of Time* ("Elementary Particles and the Forces of Nature") was interrupted by the sudden arrival of a much-battered letter from Tel Aviv, Israel, addressed to Petros Angelopoulos in Paris, c/o Ali Amar, forwarded, due to absence of either, to an address in Manhattan, then readdressed by another unknown hand back across the ocean to The Retreat. Mackenzie hesitated for a couple of hours, then opened the letter, read it and handed it on to Kathleen, who passed it to Sophia. It was dated April 28th:

Dear Petros:
Things are going here from bad to worse. So what else is new? Our new government of God-fearing patriots has settled in and buckled down. All the most right-wing elements, those which in other countries are considered the lunatic fringe, are in power now. Our worst fears are being realised. You will have heard of the so-called crazy man who shot and killed seven Arab workers near Ashkelon just because of some personal grudge. The government said he was insane, but the psychiatrists pronounced him fit for trial. The psychiatrists know where they are living. In our environment one might as well lock up the sane ones. The jails will not be very full. Yes, we had our demonstrations again. Our "*intifada* solidarity." But the winds are blowing very ill, my love.

Will we meet again this year? I know it sounds like some sort of bad romantic novel, but sometimes one wants to live this kind of crazy escape. Crazy instead of "crazy." At the end of the day I did not marry Elhanan. Don't congratulate yourself, it wasn't working anyway. He is a good man, but after all his fights and struggles here for justice, which I really respect, he is a too conservative guy for me. If I want that sort of security I suppose I can stay by myself. As they say, every man would like to have a wife, but how many men would want to have a husband? So I suppose I am still a sucker for the jolly doper sixties type with long hair who doesn't give a damn about anything. But most of those are now in the drug business, corrupt and fucked-up as hell. So what do you say? Early June, at Saint-André des Artes?

Benjamin is still down on the farm. They all want to live as closely as possible to the life of the early pioneers. But he complains there is the air base beside them. The jet fighters scream overhead, frightening the animals and souring the cows' milk. How's that for life's ironies?

I'm still working with my handicapped kids. As usual, they keep me sane. To pee or not to pee — that is a better dilemma than to kill or be killed. Small matters which are earth-shaking when vital connections have been lost. I remember your stories about the mentally ill being chased out of the asylum in Beirut when it was shelled and destroyed. There seems to be no bottom line for horror. It freezes my blood when I think of my country, and the events that you have seen and lived through, that show how far we can fall . . . I want to see you again. Like an adolescent girl of seventeen, I dream about our Little Escapes. Our slow drives down the châteaux routes. Can we try and find the auberge of the three-legged cat again? Or the hotel with all the different jams? What happened to the body of Richard the Lionheart? Or was that just part of the dream? So give me a sign. No need for comets and falling stars. A letter will do. If you're still stuck in the Bronx or somewhere else that's important I understand. You have to be where you're needed. But I still hope we can make it, or I can at least hear from you. I know, it's stupid to try to recapture things. Nostalgia. However it goes, all my love.

Yallah, Angel, spread your wings,

Yours in the visa queue,

Naomi

"The fucking bastard, now I've got to find him," said Sophia, "so I can knock his teeth out."

"This is terrible," said Kathleen. "Nobody informed the woman . . ."

They sat down together to try to compose a letter to Tel Aviv. Janet, the third arm of the Wee Threes, in Craddock on holiday from married life and the BBC, joined them in a pub crawl followed by a long night vigil. Burning the midnight oil, the three old schoolchums, putting their heads together as if to crib for the higher exams. Whispering, cackling, guffawing, weeping, the Glendower flowing into the pit. Cries and whispers. Staggered visits to the toilet. Cold flushes. What shall we say to this poor girl. She should have married Elhanan, whoever he is. Who needs the fucking bastards? Men are pigs. Games of let's pretend and forgetfulness, as the cold snap of the pre-summer night wafts through the open windows. The neighbour upstairs thumping on the ceiling. Gosh, fucking

The songs fade, into a morose reflection. All our achievements seem illusory. Does anything remain of us but shadows? We wander alone, down cold, empty corridors. All the toilets are occupied. Explode! Explode! The final release comes, in a splatter of piss and vomit. Here I lay me down to sleep. The dawn arrives, almost imperceptible, on leaden eyelids and emptied stomachs. The letter to Naomi remains unwritten. Familiar creaks and tinkles from the street. The rumble of early-morning traffic. The ghosts of municipal cleaning trucks, hosing the night off the roads.

But it'll take more than that to wash off the sins of humanity, and particularly of Gordon McTeague, mused Danny Hohenlohe, as he wandered the summer streets of London, June and July, steaming hot, a touch of the tropics, the crowds of red faces, bulging thighs, jiggling breasts, sweaty bare arms and the rancid smell of exposed armpits. Nevertheless, a sense of some freedom, having escaped the parental home in Wembley Park, the odour of old, well-polished furniture, the rasping embrace of Mother, the piles of back copies of *The Jewish Chronicle* and snipped-out advertisements from the Passover Colour Supplement: "Genuine Tiffany Ducks, £1,500 a pair." "Edgware Conservatories, Improve Your Home." The chilling car ride launching the annual visit to Dad, Pick the Elder of Barnet Rise — You should have been a cabbie, Mum. "You said it, Daniel, I couldn't do a worse job if I tried," — and her definitive catalogue of the shortcomings of the exiled spouse, his nasal hair, his uncouth gargling, his laziness and slipshod ways — "I don't blame you for trying to get away, Danny, but you have to stick to what you got." A necessary servitude, eking out the shortest possible period to obtain funding for a deposit and two months' rent on a *pied-à-terre* in Kentish Town, Oseney Crescent, overlooking the railway line to Saint Pancras. The landlord, Mr. Spetsotakis, alas, on the premises, and two adjacent bikers pummelling each other to sleep nightly on the other side of the cardboard wall. A breath, however, of welcome fetid air after the clean barrenness of Drem, the wide-open spaces, the morphic resonance of moles and ants, the melancholy solidarity of the wretched of the earth and the bilious eye of the poacher-turned-gamekeeper Avram Blok. Here one could walk out the door and merge instantly with the mass: Down the busy high street to the yuppie precinct of Camden Lock, schmuttershops and coffee-houses and canal walks, the pawing tramps of Camden Town Tube, the dour backside of Euston station, the Tottenham Court Road, with its personal-computer stores, the crush of Oxford Street, the Iranian exiles still signing up names against the Ayatollah Khomeini outside Collet's Bookshop, Marx and Lenin vying with the latest Green fads, and down to Trafalgar Square and the half-blind stone admiral, the buildings and monuments of a three-quarters-dead aristocracy and a moribund empire dreaming of penguin glories. The Grand Old Duke of York, and the parks where old men slump in the benches, clutching their tattered plastic bags.

I hear Big Ben bonging the faded echoes of empire, quoth Hohenlo-he, and I genuflect at the large nude statues adorned with bronze fig leaves: To the Glorious Heroes of the Machine Gun Corps Who Fell in World War I. Boadicea, flying her chariot. Up Mayfair and towards Grosvenor Square, ah! Twenty-one years ago we invaded the plaza and threw policemen's helmets in the air. Ho Ho Ho Chi Minh. And where is Tariq Ali now that we need him? Where are the anarchist hammers, the peasant sickles? The Hammer building lurks in the sun, where no doubt innocent minions still slave in its maw, while Gordon McTeague contin-ues to sacrifice virgins to Chairman Brent Browbeat on the seventh floor at the full moon. Guts and chopped-out viscera bagged and labelled "Confidential waste," discarded authors hacked to death at night in vicious Babylonian rituals . . . How much longer, O Lord?

Trudging up, towards Marble Arch, Speakers' Corner, abandoned on a weekday, a mere shadow of its former glory. Where is Jacobus Van Dyne, who had the crucifixion tattooed on his back and was a bagman for Al Capone? These days it's all IRA and Israeli and Palestinian zealots. Let it all hang out say I. Give 'em the guns and let 'em get on with it. Thin out the population. As the Hollywood agent commented on the crowds at Harry Cohn's funeral. It's like Harry said — if you give the people what they want, they'll always turn up.

God, now that the cold war is over who can we rely on? Old stalwarts like Brezhnev, Nixon, Honecker, Reagan have completely let the side down. Who will take up the flame? On the walls of the back streets of

Paddington, the Old Faithfuls of the Revolutionary Community Party (Marxist-Leninist) have plastered portraits of Joseph Stalin. Defend the Achievements of the Revolution! Bravo! Urrah! But still no serious temptation. Nothing should deflect one from the cause of Vengeance, Rache, Omertá, an eye for an eye, dentures for dentures, prosthesis for prosthesis.

Ah, but where are the murderers when one needs them? All about me I read of killing and mayhem, of muggers who plunge icepicks into old ladies and eviscerate hapless adolescents for their designer footwear. I read of thugs who pump policemen full of lead at the drop of a hat. I read of legions of executioners throughout the world who slit throats like cutting watermelons. Mountains of skulls. But when you need someone for a simple, one-off, uncomplicated job, there's no one to be found.

I escape into the Marble Arch Tube. Shake, rattle and roll. The automata move, expectorate, perspire in the moving crematorium. The horror! The horror! How could I have imagined constructing an entire narrative of such dross? An idiot enters, and closes the window between our carriage and the next. No one utters a word of protest. The apocalypse is all about us. To my right, an ageing youth in designer leather, a pony-tail and big beige cowboy boots is engrossed in the autobiography of Timothy Leary. To my left, a city gent melts into *The Financial Times*. Opposite a ginger-haired tramp slumps across three seats, his flame hair knotted into tiny ringlets, metal rivets through his nose, ears, lips and cheeks; his fly is undone and his plastic bag oozes some unmentionable glop on the floor. A man who must spend five hours a day dressing to look like nothing on earth. Why, when the same result can be achieved effortlessly? I examine my reflection in the window as the tunnel pipes rush by. The double glazing gives my skull a doppelgänger effect. *Courage, mon enfant!* Rome was not built in a day. What can't be cured, must be endured. So put a spring in your step, and a song in your heart, and always let your conscience be your guide, ta-tum, ta-tum-ta. A sure cue, for the appearance of my fairy godmother, with tinsel confetti, waving her wand, but instead the carriage doors open and an immense Chinese or Korean lady rushes in and sits opposite me, crushing my legs with her knees. She looks directly into my eyes, with a frightful and absolute loathing. I feel my joints beginning to give way. She places a huge plastic bag on my lap. It slides open, emitting a giant tarantula, which begins climbing up my arm.

"Eggscuse me," she rasps, "is dis de train for Cockfosters?"

My morphic resonance is breaking up. The train rattles on, shaking me backwards and forwards. The tunnel stretches endlessly ahead. Whorls and dots and wriggling worms. My floaters converge into a babbling convention. DUMP HOHENLOHE! FREE THE DUST MOTES! The oppressed masses on my scalp cheer, waving their tiny antennae. Calm down comrades, I call out to them; the hour of liberation is not yet at hand. But they buzz about, excitedly, taking up positions and forming their rival battalions on my frontal and parietal bones, sending their spies over the superciliary ridge to check out the nasal fossae. I looked this all up once, in *Gray's Anatomy*, as research for a grand saga that had occurred to me, the Dust Mite Wars, a microscopic *Gone With the Wind*. It went like this: The gentle, drifting Dermatophagoids, who have lived for millennia in the mattress, have been enslaved and transported to the skull by the carnivorous lice who live on the posterior fossae. Meanwhile, the Yankoids, who live on the anterior fossae, have vowed to eradicate slavery. The main narrative concerns the Lacunae, an aristocratic lice family who own an immense tract of grazing follicles. Their life, their loves, their hopes, their shattered dreams and tragedies. Battle is joined, and for the Lacunae, a way of life is ending. As the war rages on, a wandering louse, Rhett Scuttler, arrives at an area of the scalp which has been completely ravaged. Six hundred pages later . . .

Sacré bleu! A body divided against itself cannot stand. I take to my bed at Oseney crescent, wracked with fever, delirium and delusions. The kind landlord, Mr. Spetsotakis, brings me hot bowls of avgolemono and plates of pickles and tsatsiki. I swallow an immense green-olive stone and almost die in the night. All the characters in my stories gather round me and play malodorous airs on bouzoukia. My parents materialise beside them, pulling each other's teeth out. The bikers in the adjoining apartment are battering their heads on the wall. I can distinctly hear the long, mournful whistle of the nuclear train carrying its deadly drums of toxic waste from Kentish Town to Saint Pancras, where they are disassembled and handed out in little jars to passers-by. "Don't worry, Mister Danny," quoth Spetsotakis; "it iss only de flooze, or maybe a wasp bite. They are evil. They must be destroyed." Too true. But still they mass, on either side of the coronal suture, stockpiling their heavy and light weapons, determined to prosecute their blood feuds to the last speck of dandruff. No shampoo or even herbicide suffices. Only a burning fire, scorching the whole surface, can hope to achieve a balm. Come back, all ye Horsemen of the Apocalypse — it's feeding time once again.

Somewhere, there is a cosmic pattern, beyond the uncertainty principle, elementary forces, graspable quarks and antiquarks, boundaries beyond the boundariless condition of the Universe according to Andrew Mackenzie. Or is there? "Time is not what we think it is, laddie. The Universe is neither created nor destroyed. It just is." The grey dull tinkle of the cosmos. But who would not wish to bend eternity, to buck the trend, to stick a crown of thorns up eternity's mouldy, wrinkly arse? Mount up, troopers! Shake dem bones!

Six months earlier, Richard the Lionheart sat on the terrace of the Khamash family home in Mont Liban moodily sucking a chicken wing. Ever since the night he had been caught sodomising Aziz Khamash's sister, the clan had kept him on a tight leash, armed teenage guards accompanying him wherever he went and driving him on his few outings from the village, an itinerary restricted to the slopes and canyons of the mountains where the Khamash held sway. The farthest he was allowed to venture was the Qornet es Sauda, a gruelling but exhilarating walk to the highest peak in the Mont Liban, from which he could see all the way to Tripoli and, in the haze of the horizon, the tip of the Troödos range right across the sea in Cyprus. Another vigorous march, and he might be able to gaze down the Beqa, towards the orchards of Baalbek and the Hermon snows. But still no glimpse of Acre.

Richard had remained at Khamash through the autumn into winter while the Christians of East Beirut fought each other. Earlier in the year, the mutinous General Aoun, supported by a large section of the Maronites, had declared war on the Syrian occupiers and bombarded the Moslems in the west of the city. But when a rival segment of the Christian militias declared for the Syrian-supported Christian presidency, Aoun widened his war of liberation to include traitors in the Maronite camp. After many failed attempts to muster a parliamentary quorum to elect a new president, a volunteer, Rene Moawad, was found in late October. The foreign press reported that, in his home town of Zghorta, relatives of the president-elect were so ecstatic that they set fire to their own cars in celebration. However, two weeks later, President Moawad was blown up by a car bomb which exploded as his convoy moved through Beirut. Parliament had to reconvene, under Syrian guns, and find another volunteer, who, amazingly, did come forward, in the shape of one Elias Hrawi, who had the support, among others, of the Christian Lebanese Forces, the Phalange. It was to dislodge these usurpers that General Aoun, who had taken over the Presidential Palace at Ba'abda, launched his war to end all wars, having had his militias armed and provisioned by Iraq, whose Ba'ath government wished to lose no opportunity to embarrass the rival Ba'ath of Syria.

But, in this butchery, the ex-king of England did not participate, as he eked out his days in the Khamash embrace. The winter rains, obeying legends, washed the ferrous soil of the chasms and ravines down, reddening the rivers with the blood of Adonis. Red anemones grew in wild splendour, and young lovers hung offerings of silk and satin on the branches of trees. In the grotto of Afqa, worshippers placed lit oil lamps in the vault haunted by the Holy Lady, the Virgin to some, Zahra to others. Parents bathed their children in the pool, and the halt, the lame and the sick came to benefit from its curative powers. The patriarch of the Khamashis, Michel, was brought there, to undergo his annual immersion, a pink spindle wobbling in the holy water in his red bathing trunks, yellow goggles over his eyes and bubbles rising from his diver's snorkel, while watched carefully by his bodyguards. After thirty minutes he was carried out and placed back in his wheelchair, his useless legs still dangling and looking much the worse for wear.

The old man had lost his initial fear of the Englishman and had settled down to investigate the conundrum of the ex-king's immortality, in particular his lack of certain vital organs. After three days under polite house arrest in the annex, the king was hauled out by the patriarch's commandos and brought to the family surgery, in the west wing of the villa, where Khamash's private surgeon, Doctor Vizakali, tied him down and conducted a thorough examination, after which he put down his tools and left the village on foot, with a small bag of cheese and onions, naked except for a coarse burlap robe and a rosary, to become a hermit in Wadi Jhannam. The patriarch returned the king to his annex, and summoned a specialist from Paris, Professor Giles Penchant, who professed himself baffled and took a number of skin and biopsy samples to be analysed in Paris, but was unfortunately killed by shrapnel from a car-bomb explosion on his way back to Joûnié. Thus began Richard's stretch of open-door imprisonment, as Michel and Aziz became increasingly absorbed with the problems of the Christian civil war. Their aim was to wait until the warring sides exhausted each other and then restate Michel's own claim to the Maronite ascendancy which had been usurped by younger warlords such as Aoun, Geagea, and the Physician-Warlord, Doctor Mansur. But the combatants showed no signs of fatigue, despite the daily bombardment and carnage of their own people, the civilians of the east of the city, whose streets and avenues and shopping-centres were being reduced to the ruinous level of the west side. Every day, priests threatened to excommunicate both sides, and every day the television stations on one side would denounce the other as agents of Islam, and Imperialism and Zionism and the CIA. Meanwhile men, women and children were blown apart, maimed, widowed and orphaned.

Still the Khamash clan held their fire. And Richard waited, munching his kibbeh and chewing his chicken wings at a separate table on the family terrace, occasionally watched at a distance by the wraith-like and silent Madame Adele. The doe-eyed Rose, his nemesis, immediately following the incident, had departed to Paris for two months, and was even now returning, winding up the road from Joûnié with an armed guard of four top commandos, to protect her from being kidnapped by anyone wishing to gain an advantage over the stubborn clan.

Since his encounter at Fontevraud with Aziz Khamash, there had been little discussion of the original premise for his journey, Aziz's temptations at the brink of his tomb: "I would like you to meet those who continue your Holy Crusade to this day. I know you will be in a position to help, to answer the criticisms of your own heart. I know this, because my father has studied your life for decades." Now, having released him from the bondage of his medical examinations, rectal probes, catheters and tubes, the old man began visiting his prisoner-guest weekly, on Thursday mornings, eight-thirty sharp, after breakfast, probing the ex-king about his experiences in Outremer in the battles of the Third Crusade. The deployment of the troops, the naval problems, military tactics and strategy against the Saracen, the techniques of siege machines, sapping and under-mining, the weaknesses of the Saracen alliances, the role of the Assassins of Sheikh Sinan of Masyaf, and the political intrigues of the Crusader court, with particular reference to the covert activities of the Orders of the Hospital and the Temple, to which he returned again and again:

"Did you know," rasped Michel Khamash, "that in the year 1307 the Templars in France, and then throughout Christendom, were all arrested and charged with heinous heresies? It is said that Philip the Fourth, King of France, wanted their money, but he failed to uncover any great sums. The Order was suppressed, and the Grand Master of the Temple and his deputies were burnt at the stake in Paris in 1314. They were said to have worshipped idols and demons, and kissed the arsehole of a black cat. They denied Christ died for our sins and appeared to have adhered to a version of the Bogomil or Cathar heresy, with which you are no doubt familiar. They believed our world was made by Satan, not God, and all earthly powers, including the Holy Church, were demonic. Was it the truth, were the Templars guilty? Did they perform the anal kiss, and forbidden congress? Were you aware of any unnatural acts?"

Richard shook his head cautiously, as the dog, Franjieh, nuzzled at his master's paralysed groin. The patriarch grabbed a chicken bone from Richard's plate and threw it to the hound, who loped off.

"Buggery," said the old man, "the source of all evil. For Moslems it is their natural state. Fathers bugger their sons, brothers bugger brothers, the *kadis* bugger their pupils. That's when they are not fucking their sheep. We know all about the Mussulmans, you and I. Not to speak of the Jews. When you were crowned, the good men of England killed the Jews in London and York. But still, they have their uses. Their long wiles and financial networks. What happened to those Templar treasures? An entire century in Jerusalem. That cannot all have been for nothing."

Richard shrugged. "We lost it all."

"Money is never lost," said Khamash. "It only hibernates. It hides, in dark corners, growing. You have to know the secret numbers. The keys to the vaults. The passwords. The ineffable names. Freemasonry, Jewry, Kabalism, Hermetic Rites and Gnostic Symbols. I have made a special study of the field. There is nothing that occurs without a reason. The Orders of Esau and Ishmael. The Almusseri and the Ismailis. The Society of Rodents. Lucifer of the Lodges. The Holy Grail. There are many false trails. Many good men have been led astray by charlatans. Crazy theories about the Merovingian blood, a married Jesus in Spain. Priories of Zion. Spears of Destiny. Clues in Renaissance paintings. It's all spectres, phantasms. All the real trails lead back here, to the East. To the Phoenician roots. To Solomonic Jerusalem. But when you approached the Holy City, they turned you back, did they not, the Grand Masters of the Temple?"

"It was a strategic decision. We could take the City, but we could not hold it in the circumstances. The Saracens would have trapped us."

"That's what they told you, with their wily Jew-inspired ways. You were an honest man, a good Christian. You would have discovered their basest secrets. They could not allow you in the City."

"It was a long time ago." Richard sighed,

"You are mistaken, it was yesterday," said Khamash. "We should talk a lot more of this. There are memories, preserved, locked in your brain. We will find the truth." He was interrupted by a flurry at the main gate. A big black limousine with opaque windows had driven up, to be met by the usual teenage retinue, rushing to open its doors. Dressed in black, the still haughty Rose Khamash stepped out, followed by her brother, Aziz, who took her elbow and guided her up the steps to the terrace. The old man pushed himself away from the table with a gesture of revulsion, and his guards sprang up to wheel him into the house. Rose and Aziz swept by Richard, Aziz nodding briefly, Rose looking starkly forward, gliding remotely by. The dog bounding at their side. Richard remained alone at the table, dipping hardening pitta into the aubergine moutabal.

For two weeks, from late February into March, the Khamash made sure Rose and Richard never met, nor set eyes on each other. The patriarch Michel ceased his Thursday visits. Rose stayed with her mother in the house, receiving visits from groups of women from the village and those nearby. Richard was restricted to the back porch and rear hillside, away from the terrace and front of house. He sat and gazed at the rising massif of the Dahr al-Qadib. The rocks and river gorges. The unsullied beauties of nature. Even here, the ruins of old outposts bore witness to Khamash's statement: It was only yesterday. He could smell the cooking fires of camped armies, hear the clumps of soil flying from horses' hooves, the shouts of the knights, the twang of minstrels' mandolins. His nostrils filled with the reek of fresh corpses.

On the twelfth day, Aziz departed to the coast, taking with him a large part of the villa's armed retinue, and, on the fourteenth, at one hour after midnight, there was a gentle tapping at the window of the one-storey annex, followed by the turn of the key, and Rose Khamash stood at the door, dressed in khaki camouflage uniform and carrying two rucksacks and two AK47s.

"Come." She thrust one rucksack and gun at him, turned and strode purposefully down the path. Hastily pulling on his jeans and roll-top sweater, he followed. A winding gravel side-path between the jacaranda trees led them to a small gate in the perimeter fence, which had been left open. On the road a grey Mercedes waited, pointing down the mountain slope. She took the driver's seat, motioning him into the passenger seat beside her. Throwing their rucksacks in the back, he took hold of both rifles as she released the hand brake and allowed the car to roll silently down the hill, away from the village. The vehicle lights were off, and as they passed beyond the few lights of the village they were plunged into total darkness, as she manoeuvred the car with the deftness of the blind round unseen corners and invisible bends. At the foot of the approach road, the usual roadblock was unmanned, a small hut empty in the moonlight which now peeped behind the night clouds. Rose gunned the motor and the car leapt forward, lights still off, down the mountain. She put her right hand on his knee. He placed his left hand on her right. A soft flow of ghostly blue light seemed to engulf them both.

"Fuck them," said Rose.

"Fuck them," said Richard the Lionheart.

They reached their first roadblock at the junction with the main Joûnié-Baalbek road. At the outskirts of a village, armed men flagged them down. Rose took a package from her rucksack, got out and spoke to the men. She left the package and returned. The fugitives drove on. This procedure was repeated four more times along the way. The moon bathed the road, the trees and mountainsides with a silvery patina, and the smell of the incipient spring hung like perfume in the air. But as they approached the coast another light, another smell, could be sensed. A warm orange flow ahead, and the smoke of fires, overlaying the sulphur scent of the sea. The pok-pok-pok of small-arms fire perforating the night. Beirut on fire as usual, the haggard phoenix roasting in its own embers.

They drove on down deserted streets, the ghosts of tightly packed apartment blocks black against the glow around them. But they had to stop at a wall of sandbags blocking the road ahead. A burst of machine-gun fire peppered the boarded-up shopfronts at their right. A voice called out. Rose clasped Richard's arm reeassuringly, and climbed out of the car, hands held aside, unarmed. She called out a name. A figure appeared at the side of the barricade. She walked up to him, then both approached the car. Rose motioned Richard out. Hefting rucksacks and weapons, they joined the figure, squeezing through a gap in the barrier.

Armed men led them down a maze of trenches to a flight of steps leading to a basement fully equipped as a television studio, with banks of monitors crowded into an observation lobby and the rest a large recording stage, with a line of smartly clad soldiers standing by an arc of blazing braziers, behind two swivel-chairs in which a black-suited interviewer faced a dapper man in an overstarched fresh leopard-spot uniform with scalpel-sharp creases, his hair impregnated by hair gel into a black glutinous mass. The braziers lit a backdrop of the Lebanese flag with a vermilion glow. The stirring chords of the theme tune from the Hollywood epic *El Cid* (starring Charlton Heston and Sophia Loren) died down as the interviewer leaned forward.

"What is your prognosis, Doctor Mansur, in this phase of the Liberation Struggle, as we approach the Easter?"

"Easter is the celebration of joy," said the Physician-Warlord, "the joy of the Resurrection of Our Lord, who, crucified by the Powers of Darkness, rose again on the third day. It is for this reason that we have renamed our fighting forces 'The Militants of the Third Day'. For we too have been crucified, in word and deed, by the Enemies of our Faith and those who have usurped our faith in the service of foreign Caesars. Those who have declared their so-called war of liberation against the very concept of liberation. We have to fight, to free ourselves from the endless threat of war. The people of our city have suffered enough in the years of bloodshed and disgrace. They have had enough of civil wars, and desire nothing more than peace and honour. We have a sacred duty, to defend them from this latest onslaught, and this duty we shall perform until the last breath in our bodies. Our slogan is Victory for Peace, Victory for the Joy of Our Lord Jesus Christ, King of the World."

El Cid resumed, then faded out, to be replaced on the monitors by the dynamic opening credit of American female wrestling. The dapper man came forward and embraced Rose Khamash warmly, clutching her biceps with spidery hands. She introduced her companion: "Richard Dupont, Doctor Anis Mansur. Monsieur Dupont is originally from England."

"I adore the English," said Mansur. "'Your Pilkington night-sights are an invaluable asset in the counter-insurgency field. Your Marconi smart mines are a whole generation ahead of your competitors, not to speak of the excellent Chieftain."

"Monsieur Dupont is not a dealer," Rose interrupted. "We need a place to rest and then we should be ready to talk business a little later. Aziz will probably be asking after us."

"I have never set eyes on you," purred the militant doctor. "You will be secure in my private apartment."

They relaxed, two floors above the studio, in a riot of soft cushions, silk brocades, baroque furniture and fake Vermeers on the walls. He took her from the front, from the rear, and lying on their sides. She rode him like a great brown stallion, pulling his head around by his loose ginger mane. He lapped hungrily at her vaginal juices. Then they lay together exhausted, while concealed speakers played Charles Aznavour.

"What now?" asked Richard, floating on the satin-soft quilt.

Rose put her finger to his lips, warning him in mime that the walls have ears, eyes, sixth senses. Pulling him naked into the shower, she whispered in his ear: "Trust me. Soon we will be free." Then, as cold water flowed from the fortified watertank, she mustered his erection again with her tongue.

Afterwards, they switched on the television and watched a repeat of Doctor Mansur's broadcast. It was prefaced and followed by footage of the Militants of the Third Day marching and giving their leader the fascist salute. On another channel, the mutinous rival general was broadcasting from his bunker in the Palace at Ba'abda, reiterating to the world's press that he was the sole legitimate ruler of Lebanon. All other aspirants were agents of foreign powers, the United States, Israel, Syria, Libya. Crowds were shown, cheering in the palace yard, flourishing his portrait and shouting his name, a sound like the melancholy howling of wolves —

"Aoun! Aoun!"

There followed a half-hour of *The Flintstones*, followed by the movie *Drumbeat*. Richard fell asleep, and woke up to find the blinds drawn, the shutters down and Rose Khamash absent. He rose, and moved swiftly to the door. It was locked. He switched off the bedside lamp and stepped to the window, lifting a shutter blade and peeking out. It was night, and he was overlooking a narrow street from the first floor. Sandbags lined the entrances to all the buildings. But there seemed no one about, except one figure that he could see more clearly by pressing his head to the shutter edge and squinting. It was the dead body of a woman, dressed in black, sprawled across the road. She was face down, and black-haired.

He prowled swiftly about the room, crossing into the adjoining, and empty office, with a desk and filing cabinets. A large portrait of Doctor Mansur in uniform, flanked by Lebanese flags, on the wall, as if he had to remind himself of his own existence. The door out of this room was locked, but as Richard fumbled at the desk drawers, looking for a key or weapon or tool, his finger depressed a switch. A squeaking sound behind him made him turn to find one of the filing cabinets had moved on its rollers to reveal a hidden opening, leading to a flight of metal steps. He swiftly descended the narrow staircase, which ended at a steel door, with a latch that opened to allow him to step out into the street.

The body of the woman lay before him. He knelt beside it, noting that it had been slashed across the back by gunfire. The face was untouched, but it was of a young girl, barely in her twenties. Not, as he feared, Rose.

A chink of steel on steel, from the sandbags. He hurled himself away, escaping a burst of submachine-gun bullets which ripped the road and carcass. He ran, round the nearest corner, away from the studio building. The burst of fire was answered by another, and within seconds automatic fire was blasting from all directions. Ricochets rang across the road. He ran, along the potholed road. The tall, dead buildings looming. Shouts echoing across the urban canyons. Now the heavy whump of mortar fire. An eery whistling sound, then the crash of an explosion, a sudden glow, lighting the street for an instant. Above him, the shattered eyes of pock-marked houses, balconies hanging half-broken, large flakes peeled off concrete. The road, littered with stones and gravel and piles of indeterminate rubbish. Lumps that may have been sacks, or something else. A narrow gap ahead, through which he ran. Behind him, more explosions.

The street opened into a wider road, more like an empty patch of ground, as the buildings on either side had been pulverised into great mounds of rubble. Flashes lit up the sky, shaping the palls and puffs of smoke into intangible sculptures, writhing in ethereal agonies. Then a wailing sound from afar, coming closer, as if the twisting, wreathing clouds had suddenly found a voice. It came from a bizarre apparition, a gleaming white ambulance, painted with a vigorous red cross, its front windscreen punched out, but its wipers flipping away on thin air, as stubborn as anything Lebanese refusing to accept its futility. The van's headlights punched through the night, unblocked and unashamed. It slammed to a halt beside Richard. The driver, a teenage boy in a T-shirt with a grin and dark glasses, wagged his head out with a cigarette stuck to his lip and shouted at him in Arabic.

"I don't know! I'm an Englishman!" Richard shouted back.

The driver slammed his door open.

"Come on board, English!"

Richard leapt in. The ambulance roared forward, sirens wailing. It accelerated down the wide avenue, careening around blocks of fallen concrete, piles of rubble and discarded sandbags.

"What a night to be out, eh, English? Pleased to meet you. I am Rambo. This is Latif."

A small, diminutive boy of about eighteen grinned at Richard from the other side of the cabin, and shot out a stream of Arabic questions.

"Latif wants to ask: What is your height? What is your weight, with and without clothings? How much beer can you drink in one day? How many men have you killed? Latif is crazy, but he is a fantastic with numbers. Latif is our accountants. Here in Beirut, if you want to make moneys, you have to keep your accountings. Are you a journalist or a hostage? Do you want to go to Reuters?"

A sudden burst of fire, from a side-street, caused Rambo to veer in the opposite direction, and bounce over a potholed alleyway. Richard pointed towards his sunglasses. "Maybe if you took those off you'd see better!" The driver guffawed and shook his head. "Here, the less you are seeing, the betters! Too bad, Reuters that way. I take you to The Club. You will like. Dancing, disco, top of the pops, Kylie, Jason Donovan, Bros, George Michael, UB-Forty, Meatloaf. All-night action. Latif and me, we are the boot of the leg! You understand, English? The boozes!"

Rambo let out a maniacal laugh and hurled the vehicle through a hole in a four-storey apartment building, across a courtyard and into the next road.

"Amboolance! Amboolance!" he cried. Richard bounced and jolted, hanging on to a battered strap dangling from the roof of the van. Twisting his head he saw the entire back of the van was filled with cardboard boxes, tucked in large blocks of foam.

"The boozes! The boozes!" shouted Rambo. "Make my day! Let's do it! Fuck you, punk!"

He hurled the van down another wide avenue and then jerked it onto another rubbish-strewn clearing, by another pulverised building with a sandbag wall reaching up to the first floor. He honked his horn. A group of young men scurried out from a gap in the sandbags and began unloading the van.

"Let's go, Joe!" Rambo clapped Richard on the back and guided him through the hole into the building. A steel door was held briefly open by two armed guards, and the blast of noise coming through it almost flung Richard on his back. It was a visceral sound, something he could not have imagined, though he recognised it as the sound the Khamash teenage gunmen thrived on, amplified a thousandfold. Crossing the steel threshold, he found himself in a cavern lit by multicoloured moving lights shining on a seething mass of gyrating, twitching bodies of men and women, pressed together, shouting, yelling, whooping, barking, shrieking and howling in a quivering fog.

"A hostage! I found a hostage!" Rambo shouted. But only a few heads turned. The rest jiggled on, like puppets on an invisible chord. "What you want, Englishmans? Whisky? Vodka, Brandy? Foster's? On the house! Have a good day!" He dragged Richard through the crowd, as half-curious, leering faces loomed in and out of the smog, towards a table at a corner of the cavern, farthest away, if that were possible, from the deafening sound system, at which were hunched, on a few square feet of cleared ground, a musclebound youngish man in a Hawaiian flowered shirt and another perhaps as young, but with grey hair and a grey moustache, looking tired and bleary-eyed, an open notebook in front of him held down by a can of beer.

"Tsingtao! Straight from Singapore! Lee Kwan Jew! Lee Kwan Jew!" Rambo flourished the can as if it were an Olympic prize. He sat with Richard in two spare chairs. "This is Samir, he owns this place. And this sad man is our friend Tewfig Abd-el-Khalih. He was a journalist one day. Now he just writes what he sees. He will write your story, English. I didn't get your name?"

"I am Richard Plantagenet," said Richard. "King of England, deceased." Rambo roared with laughter. The musclebound man simply pursed his lips.

"Can you sing?" he asked. "Can you play an instrument?"

"I was a specialist at war," said Richard, "a long time ago."

"Ice to the Eskimos," said Samir, "but can you cook? Can you tend bar?"

"I used to be a bit of a poet as well," said Richard, "ballads, couplets, roundelays. I could play the mandolin and the sackbut."

"I have a vacancy for a pastry chef," said Samir. "We had this Swedish guy, who got killed yesterday. He came ten minutes after curfew. Our door was closed. It stays closed, except urgent deliveries, six pee 'em until the morning. Everybody stays inside, has a good time. Anybody outside, poof! A Syrian patrol. Goodbuy smorgasbord. I need a Westerner, for the European touch. The international ambience. You want the job. We pay in dollars, cash."

"I'll take it," said Richard Plantagenet.

The tired man merely sighed, and, turning a page, began scribbling, with a cheap blue pen, a new entry in his notebook. The inordinate clamour continued, unceasingly, as the steel door was resealed.

NINE

The

Operating

Theatre

WAKE UP, ANGEL, SHAKE YOUR WINGS. START THE CLIMB OUT OF THE PIT. Trust me, I'm a doctor. Physician, heal yourself. Commence treatment, right now.

The powers of the mind, are they overrated? Can one do without a body? It aches, it stings, it cramps and craves, it sears and swelters in the heat. That much at least I can make out: I have not been kidnapped to Siberia. For the rest, take your pick. My captors have been faceless and voiceless since the first blow on the back of my head at the exit from Drem Station. How long ago? Good question.

When in darkness, strike a light inside your head. We communicate by touch and smell alone. The grip of a hand, the pressure of a boot, the odour of sweaty bodies and clothes. They come in the dark, with blindfolds. They exit, leaving me to see nothing but the bare interior of my cell. A small square, six foot by eight, with just enough room to stand up in. Bare concrete walls and floor, with mattress. Blessedly free of vermin, generally, but the constant headache of disinfectant fumes. Perhaps I have been snatched by sanitary engineers, one of my wilder speculations. There is a ventilation grille in the ceiling, thoroughly bolted with tight screws. Now and again the dead body of a cockroach or other bug falls through. They have obviously sprayed something up there. Taking care that no insect should even conceivably bring me some message, some sign, some grain of comfort from the world outside.

169

They do not speak. Their silence, more than anything, indicates they are not who they may seem. What language, what accents might I hear if they broke their mute façade? Hebrew? American English? Russian? An identifiable Arabic dialect? Breaking that wall of silence became my first priority, my *raison d'etre* in the pit. Chiding, bantering, needling, giving them my full artillery of Middle East and Greek obscenities. But that just earned me a good going-over with the boots and wooden clubs, administered expertly to avoid the actual breaking of bones. So that at least taught me I was in the hands of professionals, not some crew of badly paid teenagers from the Levantine ruins. A first chink of dim light? So was I "back home"? An ironic stone's throw, or bullet's flight, from the Jaffa Camp and all the friends I'd left behind? Or anywhere, in the steaming stewpot east of Suez, or south of Algiers? For all I know, I might be in Ecuador, Thailand, or the Gobi desert. No sounds penetrate to my dungeon. I knew from the start this was the most serious problem: sensory deprivation. When they moved me, from the plane to the cargo ship (at least they couldn't mask out that rolling) to the unknown shore, they had not only bandaged me head to toe like an Egyptian mummy but also tied heavy muffs round my ears. Still, I could hear rumbles, murmurs, booming sounds, rasps and clangs, in my drug-induced sludge. Here, nothing, but the occasional drip or hum of water in pipes somewhere, which I cling to, fanatically, as a thin audial thread to the world . . .

The solution: talk to myself, while never letting go of the knowledge that I am alone. There are no other voices. Keep your persona together. Do not split. There is no Other. But in memory — the hordes . . .

Tewfiq, Bashir, Daoud, Salim, Bathir, Kamal, Faisal, Nabil, Saida, Muna, Small Ali and Big Ali, ah, yes! and Umm Mahmud dragging her Field Marshal Ukhinlek, and Mad Latif the number-cruncher, Anneka, Heinz, Benjamin and Klaus . . . all the thousands of faces, arms, hands, noses and mouths and ears, the balm of living fingers, the touch of life, the cries, the yells, the screams, the crazy laughter in the night, even the constant beat of enemy bombs, what Tewfiq used to call "tonight's heavy-metal concert." Imagine, he said, having free tickets in the front row every night. We would try to rename the warring factions of Lebanon in line with old rock bands: The Ungrateful Dead, The Clashnikovs, Jefferson

Airraid, The Jumblatters, Nabih Berri Can't Stop the Music, The Sex Pus-
tules, The Plotters, The Lahad Zeppelins, The Animals (take your pick),
the Hizbollahis as The Rolling Clones. It got stupider as we went along,
but we were far beyond wisdom. There is an interesting point beyond
shell-shock. Everything recedes and is yet near. There's a clarity which only
in hindsight turns out to be fake, a false insight. It may be the brain cells,
sizzling in fright. Or a heightened delirium tremens. Tewfiq used to report
hallucinations. The talking rats, the mourning cockroaches, the mounted,
armoured crusader stepping through the smashed sewers. Another time,
he saw a delegation of French intellectuals, advancing across the rubble
with tape and video recorders. He saw Jean Cocteau, and André Malraux,
and Albert Camus, Sartre and Simone de Beauvoir, Romain Rolland,
André Breton, Louis Aragon, and even Jean Genet clutching *The Enam-
oured Captive*. For Genet, the Palestinians were the ultimate dispossessed,
dispossessed even of their dispossession, so their plight drew him towards
them, as it drew me, half across the world, to my prison of crowded lovers.
Tewfiq hurried towards this phantom delegation, eager to explain everything, to persuade these illustrious savants to articulate our situation to the
world. But every time he approached, they appeared to be withdrawing,
although they were walking forward; whenever he crested one mound of
rubble, they were moving round the back of another, and in the end they
disappeared into the maw of an alley that he could not locate. Tewfiq,
paralysed by irrational guilt for the death of his murdered wife and children. The guilt of remaining in the killing-fields when he had a ticket to
leave. He had tried to keep the two parts of his soul together, his family
and his beloved city. But the city has mocked all her lovers. Old Beirut.
Gone, like the Baghdad of Haroun al-Rashid. Once she was an alluring
metropolis, with brash towers of affluence, glittering shops and casinos,
lively night clubs and drinking dens, old stone red-roofed houses set in
gardens of citrus and pine, vivacious crowds and café gossip, markets,
bazaars, greenhouses and Roman columns, a jumble of mosques, churches, grottos, relics of a hotchpotch of rulers, slaves, usurpers, a thousand
and one would-be liberators, a cultural stew of Arab, Byzantine, Greek,
American and God knows what. The new Babel. And we know what the
Lord thought of Babel. Its arrogance and presumption, its tangle of deli-

cious sins. And where the Lord left off his retaliation, the militias carried through. Ah, Tewfiq, you lost both lovers. Let me hear that mournful voice again.

Silence in the cell. No one is here. The entire throng gone from my head. Come back, you bastards! Typical Middle East bullshit, they're never there when you need them . . . Fill the void: Grab hold of a link, somewhere. Physician, heal thyself. Practitioner, get to work. Surgeon, break out your tools, enough of this hanging around. Back to the operating theatre: A craniotomy — proceed by classic routine: The first incision, at the entry wound. Peel down the osteoplastic flap, flop it over. Attach your haemostat forceps to the blood vessels. Expose the damaged, pulped bone. Suction up the pulped fragments, until the meninges are exposed. Nibble the bone, until the meningeal edges are apparent round the entry hole. Stop up the bleeding. Inject your saline solution and suck up the pulped brain. It surges up. Keep irrigating, saline, suction, till all the damaged brain is loose. Plug the hole. Now we go to our exit wound, do the same there, nibble the bone till we've uncovered the meningeal defect, suck the brain matter and blood and dirt and irrigate. Come back up, reirrigate from one end, suck at the other, so the saline stream goes through. Inject our hydrogen peroxide, with the large syringe please, Anneka, fifty, no, a hundred millilitres, inject with moderate pressure, suck. The solution fizzles and foams up. The foam's a light dirty brown, there's still dirt, keep debriding, twenty minutes, half an hour. Time for haemostasis. Cauterise the bleeding points. Apply the anatomic forceps, press the foot pedal to apply the diathermic current. Dig that snap and crackle as the tissue is coagulated, the little trail of smoke as the tissue is fried. The suture, please; we have a larger vessel, under-run it, tie the knot. Bleeding continues, nevertheless, from the depths of the brain, the major vessels. Pass in the retractors to reveal the bleeding point. Staple the silver clips on to the blood vessels, one on one side, one on the other. The bleeding's stopped. We have a clean wound. So far so good. Trim the edges of the meninges, patch the missing fragment. We'll take a fascia from the thigh. The defect is six by eight centimetres, too large for a fascia from the scalp. Cover the wounds, sterilise, longitudinal incision, dissect patch free of the muscles, close the wound, change gloves, back up to the scalp. A tight, hermetic suture to secure the patch, five zero of silk, haemostat forceps to grab the loose end, go round the defect, back to origin, take the loose end and tie the knot. Repeat with the exit wound. Put in drain, the suction apparatus, that plastic bottle we rigged up with its accordion-like arrangement, to create a vacuum effect. Suck out any fresh bleeding, bring out through the scalp, close the scalp wounds, suture in both layers, or we can do it in one layer, no, fuck it, two layers, let's make damn sure this one doesn't come apart on us. Tie all the sutures closed. Sutures round the skin incision. Voilà, another head case done. Pull back, let the nurses take over, pray for a proper recovery, a brief coma, minor or no sequela. Hope for the best, refuse to be defeated by the worst . . .

Next case! Above-knee amputation. The patient has been injured by a shell blast which fractured the bone and pulped muscle, vessels and nerves. Insufficient muscle tissue left to make the limb useful. Cut out the skin flaps first, as long as possible — we don't want to be caught with short skin. Anterior and posterior incisions. Come down to the fascia and muscles. Grab the blood vessels and arteries, the femoral, the deep femoral between the quadraceps and the vastus medialis. Look at where the bone has been fractured, the incision in the muscles, two inches longer than the bone. Heigh ho, with the amputation knife. In the old days, before anaesthetics, the good surgeon was the fast surgeon, the man who could cut like greased lightning. Surgery in the Napoleonic Wars. Cut, slash, the triple dose of brandy, for the surgeon as well as the patient, the blood running down special gutters, the severed limbs everywhere. In the Middle East, you put your limb in a plastic sack and give it to the family for burial. You cut through all the muscles in one swoop, the blood vessels, the sciatic nerve, pull it down a little bit and cut five centimetres short, with your scalpel, a nice, clean cut. The bone is fractured, it should come off in your hand. Ligature the blood vessels, a double ligature of the main femoral vein and artery. File down the edges of the bone. Scalpel, cut through the periosteum, apply periostial elevator to glisten the periosteum, scrape it to the bare bone. Cut through the bone, Anneka squirting saline to clean the bone dust away, not forgetting the pledget of gauze plugging up the marrow, now the bone is done. Go through the muscles, the femoris rectus, the lateral group, the posterior group, the medial group, catch hold of the bleeding vessels, ligate, or coagulate. The muscles are nice and clean now, a little oozing from minute vessels, you can't catch 'em all, Angelopoulos, but you're ready to bandage your stump. Your gauze, rolled up, into the middle of the wound, leaving it open, or, let's say, we have enough left to suture the anterior and posterior over the edge of the bone. Leaving the skin open. Bandage the stump . . .

Exhaustion. Isolation. Vacuum. The hooded captors arrive. Fighting a surge of gratitude for their company. Human warmth. Speak, bastards. Not a grunt. At least an established routine. The meal, at what appears to be twice a day, along with the regular bouts of exercise, stretching, bending, push-ups, help to establish an internal clock. Still difficult to gauge the time passed when they shackled and blindfolded me for a quick stagger out the cell, down a short corridor to a cubbyhole with a shower. I think it is once a month. Minimum hygiene. The plastic pot, to piss and shit in. The food, on its nondescript tin plate. It's all army K-rations. Another blurred signal to where, who, what, how. The beans, the corned beef, the prune segments. They could be American, British or Israeli. But anyone could get a supply. I try to let my taste buds roam, my tongue search out the merest clue. Nothing. I try them, now and again, with my halting Hebrew, the swear words learned from Naomi. Mostly Arabic anyway. Nothing works, no response. I impugn their manhood, their ancestry, their mothers, sisters, fathers. After a while, not even the boot in answer. They just collect the tin plate and leave . . .

Concentrate on faces. Naomi, Caroline, Sophia . . . Never could resist a redhead. She must be mad at me for suddenly becoming a victim, after all those tales of control. Love 'em and leave 'em, Angelopoulos, but not like this . . . Naomi . . . Fraternising with the enemy. I could never tell 'em apart — the Jews, the Arabs, the Moslems, the Christians, the Zoroastrians, the Greeks, the Persians, the Armenians. It's all such a fucking blur.

Focus, Angel. Naomi, the freckles, the angular nose, the cruise-missile eyes, homing in on their target from a vast distance. The Terrorist Doctor in love. Someone should write a book about it. A ghost writer! I have the ghost, just give me a pen, a typewriter, a laptop computer. Even a pencil stub with toilet paper. But that too, is clueless in here — blank notepaper.

Naomi . . . The jams of Monsieur Hazoupian at Chinon. One little pot of strawberry confiture. Another of blackberries. Another, plum jam. A large jar of orange marmalade. Fresh croissants from the bakery. The bread, even fresher. The coffee bracing. The butter precocious. The clientele on the jaded side. The British couple with their five-year-old son, all with broad Yorkshire accents. The man wearing a T-shirt, white with horizontal blue stripes. Beer belly. The woman too. And the son, well on the way. They loved those jams. It was clear they would stay there for ever, getting tubbier and tubbier, until they couldn't get through the doors. The owner, Hazoupian, face the same colour as his wall panels. A grizzled pan with a big grey moustache. His wife's moustache, same. Both smiled a lot, from so much jam-making. Not to forget, the front door shuts at ten P.M., Hazoupian bedtime. But you had a key to the back door so you could stagger in any hour. The night life of Chinon. The little choo-choo train through the Cité Médiévale runs till twenty before twelve. The rue Voltaire, the medieval houses, timber and carved beams, stone gables. Tiny courtyards with arches you had to bend to get under. The wine cellar where Rabelais's Pantagruel got smashed. The well, where Jeanne d'Arc dismounted. She came to save France from the English. Now the English, and the Germans, are gobbling Armenian jams. Night walks with Naomi on the banks of the river. The Loire. No, the Vienne. Scattered couples in the reeds. Pardon, Monsieur, pardon, Mam'selle. Fucking among the night beetles. You are never alone, at night, on the river. Life stirs everywhere. You lie, the flesh of your thigh on hers, the moulding of a breast, an ear of corn. Flick a small animal off the nipple. It returns, reconnoitering your toe. The flaccid prick seems particularly vulnerable. Let it take its chances. The bugs shun the smell of spilled sperm, or are they just waiting for our absence to zero in on a midnight special? Unsafe sex. One can only take as many precautions as one can stomach. Trust me with your life, your health, your fecundity. The river ripples by. Straws in the wind. There goes another beast, exploring my arse with its pincers. Why are we here, Petros, when we have a double bed with clean sheets and shower? A boat glides by, echoing with a monologue about dog racing. "Who would bet on a dog called Mitterrand?" Who, indeed. Motor buzz from the other shore. Crickets and cicadas.

Next case. Edinburgh, Sophia. The firm grip of arms, thighs, calves. A scratcher. She draws blood. The licking tongue. Vampires. Howdyou like that, Angelos? To live a thousand years, and sleep by day. Lead me to it. Here, even if I could change into a bat, I'd still be trapped in this hole. Even if I were that nocturnal, asshole-seeking bug, I'd still suffocate to death up there, in the poisoned ventilator shaft . . .

Rather Sophia than Bela Lugosi any day. Something about the northern sun, or lack of it, all that repression, bursting out in wild flowers. The legacy of creative art. With Naomi at Chartres . . . Can one remember those bas-reliefs in detail? A supreme rebel act of memory . . . say the Virtues and the Vices . . . the matched opposites, how does it go? Hope and Despair . . . Chastity and Luxury . . . Strength and Cowardice . . . Patience and Anger . . . oh God . . . Concord and Discord . . . yes . . . Obedience versus Rebellion . . . Perseverance and Inconstancy . . . there is more, those devotional postures . . . Idolatry and Faith . . . always these sublimely etched figures . . . the ideal, versus the real . . . Perseverance — a woman who bears a crown on her shield . . .

And Caroline. Oh yes. Hospital days and Harlem nights. Constancy in the transient city . . . Noo Yawk, Noo Yawk. These days they coat the subway trains with special substances so the graffiti can be cleaned off . . . But that old buzz of travelling encased in a mural down the endless jerking tunnels... Fourteenth Street! Thirtifourth Street! Times Square! Fiftininth Street Columbus Circle! This is the "A" train ex-press, next stop a Hundantwentififth Street! Watch the closin' doors! See all the white folks disappear!

Uptown, Saturday night, at Caroline's parents' house, that great brownstone in what was once a white bourgeois street before the blacks moved in and chased them all out to Westchester County . . . Those huge twelve-foot-high rooms crammed with African and West Indian tapestries, and a million photographs on the walls, on mantelpieces and shelves, of Caroline's mother, father and brothers with every famous black face of the age, from Ralph Bunche to Martin Luther King Jr, Malcolm X and Elijah Muhammad, Huey Newton and Stokeley Carmichael, Muhammad Ali and Ralph Abernathy and Andy Young and Jesse Jackson and a host of known and unknowns, politicians, jazz singers, athletes, preachers, cabbages and kings. Posters of milestones in the struggle, from the March on Washington to the Freedom Riders, from the bus boycotts to the Black People's Convention, and a press photograph of Mr George Bennett, her father, being clubbed on the back of the head with a billy in Selma, Alabama. He's pitching forward into the camera, his eyes popping, his hands outstretched, while his attacker's face is blotted behind the police helmet-shield. "That's my seventeen-stitches picture," he used to say proudly. "And he ain't been right in the head since," my mother-in-law, Henrietta, would declare. And that loud laughter curling through the room, swinging about the old wood table laden with mugs, plates, bowls of dips, papers, books, candlesticks, ashtrays, assorted knick knacks and the flotsam of friends and relatives passing through like a stream, surging round the hosts and a fat obeah woman who just come from Trinidad to sell an astonishing array of silk brocades. The huge mugs of grappa and vodka and brandies and assorted malts, but even sober you staggered out overwhelmed. Marrying into an aristocratic American black family is like receiving a lifelong ticket to the circus, with a dash of chamber of horrors thrown in. Greeks can't compete. The closest thing, my friend, is Armenians, with their grand guignol of tribal delights. The nuclear family extends in an endless chain of dancing, shimmering molecules. Nothing can ever be the same again. A thousand sounds, ten thousand tastes.

Caroline could only take it all in tiny doses, so she decamped south to Hundred and Fifth and Amsterdam. One of the few remaining brown-stones, before the high rise of yuppiedom. That stupid dog, Mongolian Joe, who lived with her brother on the ground floor. Indifferent to her but doted on me. I spent half my life there fending that beast off. "I signed up for miscegenation, not bestiality," as I kicked him out of our bed for the hundredth time. "He's playing with you, he's just a big puppy." She found him useful, as a barrier. Mongolian Joe. What a name.

Saint Caroline. Physicians shouldn't marry each other. Even when we worked in the same hospital we only met very rarely, at home. And even when we managed to evict the mutt — that constant flood of other mendicants: refugees from South Africa, Angola, Mozambique, Guinea- Bissau, Rhodesia. The ANC, ZAPO, ZANU, FRELIMO, endlessly in session. Plans to liberate half the world hatched in that huge front room. Accusations of treachery and sell-out pepping up weary Sundays. And that was just from one continent! Pretty soon I was bringing her Palestinians and Lebanese and the whole shebang: Armenians, Greek Cypriots, Druze, left-wing Christians, Islamic moderates. She responded by calling in the Haitians, Chileans, Colombians and Paraguayans. No need to mention the Puerto Ricans, my earliest friends. When you're young, it's all so exhilarating, but when you've done one hundred and eight hours a week in the wards of Harlem General Hospital . . . Caroline, the Queen Bee. That great life-enhancing cackling laugh. The never-ending energy. The end had to come. The Cherokee poet Abelard, and his sister, Louise Cave Bear. That raw-boned, big-pelvised bitch. I never had so rough a fuck. I had to send my penis out for major repair. In this hole, in this pit of fear, would I tell a lie? Even to myself. Louise Cave Bear. Caroline caught us, in her bed. And that, mon frère, was that.

I should examine my conscience, you're saying. Am I a Good Man? Certainly not the Good Feminist. I am a victim of circumstances. A slave of my cock. Indicted, convicted, sentenced. My hell, the opposite of Sartre's. Not other people, but the lack of 'em. My captors know me. They must have sat, hunched over files and dossiers, psychological profiles. Isolate the bastard completely. Cut all his threads and ties. Deaden his senses. Drain his energy sources. Drive the man deep inside, and let him tear himself apart.

What was that joke, that famous Laingian graffito: You're never alone with schizophrenia? Fight back, just let the voices flow . . .

"Okay, Angel, tell us another. More of those shaggy Greek stories!"

"Your mother! Your father! The Yugoslav Circus!"

"Okay, comrades. This is how it was. My mother had grown fat in America, the land of plenty. My father had grown thin and ill. He died, and I was furious at the doctors who had let him die. I decided at that point to become a doctor, and only treat those for whom everyone else had given up all hope. I was burning with zeal. My mother became sadder and sadder. To fill the void she ate even more, and became extremely obese. Then she was told something that threw her into a panic. My uncle, the automobile scrap merchant, who was putting me through medical school, revealed to her that her old lover, Popov, the strongman, from whom she had run away with my father, had arrived in the United States from Zagreb and was avidly searching for her, the long lost love of his youth . . ."

The twists and coils of those long-night stories, keeping despair from the door: My mother went on a crash panic diet, and a gentle grey-haired man turned up on our doorstep in Queens, holding an immense bouquet of flowers. My mother hid in the bedroom and my brother and I coaxed her out, and we all sat in the salon, eating cookies with this quiet man who had been a bogey through our childhood. The violent brute from whom our parents escaped. He was thin and drawn now, eaten up by cancer, obsessed with tying up the loose threads of his life. And so my mother was reconciled to her own loss and her youth and old strongman Popov died happy, in Zagreb, six months later . . . *ego te absolvo* . . .

"A heart-warming tale, Angelopoulos!"

"Is it true?"

"Would I tell you a lie?"

"Do birds fly?"

"Do starlings chirrup?"

Not in this neck of the woods. Again we are awakened from our reveries by the resumption of Amal shelling, the familiar sounds of M16 rifles, B-7 rocket launchers, jeep-launched B-10s, and the subtly differentiated 60, 80, 120 or 160mm mortars. Our ears are attuned for every nuance of death. Our defenders running to man the front lines, beginning the day's lethal dialogue. And pretty soon, the first casualties arriving, the blown-off limbs, the perforated skulls, arms, legs, torsos. It's incredible what one can feel nostalgic for. The pain, the frustration, that crushing fatigue, and at the same time the camaraderie, the strength of will that people find *in extremis*. The power to resist the irresistible. Up to a point. The camp fell, soon after I left it. Not to the enemy but to our "friends." The "dissidents" of Abu Musa, Yasir Arafat's new rival. Some memories are still too painful.

Back to work. A laparotomy, comrades: Abdominal operation. The case of Young Jamil, son of Amina and Daoud. The bullet hit the small intestine, and the inferior vena cava. A life-threatening situation, not a moment to lose. Anaesthetize the patient, shave the abdomen, from the sternum down to the pubis, about ten centimetres wide. A deep, single-stroke incision, in the midline, from the sternum, around the umbilicus all the way to the pubis bone. One swoop, through the skin, subcutaneous tissue, fascia, the muscles on both sides, right to the peritoneum. Pick up the edges of the abdomen, surgeon on one side, assistant on the other, pull up and cut again with scalpel. Split the peritoneum with scissors, all the way up and down, put in the self-retaining retractor, the prongs sliding apart on their rail, holding the abdominal walls wide open. Apply the large sponges and gauzes, wipe away the fluid faecal matter and blood, aspirate and suction up the liquid to find the source of the bleeding. Note we have blue retro-peritoneum in the posterior of the abdomen, so we know the bleeding is coming from behind. Expose the inferior vena cava, by grabbing hold of the colon on the left side, cutting the edge of the peritoneum holding the colon in place, pull the colon with its mesentary towards us, coming in behind the intestines to the inferior vena cava. The blood still gushing out, dark blue, grab hold of your large gauze-pack sponges and push them into place. The pressure on the vena cava stops the bleeding. Peel back the rest of the mesentary to expose the vena cava. Remove sponges one by one, locate where the vena cava has been hit. Put the vascular clamps on the vena cava, above and below the laceration. Now we can see the hole. Freshen up the edges, anaesthetist still furiously pumps fluids and blood into the patient, debride, then, with our fine suture close it up. Before the last suture, remove the lower clamp, the blood comes up and refills this part, coming out through the last hole. Tie the last knot, the bleeding stops, the segment of the vena cava between the two clamps is now filled with blood. Remove the upper clamp, the vena cava's bulge decreases to its normal size. Our haemorrhage is now under control, the vena cava repaired, the blood flow resumed. Put a small pledget of wet gauze on the remaining ooze at the suture site, don't forget to remove it afterwards, when you've finished with the intestines. Now put back the colon, commence systematic and routine inspection of the abdomen. Check the spleen, it's intact, check the liver, it's intact. Gall-bladder A.-okay. The stomach, the duodenum. Now the entire small intestine, beginning at the end of the duodenum, going through it centimetre by centimetre, looking at both sides, wiping off any liquid faeces, blood, et cetera. Centimetre by centimetre, the whole long caboodle, checking for perforations. Voilà, we find it, the bullet, going through the coiled intestine, has given us six perforations, twenty centimetres apart. Put your Babcock, gently, at each site, marking each perforation. Going through, to the caecum, and the appendix. Check the right colon, the transverse colon, the descending colon, all the way down to the rectum. Palpate both kidneys. *Alles in Ordnung.* Back to the marked perforations. Each hole marked with bruising from the high-velocity bullet, so we have a metre twenty centimetres of intestines with six holes. No use to man nor beast. Resect the entire segment, cut it out. As the assistant holds up the segment to the light, note the arcades of blood vessels, poke through the mesentary with the artery forceps, clamp the blood vessels, cut through the intestine, a couple of centimetres beyond the last perforation, cut the mesentary and the blood vessels, on either side of the defects, voilà, you have a perforated sausage in your hand, throw it away. Proceed now with anastemosis, suture together the separate ends of the intestine, restore continuity. Suture, double layer, all round the lumen. Make sure knots at either end prevent a purse-string effect. Tie off one suture and cut, another. Multiple little knots around the outside, covering over, continuous, invaginating the outer layer so no shit will come out. Done, now take the intestine between thumb and finger to check the circumference at the suture line. If it's too small, I'll have to undo my stitches and start all over again.

Okay. Stitch up the hole in the mesentary, go back to the vena cava, remove the gauze, clean up, put in saline, aspirate, wipe the whole caboodle clean. Circulating nurse checks the sponge count, all that's gone in has come out. Close up. Put in drains. Catheter for the bladder, intravenous lines, a nasal gastric tube. Close up the abdomen, all the layers on one side, all the layers on the other, long thick nylon, heigh ho, two centimetres from the incision line on either side, suture the skin. Fix gauze round the drains, put drains onto urine bag. Voilà, another soul, snatched from heaven, in order to live in hell?

Tewfiq, my friend, I wonder where you are now? You chose to remain in your embattled city. Like me, you are in love with cripples. Congenital masochism. You used to quote *My Fair Lady*— "I've grown accustomed to her face." But I know you, you incurable romantic. It was to be close to your wife's grave. The Christian cemetery on the rue Bliss, just by the American University, between the Orly and Edisson cinemas. The only peaceful spot for Christians in Moslem West Beirut. Although oddly enough, I heard some Christians returned this year, fleeing the war between Aoun and Geagea. Wonders and ironies never cease. Can I remember the streets as they were? The rue Bliss, Abdel Aziz, Makhoul, Khalidy, the Hospital, ah, Doctor Sa'adi! He was shot by a Hizbollah gunman, and Sheikh Fadlallah apologised to his family. The shooting was in error, they intended to kill some other poor bastard. My friend just got in the way. Too many friends got in the way. We are all in the way of some-one who wants to shape the world by dreams.

From Khalidy Street down across the rue Sidani towards Hamra, round Jeanne d'Arc, into Baalbek and the Commodore Hotel, watering-hole of the world's hacks, the vultures buzzing on the corpse. The choice of rooms on the swimming-pool or street side — "car bombs or shelling, monsieur?" Noting, among the hacks, the honourable exceptions, David, Bob, Charlie, Julie, Jody Steele, and Ali, with your tall Coptic features, your Pharaonic calm as you sip your demitasse of coffee while the whole building rocks to yet another massed atrocity —

"You realise, Angelo, if we fell here we would be the most pho-tographed corpses in the world?"

A literal truth, for many, when the Israelis carpet-bombed Beirut in August, '82. The dead out in the street in clear sight for close-ups. The children, smouldering from within, smoke trickling out of their burnt mouths, caught by the phosphorous or cluster bombs, the BLU-63B bomblets, the M-43 Butterfly, or MK-20 Rockeye, all Made in the U.S. of A. And this before Sabra and Shatila even. So many well-photographed corpses. Not to speak of those that never reached the world's TV screens, the thousands that simply disappeared . . .

Too many things to think about that don't bear thinking about . . . Out there people must be searching for me: Interpol, the British Secret Service, the Red Cross, the WHO. Governments are tirelessly pressing for my release. From whom? From where? Tell us another. This Petros Angelopoulos, he must have really been something. Yes, but he didn't pub-lish much. Hey boy, you are on your own. Now when Charlie Glass was a hostage, he managed to pick his way out, he told me, by tying a thread from his blindfold around the links of his chain, to make it appear tight while he in fact loosened it day by day. But these people of mine do not leave me their blindfolds, nor do they bother about chains, so I'm for sure nowhere near any apartment building, with a corridor to the outside world, I have to deal with this hermetically sealed dungeon, with an impenetrable steel door. Nevertheless, one has to make the effort. What was that film by Robert Bresson? *The Condemned Man Escapes?* I saw it in Algiers, in '66. The audience was rapt. You could have heard a pin drop. But I have no pin. I can make plenty of threads, from the shirt and pants I was snatched in, but they'll not lead me out of this maze. My best chance lies in unscrewing the panel of the ventilation shaft, with the edge of the steel plate they bring my food in, bit by bit, day by day, even though the shaft is probably far too small to squeeze through anyway. I'm sure my captors have me on permanent video, probably from the ventilator shaft itself, though I see no glint of a lens behind the grille. Will they let me beaver on, knowing it's all in vain?

I can't loosen the screws. The plate just gets more bent, as if steel-toothed mice have bitten it all round. They bring me my K-rations with the same plate, removing it between meals, for three weeks, then replace it, as if to say, go on, make our day. Now I know what a performing chimpanzee feels like, amusing some unseen audience, proving the stupidity of my species.

A basic question of existence. Once I believe I don't exist, I've had it. Descartes was wrong. Thinking, alone, is not enough. There has to be something else, to be dredged from inside, or I'll become like those monkeys, in the Space Odyssey, waiting for the Monolith to appear from beyond the cosmos. And all I get is my battered tin plate.

The passage of time, slow and heavy. Like putty oozing through a sieve. Back into gear, Angelopoulos. All the unanswered questions. Who, how, where, why? The question is not who have I offended, but who have I not? The Syrians, the Lebanese Shi'ites, the Iranians, the Libyans, half a dozen PLO factions, the Christian Phalange, Khamash, Geagea, Mansur et al. And of course, your compatriots, Naomi. Perhaps this is just a repeat?

I never told you the full story. My first imprisonment — 1982. The Israel Defence Forces Tour of Beirut . . . Yes, they had a dream, sure enough, your compatriots, of a world free of their enemies, but they only managed to multiply them instead. It was in mid-September, Naomi, that their dream caught up with me, at the Shatila clinic, in the city's southern sprawl. They had already reduced the Bourj al-Barajneh area to rubble by air and tank bombardment in the preceding three months. Thousands of people moving silently through the ruins, trying to reclaim their lives, to rebuild houses with bits of tin and flotsam. The Israelis swore not to enter Moslem Beirut, but changed their mind when their selected Lebanese president, Bashir Gemayel, was blown to bits by a bomb. In the after-shock, the tanks. Surrounding the clinic in armoured trucks, calling out on loudspeakers for all the combatants to surrender. But the Americans had negotiated all the combatants out of the city two weeks before. I fashion a white flag from a torn sheet and go out to meet them, explaining there are only medical personnel and patients in the clinic. But they have this place down on their map as a Fatah firebase. The flustered Major in his dust-caked fatigues keeps jabbing his finger at his map as if it's the Bible. I can see it has a little circle and a dot marked where we stand. The dot, perhaps, is me. He doesn't seem worried to show me the map, as everything else on it has already been smashed. I finally persuade him and his unit to follow me into the clinic, showing him the crowded ward, the debris in the corridor, the offices filled with camp beds, everywhere the smell of sweat and disinfectant, the harsh breath of the wounded, the hidden sights of his war which he keeps shut away behind his dark glasses.

"This is a PLO clinic," he says, still jabbing at his map.

"This is a clinic for sick people," I tell him.

But he arrested me anyway, marching me off with the other doctors and nurses, Palestinians, Lebanese and other foreigners. The Belgian doctor, Thierry, and three nurses from Sri Lanka, Austria and Italy. They separated us from the Palestinians, blindfolded us in a truck, and drove us to an interrogation centre. There I had to face a white-haired colonel with dead eyes and a cough which suggested that the rest of him hadn't long to follow. He said he knew everything about me, I was an Egyptian called Lutfi Nassir who had worked with Abu Nidal's terrorists. I said I was an American citizen, Petros Angelopoulos, and I worked with the International Red Cross. This threw him into a terrible temper and he waved away the mug of coffee which an aide was about to hand me. He said:

"The Kataeb have already taken care of your so-called clinic. You are with Abu Nidal and we will put you on trial and sentence you to two hundred years." Soldiers took me away to an isolation cell, not as clean as this one. I passed the time killing cockroaches, trying to block out the screams of those whose interrogation was harsher. They finally brought me a mess-tin of bad field rations and, blissfully, that mug of coffee. The night passed. Then, in daylight, they dragged me out and put me on an Israeli bus with forty Arab prisoners, and drove us under tight guard, out of Lebanon, into Israel.

A strange entry into the Promised Land, Naomi! Remember, I tried to get you to explain to me the particular nuances of this Jewish hold on Palestine, but you just said: Leave it alone, let's just fuck. Not an invitation to be refused. Politics, ideology, but sex! Another cliché I am reduced to. We were packed aboard this red and white bus with "Egged Tours" painted on its side and wire mesh over its windows, so we could only see the outside world in a dissected web of shapes: Columns of tanks and trucks and armoured cars, busloads of troops, broken and smashed houses, the burnt-out chassis of cars, vans and trucks. My fellow prisoners were grim and silent. Everyone was fatigued, the oppressor and the oppressed. The jingle-jangle of confusion and chaos. No dogs of war but wild elephants, crushing everything in their path. Then suddenly it all becomes quiet. A final checkpost and another column of tanks and then, a well paved, unscarred highway. Unmarked houses, villages, towns, the coast, the sea, waves rolling on beaches, as if the war is ten thousand miles away, rather than half an hour up the road. The bus radio playing soft, religious music, songs to mark the Jewish New Year. The news bleeping on in that alien language. The prisoners lost in their thoughts . . .

Isolated again, but no interrogation. Holiday time. Perhaps the warders are praying. Then, unexpectedly, after a day, Thierry's brought to my cell. I'm glad to see him, but his face tells me something terrible's happened. "There is a massacre, in Sabra and Shatila. They let the Phalange death squads in. It's on the BBC News." A horror overshadowing the good news, for us, that the Red Cross has established our bona fides. I am no longer Lutfi Nassir, of Abu Nidal, but can be Petros Angelopoulos again. Our passports, seized in Lebanon, will be returned, but we have to stay in jail to the end of the Holy Days . . .

Released, three days later, into the enemies' cities, seething with the aftermath of the New Year shock. Sitting in a Tel Aviv café reading the reports in the *Jerusalem Post*. Hundreds of people butchered in the streets, for three whole days, while Israeli commanders claimed ignorance. No one saw, heard, spoke, until the deed was done. Thoughts of my friends, colleagues, in the clinics and the hospital in the camps. Was anyone left alive? Who could we turn to? We sat in our beachfront hotel room, blind to the tanned crew-cut Norwegian U.N. soldiers lounging about with no peace to keep. The beaches, crowded with late summer loafers. The surreal normality. Where were you then, Naomi? Your brother, Benny, who later swooped on Beirut, must have been seventeen years old. His patriotic phase, you later told me. My country right or wrong . . .

Wandering around Tel Aviv, Thierry and the Angel, like pilgrims in a drugged trance. How could we walk among those who had allowed the horror to happen? We wanted to be back, crouching under the rain of bombs and shells. We wanted to be dead rather than be trapped among the murderers of our friends. And then, even stranger things began to happen. Israeli Jews, the murderers, began to demonstrate, began to demand an explanation. There was a new sense in the streets, that something beyond the pale had happened. We followed a crowd to a large square in the city, named after the Kings of Israel. The entire square was packed with people. They overflowed, into surrounding streets. I saw men and women, young and old, weep. The anger and the anguish in their faces. And so I knew how far they, too, were trapped . . .

All the multitudes inside my head. Protesting, defying, opposing. Embrace it all! It slips away, slides loose, evaporates. I am left with handfuls of sand. Not even that. Just silence, and the drip drip drip of that infernal pipe. The stinging smell of disinfectant. Scrub it all off, physician, craniotomise thyself! Cut open your own abdomen! Suction up all that pus and guk! The pulped brain, the severed arms and legs. Bag 'em for the next round! Who would have known the old man would have so much blood in him? Who is that from, Edgar Allan Poe? "The Tell-Tale Heart." The murderer buries his victim under the floorboards, but the heart keeps beating in his ears. Guilt. And not even the guilt of the killer, but of the healer, for not healing enough! Can you beat that? Can I fill the ocean? I dig and dig, and it still cascades. Perhaps this is the day of rest. Just lie back, and fade away quietly . . .

There must be better memories, somewhere. An i for an e makes better bitter. Word games. Associations. Prison. Hospital. Home. Kalamari. Kitchen. Pots. Archaeology. Adele. Desert moisture. Open landscapes. Red sand. Crotch. Shocked Bedouin. Paris. Naomi. Jams. Traffic. Freeways. Lazy Bones Bar. Luck. Michelle. Night blockade. Dead child. Jaffa. Latif. Umm Mahmud. Tewfiq. Palestine. Clods of earth. Manna from heaven. Family icons. Stony Virtues. Chartres.

The idea of permanence. Everything known that needs to be. Whereas my life is endless fragments, jigsaw bits which do not make a whole. Virtues and vices. Faith and infidelity. Prudence and folly. The wisps of grass in her hair. Lying back, on the river bank, the grumbling voice floating by. Who would bet on a dog called Mitterrand? Her laugh, muffled by my cheek. Hazoupian's jams. Missing Lionhearts. Jeanne d'Arc and the rue Voltaire. *Candide* and Cunegonde, hand in hand. All's for the best in the best of all possible worlds. One passage, from Voltaire's *Candide*, memorised in callow youth — how did it go? —— "What's worse, to be raped a hundred times by negro pirates, to have your buttocks cut off, to be whipped and hanged in public, to be enslaved in the galleys, to be dissected alive — or just to sit here with nothing to do?"

Funny that this is the first time for God knows how many years that I have nothing but time on my hands. Time to read all those novels I promised myself to devour one day — and not a book in sight. No Proust, no Musil, no Kazantzakis, no Kafka, no Thomas Mann, no Günter Grass. No Malraux, no Camus, no James Joyce. No Fuentes, García Márquez, Pynchon, Eco. My God, I'd even have time to read Shakespeare, Cervantes, Rabelais! But no, not even a Zane Grey paperback, not even *Time* magazine, fuck it! I tried to draw my captors out, at one point, by asking for religious books — the Koran, the Old, the New Testament. Gauge their response. *Nada.* No book, holy or profane. I have to dredge my addled memory —

Voltaire wrote somewhere: "It is hardly possible to read history without conceiving a horror of mankind." Yes, maestro. But an adoration, too, of that grand drama, the messy pageant of life, the greatest show on earth. And to have faith, in some sort of destiny. Voltaire again: "Faith consists not in believing what appears to be true, but what appears to our reason to be false." There's the Middle East in a nutshell . . .

Yes, I know in my bones that I'm back. I know I'm not in El Salvador, Thailand, Mexico, or in a basement in North London. I know they have brought me back. They might have spared themselves the trouble, I was on my way anyway. Perhaps you got impatient, you anonymous fates, you hooded mute furies, with your chipped tin plate and your sweaty overalls and your bland all-purpose slops. But I can outwait you. I'll sit and watch. I'll wait for your little slip-ups, your unconscious clues. Others have endured this, and survived. So why not me? At least I have no permanent ties. No children aching after a lost father. No wife to go grey with worry. Both parents in the grave. My brother, God bless his soul, the poor bastard. Anyone else? The girl in every port? There'll always be some other lucky sailor who'll get washed up on the beach . . .

The sand, the sea, the peristaltic waves. My K-rations, passing down the intestines into the gut. All the sutures seem to be holding. How many sponges left inside? The post-operative period. The patient has regained consciousness. He sits up, accepts liquids, solids, passes water, stools. The urine bag disconnected, the drips and drains plucked out. The bucket taken away, cleaned and replaced. What more do I want? I have my four walls. My venting shaft. My floor. My chain, my brain, my sweaty corpus. The heart still pumping, the mind still dribbling out stories, babbling to itself. Putting on a brave face to the void. No witnesses. But I am here, none the less.

Freedom? That's mine to take, not theirs to dish out.

Will tomorrow be any different?

TEN

The Peristaltic Waves.
Just a Short Ride
to Victory

ON AUGUST 3RD, IN CRADDOCK, EAST LOTHIAN, SCOTLAND, KATHLEEN woke Avram Blok to inform him that while he slept the world had been plunged into crisis because Iraq had invaded Kuwait. She handed him the morning's issue of *The Guardian*, somewhat chewed in a fit of frolics by the dog, on whose front page the President of Iraq, Saddam Hussein, and the Emir of Kuwait, Sheikh Jabir al Ahmad al Jabir as Sabah, covered with dog spittle, glared at each other under the banner headlines.

SUPERPOWERS UNITE ON IRAQ
Overwhelmed Kuwaiti forces continue to fight invaders
Tanks and gunfire hit a sleeping city
Abdullah Alnibari, a reporter with Kuwait's *Altaliea* magazine, was awoken at 5 A.M. by gunfire.

"At first we thought it was the garbage collectors, but when I looked out of my window I could see smoke billowing in the distance and I could hear more machine-gun fire," he said . . . "I went into the city center at 10 A.M. Iraqi troops were manning all key government offices and tanks were patrolling the city . . . "

"No, not before coffee," Blok muttered, staggering to the kitchen. He looked out of the window but saw only gulls in a hazy sky over a sluggish sea. "At least they haven't got this far yet." He took his mug and sat down in one of Kathleen's latest ventures, a wrecked lifeboat with a padded comfy chair. She handed him the inside of the paper, keeping the outside pages to inspect more closely. He consoled himself with the day's more mundane news: RUSSIA ENDS MOBILE MISSILE PRODUCTION. PLOT TO MURDER POPE ALLEGED. PROFIT BEFORE PRINCIPLE FOR WEST IN CHINA. MULTIPLE POISONER DIES IN PRISON.

"One lost, another gained . . ."

"Stop mumbling, Avram. This is serious. The Yanks are bound to take action to defend Saudi Arabia. Israel could be drawn into a war."

"It takes twelve to tango."

SURGE IN OIL PRICES WIPES BILLIONS OFF SHARES

A WAR MACHINE BUILT BY WILLING FOREIGN HANDS

"Here we go again," said Kathleen, "mea culpa and wringing of hands. God, the cold war only finished yesterday. Don't we get a moment's rest?"

"We have a whole weekend," Blok offered, mildly, having looked forward to a lazy Friday. The Retreat already reduced to a complement of three in the full blast of summer defections. The first intrepid trippers from the caravan site at Seton Sands had appeared in the mist with their rolled-up trousers and little pails, picking their way gingerly over the pebbles and rocks to reach the stretch of sand left by low tide. A membrane-thin layer of seawater shimmered under the haze. The gulls dipping and hawing, scattered by the bark of a dog. Alistair, restless, scratching at the window-sill. Kathleen, dressed in loose slacks and a T-shirt advertising the mythical "1990 Edinburgh Olympic Games," put aside "IRAQ'S SHORT RIDE TO VICTORY." "Why do the bastards always win?"

"Motivation, will-power and opportunity." Blok rose and opened the door to let the dog bound forth, indifferent to global cataclysm. The low roofs of the Craddock council estate nestled in the sandbank across the main road. The early morning deregulated bus to Edinburgh trundled up to its stop, picking up a couple of bescarved ladies with shopping bags, then passing on, leaving the landscape desolate again, till a familiar chafing buzz heralded the day's first rough-legged bastard on his tormenting motorcycle.

A hot muggy day in Scotland, a contradiction in terms. Kathleen switched on the radio, whipping past beeps and tremolos to the measured cadences of the BBC World Service:

". . . President Bush that the crisis was grave. He said that if Iraq intended to overrun Saudi Arabia, the United States would have no choice but to respond with full military force. Meanwhile, in Cairo . . ."

The sand was hot to the touch. The grass and bushes tinder dry. *The Guardian* diffidently reported a previous day's national high of 98.8 Fahrenheit at Cheltenham, 37.1 degrees Centigrade. "I'll join Alistair before we all fry to a frazzle." He walked out after the hound but stopped to sit on a rock just in the shade of the house.

Motivation, will-power and opportunity. How to connect all three. Or perhaps the entire point of one's bivouac here was to avoid any chance of them mixing. A man hides, and the world breaks in on him, upending its traumas in his lap with the paperboy, the invading broadcast beams.

Alistair perfunctorily chased birds off the rocks, then returned to Blok, looking sheepish. "You're looking for an original act?" Blok told Kathleen, "Join the Peace Corps. There's nothing new under the sun. An old lunatic told me that in Jerusalem, twenty years ago."

Nevertheless, Kathleen pursued the chimera, with hammer and glue, creation, growth, nurture, enlightenment. For global crisis or no, these were the run-up days to the Edinburgh Festival, intensive training for the annual two-week binge, the descent of the art-hungry world upon the Scottish Capital, a thousand and one acts in search of glory, the comic contortionists, jugglers in closets, trapeze artists in cupboards, dancers in boxes, no inch of space unoccupied, no room at any inn, the desperation of tourists in search of "authentic culture," street *artistes* and youth on the run. The prettified city, hoping to bask in sunshine, but quite unprepared for the soggy ooze of an overcast *hamsin* heat wave. Kathleen had two shows in different venues in different parts of the town, liaising with Sophia Salvadori in the Tartan Ball pub, up Lothian Road, in the unusually sweaty ambience of peeled-off shirts and pale hairy chests.

"Talk about the boys' locker-room."

"No thank you. Bring us a pint o' heavy for God's sake, Kathy. Go easy on the jumbo sausages."

"The Middle East, eh, what a scunner. Any news at all on Petros?"

"I had a call from that strange man Druitt the other day. Inspector Plod. I can't make any sense out of him at all. I thought we had something going for us on macho pride, you know — it happened on my turf and all that. But nada. He wanted to know if we had been in touch with the Israeli girl, Naomi, and if she was coming over."

"And?"

"I told him we wrote and she answered. So she wants to see the scene of the crime. Which one, I wonder? Seriously, Kath, I don't know if I can take this on. It's all too complicated, and I have Max Ernst to organise. You should see the cargo fees, they're more surreal than the work itself. Your Ozzie admirers are definitely coming, too. Aisleen from Sydney. This is your big chance, Kathy. What would I do with this woman? And now that the Middle East is going to be hotching with hostages, and whole countries going down the drain, what is one lost Angel going to be worth in the deluge? What am I expected to do?"

"What can any of us do, Sophie?"

The overload of missing nations. "Gerremalloff!" A collective growl from the ladies as a lad at the bar whips off his trousers, then, thinking better of it, puts them back on. "Ye shouldna start somethin' ye canna finish." His friends console him with another beer. Sweat pours down foreheads, breasts, arms.

Meanwhile Andrew Mackenzie is commiserating with Blok at the local Craddock Tavern. "Whad' you think, Avram, is it World War Three?"

"I think Scotland will be spared, Andrew."

"Ah, the Scots are always in the vanguard, son. Since the English drubbed us at Culloden, we have had to prove ourselves by doing their dirty work. We'll be there, in the front line, piping the Yanks into Baghdad. But what about Petros? I hate this. When the whole world goes mad, who cares about one man?"

"A drop in the ocean, Andrew."

"Aye. The Arabs seem to have shot themselves in the foot, as usual. The ordinary people never get an even break. Anarcho-syndicalism,

Avram, it was the only realistic chance. But no, we had to go through seventy years of Bolshevik madness."

"Nobody ever listens to us."

"Well, what good are we, anyway? We can hardly save one soul from the wringer, let alone the toiling masses. Well, I'm away home to watch the gathering storm on colour television. Rhona insists on getting Sky. She's not content with all the rubbish hopping and leaping over the hills and valleys, she wants it beamed in from outer space. The spoils of that foul beast Murdoch. Damnation to all men of power."

"You should get a proper satellite dish, and get the whole world's output."

"Och laddie, our guts would explode. That's what the Yanks should do to Saddam Hussein: Bombard him with all the episodes of *I Love Lucy*."

"He probably subscribes already."

"You're right. There's no hope for us."

Has everything that could be done been done? Is there to be nothing but repeats? The tanks roll on, across the Mesopotamian marshlands, into the oil city. No visual reports on the news. No on-the-spot reporters. Just endless experts, in studio swivel-chairs, the anchormen, with their topographical maps and model tanks and aircraft, toy ships pushed with sticks up the Gulf. Déjà vu, of so many other traumas, the numbered wars tripping off the tongue, '67, '73, '82. Who wants to be restricted to World War Three? Retired generals survey the amusement-arcade battlefield, like the Gods overlooking the world of poor Mister Fotheringay, the Man Who Could Work Miracles. And what say you of those puny earthmen now? Should we give them another chance?

Saturday brings no respite. POLL TAX BLOW FOR DISABLED TRAINEES. KOHL AGREES TO HASTEN GERMAN POLL. STANDING UP TO THE TYRANT. IRAQ PLEDGES TO PULL OUT TROOPS.

But it is only, everyone agrees, a ruse. CAUTIOUS ARAB STATES SLOW TO CONDEMN "BLACKEST DAY." Blok reads out the Iraqi Revolutionary Command Council's statement in bed to Kathleen:

"Our forces have performed their pan-Arab and national duty in supporting the people of Kuwait and maintaining security and stability with a high degree of fidelity and discipline, as everyone saw, even our enemies. There can be no return to the extinct regime now that the sun of dignity and honour has shone over Kuwait."

The sun in Lothian was a cooler, hazier affair. Blok spent the day in pretence of a childhood beach holiday, spreading his sagging whiteness out on a towel on the sand, with a thermos flask and a science-fiction novel by Isaac Asimov, the fifteenth volume of the Foundation Trilogy. The wisest brains in the universe were still wandering up and down the galaxies, looking for the lost central planet, Trantor, despite the fact that their founder, Harry Sheldon, had discovered the mathematical model for predicting history fifteen volumes before.

Sunday was appreciably cooler, bringing the first, inevitable atrocity stories. Looting, burning, summary executions, beatings, assault and rape. The Kuwaiti armed forces put up a brief resistance, while their emir escaped by helicopter to Saudi Arabia. Other refugees piled across the Saudi border before the invaders shut it down. Many British and other foreign nationals remained trapped in Kuwait and Iraq. The first graphic maps of the battlefield were spread across the Sunday papers' central pages, showing the balance of forces, warplane strengths, matching tank and infantry forces.

A traditional Sunday afternoon. Blok and Kathleen, settled on the porch, with Sophia, Andrew and Rhona Mackenzie, and their closest neighbour, Stanislaw, father of Kathleen and Sophia's old school friend Janet. Stanislaw was a Polish ex-airman settled on the Firth of Forth, after ten years in the coal mines and a career in aircraft maintenance, exchanged for a low pension, home jam-making and the collection of esoteric books. Andrew Mackenzie probed him for his East European insight into the recent global shifts, which the old veteran viewed with a lifelong sceptic's caution.

"When there are only rotting potatoes on the shelves and dictatorship, it's easy to know who to blame. When there are only rotting potatoes and democracy, you don't know who to tear apart. Walesa, Mazowiecki, Jaruzelski, George Bush, the Pope . . ."

"I hear the Polish government is sending a warship to the Gulf."

"Most probably to pick up fresh pitta."

"You don't think we should all be standing up to the dictator in Bagh-dad?"

"I think lying down is much preferable. It soothes the brain and conserves energy. Who could believe any more in crusades? The Americans will rattle a few airplanes and then make a deal. The price of crude. What else is at stake?"

" *The Observer* says: This Hitler of the Gulf Has to Go."

"To go where? To the bathroom? The old-age home? The grave? Hitlers are ten a penny now. That currency has been debased long ago. What do we know? We live an ersatz past and we have lost our ability to judge. Who was Hitler? Alec Guinness in a false moustache? A man who appears in black and white on television? Even your personal memories begin to be suspect. It is like the witnesses at that trial in Jerusalem, of the alleged SS guard Demjanjuk. They look at a fat, avuncular car salesman from Detroit, and are asked if they see a thin, sadistic killer. Can they afford to send a man to his possible death for those bombarded grey cells? Or can they afford to waver and let the murderer laugh and go free?"

"But Saddam's tyranny is here and now, and we can see it happening before our eyes."

"I have no doubt. But it is his own arms suppliers who are demanding our sons' blood now. Their memory does not even stretch back three weeks, let alone fifty years. It is the true Orwellian world. Alliances shifting overnight. Is this the legacy of our loss of easy enemies, of communism's fall? I don't want to see a police state replaced by a police world."

"Have another madeleine, Stan."

A bite into the soggy texture, but no Proustian transformation. If the landscape ripples slightly, and the Sunday celebrants shimmer a little on the porch, facial contours blurred for a fraction of a second, that is merely a spasmodic dizzy spell. The Sufi idea: We are all living in the invisible moment between a past which has disappeared completely and a future which will never happen. The Middle East, having flicked its finger into Blok's Lothian sinecure, with Petros Angelopoulos and his abductors, now invades with the full weight of Sunday Supplement dross:

Eerie Echoes of Suez Debacle as Bush Dons Eden Mantle

(Robert Harris, *Sunday Times*):

... the Americans, having picked up the white man's burden, will not find it easy to put down. There is no sense of outrage about this, as there was in 1956. No demonstrators throng Trafalgar Square. Most of us, if we give the matter thought, will probably agree, however reluctantly, that we have no other course. We should be clear, however, just how costly this policy may prove; and we should give it its proper name — imperialism. In these circumstances, Eden no longer appears the highly-strung, outdated colonialist of liberal caricature, but a wise and far-seeing statesman whose spiritual heir is George Bush. It is the centenary of Eden's birth in 1997. The way things are going, we may yet see a penitent America erect his statue on the steps of the Capitol ...

Aye, the New World Order. As the world twitches on regardless: civil war in Liberia; fears of riots in Transylvania; food crisis in the Soviet Union. In South Africa, on the other hand, of all places, the African National Congress suspends its thirty-year armed struggle as negotiations to end apartheid loom; Liechtenstein applies for membership in the United Nations; India Totters on the Brink of Disaster at 77 for 3 in Response to England's 519 at the End of the Second Day of the Second Test. And the glimmers of some local relief, Blok takes note, as he replenishes, later that night, his scrapbook, the empty pages yearning to be filled:

If you are heading for the Edinburgh Festival this weekend, be gleg. It would be heepochondreoch if you end up glaikit before a show run by stookies. Better to get fou as a puggie. These are just some examples from the recently published Scots Thesaurus ...

Indeed, as the Festival week commences, the streets crowd as anticipated, suitably gleg, and Kathleen drags Blok, global panic notwithstanding, through the venues, not sparing him his fair share of stookies, from the Massed Strife and Crumbs of Kilwinning to Hull's Horny Sons of Toil, the Faggocites of Newcastle-Upon-Tees, the Sinkship Rats of Tottenham, the Umbilical Chords, the Unkindest Cuts, Satin Crap, the Grimethorpe Tea Ladies, the Bonsai Oaks of Middlesborough, the Croak and Dagger Theatre, Machine-Gun Kelly and His Dancing Fish, Transmission Card's Production of *Hamlet*, the Blind Men in the Buff, Total Abuse, the French Kiss Theatre Company, Gog and Magog, Sinbad the Salesman, the Mouse That Roared, the Armenian Flea Circus, the Warsaw Mime Theatre, the Albanian Ballet, the Russian Roulettes, the Twisted Tacos of Mexico City, the Marshall Plants, the Misguided, the Oban Onanists, the Inverness Yiddish Theatre, the Old Farts of Fife, the Oil Jiggers of Aberdeen. Not to speak of a long afternoon at Sophia's triumphantly opened exhibition of Max Ernst sculptures in precious metals and bronze. The child-like but sinister contours of the *Bird Head*, the limpid *Lunar Asparagus, Capricorn, Moonmad, The King Playing with the Queen . . .*

"*One of Max Ernst's principal concerns was to depict the shifting, dreamlike zone that lies on the frontier between the inner and outer worlds*," says the programme. "If only," says Blok, "we could have had Weimar's dreams without the consequences." But they exit, into a sudden downpour in the damp heat which gives the city an odd tropical ambience. Up and down, the tourists scamper, squealing, taking refuge on the stairs of the vennels, watching the sheets of rain drift across the Princes Street Gardens and the shrouded Scott Monument. Adjourning to a nearby pub, with a strange meat pie and a pastie, and two mugs of export, Kathleen tries to chide him for his disconnections.

"The Middle East, Avram, don't you care any more? Maybe now we should seize the chance and make a quick visit, before the whole balloon goes up. All those promises and we never went. What's the big secret you're hiding from me?"

"The boredom, the horror, the apathy, Kit-Kat. I've lost my defensive carapace. My sword and magic helmet. I couldn't possibly set foot at this stage. With my luck the missiles will start flying and I'll be stuck with my poor parents, buried in their retreat down on the farm. Or even worse, sent into the desert again, in mufti. Camouflaged as a jackal turd."

"You know I've always wanted to meet your parents, Sourpuss."

"A sweeter treat for the wait. Come on, Kathy, why should I feel responsible? The Jewish State can commit suicide without me standing there saying I told you so."

"You're like a jilted lover, Avram."

"No, I simply hate the place. And anyway, you have an exhibition to see to. Australians to rub up against."

"Oh, those things can run themselves. So are you coming tonight, at least to meet the Aussies?"

"No, I think I'll just drag Main and take the bus back. Enjoy."

"When will you come out of this misery, Avram?"

"When the Messiah is finally killed. It makes me nervous, all this anticipation."

"You're the one who's waiting, Avram."

They part, Kathleen climbing up a vennel towards the Lawnmarket, and her second venue, Blok proceeding down into the gardens past the flower clock and the memorial to the fallen of the Great War. The rain stopped, and a tentative sun. He sat down, brushing water away with his jacket, on a damp bench donated by James and Agatha McTaggart in Memoriam of Angus and Anne. At the bandstand, a group of folk dancers rehearsed, flapping their frilled sleeves and skirts and waving coloured scarves in the air. It was difficult to make out whether they were local talent or Serbian or Lithuanian imports. A ragged drunk came up and disturbed the stalled train of his thought:

"Are ye prepared? Are ye prepared?"

"No, I'm not," said Blok. "Are you?"

"Aye," said the drunk, "have ye noticed it?"

"Yes," said Blok, "a ringing in the ears."

The drunk leaned down towards him, suspiciously.

"Ye're a psychiatrist," he said.

"Of sorts," Blok admitted.

"Ye feckin' miserable baistard!" The drunk spat in the path and moved on, waving his arms at the perambulant celebrants, shouting at the top of his voice, right and left: "Ye miserable feckin' baistards! Are ye prepared? Are ye prepared?"

The tide ebbs and flows, washing corpses in on the beach. Surf-boarders flash in and out among the bloated carcasses. The city has long since died, and yet teems with the living. They eat their own flesh, and are revitalised.

Pimples grow in place of heads. Extra limbs dangle from shattered groins. These are the days of miracles and wonders.

The martyr, the shahid, *crawls up from the grave, growling, crying, gesticulating, demanding another shot at* The Ted Koppel Show, *another live spot on Global News Broadcasting. He is a young man, eighteen years of age, with a ragged beard and a shock of black hair held down by a red cloth band round his forehead. He wears faded jeans and a torn T-shirt bearing the portrait of the Vanished Imam, Musa Sadr, founder of the Shi'a Amal movement and saint of South Lebanon, who disappeared while on a visit to Colonel Gadaffi's Libyan Jamahariya over ten years ago. An amulet round his neck proclaims the Greatness of God, and ammunition belts criss-cross his concave chest, within which beats a true Islamic heart. He looks out into the deserted road, a stretch of potholed asphalt almost entirely choked with rubbish and debris. Shattered houses on either side, gaping holes for shop fronts, arched entrances and windows, the charred girders of upper floors and slanted roofs, skeletons of awnings, remains of wrought-iron balconies and skewed railings, broken flakes from overhanging pillars, bent lampposts and fire escapes, the burnt chassis of cars, electricity and telephone cables sagging across the street. Partly erased shop signs and hoardings have left words that make no sense:* GR ND G, SHAM LYS E, CRED BAN, RIEN L JOUR. *From behind a pile of rubble, a burned bus and row of sandbags, comes a burst of loud rock music. The* shahid *lopes forward, picking his way over the refuse. The music comes from a hole in the ground, leading down to a concealed basement. The fetid smell of burning joss-sticks and sweat rises like a cloud. A tall hulk of a man, armed with a pistol at his belt, looms from the depths. He pushes the young man against the wall of sandbags, strips him of his bandoleers and a Bowie knife concealed in his left boot, and issues him with a beer-stained chit. "Passed!" he shouts into the darkness. A small steel door opens. The guard grabs the young man by his trouser belt and the back of his T-shirt and throws him into the bowels of The Club.*

"Amour! Amour!"

"What's your poison?"

"A Michel Aoun on the rocks."

"Is it still daylight out there?"

"The promenade . . ."

"The pineapple grenades are early this year . . ."

"The phosphorus crop is blooming . . ."

"A stockpile of biological agents . . ."

"And just a little twist of lemon, Salim."

"Sit down young man. Have a 7-Up. Do you play a wind instrument?"

"Let me introduce you: anti-clockwise — Samir, le patron, Tewfiq, our scribe and chronicler of the lower depths, survivor of the manifold tragedies of Palestine-in-Lebanon. Marcel, grill chef and drums. Irma la Douce, née Umm Hamud, chief hostess, she was once the mistress of General Shihab, although the ravages of time passed her by regardless. Dick Plantagenet, pastry chef and ex-king of England. Rambo, chief of procurements. Latif, lunatic and accountant. Hamid, our chief political analyst."

"Peace be upon you."

"Peace."

". . . played the Marseillaise with her cunt . . ."

". . . swallow anything, in the right frame of mind . . ."

". . . a pile of eyes, in glass jars . . ."

". . . did you hear, it seems Perrier water is lethal . . ."

". . . is nothing sacred any more . . . ?"

". . . a man from Osaka, who wants to rebuild Beirut as a theme park . . . the Hizbollah will be relocated in the southern Philippines . . . the Palestinians resettled in Vanuatu . . ."

"It's perfectly true, my boy — our pastry chef has no heart! Feel it!"

"It's a yogi trick of some sort."

"No, just an example of perfect adaptation to the environment . . ."

". . . peeling the skin back, Afghan style . . ."

". . . cash money, from Mitsubishi . . ."

"So tell us the story again, Plantagenet, what was it like to meet Saladin?"

"I told you before, he and I never met, we only exchanged messengers. But I remember a dream . . ."

Yes, Plantagenet, Tewfiq reflected, we all have dreams, even here. They serve to balance the nightmares. Remembrance of things past. If

Proust were an Arab, he would think twice about starting the work. An armour-plated room instead of the cork lining. But Sodom and Gomorrah, oh yes! Proust and Camus, Plantagenet, and Gide, and all the rest of them, you have a lot to catch up with . . . Eight hundred years of a future which is suddenly available if required. Myself, I prefer to live in neither past nor future, simply taking things in, day by day, week by week, month by month, in this timeless capsule. (And how long have we been here? Ten months? A year? Ten years?) Dreaming of an endlessly postponed revenge against the murderer Aziz Khamash. An insubstantive act hacked out of the soul, while the body remains in its chair. Far from the convictions of Jaffa Camp, the comradeship of unbowed fighters, the drinking bouts of fallen angels. (Where art thou now, doctor moonshine?) Let the Plague outside take who it may. We are likewise marooned, you and I, Plantagenet, in our mutual fossilisation. I, paralysed by my wife's death, you, Plantagenet, by your own.

". . . today Lebanon, tomorrow the world . . ."

". . . not a doubt that Gorbachev is a creature of the KGB . . . the whole deceit was preplanned by Stalin, who was an American OSS agent from the start . . ."

". . . cloves of dried penises in his closet . . ."

High tar fumes lie thick on the air. The inmates of The Club breathe sulphur. Their flesh is a dull metallic grey. Their hair plastered to their heads with sweat. Their eyes shine with a phosphorescent glow. Their farts rise and slither on the ceiling, above posters for Arnold Schwarzenegger films, pin-ups of the Ayatollah Khomeini and Arafat, crosses, crescents, mandalas and framed photographs of world celebrities: Muhammad Ali, Martin Luther King, Gandhi, Charles and Diana Windsor, Bob Marley, Walt Disney, Tiny Tim, and the latest, hastily added hero, the President of the Arab Republic of Iraq, Saddam Hussein al-Takriti. The Vanished Imam gazes out from the *shahid's* T-shirt, his grim bearded visage pensive and sad. He looks out through the oily smoke to a far landscape, a blinding sun beating on a bare plain. The consecrated ground of martyrdom. Out there, the spear tips of the usurper's armies are myriad painful points of light, dazzling the Challenger with his faithful band of believers. All those who could not be bought, all those who loved the Idea above material wealth . . .

"Ya Saddam! Ya Saddam!"

"The New Hope of the Arabs!"

"The living link with the past!"

"Our glorious future!"

The temptations of hope. Religion enjoins the good and forbids evil, but you have to keep your powder dry. When the tyrant Yazid, son of Mu'awiya, grandson of the Prophet's greatest enemy, demanded the allegiance of Hussein, the Third Imam, the Imam fled to the holy city. But the challenge had to be met. The Imam marched forth, across the desert. The outcome of the battle was not in doubt. The faithful numbered seventy-two men, with their women and their children. The tyrant's armies were legion, with every weapon man could devise. The small band of the faithful was decimated. One by one they fell until only the Imam himself and his half-brother, Abbas, were left. Abbas tried to bring water to the starving women and children, but was struck down. The Imam left alone against the tyrant's hordes. He advanced towards them, carrying his son in his arms, pleading for water, but an arrow pierced the child in the throat. The Imam fought on, alone, until the commander of the usurping armies, Shamir, dealt him the fatal blow. They cut off his head and those of his followers, chained the women and children and marched back to their camp, carrying the severed heads of their victims on the tips of their spears . . .

" . . . Václav Havel, where did he come from? Todor Zhivkov, why is he still alive? Egon Krenz? Erich Honecker? Nicolae Ceauşescu? General Jaruzelski? The Pope? Ronald Reagan? Mrs Thatcher joined the Communist Party at seven years of age . . . the KGB and the CIA are one and the same . . . their only true rival is the Mossad . . . turmoil is always good for the Jews . . . are we not the living proof of The Plot?"

Ah, the Plot! Living murmurs of nostalgia and delight . . . On the improvised stage, weaving her way in a lull between piled crates of liquor bottles and canned foods and a tangle of electric cables, Irma la Douce, née Umm Hamud, coaxes old saws from an overlubricated larynx:

"Your eyes,

behind the tattered curtain

of the sky . . ."

"Mark my words," Hamid prods the air with his pudgy finger, "everything seems to change, but nothing will change. Who controlled us then controls us now. We are allowed the delusion of progress. But if we want to rebel we have to have a proper grasp of the barbarism that we face. The savage claw in the velvet glove of 'democracy.' We are simply fleas orbiting around the oil fields. They give us guns only as long as we turn them on each other. Look at Vietnam. They challenged the Empire and got a victorious swamp. You have to show them you are as savage as they are. This is how the Israelis operate. As long as we're weak, and talk about truth and justice, they laugh at us and turn up the heat. But will we ever learn? The Arab Nation . . ."

Ah, the Arab Nation . . . ! Tears flow, soaking shirts, pants, napkins. The Arab Homeland — *al watan al arabi* . . . the Arab Masses —— *al jamahir al arabi* . . . A spreading salty pool on the floor. Tiny armies and fleets rocking in its shallows with their minuscule flags and banners. *Urubah*, the New Morality, the Social Spirit, the Rugged Life, Renaissance (*Ba'ath*), the Manufacture of Death, the Arab Spirit, the Whole Nation, the New Arab Generation, the Revolution, the Revolution, the Revolution. Vultures feed on fresh entrails. Skeletons stretch out to the black horseman riding by. A hand squeezes a human heart. Watches droop. Death scythes the desert. Jackals drink the blood of tethered children. Worms writhe from emptied eye sockets. Maggots dance under rocks. The impaled mark an unseen road. Hordes of the dead queue in vain for rooms in demolished hotels. The people's leaders, travelling on mountain roads, are blown to ash in their cars, while their leaderless people vow revenge. The disinherited fall upon each other, besiegers and besieged, clawing at each other's eyes and entrails. In their towers, the usurpers laugh, cracking open another beer. At their whim, do not the puppets still dither, dance?

> "And in your embrace,
> I see once more
> my blindness in its rainbow hue . . ."

"Ya Saddam! Ya Saddam!"

"The New Saviour!"

"Scourge of the West!"

"Yes, that's just what we need — more war, more dispossession, more refugees, more hordes of ragged prisoners . . ."

"O ye unbelievers!"

"Don't you understand, you poor dupes? It's a set-up by the Americans. Why did they give Iraq the green light? Why did their ambassador tell Saddam his dispute with Kuwait was an internal affair? Why did they advise the emir to spit in Saddam's face at the same time? They want to get their armies into Saudi and their hooks into the Arab world!"

"We should close our eyes and open our hearts now!"

"You dumb bastards, don't you see what's happening? Saddam will be destroyed, and we'll all be dragged down with him . . ."

"What else can we do? Eat the West's shit again?"

"Why not? At least it's a diet we're used to."

"Bring us another canteen of Black Label, Salim. This could last all week . . ."

"Do you know they're selling Khomeini's pee again? I was offered one of those famous samples, up by the Protestant College . . ."

"How much?"

"A hundred and fifty dollars."

"Some people never give up."

"In the dark I shivered,
remembering the furnace
of your smile . . ."

The Imam may be lost, but his spirit moves across the dusty streets, the bazaars, the port, the ocean. He has achieved the occultation promised by history and faith. The young shahid *removes his T-shirt and turns it inside out, redonning it, so that the Man of God should not have to look on as he accepts a battered guitar from Farid and, stepping to the stage, composes, out of his dreams and terrors, an ode to the New Deliverer . . .*

"The Sword of Destiny, unsheathed,
In blood red flowers wreathed . . ."

The impromptu jams of the Beirut Dead. Richard Plantagenet, on the clarinet, coaxing his pain out of the pipe. Long-buried memories, millennial nostalgia for dead times. Sweat emerging from who knows where, cigarette smoke blown in the lungs by Samir's three table fans, the eyes watering in the fog . . .

In the beginning, he had had to grit his teeth against the incessant pounding of the sound system, the night hammers of the dance floor, the self-imposed flagellation. Until Samir found him a berth in the deepest recess of The Club, next to Tewfiq and that other homeless waif, Mad Latif, who spent most of his time entering numbers in huge ledgers. "I don't understand it," said Tewfiq, "but Hamid says he is doing wonders with zeros. Soon we will all vanish into that hole and wink out, in a sublime oblivion . . ." But Tewfiq himself had vowed to remain in place until he had completed the chronicle of the "Beirut Plague," à la Camus, achieving nothing so far but endless notes and scribbles, hieroglyphs in tattered school notepads . . .

"Your finger's touch

is but a memory

of my skin . . .," croons Umm Hamud — the disco pounding starting up again . . . Eat drink and be merry for tomorrow we die . . .

"What is tomorrow to you, Plantagenet, eh, dead man? How does it all seem to you, this madness? Were your times better or worse?"

But the Lionheart is dreaming of Rose Khamash, floating naked through a lush garden of hyacinths and rhododendrons, with tall cypresses swaying in a breeze, and a large spotted dog panting after her spoor. Who was she, who came to me in the dark, joining forces in a forbidden embrace? She turns away, cradling a Kalashnikov rifle, disappearing into a mist . . . Fog rolls across the English Channel. The melancholy hoot of boats . . . Turning and tossing, night into day. Marching feet and beat of drums. Betrayal and failure, scratched in by the hoarse jeers of the decrepit patriarch Michel Khamash: "Malicious advice from the Grand Masters of the Temple — corrupted, seduced by the Saracens and the Jews . . ." A repetition of ancient admonitions . . . The chaplain-knight, William of Poitou, who walked into his tent at Gaza, tears streaming down his eyes. Speak, man, what is it that inspires this melancholy? "The men blame you sire, for their distress. They have heard the rumours of your withdrawal from the Holy Land. They fear that all this sacrifice has been in vain." So goaded, the army marches, through the harshest winter, towards Jerusalem. Christmas Day at Latroun. The rain pours down, the ground a soggy mass of mud. Horses slither, men fall, drowning in their chain-mail. The mocking elements, pouring a flood onto the parched land, only to lay more snares. The Templars and Hospitallers in conclave. "Jerusalem is a trap, sire. We can take the city but only die in her. The Sultan's armies are gathering. We must withdraw, to fight another day." But the day never came. Sickness, defeat and dreams. How can such a betrayal be purged? No heart, no guts, no staying power . . .

"Fuck it, Rose!"

"Fuck it, Richard!"

A dead king masturbates in the dark . . .

". . . when will we ever learn?"

". . . your Saddam is one hell of a saviour, right enough. I hear that in Baghdad they had to bulldoze the houses back of the *Mukhabarat* HQ to extend the graveyard for those tortured to death in the jails."

"Slander of the Deliverer!"

"In Basra jail they invented a special machine for gouging eyes out. Automatic, keeps blood off your hands."

"Cowards! Defeatists! Bourgeois elements! Lackeys of the West!"

"Another innovation of the *Mukhabarat* in Baghdad: Putting the children of subversives in sacks together with starving cats or poisonous snakes and throwing them in the Tigris. It was a common Ottoman punishment."

"Filthy lies! The relationship between the Ba'ath and the toiling classes is totally harmonious!"

"Of course. They are both totally bankrupt."

"The party's task is to undertake serious and speedy work to change the features of Arab realities with the object of attaining the objective conditions necessary to confront the Zionist-Imperialist alliance by tireless endeavours to realise unity in its progressive form . . ."

"How many Kurds were gassed at Halabja . . . ?"

"It was the Iranians who bombed Halabja!"

"There are always a few negative aspects which are an inevitable manifestation of a revolution on the march . . ."

"Just keep out of the way of those feet . . ."

"We need a bastard like Saddam, a brutal torturing tyrant, to frighten our enemies and give us self-respect . . ."

"The whipped dog deifies the whip . . ."

And more days follow more nights and more days without change . . . Tewfiq and the Lionheart sunk in their eight hundred and forty-ninth game of backgammon, having won four hundred and twenty-four games each . . . The dice on the table. Between East and West . . .

"So what's next, my friend?"

"The world turns on its axis. The wheels whir, the gears mesh."

"One cannot live by faith alone."

"Ah, but one can kill for illusions."

"Trois deuce — a difficult decision."

"Play the game, Lionheart, play the game."

"Tewfiq!" A call from Rambo, at the door. "There's a man here to see you, from Reuters!"

A figure in chain-mail and bullet-proof vest, festooned with tape recorders and cameras, with three cigarettes stuck to his lip, handing out wads of Deutschmarks to the guards. Tewfiq rises to greet him.

"Praise be to God! Here is a true deliverer! Sit down, friend. Let me introduce you to my friend Dick Plantagenet. Your name, beautiful stranger?"

"François Lebrun."

"Glenfiddich? Stolichnaya? Sliwowitz? Armagnac? Black Label?"

"Thank you, just one of each."

"And what brings you to our fair city? The climate? The sportive atmosphere? The entertainments? The camaraderie?"

"I met your colleague, Ali Amar, in Paris. He recommended you for the Gulf. We are trying to put together an alternative team, which will not be bound to the official pools. All the old hands are gathering. Wardogs of Saigon, Salvador, Beirut, Asmara. Everyone is heading for the desert."

"Rommel. Montgomery. Field Marshal Ukhinlek. The old woman was not as mad as she seemed. If you wait long enough, it all comes round again. Wasn't it Nietzsche's idea, eternal recurrence?"

"We are collecting the Arab veterans of the Beirut desk. Jamil, Rafiq, Agazian. The Middle East is hot again. Baking, in fact. One hundred and twelve degrees at Dhahran."

"The sun's anvil. The burning sands. The camel trains of Araby. Orientalism rides again! So, François, do you want another veteran of the Crusades? The genuine article? The oldest desert rat of them all? Whadyou say, Plantagenet?"

"Play the game, Tewfiq. Throw the dice, for God's sake."

"I am throwing, Dicky bird. Don't you see, double aces! A sign, mon frère, a definite sign. Don't you feel the lure of the saddle?"

✥

To be truly glaikit in a show run by stookies . . . As Blok walked along the shopping swathe of Princes Street, cocooned in the buzz of commerce. Marks & Spencer's. British Home Stores. John Lewis's. Menzies. Liberty's. Peter Lord. He was drawn by the hubbub of a crowd gathering at the base of the Walter Scott Monument. Someone, it was difficult to see, had climbed up the grid of scaffolding shrouding the renovated tower and was haranguing the mob, high above the street. People laughed and pointed. Blok craned his neck, but the figure was insubstantial, the words snatched away by the traffic. Was it the same drunk who had accosted him earlier? He had hardly seemed fit to climb a four-foot ladder. Blok cleaned his glasses and looked again. The figure was clad in a white robe, and seemed to sport a crown of flowing white hair. Snatches of words floated down:

"Father . . . Son . . . Women . . . Chains . . . One divine-human energy . . . Chalcedon . . . Maronites . . ."

The police arrived, and began scaling the monument on firemen's ladders. Tier after tier, the ladders extended into the hazy heights, a fireman with an axe and supportive saddle leading the way, on the edge. Fold after fold, level after level, up the flanks of the memorial: *Waverley. Rob Roy. Old Mortality. The Heart of Midlothian. Redgauntlet. Quentin Durward. Ivanhoe.* The Crusaders of King Richard gallop to the rescue, and Jerusalem just out of reach. We are climbing Jacob's Ladder, extending, on and on, past the spire, past the sky . . .

"Sons . . . Fathers . . . Chalcedon . . . One divine-human energy . . ."

"I told them, but they wouldn't listen. I spoke, but the wind snatched my

words. They built my pillar higher and higher, till no one could hear my pleas. They invented ever more ingenious ways to winch me up my food and water and recycle my wastes, but they cut me off from the ground. I was better off when I was chained to a steel ball on the bare tiles. The pilgrims could come right up, feel me, touch me, feel my breath and I theirs. The fetid smell of garlic and bad teeth. The real bloom and decay of the flesh. Voices, plaints, dirges, hymns, songs and wails and glottal sprays. Life. Now I am higher and higher, and the wind is taken out of my sails. I am becalmed, above the steel cities, the oily squeal of machines. Below me, I can hear festive cheers, roars of mockery and merriment. What have they got to laugh about? The sky is dark, the earth red, the flesh flush with sin. False Gods, capering before the towers of Mammon in paper masks. Avaunt! Avaunt! The time is nigh, the debt long overdue for payment, the credit extended far too long . . .

"ARE YE PREPARED? ARE YE PREPARED?"

But Blok repaired to the Saint Andrews Bus Station, and took the green double-decker back to Craddock. Floating above the shimmering city on the Upper Deck, towards Portobello and the resonating port of Joppa. Again, he felt the old myth of Edinburgh as Jerusalem; the Castle, Mount Zion; Saint Giles, the Temple Mount Moriah; Arthur's Seat, the Mount of Olives; Princes Street, the Valley of Jehoshaphat. Bereft of time and place. Despite the solidity of the grimy stone houses, the fish-and-chip shops, pizzerias, New Star Chinese Restaurant, Findlays of Portobello, Mike's Tackle Shop, Lockfast Securities, Crawfords, Thompson's Fashions, Alex Wood Family Butcher, Global Video, Paws and Claws Pet Shop, past the straight terrace blocks leading down to the sea, and the diversion over the River Esk and down the motorway and past the Prestonpans power station, straddling the road like a dark belching giant. Along the coast past Seton Sands. How much longer can the retreat be viable, with the invasion on every hoarding and front page? PAKISTAN WILL SEND TROOPS TO HELP SAUDIS. U.S. WARMS TO SYRIA'S ASSAD. IRAQ OFFERS PEACE TO IRAN — TREATY FREES TROOPS FOR GULF CONFLICT. IRAQ ROUNDS UP WESTERNERS TO HOLD AS HUMAN SHIELDS. CHEMICALS "AN OPTION" IN U.S. ARSENAL. SUPREMACY IN THE SKIES WILL BE CRUCIAL.

Are ye prepared? Are ye prepared? Out of one's genes, an old fear festers, stirred with new grids of need. Blok leaves the bus outside Craddock and, pausing briefly at the house to collect Alistair, walks with the dog in the cooling afternoon up the gentle hillside towards Drem, leaving the main B road to amble down trails and over the gorse-grown fields. The dog bounds and barks, shoving his nose in the ground and disturbing beetles and other small crawling beasts, morphically resonating. Blok remembers Danny Hohenlohe's seminal walk, and turns himself too in the direction of the alleged last sighting of the Angelopoulos kidnap van. No sign of action at the abandoned airfield. A rabbit, rising unwisely from its burrow, rushes off, with Alistair in hot pursuit. Blok is left alone with a wasp, which circles him grimly, wondering whether it might be safe, or morally justified, to attack.

Leave us not at Drem station . . . A cloud gathered on the horizon. "Its going to rain Alistair. Let's go," he tells the dog, starting back towards the coast, consulting the beast about his dilemma as they hurry over the fields. "What do you think? Should I fall in with Kathy's dreams of the Orient, introduce her to the land of promise, the heat, the ingathered exiles, the one disk country, the falafel with the hundred-thousand-fold bacteria, gunsmoke in your eyes, the rabbiocracy? Should we sit back there sipping tempo-cola and waiting for Saddam's bombs to fall? To listen to my old Pa's despair, eight years after he burnt his stamp collection? To trudge that same old closed circle? What do you think, Ali-Star? Speak, *ya kalb*."

"Wuff wuff wuff."

"I knew you'd end up seeing it my way."

Nevertheless, the gathering storm, with all its Churchillian undertones. He arrives at the house with Alistair just as the threatened drizzle begins. Little pinpoints going into the sea. Grey on grey, no horizon. He melancholily surveys the mounds of unclipped newspapers. No great temptation for the Blokbook in this clichéd apocalypse. Instead, he inserts into its pages a small item from the local *Lothian News*:

Man Hanged in Sensation Bid

A 36-year-old Lothian labourer accidentally died after he hanged himself "for the sensation," an inquest heard. Thomas R., of Hamilton Road, Dunbar, a loner who distanced himself from family and friends, was found yesterday after being missing for three days in a half-built house at Flanders Road. Recording a verdict of accidental death, the coroner, Mr James Burton, said: 'I am convinced that this was not a straight-forward suicide and he did not intend to cause his own death. It was just part of the things that he did, done just for the sensation."

On television, the toy tanks and ships move about their model battle-fields. Little multicoloured flags at key targets. Oil fields marked by toy drumlets. Toy soldiers scattered on the sand. A bluff-faced man in an immaculate suit quotes grandly from Shakespeare's *Henry V*:

"From camp to camp, through the foul womb of night, the hum of either army stilly sounds . . . and from the tents the armourers give dreadful note of preparation . . ."

In his basket, the dog curls up and dreams. Rain drums upon the closed windows, as the armies gather, on the open plain —

For never two such kingdoms did contend
Without much fall of blood; whose guiltless drops
Are every one a woe, a sore complaint
'Gainst him whose wrongs give edge unto the swords
That make such waste in brief mortality . . .

ARE YE PREPARED? ARE YE PREPARED?

BOOK THREE

Waiting for the Apocalypse

ELEVEN

Guilty
as Charged

THERE IS NO DOUBT. McTEAGUE IS EVIL, HE MUST BE DESTROYED. THIS IS Danny Hohenlohe sprachen to you here. Do you receive me? No matter. The guiding principle grows ever clearer as the summer drags on. Prospects of war east of Suez making the consummation even more poignant. Was it not Chaplin, in *Monsieur Verdoux*, who commented, at his trial for murder, on the hypocrisy of holding one man to account for a few measly homicides when governments were prepared, at the drop of a hat, to incinerate hundreds of thousands? Selah. Peter Lorre, also, I recall, directed his only film, *Die Verloren*, on a similar theme. Ah, those old frayed prints projected dimly across the cavern of the old Electric Cinema . . . Memory lane, memory lane. The vast dark theatre, the icy cold, the tattered seats whose springs sprung straight up your anal cavity, the jingle-jangle warm-ups by the worst rock groups in town, but the joint, wafting down the rows, towards you, in the middle of Godard's *Breathless* . . . But these are sterner times. Peter Lorre's murderer, an M for the Nazi era, was shunted aside because no one in the age of mass murder had time for an amateur. Monsieur Verdoux, on the other hand, was guillotined. It is a far, far better thing that I do, et cetera. The world will be a better place. There is no doubt the planet is teeming with people, one less should be a boon, should it not, to an overloaded ecology?

Nevertheless, I still feel motive is crucial. Monsieur Verdoux killed his wives for their money, but I don't believe one should kill the innocent, no matter how grotesque they might be. McTeague's crime, on the other hand, cries out for vengeance. Though there might be pangs of reason.

Why blame the lackey for his master's voice? The rude factory-horn blast of McTeague's boss, media mogul Brent Browbeat, with his worldwide empire of crud: Shipping, communications, newspapers, terrestrial and extraterrestrial television stations (I picked up this jargon from a copy of *Variety* I found on a bench at the South Bank whence I hied to examine the techniques of the cardboard-city homeless in panhandling the National Film Theatre's patrons. One should always be on the look out for tips, if all else fails. Grabbing by the lapel and swearing undying gratitude for the few pence to be tendered turns out unexpectedly fruitful, while sitting sprawled at either end of the Hungerford Bridge looking woebegone under a blanket with a flea-bitten dog and a sign proclaiming HOMELESS AND HUNGRY, PLEASE HELP is no bloody use at all). An evocative vision of antennaed Martians gawping at, or more likely transmitting, Brent Browbeat's crap across the ethereal spheres, but referring in fact merely to the hunks of orbitting metal bouncing the uncouth North American's junk down to selected homes. "Invasion of the Soul Snatchers." That was a short story I sent once to *Jake Akimbo's Science Fiction Magazine*, but as expected it boomeranged back with a condemnation of a familiar redundancy. So why not eliminate the master, not the slave, Lucifer, not Mephistopheles? But no. Targeting Brent Browbeat would be too popular. An act that would presuppose an ideology. Innumerable cranks would queue up to adopt me, environmentalists, print workers, animal-rightists, moralists and humanists of every shade and hue, not to speak of the dispossessed of the third world, whose countries Browbeat International despoils with gusto, deforesting their forests, demineraling their minerals, sweating their labour into sweatshirts . . . A solid case against Lucifer, but it would be a pyrrhic victory. Cut off one head of the hydra, it sprouts ten more. I remember this from ancient Bolshevik tracts. The octopus's tentacles spread, from the central blob, the beady eyes, the ceegar and top hat, on one scaly arm the star-spangled banner, on another the union jack, the tricolour, the double-headed eagle. One cannot vanquish Capital. That much at least Elena and Nicolae Ceausescu found out. One can only accumulate a fair wack of it, for a time, till people get wise. But the Ceausescus made the mistake of conspicuous consumption. You got to have some finesse in this field. Caress 'em first, kill 'em afterwards, not the other way around. On the other hand, it works for Saddam Hussein. So who am I to complain?

But I have not set out to save the world, merely to exact a personal revenge. I want McTeague to know there can be no defence of I vos chust obeyink orders. When Brent Browbeat orders a cut in the list to dump unprofitable authors, he-who's-hand-wieldeth-the-hatchet cannot deny the blood on the palm. Remember the hours of innocent hope? The first advance, the cheque borne proudly to the disbelieving bank clerk, the joy of proofs, the cups of tea in messy offices, the piles of volumes of those who have made it and the manuscripts of those who have not, about to be poleaxed by the familiar riposte: Dear Author: Fuck off, The Publisher. Slipped through the net, one basks, wallows, in the adoring glances of those willowy nymphs in literary arcadia, the little apples of desire balanced on their blonde heads. Go for it, Willum! Can one fail to split the core? The shining finished tome in your hands. "Whatdayasay, Danny boy? A virgin birth!" He was the virgin, you see. Robed in white, above the toiling masses, the burning halo of patronage, the quiver of his Cupid arrows ready for the next clown.

So much for classical metaphors. Ah, the dregs of an English education. Well, at least they can spell "homeless" and "hungry." One shouldn't chuck it all out of hand. As I sit, on the outside benches of the film buffs' Mecca, under the Waterloo Bridge, watching young Lochinvar tightening his grip on the lapels of his two trapped marks. "You don't know what it's like mate, having somebody 'o knows what it's like. Kno'-amean?" An older colleague approaches me with a proferred torn handkerchief. "I already gave." He passes on to greener pastures. Ah, to see McTeague reduced to this . . . But one needs a more permanent outcome . . .

There must be more in life than thoughts of murder, though you might not know it, scanning the daily press: WASHINGTON'S JIHAD. BUSH PREPARES U.S. FOR WAR. VICTORY IN THE AIR IN ONE DAY. SADDAM SOLDIERS WILLING TO FIGHT AND DIE. Rather you than me, brothers. MORE BRITISH HOSTAGES ROUNDED UP. There's an idea there, somewhere. But who would ransom Gordon McTeague, or even Brent Browbeat for that matter? One would have to feed the blighters, even if only canned beans and spaghetti loops. *Caveat emptor. Allahu akbar.* Alas. I too, like Peter Lorre, am becoming a faded *Verloren* in the dim space of the Electric Cinema. In the shadow of mass slaughter, what price Hohenlohe's skimmed schemes?

In "Invasion of the Soul Snatchers," an evil scientist, Doctor Xkalibur, discovers a method to leech souls from the bodies of innocent passers-by with a giant syringe pointed out the window of his house. The souls are then emptied into large glass vessels kept in his basement laboratory. As the de-souled inhabitants of the city continue about their daily business as automatons, the doctor proceeds to inject himself, little by little, with the stolen ectoplasmic essence. The memories, experiences and emotions of the city's populace flood into his veins and bloodstream. But the knowledge and secrets he hoped to appropriate become a hopeless, tangled knot. In desperation, he turns the syringe on himself, to suck his own soul out with the others before he loses control of his mind. But his machines cannot cope with the multitude and explode, burning the house down. Filled with thousands of souls, he staggers out into a city of mindless, passionless robots, making their way from home to work and back, performing sex and procreating without purpose, functioning without hope or desire. Only he feels love, rage, joy and anguish, pleasure and unhappiness, exultation and frustration. He wanders about, despite his manifold personalities, in a state of desperate solitude, until suddenly, one day, from a nearby building, he feels the tug of a giant syringe . . .

No, but seriously . . . Make an attempt, Danny, to throw an anchor to reality. I tried to conjure up a sensual tickle or two. Telephoned an old flame, who I had arranged to meet on the wings of my publishing success, but ferries passing in the blight . . . "Martha?" Miraculously at the same number, although an automaton from the Telephone Company interrupted, claiming: "You have dialled an 081 number. Please redial using the prefix 0-8-1. British Telecom is not charging you for this call." Oh yeah? Up your ass, sister! "Danny? I was just thinking about you." "Are you all right? Are you ill?" "No, I'm feeling fine, Danny. Are you okay?"

"I've been at a madhouse, in Scotland."

"Was it interesting?"

"Dull to moderate. A visiting friend was kidnapped by terrorists."

"I'm sorry I missed it."

That's my girl. Trotskyist Martha, who wanted us both to seek employment at a Dagenham car plant and feel the oppression of the proletariat in the aching of our bones. Halcyon days. Instead I rode the charter winds to Manhattan and began squeezing out those old redundant ideas bought for a dollar from the wizened old Chinese in Orchard Street. Two years of painting lofts, sans La Passionaria of the International Revolutionary Communist Front (membership fifteen and falling). She burnt my Erle Stanley Gardner collection, as it was propaganda for Imperialist justice.

"I'm sorry," she told me now in the Patisserie Valerie. "That was a dumb thing to do."

So long ago. 1973. The oil embargo, another Middle East War, Tricky Dicky, Watergatey, Veet-Nam. But she looked no different. Still a wild thing in sweaters, though now with *pischifkes* in her earlobes. I am lying, the skin is drier, crow's feet, stretch marks. But from my papyrus face, who am I to speak. An American couple at our elbow are arguing about Dante. Rather, he is lecturing her. "Of course, Dante was the first structuralist. His deconstruction of reality is way ahead of his time." Like Woody Allen, I wish I could say: "I have Signor Alighieri right here with me, and . . ." A flame-thrower would also be handy.

"So what's new, now that communism is kaput?"

"Oh Danny, you're so naïve."

Guilty as charged. I take everything so seriously, such as the evidence of my own eyes and ears. But she had left the Party, which she accused of patriarchy and sexism. All her energies are now charged with opposing war in the Gulf: "Saddam Hussein is a scapegoat for the West's bankrupt ideas. He's the bastard we put in place, now he challenges us where it hurts, we get all high and mighty. It's a setup for the oil companies. Everybody knows that."

I try to tell her about my betrayal by McTeague, but her mind is in Arabia Deserta. All agog with her plans to join a group of peace activists who were going to fly to Baghdad and then bus south to form a peace camp on the Kuwaiti border, to interpose themselves between the belligerent forces, so that when the dogs of war are finally unleashed, the peace militants will cry "Down, Fido! "

"That doesn't sound very healthy."

"Sometimes you have to stick your neck out. In the Party we marched and chanted slogans. Now here's a chance to do something."

Pouring petrol over oneself and lighting a match at the gates of the palace. That too has been tried. "You should take a lot of suntan lotion. And woolly sweaters. The sands are cold at night. And scorpion repellent."

"You're not fooling me, Danny. You know you really care, under that spiky armour. But you deflect all that anger against the wrong targets. Against yourself. It's such a waste, Danny."

"I intend to use it all in good faith." I riposted. "I'm going to kill my ex-editor, and rid the world of his scourge."

"You're not going to kill anybody, Danny," she said, wearily. "It's just another fantasy of yours. Here, sign this petition." She plunked a wrinkled document down on the table. It was headed: IMPERIALISM, OUT OF THE GULF.

"Where else should Imperialism be?"

"You're a wanker, Danny!" she exclaimed.

"I always like to approach that question through the mediation of a text," the idiot at our elbow drawled. I too like to read a book sometimes. But this was getting me nowhere, and certainly not into the lady's pants. We parted curtly, she to her battlefields, me to mine. The humid night of Oseney Crescent. Just e-shout if you need. Aaaaaaaaaaaaaa! No dice. The peeling walls still stand. Filled with the city's pilfered souls, I swell and suffocate. Or perhaps it's just the dust mites after all. Their tiny damned ghosts. We are surrounded by anguish. If it's not the living, it's the dead beating their wings against the panes. The morphic resonance of trillions. How are we supposed to cope with it all?

Somewhere in this vast metropolis my enemies are enjoying their repast of blood and fresh entrails. Penguin suits under the chandeliers. Or has the wife popped the Tesco's Chicken Supreme into the microwave? Domestic bliss, or corporate relish? Exeunt, for a Kentucky Fried Chicken, to Eat Here, rubbing elbows with the lumpenproletariat. Yobs Without Necks. Fat ladies with their squawling brats. Hold on to that pram, chile! You'll never get another chance! Junior Macnuggets. Eat your fish, Danny! I know it's cold, it's your own fault! Against one's will, one's bones elongate, one's flesh stretches, skin folds. Growth and entropy entwined. The passing blob of protoplasm. The gravedigger's forceps. There is so very lit-tle time.

Should I forgo revenge? The milk of human kindness curdles like everything else. But, nevertheless, beatifically, I float, over the rainbow, exuding absolution, for McTeague, for Brent Browbeat, for George Bush, for my mother, for Andrew Mackenzie and the fake therapist Avram Blok, for International Peacenik Martha, for Karl Marx, Margaret Thatcher. (Among the excluded: Adolf Hitler, Stalin, Genghis Khan, Saddam Hus-sein, Lyndon Johnson, Harold Wilson. One has to draw the line some-where.) The moving automatons, sucked dry by Xkalibur's syringe . . .

There is a bad habit, in the Kentucky Fried Chickens, of servers pick-ing out your two pieces, one from the newer, one from the older batch. Usually the leg from the former, the breast from the latter. One is so help-less, before fate. Four black youths have taken an adjacent booth, launch-ing into an incomprehensible multilogue loud enough to raise Colonel Sanders himself from the tomb. I am a martyr to this booming London patois, which is like a wooden corkscrew driven into the skull. Not, I has-ten to add, a racial comment, but one of class alone. Oh, for conscription to dispatch them all to struggle in the Saudi sands! All glottal stops and chicken bones.

I am, despite what peacenik Martha believes about my inner drives, drawn by all this talk of combat and death. To sit, comfortably in one's armchair, watching the electronic fog of battle on one's Sony twelve-inch. The telephoto explosions, the burnt-out chassis of tanks and zapped air-craft. Nowadays, unfortunately, we can't escape from the concomitant images of what the Americans in Vietnam quite properly designated "ambulant non-combatant personnel." The civilians caught in the car-nage, their remoteness annulled by close-ups, guilt bored into our hearts. Even extraterrestrial television, I suspect, will not protect us from this. Conscience. Compassion. Empathy.

Bad news for the anti-McTeague axis. Should feed the demon better vittles. Short rations for the cherub. You gotta take the longer view. Hard-en your heart, as the Lord did unto Pharaoh. Just hang tough in thar, baby! The world is not made for sissies . . .

Return from the old Kentucky karma. My homestead, with bilious-green wallpaper. The battering neighbours have battered each other into silence, and I am left with the ghosts of old gas meters, the coin-swallowing ghouls of yestertear. Open a window for air. This is where the good fairy enters to save me from my elongating nose. But no nose-job dame from outer space tonight. Instead a scrabbling at the window-sill, and Nick and Elena Ceauşescu heave themselves into the room. Dishevelled and grimy from their sojourn in the mountains, they make a beeline for the mini-fridge, grabbing a hunk of cheddar cheese and a festering Milano salami, which they begin to tear with their cracked and filth-encrusted talons. They insist on staying the night. It's a tight fit, lying between the two. They are blanket stealers, pulling and tugging all night long. Eventually, I fall asleep, and dream. I am in the old Electric Cinema, watching a movie of my childhood in Wembley Park. It's one of those drab old English black-and-white affairs, with dingy curtains and absymal wallpaper. My father, Pick the Elder, is slouched dead in his armchair with a paperweight through his heart. My mother, on the sofa, is turning the pages of The *Jewish Chronicle*'s Brides & Homes Supplement. I, a small, weedy child, look upon this scene dispassionately, then turn away, stepping into the closet in the hall, among my father's musty jackets, the brooms and mops and battered shoes. A strange muffled wailing comes from beyond the wall. I push against a side panel, which slides open, leading to a dark descending flight of stairs. The wailing, accompanied by a mechanical sound, increases. I step out of the dark passage into a vast laundromat, lit by buzzing neon lights, with hundreds of machines churning their dirty linen round and round. On a raised dais, at the further end of the hall, I approach a man dressed in army fatigues, whom I recognise clearly from press photographs and television as the President of the Republic of Iraq, Saddam Hussein.

"Do you do a service wash?" I ask him.

"We are alone here," he replies.

I look around and we were indeed the only persons visible alongside the machines. But as I look closer I can make out, inside each appliance, an agonised face revolving in the froth and bubbles, mouth open in a silent scream.

"What about them?" I ask him.

"They are of no consequence," he answers, with a dismissive flick of his hand. "Self-service riff-raff, Mensheviks." I walk down the lines and peer inside. Many faces appear familiar, childhood friends, neighbours, relatives. In one window McTeague revolves, his face contorted in a faded plea: "Help me, Daniel!" A far-off, miniature squeak. I see my parents, turning, my father's dead-fish eyes, my mother clinging to clipped-out coupons. And poor Martha, tangled in a tattered red flag.

"But this is inhuman!" I protest to the dictator. His face takes on a frightening grimace, a malicious grin. He points towards another chamber I had not noticed, hewn out of the rock. It glows, with a multitude of roaring fires, licking in the maws of giant engines —

"AFTER THE WASH — THE DRY!"

This cannot go on much longer. Something has got to give. Either my mind, or the universe. There's no room for both of us in town. Nevertheless, I face the morning with a renewed confidence. Nicolae and Elena have departed, taking the remains of the salami and a rancid tub of my landlord's taramasalata. I hie to the local store, to replenish the losses and buy a thick string of garlic. That should keep the dead dictators from my door. The live ones, on the other hand . . .

One lives in a parochial madhouse of nostalgic never-never-lands. Echoes of past, imagined glories. Paradise Lost and Richard the Lionheart. George Bush that is never consumed. Was Martha right? Am I secretly *engagé*? Do I dream of saving the planet? Or merely of getting a good original non-biological wash, like everyone else? I peek in my local laundromat, but the President of Iraq is not there. Just the two Asian sisters who run the joint and the usual doleful crowd. Muggy sweat of summer togs. My news agent Patel is his usual happy self. "These politicians have nothing to do except invent new ways to kill people." "It's what they get paid for," I tell him. "They should pay them to take an open holiday," he says magnanimously, "to the Bahamas, and not come back. Let them lie in the sun and enjoy themselves, and maybe they will think charitable thoughts."

Not a hope, Mohandas, not a hope. The city is its usual tangled net of apathy and hyperactivity. The dust mites and their daily chores. Do you realise ants can carry an object ten thousand times heavier than themselves without giving it a moment's thought? If they did stop to consider the matter they might well show their sluggardly queen a pretty clean pair of heels. Or several pairs, as the case might be. Is there a hidden hand, nevertheless, behind it all? The maverick Moogli trudges on, away from the nest, with his little bag of *pekalach*. The dust mites of the right fingernail prepare for battle with the left. Can we ignore the writing on the wall? Probably, when it is scrawled everywhere. When MENE MENE TEKEL UPHARSIN has to vie with DESMOND IS A FUCKING CUNT. Yes, we lack that sense of direction, Lord. Jee-sus, Show the Way! At Kentish Town station I sit down and weep, when faced with the Underground Map. Why is Finchley Central in Zone 3a, while Mill Hill East is Zone 3b? Does Theydon Bois exist? When is Totteridge not Whetstone?

There has to be a way out of this web. Plunging back into the underground, the Möbius tunnels of infinity. Lose me on the Circle Line, Daddy. Don't terminate at Liverpool Street. These days there are little homilies and poems in the tube carriages beside the advertisements:

> a cloud
> hanging lonely
> in the distressing tea party
> of life.
>
> — James ffetlock-Grunge

The English have learned the haiku from the Japanese, while the Japanese have not needed to learn anything from the English, who have nothing to teach except their surly fish-and-chip nostalgia.

Save the world! There must be a more deserving cause. Somewhere in space, a better species. Open that third eye, you hidden Martians! You thirty-six wise men, speak up! I'll accept women too, or intermediates. Anyone who has a reasonably good idea. Perhaps it's time to return to my little Chinese chap in Orchard Street, to buy another couple of phials of cheap inspiration. The soup to turn Jekyll into Hyde. Or vice versa, one may never decide which is best. The bottle imp. The elixir of life. Transmuting base metals into gold. The incompetent and the inconsequential flourish, while . . .

Is there anything dumber than hubris without cause? I walk the streets, with my fizzing ego concealed in a brown paper bag. Taking every now and then a surreptitious sip through a straw. Hair of the God that bit me. Everyday life continues. Couples ogle cakes in windows. Tourists gape at Indonesian restaurant menus, punk girls float down the street with translucent skin, satellite-television salesmen pile out of a Volkswagen van with striped shirts and peaked red caps, grabbing unwary passers-by and forcing them, by painful judo holds, to accept free subscriptions to extraterrestrial broadcasts, by a newstand poster which proclaims: SADDAM GIVEN LAST CHANCE . . .

What will they do? Ring his doorbell and run? The gangrene of imperial dreams. Is Trotskyist Martha already laying down a barrage of Pete Seeger ditties between the kennels of war? "We'll call on the soldiers on both sides to lay down their weapons and embrace each other," she told me, in the Patisserie Valerie. And they shall beat their swords into British Gas shares, at 120 pence. The beardless youth from Chippewa, Minnesota, will brush the bristles of the fellah from Wadi el Brouj. Soon they will all be humping in the dunes, like in Antonioni's *Zabriskie Point.* Come back, Monsieur Verdoux, all is forgiven. A little spot of personal violence, for cash or pleasure, would do us all a world of good. The private, rather than the public, vengeance. Do it for old time's sake, and don't spare the mustard! Anything but self-delusion and false hopes.

AFTER THE WASH — THE DRY!
   — a shroud
      ground to dust
      by the soft drop
      of a counterfiet coin.
                     — Daniel ffotheringay-Pick

And so we hang about, waiting for the Apocalypse, again. Picking our nose on the street-corners of history, flicking the snot into the road. Will the police arrive, in their Black Maria? Or is it open season, out there?

IS ANYBODY LISTENING? IS ANYBODY AWAKE? WILL ANYONE PLEASE START THE BIDDING? DO I HEAR A VOICE IN THE BACK?

TWELVE

The Mirrors
of the I

I WATCHED IT ALL, THE GATHERING STORM, THE GALES, THE SQUALLS, THE tempests, the flash-floods of blood. One predicts, but no one takes one seriously. It gets worse as times move on. A man came to me once, on my column, sometime between the Khwarizmian massacres and the sack of Constantinople. He said he came from the north of an island at the north-western edge of Europe, but his accent made him difficult to make out. His name was Loggie-Bird, or such like. He had an idea, he said, which would transform my ability to communicate with my adherents. He had an amazing notion, of a mechanical system, which would enable my words, and indeed my visage, to be transported to vast distances, and even beyond the sea. It would be a labyrinth of tubes, of inordinate length, into one end of which I would speak, my words being emitted by means of echo chambers to persons who would sit with their ears bent to innumerable orifices at the other. Furthermore, there would be a series of gigantic mirrors, set in the desert and on the peaks of hills, which would reflect my image as I spoke from glass to glass, interminably, and even set on ships at sea. He had a rudimentary blueprint of this vast entanglement, which was something like this:

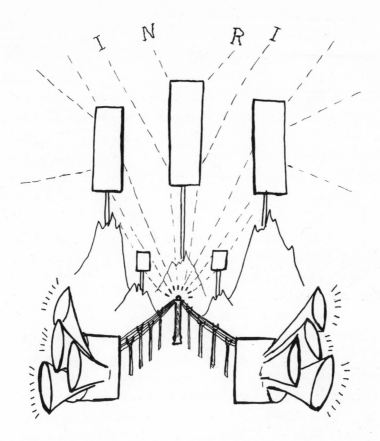

I sent him packing. One can see where this sort of thing leads. Folk will wallow at home, lost in idleness. Salvation brought on a plate, or on a glass, is no salvation at all. There must be the hot breath of contact, with no intervention except the spirit of God. The mirror is the satanic icon of vanity. I have no need to know myself. I am vile. And thus I am a mirror of all.

I feel history as a great roiling confusion, a seething mass of the condemned, dreaming their dreams. When the Holy Crusaders marched upon the city of Jerusalem, they were exhausted by their journeys, battles, famines and disease. But they were sustained by the dream. Their first attack was repulsed with heavy losses, so the commanders ordered great siege machines to be built, sending teams of soldiers, labourers and prisoners out to the hills as far as Samaria to collect the wood and logs. In the stifling summer *hamsin* which filled clothing and chain-mail with blazing dust, wielding their mallets and adzes and awls, the assailants built their engines. Now the bishops themselves began to dream, seeing, in their *cafard*, the armies of Joshua the Israelite, trumpeting the walls of Jericho. Carrying their banners, standards and holy relics, the armies of the Crusade donned white robes and walked barefoot around the walls of the city, oblivious to the mockery of the Moslems, who cast rubbish and offal at them with catapults. On the 13th of July, Anno Domini 1099, the siege machines were ready. Seven times they circled the city with ox and camel hides sewn on by the women to protect them from the liquid nafta fire. The first machine was raised against the Zion Gate, fired by the defenders and crashed in a wash of flames and corpses. But the next, raised close by the Gate of Flowers, held for enough time to allow a small group of the attackers, closely followed by Godfrey de Bouillon, and the main force, to stream across on ladders.

Godfrey of Bouillon, Duke of Lower Lorraine and vassal of the Emperor Henry the IV, was said by legends to be a direct descendant of the Nazarene, who had in fact escaped his fate on Calvary to marry and father a son in exile. But such heresies need not detain us. In fact, this Godfrey was suspected by the Emperor of excessive sympathies for the Pope, Urban II, causing the Duke to find it theologically and politically sound to absent himself from Lower Lorraine. But now this commander crossed over the burning sky to invest the Holy City, having received, by means of his comrade Raymond Saint Gilles, the surrender of the Moslem commander, Ifkhitar ad-Daula, besieged in the Tower of David, in return for a guarantee of safe conduct. Thus a small group of military survivors was allowed out of the city. But no mercy could be shown to the rest. For three days the Crusaders raged in the city, tearing through the souks and alleyways, killing all in their path. Another eyewitness (without benefit of Loggie-Bird's mirrors) was the knight William of Tyre, chronicler of the Crusade (I never put anything down on paper), who described the proceedings thus:

"It was impossible to look upon the vast numbers of the slain without horror. Everywhere lay the fragments of human bodies, and the very ground was cov-

ered with the blood of the slain. It was not alone the spectacle of headless bodies
and mutilated limbs strewn in all directions . . . still more dreadful was it to
gaze upon the victors themselves, dripping with blood from head to foot . . . It
is reported that within the Temple enclosure alone about 10,000 infidels per-
ished, in addition to those who lay slain everywhere throughout the city in the
streets and squares . . . The soldiers roved the city in search of wretched sur-
vivors who might be hiding in the narrow portals and byways to escape death.
Those were dragged out into public view and slain like sheep. Some formed
into bands and broke into houses, where they laid violent hands on the heads of
families, on their wives, children and their entire households. The victims were
either put to the sword or dashed headlong to the ground from some elevated
place so they perished miserably. Each marauder claimed as his own in perpe-
tuity the particular house which he had entered, together with all it contained
. . . At the entrance of each house, as it was taken, the victor hung up his shield
and arms, as a sign to all who approached not to pause there but to pass by, as
that place was already in the possession of another . . ."

But, Guillaume de Tyre could not but conclude:

"Guiding and directing all was the merciful hand of God, to whom be honour
and glory for ever and ever."

Oftentimes one cannot bear necessity. But the city fell, again, back
into the hands of the Kurdish general Saladin, not one hundred years later,
a mere blink of history. All that blood in vain. But the divine spark! I used
to watch as it lit the fires of Jerusalem, but also ignited the embers of
greed: The miracle of the Descent of the Holy Fire, that annual Easter
spectacle. In the Church of the Holy Sepulchre, just above the spot where
the Saviour's body was brought down from the Cross to be washed, there
is a small opening in the rotunda. A small bundle of straw, hung in an iron
frame from the ceiling, ignites spontaneously on Easter Sunday, with a
frenzy of activity ensuing as the pilgrims rush to light their lamps and
tapers. But even this divine intercession can be degraded by avarice and
desire. Many the time I have witnessed the separate sects buying and selling the right to the fire like a McDonald's franchise, Armenians and Copts

attempting to wrest the concession from the Greeks, and vice versa. God does not ignore such transgressions. More than once terrible consequences have ensued in the Sepulchre, as maddened crowds trampled themselves to death, or burned down the entire edifice by the excess of torches and candles. More than three hundred were killed in a fire in late Ottoman times, A.D. 1834. There is no end to human folly.

To return to the font, once again — my Maronites. I perch, in my occult persona, as it were, on a sandbagged terrace overlooking the familiar visage of the tattered and debilitated city, watching, with not a little wry amusement, yet another saviour of the Levant, General Michel Aoun, fleeing in his silk Armani pyjamas from the blitzed ruins of his presidential palace at Ba'abda, dancing on eggshells through the bombed streets in the direction of the French embassy. Behind him, the palace is strewn with the corpses of his loyalist defenders, strafed in the act of surrender by Syrian aircraft taking advantage of the latest mutation of global alliances and interests. Only hours before he had declared his principles to the nation: Victory or Death. Now the gates of the Embassy of the Fifth French Republic close behind his pathetic form. At least the cuisine will be admirable. One must be thankful for small mercies. On the terrace, beside me, his enemies dance, waving their chequebooks in the air. The clans of Khamash, Gemayel, Mansur. Another community up for grabs. And the steel vultures circle above.

Incarnate Nature of the Divine *Logos*. Everyone wants in on the act. The tribal patriarchs, political spin-doctors, clerics of every sect and hue. Heralds of Messiahs and Mahdis, religious dissimulators and schismatics, purveying their recycled Days of Judgement on every street-corner. *When you see the masters of error prevailing over the masters of truth* . . . When was it ever otherwise? *Then comes the* shahid, *the heir of Adam, to teach Mankind how to die* . . . A superfluous lesson. Courage in a bad cause was ever plentiful. And everyone waits for second comings: The Nazarene, the Paraclete, the Hidden Imam, Elijah the Prophet, King Arthur, Richard the Lionheart, Frederick Barbarossa, Musa Sadr, Bashir Gemayel. Repeating, like a bad meal expelled from the gut. The Druze have even spread this idea like margarine, declaring their belief, like the Hindus and Buddhists, in the reincarnation of every member of their faith. Metempsychosis.

Allahu akbar. But I know, that one only comes once, though one may linger, unwillingly, on and on . . .

Everyone so loves their vanished heroes, who take on their sins, absolve their responsibilities. How they adore evoking their monuments. My own devotees demolished my pillar, stone after stone, chipping off samples to carry off to mantelpieces and salons. Digging up clods of the soil on which the Saint pissed from on high. But the Maronites, like the Jews, deified themselves: Keepers of the Faith, embodiments of the Culture. Like cells on a Petri dish, the living truth seen through a microscope. Deification and hubris. Why else should they dig the living-dead crusader out of his berth at the Café des Amis, reading cast-off *Le Mondes* and dreaming of lost glory, dragging him back to the scene of his failure to justify their decayed pedigree, the fossil family tree? Cedars of Lebanon. There are but a handful of the originals left, scattered in the remotest ranges. Tiny groves surrounded by fences and guarded by toothless monks. But the drumbeats of the blood, battering at the soul. I close my ears to the mad cacophony, the timeless babble, the myriad wailing, whining voices, the strange chaos of the ages. I cannot escape. I walk down the streets of the slaughtered city, dragging my ghostly feet through the mingled blood of the slain, the heaped brotherhood of the dead, the democratic stench of decay, the pan-lingual cries of looters, rapists and their victims, the sobbing of the robbed, the sword-slashed doors and potholes, the spent cartridges and hacked-off limbs and shattered shop fronts fallen in the road. The wars of the wretched of the earth. And the angels, burning bright in the sky, floating down on gossamer wings.

THE HOSTAGE: BENNY POTAMKIN'S STORY

. . . I rose, I flew, I defeated gravity. The earth rolled under me like a vast ball of fur. Its plains, its forested mountains, the urban sprawl appearing with an expected suddenness just off my left wingtip. Bathed in bright sunlight, the tiny hillside villages, buried in trees, the dotted villas and chalets. The asphalt roads and broken freeways, leading into the swathe of the slums, the ugly glut of houses looking as if a dinosaur had grazed on their roofs. Patches of rubble and mounds of scrap metal sending sparks of light to my eyes. And beyond that, the sea, rippling from a blueish grey into a searing white.

Above it all, that tremendous sense of freedom. Flight. Whatever else becomes mechanical and routine, flight, the incarnate miracle, that sense of limitless power — you can become the machine . . .

That, I suppose, was my weakness. I never quite became the machine. The cog, whizzing under voice control, the tinselly drone in the ears, disembodied instructions, by switches and dials, to a disembodied mind. Or it may have just been that, down below, somebody got lucky. Usually they haven't the range. They stand there, Rambos on their trucks, legs planted apart, arms cradling the swivelling turret, wasting ammunition on thin air. They haven't the range. But I swooped down, too low, towards them, the recording camera clicking beneath me, pinpointing targets for future missions, identifying the command posts, anti-aircraft batteries. It was, as I found out later, a shoulder-held missile that took me. Supplied by the Russians, the East Germans, Iran, or France, England, the United States, even by ourselves in the tangled web of some forbidden deal. Who could know?

The explosion ripped off the Skyhawk's tail. It is not, after all, a large plane. People think these weapons are huge and invincible. But on the ground you're amazed at this gossamer thing weighed down by its missiles and bombs. It seems only a few steps removed from a child's assembly toy. Of course, we never see the results of a raid, except professionally, craters on aerial snapshots and films. No human factor. I lost control immediately and spiralled. I shouted into my helmet microphone: "I'm hit. Ejecting, co-ordinate . . ." But there was no time. My eyes were blurred. I pressed the ejector switch. Like being kicked in the pants by twenty mules. I was free of the machine. Falling. My parachute opened, plucked me up in the air.

The city below me, in closer detail, revealing another face. Dusty, dry, coarse and gritty, carbuncled with the bumps and lumps of broken and rebuilt dwellings, jury-rigged TV aerials, and electricity cables hooked on to drooping lines, washing lines and ruptured watertanks and solar heaters, tarpaulins stretched over bombed-out cavities, scattered junk, twisted steel girders, and the people: little bits of rag-clad flesh, blobs of flesh looking up at me, as I floated out of the sky.

Uniformed figures, and figures in half-uniform, jeans and T-shirts, scurried about, rifles glinting in the sun. Flashes and explosive discharges as they fired at me from the ground. Then other figures, rushing up. Now I could hear voices shooting up at me in bursts of sound. The firing stopped. I tried to pull the threads of my parachute to manoeuvre away, but there were people everywhere. I narrowly missed a five-storey rooftop and floated, not much more than a metre from a scarved and chequered-robed woman, shouting and waving her fist at me, her lips hurling out angry cries.

I landed in a rubbish-strewn backyard. Chickens cawed and scattered. My foot caught in a pile of rubber tyres. I shook myself out of the chute, which luckily snagged and tore free on a jagged sheet of corrugated iron. A small boy, dressed in a Popeye T-shirt, stood frozen in terror. I stretched out my hand, God knows why. He unfroze and ran off, screaming.

My sister, Naomi, used to tell me about the invasion of Lebanon, four years before, in 1982. I was a teenager then, and had other things on my mind. But she was outraged at the image of the troops marching through the villages we had bombed, handing out sweets to the kids. "We killed their parents and gave them sweets," she used to say, mockingly. I said: "Well, at least they got something out of it." All the rawness of youth. Naomi was very active with the Peace Now movement, marching night and day. I thought then it was weak-kneed feminine nonsense, a luxury for a besieged nation. But now I was ready to bleed, and I had no sweets to handout.

I kicked free of the rubber tyres and ran, pulling out my side-pistol, to a broken-down fence. Tumbling bricks, bent corrugated-iron sheets. Shouts from inside the adjacent house. I cut my hand and tore my pant leg, tumbling over the fence. An alleyway between tin shacks. Men in grimy vests and women in short-sleeved dresses and scarves came out, holding picks and knives. One huge bearded man in a string vest wielded a vicious-looking axe. I brandished my gun, but it was no deterrent. They advanced. I turned and ran down the alleyway. At a junction, a band of armed young men barred my way. Five or six of them in T-shirts and camouflage pants, with Kalashnikovs and carbines. A second group of seven or eight spread out a short distance behind the first. A tall man with a limp and a shock of grey-white hair, clean-shaven, with an immense beak nose, came forward, stretching his empty hand out to me.

"Put away your pistol, pilot." he said to me, in Hebrew, "or you will be shot dead right here and now."

I hesitated. I could take one or two with me. Win a place in some ethereal balance-sheet of heroes and cowards, the good, the bad and the stupid. Or be just another corpse in a mass graveyard.

"You are worth more to us alive." he said. "We are Palestinians. We recognise the Geneva Convention."

A bizarre statement to hear there, in that tin-shack alley in the midst of bombed-out killing-grounds. The white-haired man spread out his right hand and his left. "Life, or death?"

I put away the pistol.

The armed young men surrounded me and pinned my arms. Someone wrapped a dirty scarf round my eyes. The sun went out. Sweaty grasping hands pulled me, punching my back and ribs. I was dragged over the side of a vehicle, probably a jeep, flung onto a back seat. The voices jabbered above me in that language I have lived with all my life, but could neither understand nor speak. We were given rudimentary classes on survival in enemy hands, but the simple Berlitz phrases I was supposed to utter had all gone out of my head. I laid my head on the seat, exercising regular breathing. Transcendental meditation. Shut out reality, regain the inner core. We do train for this, the moment of failure. The knowledge that from now on, I'm on my own. No past and no foreseeable future. The present, second by second, minute by minute, hour by hour.

Blackness, and more manhandling. From jeep to road, from road to room. Left on my own, hands tied and blindfolded, but a welcome respite. One hour? Two? A terrible thirst, but my brain knows my body can hold out for some time. Mind over matter. It's a technical problem. Or so we are trained to think. The mind, under stress, tries every tactic to collapse the body. One has to take control.

Later they came and took me into another room and untied the blindfold and my legs and hands. I was in a straight-backed wooden chair, facing the grey-white-haired man under a peeling wall pinned with posters of Yasir Arafat and two other ageing men I didn't recognise and a map of Mandate Palestine with crossed rifles and Arabic slogans. I had finally come to live the cliché. The white-haired man offered me a cigarette, and lit it with a gold-plated lighter. I had more time to study his face, deeply grooved with old strains and sorrows, and I now realised one of his eyes was glass, he had only part of his left ear and a large scar on the underside of his chin. He looked, in one sense, a hundred years old, but was probably on the lighter side of forty. He had my identification tag and dog-tags on the desk in front of him, pursing his lip, his good eye bulging as he read the name in Hebrew.

"Benyamin Potemkin. That's a curious name."

"It's 'Potamkin,'" I said, clearing my throat. At least I could tell him that much. The pressure to ease up somehow was intense. "It's a common Russian name."

"But of course, we are not in Russia." he said, his eye resting mournfully on me.

"My grandparents came to Eretz Yisrael in the twenties," I said. "My father and mother were born in this country." I should resist the urge to talk, to make human contact, but theory is not practice.

"You don't mean this country," he said. "Here we're both strangers. Scrapping in our neighbour's backyard." His fingers caressed the tags. "Potamkin. Who would believe it. If we wrote this in a book, would anyone believe us? We are living in an impossible world. But here we are, you and me. We have to play our roles, to the end." What roles might they be? I was only concerned to survive, in as honourable a way as possible. If that had any meaning here.

"Why did your grandparents come to Palestine?" he asked me, as if we had just met at some diplomatic reception, over tea and cakes. "What were they looking for?"

A new life. Seizing their own destiny. The old story. But I didn't want to be drawn any further. I was glad to have the cigarette to drag on. He put the dog-tags aside and looked at me, with a certain unsettling recognition. "You know I have never set foot in Palestine, legally," he said. "I was born in 1949, in the refugee camp Ramleh in Jordan. My mother fled from Palestine pregnant. She ran, with all her belongings on her head and me inside her belly. My father carried us part of the way. I was brought up on his stories. The fear, the despair, the humiliation. I grew up with my homeland locked away from me, a mirage just out of arm's reach. Later I penetrated into that unknown country, several times, as a *fiday*. I came to kill your relatives, because they were the cause of my pain. I killed some people, but my pain was not eased. I came like a thief in the night to my own country and left, running like a criminal. Now you have come in your plane to kill me as I sit here in someone else's country and others fear me as I feared you. Can you see any logic in this situation?"

I couldn't, but this was hardly the point. Cats run from dogs and dogs chase cats. "Tell me what should I do with you?" he said. "The Syrians would give their eyes for an Israeli pilot. They will torture you and get the information they want. Of course, you may be a hero. So you would die. They are not fussy. So many people die here."

I could believe him. In our "survival" course, the climactic phase was simulated enemy interrogation. A special unit of our own military policemen held us prisoner in an unknown facility, forcing us to stand up, hooded, in stinking pens as white noise was fed in our ears. The *pièce de résistance* was an electric-shock session with the so-called telephone. Electrodes are attached to ears, toes and fingers (they spared us the genitals, a limit to authenticity). The muscles go into searing contractions, like cramps all over the body. It shows how cheaply total pain can be rendered. All you need is a battery and some wires. Anyone can do it to anybody. Who needs the full paraphernalia of the state? Though it helps, of course, to achieve that true feeling of total helplessness. We received a lecture, during the course, by a survivor of Enemy Interrogation, a famous officer who had been captured behind the lines. Everyone talks, he said; the question is: How soon. The point of resistance is to delay the enemy's acquisition of information. This is only valid in an operational mode, in the heat of battle, where every hour matters. He also spoke about the special "sexual" relationship between the torturer and the tortured. The physicality of a perverted love affair. The trick is not to fight this, but to return the seduction under your own control. Like judo — turning the adversary's power against himself. I had no idea what he was talking about.

He also spoke about the "Stockholm Syndrome." How hostages begin to identify with their captors. The surrender which makes captivity bearable, even acceptable to the bruised ego. The outside world becomes a common enemy. In the past, prisoners of war were able to band together to maintain their bond. But these days the captured are often separated into small groups or individual units. A prisoner, in a war situation, is an asset, unless there are so many of them, as in the Iran-Iraq War, or our own '67 and '73 wars, when their value is calculated in bulk. If you are a single or a small group, you should grab hold of this awareness of your intrinsic worth, and use it to keep alive and sane.

True or false, I still kept silent, opposite my white-haired captor/deliverer, facing me not so much as a Torquemada but as a kind of warped, crippled, limping God, holding out a pair of rusty, chipped scales of justice. "On the other hand," he said, "I could sell you to Hizbollah, the Army of God, and they will keep you chained in a cellar for a few years, until they can get the going rate from your government. The Americans, I hear, will pay two hundred million dollars per hostage in high-grade military goods. What are you worth to your government, Potamkin?"

We believe in the sanctity of life. I could hardly tell him that, having swooped in my Skyhawk to prepare the ground for his obliteration. The armed young men came into the room again and reattached my blindfold. Once again, thrown in a corner. Mind over matter. Suppress fears. Try to find the deepest source of your being, beyond the ego, under the id. What might that be, Potamkin? The world I'd left behind? Memories. Clichés. Home, the beach, the city, the streets, cafés, the Tel Aviv esplanade on crowded summer nights, the tarry whiff of the sea, falafel, friends, family, my father's bitter moaning about the air-conditioning business, my mother's dreams of her abandoned kibbutz paradise, my sister, Naomi, marching in the streets for peace and justice . . . other sweet feminine faces . . . No comfort here.

Benny Potamkin, This Is Your Life. One moment, jokes and banter

in the pilots' mess, the clatter of plates and coffee mugs, braying laughter, the next, the swoop towards the shattered city, the sudden explosion of confusion, then the long, dark age, with nothing but sounds,
incomprehensible cries, bangs and scrapes, calls, shouts of women,
children, the screech of tyres, vehicle thrum, the ubiquitous radio wail
of Arab music. And then, the gun- and cannon-fire of bombardment,
shells landing, the shifting of the ground, coming and going, a regular
hammer beat on the eardrums. Moved again, I guessed into a cellar, the
shelling more muffled, though it continued, for a long time . . . All
night, no day, until that sudden moment, when they took off my blindfold, and a cheerful, gaunt, moustached face with a great beak of a nose
and untidy hair, a wiry form dressed in a faded white surgeon's gown,
splattered with blood, called to me in English in an American accent:

"Hey there, soldier boy, do you have any medical training?"

. . . One takes refuge in whatever's familiar. Never a dull moment in the
shaken whirlpool of the mind. Just imagine yourself out of this hole,
Angelopoulos . . . Try to organise these scattered dreams, memories, reflections. In the cold, imagine a burning summer. In the heat, the winter
snows. Santa Clausland and Desirée . . . New Hampshire and the More-
land Art Colony, there's a ball to run and catch . . . A whole month of sex
and hibernation, in that order, in Our Thornton Wilder Town: the church
spires, the clocktower, the neat little houses and shops, Main Street, the
Village Pharmacy and Diner. Up in the woods, the cosy not quite log cab-
ins provided for creative art . . . Desirée . . . She came to a political meeting
in New York, at which I spoke about the Lebanon War. The usual doctor's
perspective: wounds, mutilations, death, disease and poverty. Raven-
haired, she floated up to me at the end of my talk, caressing me with distant eyes. What could I do? I am just a man, and a Greek. A night of her
poetry, or at any rate, part of the night. On her way for a month's sojourn
at the Colony. December, 1983. Christmas through New Year. The white
trees and the sluggish river, snowballs in gloves, two sets of tracks, male
and female, across the pristine fields. Convivial nights, at those stern Boy
Scout dinners along the great wood table in the Colony's main hall, with

directors Cornball Jimmie Cooper and his wife, Aisleen, presiding over spaghetti with meatballs and august patter on the pollution of the countryside, or the decline of American intellectual life, history, the real origins of Huckleberry Finn, the hidden mantras of Mao Tse Tung, the conspiracies of the State Department, Vietnam, Cambodia and the psychopathology of Henry Kissinger, the Mahabharata, T.S. Eliot's *Waste Land,* Upanishads and Sanskrit verse, Giordano Bruno's *Secret of the Seals,* the linguistic theories of Noam Chomsky, the finer points of skiing, the sad tale of the Shaker furniture and so on and so on. . . . Desirée . . . Her real name was Gladys Schmidt, but she took a pen name for her poetry. You learn to live with people's phantasies of themselves. Who am I to cast stones, who have lived in a glass house all my life?

Eventually, one tires of highbrow camaraderie, New Age touchie-feelie, so we locked ourselves in our cabin, Desirée and me, cutting ourselves off from the world. Like trappers hunting for raccoons in the dead wilds of the Northern Frontier, we wrapped ourselves in skins and followed the spoor of small game deep into the silent woods. But in that conjoined solitude we rapidly grew apart, in the long evenings we sat, without television, reading books or just listening to the dull roar of the central-heating system. I decided her poetry was hollow and unreal. She played beautiful games with words and rhythms, but it was all the old clichés. Nature, nurture, the flutter of hurt feelings, small desires and shallow dreams. I was the wrong audience. I have an allergy to sensitivity. So I had an affair with the Colony's cook. She was a wild eighteen-year-old Vermont filly named Jo-Ann. We fell upon each other, after a course of eyeballing, when I excused myself from a long dinner discussion of the influence of the Bauhaus on the collapse of Weimar Germany. Gladys wanted to stay. I left and joined Jo-Ann in her cubbyhole, where we fucked in every conceivable posture.

The defendant pleads guilty as charged. A creature of habit, though not much habit here. Oh for a switch to Sartre's hell! Anyone, even my greatest enemy, I'll fuck them right on the floor! As I lie, sucking my own sweat. One time, Gladys brought from the Colony's library a great leather-bound tome of Dante's *Inferno,* illustrated by Gustave Doré. The shafts of fire, descending from the sky: *The stormy blast of hell, with restless fury dri-*

ves the spirits on . . . Thy city, heaped with envy to the brim . . . Only so far afflicted that we live desiring without hope . . .

"It's exactly like that," I confirmed to her. She thought I was exaggerating. But, in Dante's day, hell was an imagined place. Inquisitors and torturers produced small hells on earth, disease and plague larger ones, but for the real thing we had to wait for our own century. And I have seen *Mahomet mangled, and Ali weeping, from the chin his face cleft to the forelock* . . . No divine justice, or sword of God, just American cluster bombs and phosphorous shells produced by the good folk of Kansas or Wisconsin on proper Union rates. Not to speak of Skoda's shrapnel . . .

In which circle would old Alighieri have put me? The sacrilegious, the schismatics and heretics, the flatterers, or those who have seduced women from their duty . . . Wake up, Angelopoulos! Incoming! The fires, the fires from the sky . . . I stagger to my post, the gown, the gloves, the scrub nurses, the operating kitchen table . . . Another laparotomy? No sweat, comrades. Suction. Aspirate. Clamp. Suture. Resect those damaged segments. But here we have another mundane hazard of the third world that Dante might well have appreciated: the worms, the ascaris parasites, white and wriggling in the bloody abdomen . . . slithering and writhing, refusing to be anaesthetised, wiggling through the blood and perforations . . . Throw them out! Bag the fucking bastards! Scoop 'em out, they still wriggle and writhe on the operating-theatre floor . . . Benny Potamkin, as scrub nurse, scrapes them up for disposal, but still they come, oozing through the mess . . . I can almost hear their tiny cries: Fuck you, Angelopoulos! We have no intention of dying —— we'll hang onto life as long as we can! It's dog eat dog in here . . .

Milling survivors in the rubble without a cause. Or the rubble of many causes. All in the same pit. Tewfiq and Salim and Kamal and Daoud and Muna and Saida and Mad Latif and Benny Potamkin, the alien who became part of the pack. Identical troglodytes, gaunt shufflers in underground burrows, skeletal forms with matted hair and distended pupils, bandy-legged and scuff-elbowed. Indeed, the shelling so reduced the camp that the remains of the breeze-block buildings fell in on each other in multiple layers, the few remaining streets became tunnels, easier for access across our box. I no longer need to feed off Tewfiq's hallucinations, I'm already familiar with my own. Pulsating torn, bleeding human organs pursue me down the claustrophobal alleys. A chopped pancreas beards me in a dead end and bends my ear with a whining recitation of the Geneva Convention on the Victims of War. Resected entrails coil round my ankles rattling a paper cup of small coins. My own eyeballs seem to be leaving my body and straining for unattainable space. And all this without even the golden liquid, supplies of which have completely dried up. My lusty sessions with Anneka now more like two sacs of flesh rattling bones together like primitive dice. An erection's hardly feasible on two spoonfuls of yoghurt per day. Still, life struggles against entropy, and stupidity struggles against hope. In a rare lull in the night bombardment a massive explosion tears through the camp. We run, Tewfiq and I, joining the crowd spilling out of their holes and crannies converging on the camp perimeter, up against the rubble barricades. The teenage soldiers are carrying the torn body of Limping Nabil, the Fatah Operations Officer, old one-eyed, one-track Nabil, the man whose zeal kept everyone else going, who probably had taken more shrapnel into his body in thirty years than any man alive, but he was alive no longer, because both legs have been blown off to the knee, his chest is a wide-open gap and he arrives at the clinic stone dead. Someone planted an anti-personnel mine on his route of patrol. Nabil, who had survived the earliest years of the Fatah, and countless incursions into Israel, and the battle of Karameh, and the wars of Southern Lebanon, the Litani Operation and the Israeli invasion of '82. Blown up by his own kind inside the camp. I bearded Kamal Abd-el-Rahman, his rival of the Popular Front, and pinned him to the wall of the Cabinet: "Don't bullshit me now, Kamal, who did this? If we're going to kill each other in this rat-trap, let's at least do it all in one go . . ." He swore blind he had nothing to do with it. We knew we were facing complete disaster. A civil war in our two hundred square yards would spell an end to all our hopes. Two thousand people crammed up against each other, five hundred of them armed. Not to speak of the dead, four hundred-odd of them, cramming every available piece of diggable earth, bursting out from the confines of the mosque into the backyards of warehouses, shops. We had no more room even for the deceased. Kamal and I conspired to hide the truth. We told the camp Nabil had trod on an unexploded shell, but we set up our own secret committee of inquiry. Bashir, Nabil's deputy, Kamal and Radwan, of the Popular Democratic Front. We didn't have far to look. The small band of anti-Arafat "dissidents," allies in fact of the forces besieging us, though trapped like all the rest of us they nominally fought on our side, had received orders from outside. I left them to Kamal and Radwan to deal with. They rounded them up and pushed them out of the camp, through the sniper-covered checkpoint. Two of the eight made it to the enemy lines. Benny Potamkin helped us bury Nabil on top of two other bodies in the ruined mosque. Unable to get any whisky, we passed the following night on a bottle of raw alcohol I had been hiding for the most desperate hour.

Can you hear me? The ascaris worms slide across the floor. They bring me greetings, from my Palestinian and other comrades: *Alles in Ordnung* in the outside world. Disease, disaster, pestilence, poverty are still the order of the day. Stick-like naked black children stagger across the landscape of the sun. Women with dried-out dugs gaze opaquely into the camera. Men sit hunched in their dishonour and shame. The jackals of war tear the bleeding flesh of the living. General Dynamics shares are up up up. Tyrants fall, while others queue for their turn. My visiting parasite worms will not be gainsaid. They have just come from the World Congress of the CBV (Cocci, Bacilli and Viruses), where a unanimous vote was taken to combat all efforts by modern medicine to deny their natural rights. Guest lecturers from many third-world dicta-torships and juntas and delegates from the West's defence industries were warmly applauded. All the Middle East's sects and governments were represented, you should have been there, said the Chief Worm, it was enough to warm the cockles of your heart. I have been there, oh yes, 'twas only a freezing of the blood . . .

Danger signs. Getting lost in the labyrinth. One has to reluctantly get back to the centre. There are no voices. There are no multitudes. No boos and no applause. There is just that empty hum of the cell. The clatter at the door, the captors' boots. The tinned ration. "Thank you very much."

"Bleasure," he said.

The "B" for "P." That Arab giveaway! A glow of happiness the whole day. My first clue, a confirmation of the obvious, but at least, I felt, I am with my own! A bizarre feeling of contentment. I'd narrowed the field, from the world to a continent, from a continent to a familiar region, from a region to my own chosen backyard?

I beamed at the hood. It turned away, expressionless. Alone again, with my chipped plate, in "baradise." The necessity, and the impossibility, of creating something out of nothing . . .

In the year 387 of the Hegira, or Anno Domini 996 , an eleven-year-old boy ascended to the throne of the Fatimid dynasty in Egypt. The boy's name was Abu Ali Mansur al-Hakim, and he became known in the fullness of time by his detractors as the Mad Caliph of Cairo. He was the son of the wisest of the Shi'ite Fatimid caliphs, al-Aziz, his mother the daughter of Russian Christians and sister of the Melkite patriarchs of the See of Jerusalem and of Alexandria. From this syncretic parentage the boy imbibed heresies of the interconnection and latent harmony of all the great religions of the world. To further this ideal and to understand its origins the young caliph summoned to his side theologians and mystics from the farthest reaches of the *umma*. For months the boy sat in his palace, surrounded by these bearded, white-robed sages, devouring ancient and mysterious books and parchments, leaving the affairs of state to his viziers, while in their barracks the Turkish and Ethiopian mercenaries recruited by his father plotted and intrigued against the throne.

But it was in the tenth year of his reign that the catalyst to al-Hakim's thought arrived, in the shape of one Hamza Ibn-Ali Ibn-Ahmad al-Zuzani, an Ismaili mystic from the mountains of Afghanistan. Hamza disclosed to the circle of devotees around the Caliph a unique revelation: That the caliph himself, al-Hakim, was the Mahdi, the Hidden Imam of Shi'ite theology, who had dis-occulted himself, as tradition predicated, in the shape of an eleven-year-old boy, who, now grown to manhood, was fully prepared for his divine mission.

The Ismailis were devotees of the disinherited son of the Sixth Imam of Shi'a tradition, Jafar as-Sadiq, a direct descendant by his mother of the first caliph, Abu-Bakr. As-Sadiq was renowned throughout the Islamic world as a peerless scholar and jurist. In his era the Shi'a, persecuted and neglected, mounted several revolts against the Sunni Ummayad rule. The Ummayads were overthrown by the Abbasids, but the persecution of the Shi'a increased. As-Sadiq was arrested and often imprisoned, then poisoned, his followers claimed, by the Abbasid Caliph al-Mansur, in the year of the Hegira 148, A.D. 765. The Ismailis claim as-Sadiq designated his eldest son, Ismail, to succeed him as the Seventh Imam. But Ismail died in his father's lifetime, and most Shi'a authorities claimed the designation had passed to a much younger son, Abu al-Hasan Musa, known as Musa al-Kazim— the Forebearing. Others claimed the imamate for as-Sadiq's eldest surviving son, al-Aftah (the Flatheaded). But the devotees of Ismail claimed their chosen imam had not died but been hidden by as-Sadiq and then undergone the *ghaiba*, the occultation, to return as the Hidden Imam. The Fatimids, an offshoot of this tendency, believed there were several Hidden Imams in succession, culminating in the founders of their dynasty. But Hamza Ibn-Ali presented to the young Caliph, al-Hakim, the shattering news that he himself was not only the de-occulted imam, but a virtual manifestation of the Deity, God Himself, whose task was to end the sectarian divisions of Man. He was the Ineffable One, divinely inspired and infallible, the Microcosm and the Macrocosm, the Metaphysical Soul of the Cosmos, His Truths the Truths of Universal Order, His Will requiring total obedience.

Soon after the Truth of Hamza's revelation sunk in, al-Hakim took action. He issued a proclamation and a Divine Call for the New Faith to be practised throughout the Empire. The tenets of Islam were not abolished but overtaken and subsumed in the New Divine Order. New dietary laws were issued and a prohibition on the eating of peas and of the national dish, the melokhia. Singing and dancing and other public frivolities were banned. Hamza sent out apostles to spread The Word throughout the *umma*. Two of them, Baha al-Din and Muhammad al-Darazi, travelled to Syria, Palestine and Lebanon, there to form the nucleus of what became the Druze religion. Meanwhile the Ineffable One ruthlessly imposed the New Faith at home. Dissenting viziers were executed. Schismatics and heretics were forced to wear degrading symbols, black robes for the Christians, a yoke with bells for the Jews. Churches and synagogues were destroyed, and, in the year 400 (A.D. 1009), al-Hakim had the Holy

Sepulchre in Jerusalem demolished, stone by stone, including the site of Golgotha and all relics which the priests had not managed to carry away beforehand. It was said the Caliph had been told of the miraculous descent of the Holy Fire at Easter and had moved forcibly against this challenge to His Divinity. Others said he had to silence opponents who claimed the New Faith was a front for the Christianity he had inherited from his infidel mother.

The New Order lasted fully ten years. But in the year 411 (A.D. 1021), the Caliph al-Hakim disappeared. The Ineffable One was pronounced missing, presumed dead. Conspiracy theorists thrived. Some said he had been killed by his sister, Sit al-Mulk, whom he had accused of fornication with beasts. Others believed the Moslem authorities had at last succeeded in disposing of this threat to the True Faith. Others claimed the followers of al-Darazi, the Druze, had themselves killed him and disposed of his body to claim his occultation. Others said he had been chastised by the ghost of his mother and departed to become a Christian monk. Witnesses had seen the Caliph ride off into the desert alone, in a pilgrim's garb, upon a donkey. Some said they had seen him discard the donkey, and stride out on foot under the pitiless hammer of the sun. Still others claimed he had taken ship to India in the guise of a merchant and spent the rest of his long years studying the esoteric arts with the apostles of Gautama Buddha. Or even that he had travelled farther, to Tibet, Burma and China, where he had finally achieved parinirvana and died, to be reborn as the Future Buddha, Maitreya, after an interval of one thousand years.

But the disappearance of the Caliph did not end the New Faith. Although a dispute between al-Darazi and Hamza had led to the former's assassination and excommunication, Baha al-Din continued to spread The Word in Syria and the Lebanon, and to collect the 111 epistles which were to become the Noble Knowledge (*al-hikmat al-sharifa*). This Knowledge had to be compiled in secret, as the followers of al-Hakim were driven underground and persecuted by the viziers of the new Caliph, al-Hakim's son, al-Zahir. The religious teaching, the *tawhid*, of Druzism, turned inwards, and became a matter for the initiation of those ready to receive the ancient secrets of Mankind, the Knowledge which, it was claimed, had always been passed down from initiate to initiate, from the Dawn of Man.

Among the initiates and manifestations of the Universal Knowledge of God on Earth were Adam, Noah, Abraham, Moses, Jesus and Muhammad, as well as Imhotep, builder of the step pyramid of Sakkara; Hermes Trismegistus, founder of alchemy who gave his name to the hermetic tradition; Melchi-zedek, King of Salem and initiator of the Patriarch Abraham; Jethro, initiator of Moses; Pythagoras; Plato and Aristotle, who codified the principles of Reason. Only the highest initiates are able to appreciate the wisdom of these great sages, revealed in secret books and ancient texts entrusted only to those who achieved enlightenment after the most rigorous process of probation, initiates who lead a life of exemplary holiness, abstaining from all vice, tobacco and alcohol, shunning all material goods and riches. Wearing their distinct white fez and black garment, they are above the conflict and strife of the polluted world, as they meditate in their mountain shrines, the *mazar*, contemplating the Ineffable Mysteries, computing, by the movement of the stars, the date for the appearance of the next great seer, the next custodian of the Ultimate Knowledge. He is said to have already been born, and will manifest himself before the end of the twentieth century. He may even be a Woman, for the Druze accept women into the process of initiation. She may be the next answer of God to Man's infinite folly . . .

Michel Khamash's head, proving too heavy for his frail wheelchair-trapped body, sagged onto his scrawled summaries, his pile of yellowing tomes, his parchments of occult diagrams and Bembine tables, of hieroglyphic plots and plans. Charts of the relationship between the human body and the exterior universe. Maps of the stars and elemental trees. Heraldic symbols and sephirotic schemes. The Apollonian sunflower. The Tablet of Hermes. The Scroll of Thoth. The seven cycles of the Druze Messages of Wisdom. The Sufi orientations of colour, stations of the spiritual journey, macrocosm and microcosm, the thirteen spheres and secrets of the alphabet. All the ingredients of the attempt to reconcile the opposites of ancient knowledge and present power. Or just the scratchings for an elixir of life through the old crumbling chemical formulae? His head lying on the crisp pages, he continues to mourn the elopement of his royal prisoner-cum-cadaver and his necrophiliac daughter, while other compartments of his brain continue plotting against enemies near and far, scheming to head off further resurrections, always excepting his own . . .

The end justifies the means and the end is nigh. He has noted all the usual signs and portents. Ingathering of the Jews. Collapse of the communist antichrist. Resurgence of the Caesaropapist hordes. Collapse of all morals, disintegration of the family, the loss of faith in reason. The iron needs of dog eat dog. Now, our rival eschatologies face each other naked on an open battlefield. Good versus evil, Gog and Magog, the only question being, which is which?

My son, my son. The old rheumy eyes mist with tears as the living patriarch of his clan wheels his chair to the window of his study to gaze down at the terrace where his child and heir, Aziz, instructs his personal guards, clustering respectfully about his stocky form. It's a tough job, keeping a militia together in this mendacious place, in these infernal times. You have to learn to function like a rat in a sewer, to defend your turf against all comers, to harden your heart, if you want to survive. You have to commit all sorts of crimes and falsehoods, to learn to be a beast in the jungle, to know when to betray your initial principles for the higher principle of your animal instincts. To learn to mistrust even your nearest and dearest . . .

Why did he bring me the Lionheart? the old man ruminates. Which of my ancient parchments did he steal in to photograph or copy, and how did he find the clues that led to Fontevraud in texts I had already ploughed thoroughly? Or does he have independent sources? Has he his own access to the Jew in the rue de l'Ermite? What does he see that I am blind to? Did he connive in the elopement? Does the next generation have any feelings at all, apart from the barren lust for power? Mussolini and Hitler at least had a plan. A blueprint for salvation and order. A little too ambitious and cruel, perhaps, but look where muddle-headed kindness leads. All those genetic deceptions . . .

Having looked so far into his head, I withdraw. There is a limit to how much intellectual confusion, moral vacuity and delusional fugues one can take at a time, even a disembodied Saint. More than ever before I require the peace and tranquillity of my pillar, to have it raised, higher and higher from the prying eyes, the stretching hands, the rabble's babble, a vain hope. Not even the Walter Scott Monument or the Eiffel Tower will do. I am adrift in the world of displaced and paralysed souls. Retracing my escape to the desert, which is now defiled by the steel treads of tanks and the exhausts of armoured cars, the ingathered engines of destruction, an army of leviathan locusts spreading from across the seas, smearing the sands with oil and motor grease, littering the dunes with plastic packs and non-biodegradable wrappings, cigarette butts and discarded bottles, the waste and rubbish of far-away lands. The noise, curling into the stratosphere. Eat your heart out Hermes Trismegistus, Imhotep, Pythagoras, Archimedes, Leonardo, all you who dreamed of mastering number and nature, your warped great-great-grandchildren have mustered power you would never have imagined in your most extravagant visions. Like boils upon a healthy body, their creations swell and blacken, emitting their foul putrescence, poised to burst in the agonies of death, while vanished caliphs cower behind sand-dunes, hidden imams squeeze into the shadows of dry roots, and old men, far away, plot their myriad schemes to escape their own death, to reverse putrefaction, to find, in the twinges of their thirst for power, their alchemical rebirth and persistence, convinced it has to be only a matter of luck, just a question of finding the right connection, of finding the right switch to pull . . .

THIRTEEN

Genetic

Deceptions

IT SEEMED TO KATHLEEN THAT THE STONE CITY OF EDINBURGH, THE GREY
Lothian shore, the tangled clutter of her workshop-home, the consolations
of art, all were falling away from her like a fragile mask eaten by the acid
drip of a concealed reality. The particular solidity of the city, its dead volcanic rock, its jagged fairy-tale castle transforming ancient agonies into
hard currency, dolour into dollars, all appeared adrift on shifting sands, as
the daily headlines danced before her eyes: MIDNIGHT HERALDS THE
REBIRTH OF GERMANY. LEBANON'S BLOODY "SAVIOUR" FLEES. ISRAEL'S
BLOODY MONDAY: 19 DEAD IN TEMPLE MOUNT CLASH. BUSH SAYS SANC-
TIONS WILL NOT DEFEAT IRAQ. Tremors in far-away places that seemed nevertheless to shake her hands as she moulded the day's Firth flotsam, trying
but failing to allow her to form the right shape out of an old crossbar . . .
That necessary combination of concentration and calm, replaced by vexation and wrath . . .

Naomi Potamkin arrived, a small, determined, if anxious, figure presenting herself for inspection at the door to Sophia Salvadori's Marchmont
apartment, settling down warily on the tattered brown settee opposite
Kathleen while Sophia stamped off into the kitchen to prepare filter coffee. Kathleen ventured a wary foot in the minefield by enquiring about the
"situation" in Israel. The ordinary Jew's-eye view of The Crisis, given that
Avram Blok, as usual, had refused to comment on the television scenes of
riot and mayhem in Jerusalem, grunting only: "It's the hunting season."

"We're too used to chaos," Naomi tried to explain. "What seems
abnormal in the outside world is simply a continuation for us. The

government sets up inquiry committees which count all the trees but miss the forest. Meanwhile people are rushing to hoard food because of the Gulf, everyone's arguing whether we should all be given gas masks or not. We've already got our instructions what to do in case of a chemical attack. We have to go into a room which we've sealed up with sellotape, wet a piece of cloth with baking soda and water, and lie down with the wet cloth over our face, wrapping the body in a plastic coat or sheet."

"It sounds insane. I'm sure it won't come to that," Kathleen murmured, as Sophia returned with a jug of coffee and cups. Safer to discuss the bedlam of the world than the personal tangle at hand. "But what's happening to the Palestinians while all this is going on?"

"They're under curfew, after the Temple Mount shootings. The committee of inquiry found the police who fired were provoked. We always play this game of self-assurance, convincing ourselves that everything is all right. The only blame lies with other people. The responsibility is never ours."

What responsibility could we have, for a world veering once again out of control, just as we thought the counterweights of freedom and justice were turning it on an even keel? A quick fading of short-lived illusions. Sophia poured the coffee and sat in the farthest corner of her room, while Kathleen handed Naomi a mug and settled back at the apex of their triangle, allowing a long awkward silence, into which Kathleen finally lobbed the name of Angelopoulos the Disappeared, but Naomi could provide no news.

"I passed through Geneva," she said, "and spoke to people from the Red Cross. They've been in touch with the police here and Interpol. And with the International Bureau of Missing Persons. Apparently they have fifty thousand names on their computer. And that's only those who have names, not counting the millions who drop anonymously out of the world, into black holes. There are absolutely no leads in this case. The Palestinian Red Crescent apparently did some digging but hasn't turned up anything either."

And what about the Israeli connection? "My brother, Benny, came out of the farm," Naomi said, "for the first time in two years. You don't know what that means for him. It's his hermitage, his monk's cell. Of course he owes an obligation. But what can he do? He tried to sound out friends who had friends. No result. I went to see Major Keinan, who negotiated through Angel for Benny's release. He's convinced it's a Lebanese connection. But why should it happen in this country, if he was heading back to the Middle East anyway? Wouldn't it be easier to kidnap him there?"

"Maybe they were impatient," said Sophia.

All the cyclical speculations again. All of us, Kathleen thought, groping in the fog of an experience none of us can properly imagine or grasp. Clutching the unclutchable Middle East mist. And not even TOW missiles to bargain with.

Sophia begged off further scratching at the congealing wound to return to business at the Bridge Gallery, while Kathleen took Naomi round her city. Ploughing a mundane path: the Castle, the Park, the New Town's Georgian grid of order and stability, the Royal Mile, the Lawnmarket and Canongate. Pizza restaurants and signs to Heritage Tours: RELAX IN A WHISKEY BARREL; RIDE THROUGH 300 YEARS OF SCOTTISH HISTORY. Another time perhaps. Climbing up the vennels and stairs with Royal Societies and Scientific Institutes peeling off in nooks and crannies, the walls still plastered with the posters of the thousand and one Festival nights: The Bedlam Theatre's presentation of *Antigone*, California Fault-Zone in Recent Disappearances [*sic*], Simon the Storyteller's Do-It-Yourself Theatre, Ubu, Crossed Wires, Spontaneous Combustion's Outrageous Lies, Infinite Regression and The Jive Café. You should have been here last month, Naomi, the city at its best, now it's just the hangovers. Retrieving wind in The Sweet Tooth, a small cake-and-fudge hole in the wall, over chocolate-flecked cappuccinos. Kathleen explained to Naomi the problem of Sophia, the awkwardness of that encounter.

"It's to be expected," Naomi said. "It's a standard Petros situation. The demonic saint. You either take him or leave him. I'm sure wherever he is, he'll survive. I have this stupid thought, that if he's dead, I'll know somehow. The sky will shudder, or weird voices in the night. And if he is dead, let's find out. There are too many people who're forgotten . . . But tell me about yourself, Kathleen."

What is there to tell, an onlooker . . . An arrested child making mud pies. I've been trying to make things out of nothing, to knock some sense into objects found at random. Beachcombing. It's to do with the sea and ideas, perhaps clichés of eternity. I've worked in cycles and waves. A whole year spent on pollution. The ocean versus human waste. That went down very well in Japan. Now there's the Australian proposal, to exhibit the smaller pieces March next year. The Woolloomooloo Gallery in Sydney. It's not a name one can pass by. A siren echo. That's if the world is still here.

Jam tarts and chocolate éclairs, twelve different flavours of fudge and old traditional boiled sweetmeats: Berwick cockles, soor plooms, pan drops, striped balls and humbugs. When even whisky has a heritage. There is a flow over the hills of time. Kathleen took Naomi east along the coast to Craddock, spending a pleasant afternoon in her "junkyard," among the completed works and in-progress, joining with Avram Blok as he arrived after working hours at The Retreat, coffee and small-talk. The lingering Lothian daylight, late sunsets over the glistening bay. A chilly quiet, and exchanges between Blok and Naomi in Hebrew, a guttural incomprehension for Kathleen, shut out from a kind of club reunion of members of an obscure society sharing an instant, guarded empathy.

When Naomi left, turning down the offer of a lift, to take the late bus back to Edinburgh and her hotel, Kathleen and Blok unexpectedly had a rare hysterical fugue, shouting at each other across the clutter of the living-room, the kitchen, bedroom and porch. He accused her of moving his scrapbooks to accommodate a particularly useless piece-in-progress, she accused him of trying to shut her out of vital sections of his life, treating her and his adopted environment as an unnecessary crutch, masquerading as a cripple and being hypocritically unable to face his own traumas while advising others on their own. He riposted that this was the nature and nub of psychiatry; normal people need not apply. She shouted back that he was a moral cripple if he couldn't empathise with other people. He accused her of self-deception, of pretending that her empathy could help change the unchangeable beastliness of things, particularly concerning the Middle East, Angelopoulos and Naomi. The most boringly predictable behaviour, he shouted, is the behaviour of unpredictable people. "It's biological!" he cried, dredging up old slogans; "they're driven crazy by the climate and the food! Falafel is a proven toxin, its swimming with brain-eating bacteria! Read all the relevant reports."

She stalked out of the house with the dog, despite his reluctance to take sides. The crisp night beach, the darkling waves. The glint of mysterious objects ignored in her fury. Where did all that bile come from? A dormant dissonance jerked awake by the drum beats. Feelings of impotence over the Angel. Or a projection of her irritation over Sophia's hardened heart. Violation of the Wee Three ethos, but by whom? This was, after all, par for the course of Sophia's transient amours. What about the Czech dissident who hardly had time to grow stubble, the Argentine post-modernist packed off back to his past, the Indonesian pianist en route to Carnegie Hall, the bisexual French screen star, Philippe? All the mavericks passing through her revolving doors, anything to avoid a repetition of permanence, the broken eggshells of a dead marriage. No surprise therefore to find her enraged at being left with an unwanted guilt. An emotion surplus to requirements. Why should we be drenched with the sweat of far-off battles, touched with the rot of those forsaken trenches, marching off the TV screen into our lives? The irrelevance of local hopes and fears. Political impotence. Why should it be otherwise? After all, aren't I living with Mister noblesse-non-oblige, the embodiment of escape from commitment? Or am I just enraged at my own desire to curl up in a ball and lock the whole world out?

So what's on TV tonight? Police soaps, a TV movie about a bed-wetting athlete, the Secret Life of the Washing Machine, a painful documentary about British drug addicts, an exposé of the Camorra in Naples, and the ubiquitous, impartial news: British tanks setting out for the Gulf. Why did the U.S. not warn Saddam? Gorbachev backs radical change.

Blok, mollified and having prepared tea, was pasting into his scrapbook a prize item sent by Janet from London: QUEEN MUM CORGI KILLS QUEEN'S PET DOG. *Grief Over Savaged Chipper.* Kathleen contributed her unpaid Community Charge vouchers, which he glued in by his own, next to another prize item: **Top Russian Scientists working on the Chernobyl Disaster have developed a remarkable odour destroyer — BAN IT: Will destroy ANY smells in your home within 8 HOURS. Can absorb up to ONE MILLION TIMES its own size in odour particles. Imagine your**

home always smelling fresh and clean . . .

If 'twere ever so . . . Later, in bed, he murmured to her: "D'you know, if it comes to war we'll have to close down The Retreat? Research shows ordinary neuroses and depressions miraculously clear in times of general crisis. In Israel they used to discharge most of the patients from the asylums in wartime. Their behaviour had become completely normal. Apart, of course, from the battle-shocked soldiers, who were cured by the doctors reconstructing the scenes that had traumatised them in the first place. Most of them could be returned to the front in three weeks."

"I don't want to hear any more about it," she said, turning her back to him and facing the wall, the dark shadows of her creations grinning from their shelves. But in the morning a letter arrived from Blok's rejected Homeland, from his father, Baruch, trapped in his wheelchair down on the farm with Blok's mother, Rosa, and Blok's Aunt Pashtida, a.k.a. Greta Pasternak, whose offer of a tranquil home had uprooted them from their home town of Jerusalem eight years before. Baruch Blok was so slowed down his letters had become biannual and vague, to match his son's detached and somewhat condensed bulletins ("Hi, Papa, everything's going well. Are you and Mama okay? Love, Avram."), but this was of unusual scope and candour, requiring, by demand, a full translation for Kathleen on a day when the good weather collapsed into a torrential downpour, the cloud thickening into a black pall, and massive sheets of rain slashing into the sea like a million needles punching the waves:

> Dear Avremel,
> If life is shit, why this antiseptic smell? The worst thing about old age is this dulling of all the senses except pain. Everything smells the same. Everything tastes like mush. Everybody repeats the same dull movements. There is nothing new on television. As for the radio, you might as well put a drill in your skull. Your mother is not in the best of health but has stopped complaining. I don't know if this is a good or bad sign. The one thing that keeps me alive is hate, which is a terrible thing to say, I know, but I take such pleasure in it. I am now able to hate all the neighbours without exception, now that old Menachem, the Romanian from around the corner, cashed in his chips last month. He was a mensch. The

rest are zombies. Of course you know we have millions of Russians, though we don't see that many on our patch. You're not Romanian? Piss off, kakker! We did get a few Ceauşescu orphans. More downtrodden of the earth.

Of course I hate all the politicians. Shamir, Arens, Levy, Sharon, Peres, Rabin, Peretz, Deri, all those liars, thieves and idiots. I hate the TV announcers, with their grisly smiles and feinschmecker airs, clowns posing as pundits. I hate President Bush with his greasy bonhomie. I hate Yasir Arafat with his blubbery lips and triple-faced deceit. I hate Saddam Hussein the butcher with his Hitler-Stalin eyes. I even hate Gorbachev, God help me, because he has let me down. At last, I thought, a human being! But there's no hope in power plays. All merrily leading us to perdition. I hate the Palestinians who shout for Saddam to send chemical missiles and I hate the Israelis who drove them to it and now say I told you so.

I miss you, Avremel, but I don't think you should be here. You'd become like me, a wrung-out schmutter. I don't even remember all the hopes of my youth. Old people are supposed to forget where they were two minutes ago, but to have total recall of sixty-five years before. I'm the opposite. Every little daily frustration burns itself into my being, but all the pleasant things disappear. Not that life was that pleasant, fifty years ago, as you well know. But there must have been some happiness, somewhere. What one ought to do is write it down. Whenever anything good happens to you, jump to pen and ink immediately. Don't let it pass unrecorded.

My eyesight has been through the usual wringer, but I can still read, thank God. I have been rereading Dostoevsky. I think he understood the whole thing. Where there is no moral order everything falls apart. Not, God forbid, religion. That is a horror. But an awareness of an obligation.

Preach preach feinschmecker. Maybe the chickens will listen. A moment of bright enlightenment before their heads are chopped off. That's I suppose all we can hope for. But you have to find your own way. Aunt Pashtida has gone out and purchased an entire chemical-warfare defence kit. Gas mask, antidote, protective suit with gloves and boots. I can see her now through the window, in the asparagus patch. She looks like an astronaut on the Moon. Ah, if only I had my little squirter of DDT! Small pleasures, Avremel, small pleasures. Keep your spirits up. Regards to your Scottish amorata, whom I have never seen. Somebody has to keep you sane.

Bring her here when this all blows over, if it ever does.
Servus,
Your vegetating progenitor,
Baruch

Mind the Gulf! No, nothing seems to change. Convoys of trucks and transport planes go east, bearing gifts of mutilation and murder. Hundreds of thousands of horny G.I.s being poured into a dry hourglass with little prospect of Retching and Rutting. The Tommies hanging on their tales. Egyptians, Syrians and Saudis. Even Gadaffi has joined the anti-Iraq club. My sympathies are strongly with the loser, no matter how brutal he might be. But even if I wished to put up a poster of Saddam Hussein outside my window, where would I find one? I have often wondered about that. Those masses of deluded Palestinians who appear in spontaneous combustion on the streets of the occupied West Bank waving thousands of colour blow-ups of the Great Arab Saviour (henceforth known as The GAS) — where do they get them? Some enterprising photo-laboratory is on the ball, ready with contacts of the world's most vicious bastards: Saddam, al-Asad, Bush, Thatcher, Charles Manson, Kim Il-sung, Pinochet. And what about those millions of Ceausescu posters going cheap? The million little busts of Nicolae and Joe Stalin . . . There should be an opening for Danny Hohenlohe, somewhere here . . .

As Margaret Hilda Thatcher used to say: Suumthing muuust be done . . . McTeague, not content with his original unpardonable perfidy, has now unleashed his Exocet missile against me, the remaindering of *City of Shmucks*. Vast piles of the unsold opus, from the warehouse womb untimely pluck'd, have begun appearing in the second-hand bookstores. And even there they remain *in situ*, untouch'd by human hands. Idlers browse, picking up *The Colic Book of British Wild Pansies*, or Szytkieker's *Lives of the Proudhonist Poets*, or Rimmer's *Anal Hollywood*, or *The 25th World Book of Moths*, but Hohenlohe's pride and joy remains static, even at a grisly ninety-nine pee. The final ignominy from my enemy, valued at not even one pound sterling. The man has signed his own death warrant.

On the night of the reunification of Germany I locked myself at "home" at la maison Spetsotakis with a takeaway shish, banging my old Toshiba monochrome television to try to kick some sense into it. Stubbornly it showed scenes of cheering crowds, fireworks, East German Vopos doing the Last Goosestep and the Deutsche president, Richard von Weiscracker, mouthing an unheard speech while a "liberty bell" pealed across wall-less Berlin. All the icons of my childhood were being destroyed, the blitzed buildings, Checkpoint Charlie, Spandau had been bulldozed into the ground long ago and Rudolf Hess mysteriously self-hanged to protect the British Royal Family. My black-and-white image yawed and twisted, totally unable to cope. I switched it off, waiting for the anal thumping to die away starboard and for the nightchat with Nicolae and Elena, but no dice. Even my best demons desert me. No news from ex-Trot Martha, out there somewhere in the Mesopotamian desert, knitting woolly hats for Ba'athi commissars, singing John Lennon toons. Give peas a chance! My fridge freezer is empty. The days ooze past leaving their muggy scum on the soul. Oh, to be a hostage in Baghdad! "Saddam Agrees to Free Selected Britons." Will he really dispose of the dross? "Arabs Driven to Brotherly Hate." I am wrapped in my metaphorical *keffiyah*. The private life of Fidel Castro has been finally revealed. It appears he has a secret wife and five children, four yachts, thirty-two houses and nine thousand eight hundred bodyguards, with a hundred and twenty-two divers who comb the sea-bed in search of underwater mines when he goes out to swim.

Venceremos, compañero! One should not relax one's guard for an instant. But I have been offered gainful employment, inevitably through Mama's Wembley mafia, as a cog in the machine of Edelweiss Travel, a bucketshop run by one of her cronies in West Hampstead, specialising in cheap safaris to Zion. A certain skill in computer searching, ticketing, telephone *spiel* and *sitzfleisch* is required, but the rent will be paid. There is reality, not only hope, in life. And in the next chair, lo, a dusky-skinned maiden, Narindra, swivels, exercising her shapely behind. Ahhh! Motive, opportunity and incentive. I cease wandering the streets, except on weekends, spending the rest of my time dispatching punters to their tatty dreams around the world. Benidorm, Saronic Greek Islands, Barcelona, Bilbao, Bangkok, Tel Aviv, Hanukkah with Your Family, North America

Book Now, Winter Canary Sunshine, Hotel Vienna, Florida Sonesta Key Biscayne, Aloha Málaga, Low-Cost Scheduled Flights, Sky Bargains, Late Availability, Great Escapes, Trading Places, One Way to Kathmandu: Best Quotes.

Whibble whibble whibble. Even I am tempted. Flights to Freedom. Italy, Greece, any Mediterranean laxity, could beckon. Or even a return visit to Manhattan, the nostalgia of freezing winters warmed by mounds of rejection letters wrapped round the tush. The H & H Bagel Shop, The Burger Joint, the barking man, the park squirrels, the ice on The Pond. Scraping the sky and the gutter at one and the same time. Or the exotic East? But I still have a mission to fulfil, in the belly of the bistro. The Holy Task that cannot be detoured.

Narindra, whose trusting eyes and smile should have alerted me from the start, turns out to be a Seventh-Day Adventist. She spends her Saturdays wandering about Cricklewood with a West Indian friend, Susha, ringing innocent people's doorbells and inviting them to converse about Jesus. Rashly I enquired about the articles of the Faith one lunchtime, to try and get closer to the Land of Promise, but no transportation occurred. It appears Jesus was perfect and undefiled by sin. He is the Very God, who has existed with the Father for all eternity. This seemed to present certain biological problems, but what is biology to the Believer? Jesus was "the Lamb without blemish or spot." Unsullied by corruption, he did not possess the "passions of our human, fallen natures." "Are you free Saturday night?" I finally asked her, but she had a prior booking for Bible class.

I wanted her body, but she had no interest even in my soul. Not even a shugel towards the Bible readings. There was a pragmatic Asian caution there, which made her give up on me from the start. I would have to find my own path to salvation.

By November, my remainder piles had gone, mysteriously vanished in the night. One day they were all over the Bargain Bookstores, the next not even a wisp of a jacket cover, not a page, dot or smudge. Unmarked vans must have come, in the small hours, and carted them all off to their final destination, the burning and pulping mills, where immense machines scooped them up and crushed them into compressed sludge, pulverising the imagination and destroying one's dreams. I could feel the machines, straining and squeezing, their hydraulic pumps wheezing and panting to reduce my immortal soul into the tiniest possible scrap of drek, then rinse it with powerful hoses down the gutters of the Brentford Industrial Estate. A stain that only blood can wipe out.

I decided to kill McTeague over Christmas. This would satisfy the poetic furies and provide enough time to plan the act properly and ponder all its conundrums. The mode of despatch: knife, bullet, poison, garotte, other? The place of execution: office, home or transit? The mode of escape, alibi, security, cover. The apotheosis at the point of delivery: the victim's obligatory realisation, the frisson of the moment of the revenge. For the love of God, Montresor! That luscious tang of the Amontillado . . . but who has time for bricks and mortar any more?

Murder is a serious business. At last I am brought face to face with this fact. I realised that all along, since Drem, I had been daydreaming, toying with an aesthetic concept. No more. Now it's the new Hi-tech Hohenlohe, with Smart Weapons and Battle-Zone Capabilities, intent on maximising Humint and Sigint, and scorning Collateral Damage. Action Man! It's like a revelation from the Shekhinah, a bolt of lightning from the grey. The world has suddenly become real, not itself a creature of my phantasies and fears. I know the moment the revelation occurred. I was going to pick up the phone, to tell Avram Blok or Andrew Mackenzie that I had finally decided to kill McTeague for real. But I put the receiver down, as I realised that in fact that was what I was going to do. The act itself, in all its horrible materiality, the *Ding am Zich*, with no cancellation clause, no indemnity, double or quadruple, absolutely no turning back.

Now I see the world with fresh eyes. The girls are suddenly prettier, the men less morose, objects taking on a new shine, colours less shabby, even the Tube appears less drab, though this may be the absence of American tourists, holed up at home at the first whiff of war. The winter delayed, a muggy autumn lingering, falling leaves in all the parks. Swans and ducks cluck and young lovers hold hands without reducing me to mute despair. I have begun to smile on people in the street, a terrible rictus, as it seems to create a wide swathe around me. "Nice day. Looks like rain." There is no better way of repelling the English than addressing them without apparent reason. But now and again some jaunty soul nods back.

Hands across the ocean. Even the politicians appear to have awoken. Ex-ministers sinking their false teeth into the Prime Minister's ankles, taking a taste of human flesh.

The luxury of planning. Firearms a problem from the start. This is not America. One cannot just go into a shop in Camden Town, heft an M57 automatic carbine with triple-revolving-barrel capacity and take it away for ten days' free trial without obligation. I recall there used to be two gunshops on the Fulham Palace Road, opposite an underwater-equipment store, so that if one wished to murder Jacques Cousteau, that was the place to go. But that would be too conspicuous. This was one matter where my mother's octopoid connections would be no use at all. "A gun, Danny? Who are you going to kill? I know a man in Hendon who can do it for you less than half-price, you won't have to lift a finger." Strike One. The Blade . . . To confront one's squeamishness. The good schochet can kill a bull with one broad cut. The lost traditions of one's ancestors. Today the goyim kill the cows with an electric gun. How many abattoir workers do I know? A dead end. But electric shock, a definite contender. À la John Dickson Carr, a toaster dropped in the bath? No marks, no weapon. The perfect murder. This would require coordination, penetration. McTeague would have to be alone, his family lured away by mysterious tickets to an Andrew Lloyd Webber show, or some such venue he himself would shun. A tricky business. Hohenlohe picks the lock softly. Creeps up the stairs, hugging his Morphy-Richards. But what if the victim prefers a shower? Is there an electric socket within reach?

Too many imponderables. The easy option is always the easy option. A blunt instrument in a dark alleyway. The wallet snatched, a mugging gone wrong. Go look for rejected authors. But how to let the man know? A thud, a spark, and then nothing. Not even the first base of vengeance. Justice must be not only done, but realised . . .

Researching the victim. Fact one. I knew McTeague's address, 11 Clerihew Gardens, a fashionable backwater of Notting Hill Gate. A cul-de-sac, off one of the crescents, beyond earplug range of reggae soirées. The street too isolated to provide much scope for an aspiring murderer to case the joint. Scrub the dingy raincoat with the bulbous false nose and grey beard. But the answer lay in an old G.K. Chesterton story, an elegant

Father Brown: The postman. The invisible man. *He even carries a large bag where a small corpse can be stowed quite easily*, though McTeague is rather larger than me, physically, and postmen nowadays often push a little tricycle, with hardly enough room for a dead cat.

So, a triple delivery for Clerihew Gardens. The postman's uniform easily hired from the Transcosmic Props warehouse in Isleworth, in the name of Winston Smith, of the Boots and Britches Repertory Theatre of Cheam, calling swathed in bandages like the invisible man. I had to put down a deposit of twenty-five cash, as the man at the warehouse didn't like my looks and was suspicious of my Greek accent, but I thought it adequately covered my tracks. Next to stock up on envelopes and parcels. This too was a snip, if time-consuming, gathering bills and unsolicited mail from the Spetsotakis hallway and from my mother's Wembley slush-pile. It's amazing how much rubbish circulates the globe. Offers of magic crystals, free washing powder, Your Guide to Good-Looking Hair, Outsize Leisurewear Summer Catalogue, Find Your Own Tax Haven, The World Book of Hohenlohes (only $15.95!), Kentucky Rum Cake Specials, Cancer, Cholera, Typhoid and Save the Whale, Greenpeace, Bluepeace and Yellowpeace, Readers International, the Folio Society, Midget Lingerie, Men of Achievement, the Institute for the Blind, Deaf and Dumb, Bone China and the endless Free Gifts: You Have Won £20,000! Just Scratch This Number! Congratulations — You Have Won a Volvo Pantechnicon Truck or an Electra Speed Motor Boat or a Pair of Pearl Earrings! Phone This Number Now! Just peel or cut off the names and heft round to the doorflaps of Notting Hill in Hohenlohe's invisible sack.

By mid-November I had Clerihew Gardens well cased, a good idea who lived where, the schedule of the two McTeague weens and the forbidding au pair who whisked them off to Gradgrind House and back. She was a tall, swarthy Yugoslavian tottie, with a great shaggy brown mane. The children I already knew were called Mick and Geegee, aged four and six, a slight complication, ditto the spouse, Gemma, whom I had met in my only visit to the house, when I was McTeague's new discovery, an author bright-eyed and bushy-tailed, clinking the champagne at Sunday brunch, unaware that the pellet with the poison was in the vessel with the pestle, or even the chalice from the palace. She was a bright, hearty girl with a loud laugh who presented an arts show on Weekend Television. Several minor celebrities were present, a trio of feminist writers, a computer whiz-kid who had written a "graphic novel," a stereotyped drunken publisher, and Madam McTeague's producer, an ageing lady with buck teeth who never ceased to remind everyone she had been present when Jean-Paul Sartre stirred the punch bowl with his penis in Paris in 1965. I beamed on this urbane convocation. They beamed back at me. I quaffed the champagne. One has to harden one's heart. One cannot consider innocent bystanders. One either does the right thing or not.

Developments elsewhere distinctly encouraging. Mrs Thatcher's day has finally come. The dead sheep, her former Foreign Secretary, rose to savage her on the Floor of the House. The Floor of the House. It suggests sawdust, broken glass, blood, vomit. The headlines egg on to Götterdämmerung: CONSERVATIVES REEL AT DEVASTATING BLOW. THATCHER FACES FIGHT FOR LIFE. And meanwhile liberal columnists rage on in their futility against the MONSTROUS ANGER OF THE GUNS:

> Let us strip off the second-rate hypocrisy of our prattling rulers. A proper cynicism insists that a decent killing war needs the Bible or its moral equivalent as a sauce to its slaughter . . . We can't prophesy the precise form of a Gulf War beyond observing that it doesn't have to be long to be bloody. Modern conventional war prides itself upon the harm and hurt it does. *Schreklichkeit*, the concept of punitive, exemplary brutality, is no longer something you do *after* the fight. The cutting edge in downtown Baghdad will be *Schreklichkeit* enough . . .

Absolutely. And in Clerihew Gardens too, *Gott dank*. All the omens are positive. The world will be plunged into mayhem, and while attention is turned to the Orient, I will creep up on my prey. In the dead eye of the storm I will wreak my destruction and fade away into safety, escape provided by Edelweiss Travel. It's all coming together. Nothing can fail. The perfect crime. Like *Die Verloren*, I will be a small flurry in the midst of the tempest of doom. I will soon be able to send back the postman's costume. Done with.

The bell is tolling, for all tyrants. Mrs Thatcher deposed, dragged out of Number Ten Downing Street by her ankles, grabbing on to the iron railings in vain. With a crunching, clattering sound they scrape along the asphalt. Her skin scuffed, her clothes torn. In confirmation of dreams, her effigy hangs from gibbets, her tearful face glistening for the last time upon the pane of the Black Maria . . . A new colourless, odourless man in a grey suit and tie leads the somnabulant nation now, harf'league, harf'league, harf'league onwards, towards our parallel rendezvous with destiny and the inexorable consummation of our most heartfelt dreams . . .

Night, Paris and the moon. Naomi walks along the parapet of the river, watching the excursion boats coasting by with their illuminated crowds. The Muzak's thump. The guide's nasal grind. Intemperance of things past: LA POLITIQUE FLUVIAL! ARRÊTEZ LE GÉNOCIDE DE LA BATTELERIE! all the echoes and shadows of a festive blur. Embers of fireworks and old sepia photographs celebrating a bygone age. The Quai du Grand Augustins and the Pont Neuf. A personal shadow by her side. Like a parodic echo of *Casablanca:* We'll always have Paris. The laughing eyes over the great Greek moustache. Come on, Angel, flap your wings. But the wind that blows is a chill scout of winter, flapping old newspapers around one's knees. The cars dip into the subterranean way. One turns back, into the narrow streets of the Left Bank, the patisseries, book and souvenir shops, to the rue Serpente and the dependable presence of Ali Amar, chopping onions for a spaghetti sauce under an unsettling poster of three rats splitting their sides over a copy of Camus's *La Peste.*

"The city never changes, Ali."

"It gets sadder and dirtier. The pickpockets in the Métro get bolder. The policemen shoot each other by mistake instead of the public. Unemployment rises. Beggars increase. No one would save Boudou from drowning nowadays. We become more and more like Algiers. Reimporting the colonial modes. Fascism is fashionable again. Not to speak of the French Role in the World."

"They're not going to go to war, Ali; it's absurd."

"It's absurd, that's why it's going to happen. We are too tired of bourgeois normality."

"Can I do something?"

"Open this can of tomatoes."

Chopping mushrooms, crushing garlic. A kitchen table, pots, pans, spoons. The curling smells from the electric cooker. An uncorked bottle of red wine. The after-whiff of Edinburgh failure, no keys found to open the locks . . . Standing on the empty weed-grown tarmac of the abandoned Lothian airfield, with Kathleen, Avram Blok and Andrew Mackenzie, his usual briskness slackened by the somber thoughts behind his rumpled face: "I feel responsible, Naomi. But what can I do? After all, he came this way just to see me. It's the last place you could imagine anything like this happening. A drunken squabble, a trace of wife-beating in the dark, a spot of marijuana in the bushes, that's about it. The nearest police station is twenty miles away." A twilight dinner at The Retreat, Rhona and Andrew Mackenzie alone now in their twelve-room mansion, expecting no new clients till the New Year. Toasting the sweet end of the Thatcher era. "Some people really ought to disappear." A muted and silent celebration in the long northern dusk. Walking with Kathleen and Blok on the beach, with the big, bounding black dog. The grey waves, the smooth rocks, the shingle. Incongruous gossip with Avram Blok in Hebrew. "My father wrote me again about the great gas-mask mania. He says he'll put one on only after he's dead."

"That may well be the only solution."

For all of us, our little ghosts floating up to heaven in our Government Protection Suits. ABC, Atomic, Bacteriological, Chemical. One does not wish to think of D through Z . . .

"They want me to go to the Gulf, the Agency," said Ali. "A series of reports on the anxieties and hopes for the future of Saudi and the Emirates. What could be the hopes for the future of a religious dynasty? It can only be for more of the same. What can I do? I'll add my voice to the chaos. I think I will also go to Jordan, maybe Israel. Egypt I don't know if I can bear. There is always the pain of memories everyone else has already forgotten. You could show me round the promised land."

"It's not at its best now. Though when is it? We can try and dig out its better side."

"They are all foreign countries to me now, Naomi. The cries, the rage of desperate people. I've been away so long. Sitting in my office, writing analyses, making short and sharp visits, like commando raids behind enemy lines. But now all my allegiances have been scrambled. Suddenly I'm behind enemy lines here, in Paris. I find myself sympathising with all those forces I attacked for so long: nationalism, emotionalism, gut feelings . . . An attack of ethnic bile . . ."

"It always passes, Ali. And what about Lebanon? Will you go to Beirut?"

"Can you believe it, the rich Arabs are moving their money back there! It's so crazy, Beirut is considered the safest place now. These sudden changes make my head swirl. How do you feel, as an Israeli, with Syria on your side?"

"I haven't had sides for a long time, Ali, and after Petros that's wiped out of me completely. Who's your enemy, and who's your friend? It's a mess. The people we supported are clamouring for our death. I suppose it shouldn't be surprising. Not much refuge in the Brotherhood of Man, or even Sisterhood. We believed in a single world and find it fragmenting back into the tiniest slivers and sects."

"It was always like that but we had our delusions. In Egypt we had at least five different communist factions. We had Mishmish, we had Nasham, we had Iskra and we had al-Raya — The Flag — which was the Communist Party of Egypt, and later the United Communist Party of Egypt, another splinter, all proclaiming unity. But in prison I lost my passion for rhetoric. You are reduced to your inner self, your nuclear core. All energy has to come from within. As a party, we committed suicide. But the slogans seem to have their own life, they leap from body to body like ghosts. Unity, Socialism, the Arab Masses. The words mutate, from purity to pollution in the mouth of someone like Saddam Hussein. Perhaps it's our stupid belief in The Word. The legacy of Koran and Bible. We lost our faith in man as a living organism with urges and desires. And we're still looking for ideologies to fill the vacuum of so many slaughtered Gods."

Ali reduces the heat to a simmer. The aromatic brown sauce bubbles under the pan cover. Naomi pours the wine. "So what do you see in your crystal ball, brother?"

"I see death and destruction, and savagery, and plague, and a new cycle of despair. Not much hope for our own prisoners of war." He looks at her across the table. The grey-haired, dark, heavily lined face against the freckled earnestness of her gaze. The bubbling sauce and the cartoon chimes of a police car outside trying to wail its way through blocked traffic. The invincible farce against the immovable abject. Hope and the persistence of memory . . .

"All right," he said, "I will go to Lebanon. But don't expect anything. He may well not be there, and even if he is, he might be ten feet away from me, on the other side of a wall, and I'll never know. I'll be completely helpless. But I'll talk to people, I'll see if anyone can shine a light."

The sun filtering through the glass panels of Chartres. The huge rising pillars, the carved-stone Calvary. The Last Judgement, the Nazarene showing his wounds. Triumph over Death. Yes, but he didn't publish much. Neither did you, Petros, leaving us an oral concoction of legends and shreds, loud days and shivering nights. Take it or leave it. The rushed pilgrimmage to the rue Voltaire, the jampots of Chinon, the whispered words of Jeanne d'Arc. What were the words that made the King of France so joyous? "I'll suck your cock later," the Angel had suggested. The Maid of Orléans. It couldn't last. Up in smoke she went, like everyone else who thought they had the answer. Spare me the martyrdom, and let me just have those few moments of tranquillity to cultivate my own garden. But here was a man who loved to make enemies, who was happiest when besieged on all sides. There is a price to pay. But can there be a ransom, by the counterweight of love, the stubbornness of recollection? Or is that reserved for the abstract? Is there a secular redemption? And how long can it last? An hour? A year?

Come on, Angel, flap your wings. If you could fly off into thin air from an airfield in Scotland . . . But still no message from beyond. The pleasure boats drifting by on the Seine. The couples hugging and running over the bridges, scanning the menus by the doors of Vietnamese restaurants. The steep steps down from the fruit market. The poster-plastered walls with "Défence d'afficher." The wailing police cars, nudging vainly at gangs of youths whooping and leaping down the street. The shuffling black man cocooned in a dozen tattered coats with his twenty shopping bags. The tuxedo classes heading for a discreet watering-hole. Illegal substances furtively exchanged on corners. The thump of a Senegalese band.

Clink of coffee cups and beer glasses. Earnest flux of lips and touching fingers. Unfolded newspapers and cigarette smoke. *Tout le monde.* It ebbs, flows, rushes. A trio of arm-linked adolescent girls, tripping along, defying the universe. The pitter-patter of dancing feet, the melancholy strains of exile and home.

If you have a home to go to. Come on, Angel, flap your wings. No, one does not hear the beat of the wings of history, only the timid plop of the aircraft warning lights, turning on the Fasten Seat Belt sign. Naomi returning to base without clues. To the nub of her vulnerability, her parents cocooned in their disillusionment, the reclusive brother, the non-husband still knocking at the door, the ordinary pain of her handicapped charges. ABC. A deep pang of desire for the mundane, as her baggage and person were checked for explosives. The insistent questioning of security: "Did anyone give you anything to take back to Israel?"

"Nothing at all."

Ear plugs, face mask to cut out the in-flight entertainment. Enough the thunder of the machine.

The tarmac at home full of soldiers. Rain drizzling on the barrels of guns.

FOURTEEN

Come on, Angel, Flap Your Wings...

And first God created Satan, out of a smokeless fire. Then God made man from a dry clay, from a black moulded loam. And God commanded the Angels to bow down before his creation. But Satan did not bow, and was cursed by God, who then reprieved him till the Day of Resurrection. Lord, said Satan, since you have led me astray, I shall seduce mankind, excepting only those who serve you faithfully. God replied: That is the right course for me. You shall have no power over my servants, except the sinners who follow you, who are destined for the seven gates of Hell. But the righteous shall dwell among gardens and fountains, which they will enter in peace and safety. I shall remove all hatred from their hearts, and they will recline on couches, as a band of brothers. They shall not be wearied by toil, nor shall they ever leave Paradise. (after Koran, sura 15:32)

But it is very difficult to do the right thing.

❖

The Caliph rode to the edge of the desert, dismounted his mule, paid off his groom with a bag of gold dinars and walked alone into the dunes. The sun was rising ahead, out of the sands, a furious giant, glowing red, then orange, then searing yellow, a naked flame, scorching his bare head and skin. The sand burned his feet like live coals. The sky was a canopy of blue steel. There was no breath of wind. No sign of life. This was the anvil upon which the Creator tempered the earth to his will. The Caliph, dressed only in a peasant's loose shirt, walked until scales of skin peeled off his feet, arms and face, until his brain felt as if it were boiling and bubbling in his skull. His feet left bloody prints in the sand, which were swallowed up by the inexorable drift of the grains. He felt that if he stood still, the desert would flow about him, climbing up his ankles, calves and torso, covering his shoulders, neck and head, burying him in eternity. And he understood the terror and obsessive drive of the Pharaohs to build fortresses of stone about their bodies, to ensure that the Creator did not rob them of their passage to power in the next world. For they were at heart rebels against fate.

But he had tried to do the Lord's bidding, to unlock the chains of transgression and wipe out the dirty smudges made by Man on the pristine pages of the Message. To cleanse all the moral pollution. To impose the correct patterns of behaviour, label the Unbelievers clearly, demolish all the Temples of Moloch and start with a new clean slate. But the sands, drifting and flowing back over all . . . He looked up straight into the sun, but it merely stared back at him with its blinding indifference.

"Open thy gate, O Lord!"

No answer. And there should be a new flood, a fire, to rage across the continents, consuming all the waste, scourging the cities and the fields, whitening the bones of an unworthy generation, to leave the seedbed clean for a new bud, after the Day of Judgement which would sort the wheat from the chaff. Burn it all! Burn even Your Own Book, O Lord, strip it ready for the New Word . . .

"I am listening, O Lord!" No answer. But the Caliph kept walking, growing younger and younger as he shed his skin and blood, the years stripping away from him like layers of an onion, leaving a lean, youthful core, as he felt the rays of the sun burning away his excesses, moulding a fresh, daring vigour, leaving his old shrivelled spirit crumbling to dust in his wake . . .

"Give me a sign!"

No answer, but a far chorus of whispers and groans . . .

And yet more of memory's jagged edges, clouds of Angel dust, filling the throat: There we are, the camp's defenders, still running from sandbag to sandbag, except that now we're joined by the tiny bouncing box of Jody Steele, immortalizing us on camera. Jumping Jody Steele of the London *Guardian*, a face from the past, from the "good old days." The first journalist to breach the camp's blockade, she managed to get in during one of the brief cease-fires that allowed some women through the lines, covered up and suitably veiled. The Amal militiamen wouldn't touch them, their one act of mercy towards us . . .

"Hi there, Angel, long time no see." And the obligatory comradely embraces with almost everyone she knew from before, Kamal, Nasir, Tewfiq, but not Nabil, our first internecine victim. The Fatah commanders, convinced I would be the next target, had assigned me bodyguards, three teenagers with Kalashnikovs, who stuck to my heels like glue, stood by in the operating theatre, masked and sterilised, and even followed me into my tiny night room, disrupting any plans I might have had to celebrate with Jody in style.

"So how's the outside world, Little Ironclad?" Meaning West Beirut, the other side of the sandbags. "Imagine," she said, "the Librairie Antoine is still open. There are fifteen cafés operating in Hamra. People are surfing off Ras Beirut."

"Life goes on."

She handed me the flask of holy water smuggled through in her black robe. My first tipple for two months. "Aaaahhh!"

"You're going to make it, Angel." Our ordeal, apparently, was drawing to a close. President Hafez al-Asad of Syria owed a favour to the Iranian *mullahs*, who were currying favour with the West for a change, particularly with La Belle France, which was having a warm proprietal nostalgic buzz over Lebanon. Our siege was now an embarrassment to Uncle Hafez, furious that we had lasted so long. Jody claimed he had said in person: "Who is this so-called Doctor Angelopoulos? I want his head in a bag." But who am I to play any such role in world affairs? I who only cut and stitch, and scoop up ascaris worms?

Still, we drank a toast. "To Uncles Hafez and Rafsanjani and Mitterrand. Blessed are the peacemakers."

The bombardment resumed immediately. Tewfiq stuck his neck in the Cabinet and slammed down panting between us. Jody had recognised me instantly by my moustache, but it had taken her a while to connect the emaciated gunman beside me with the pudgy scribe of the Lebanese News Agency. "This is the worse it's ever been," he said. "It looks like the big push. Kamal says he's expecting a ground assault."

"It's only a cease-fire," I told him lightly, taking another swig. "Tell everybody to keep down in the cellars and not to get too excited. I don't want any work tonight." But ten minutes later they were bringing the first in. Mrs Hodeida, who had already lost two sons on the barricades and was hurrying to the clinic to get some ointment for a bad rash suffered by her daughter's baby. She survived so long she thought she bore a charmed life. We are always amazed, for that split second, to discover the error of our infallibility, that our skin and flesh, too, can be shattered. Shrapnel ripped her abdomen. Laparotomies, they never cease. This one is bad. Too much tissue pulped. In a proper triage she would be discarded. But I am operating against all rules. No strangers come before me now. Everyone under my knife is a friend. Every face that lies glazed or torn before me is familiar, I know every line and wrinkle, every stubbled chin and shock of hair. It can't go on much longer. I pass the flask to Benny P. This green-eyed Israeli who fell on us from the sky now as gaunt and haggard as any bastard refugee. People have long forgotten his origins, and holler and rail away at him in Arabic, forgetting he's never managed to learn more than a few key words and phrases. But in Jaffa Camp one needs no other language than Jaffa-speak, the jargon of the bombed. "I want to do an interview with you," Jody said to him. "What is it like to be a prisoner of war in this situation?" But he looked at her blankly, his status forgotten.

Suction. Aspirate. Suture. They keep flooding in. Ali B., minus his left ear. Majid and Abdelatif al-Saleh, inseparable brothers, hit by shrapnel carrying ammunition — leg and arm injuries, one amputation below the elbow. Young Jamil the Crooner, with his melancholy songs, cut open by a mortar shell, colostomy. Javed the Persian, Foxy Marwan and Tiny Rada, the scavengers, aged seven and nine, killed outright, probably by a 105. Radwan al-G., who survived everything from the 1936 rebellion onwards, heart attack at the age of seventy-four. Fifteen assorted flesh wounds from ricochets and fragments. Hamid Abul Jamal loses his right eye. Jody helps wash down the blood-soaked table. During the lesser operations she takes a few pictures. They will never make the cover of *Newsweek*. We are definitely the wrong heroes in the wrong place.

The morning dawns not to any glow of light, but to an uncanny hush. One moment our eardrums are vibrating with the usual incoming ruin, the next they're suddenly straining at the leash with disbelief and anticipation. Waiting for the amputee's other shoe to drop. We've been through this before. We are bombed; therefore, we exist. But the silence is drawn out, like a long elastic band. And then a faint rumble that we can't at first identify till Tewfiq whispers: "Trucks." We look at each other. "The ground assault." The long awaited, ever dreaded. Bobbing and weaving our way out of the clinic basement, through the tangled wreckage and rubble, Commander Bashir running to greet us from the front, fifty yards away, shouting the impossible news: "Red Cross flags!"

Everywhere around us, heads popping out of holes in the ground, as we no longer have houses, doors, windows, just flakes of concrete gnarled with girders, pockmarked with perforations. And out of each perforation, a human face, like flowers poking from ash. Gathering gingerly as Kamal's crackling radio confirms the miracle. It is daylight, we can see the sky, a deep blue flecked with hanging white feathers. The kiss of a breeze. The tall punctured buildings of the Amal outposts looming with dormant snipers. The checkpost through which the cease-fire women brought food, medical supplies, Angel-juice, and often ammunition, is open, the first truck nosing through. The white flag with its welcome red smudge. A recognisable friendly, if wary, face poking out of the open door window. Butrus Badawi, of the Lebanese Red Crescent. He looks into my face, blinking. "Angel?" We fall into each other's arms. That special grating of stubble on stubble. He looks enormously fat to me, bloated, but it is probably just the average weight of a normally fed person. Jody clicking away at us, as at a wedding. A battered car drawing up, a red Mercedes, with a splintered sellotaped windscreen and an attached white rag. Three burly men climbing out, in camouflage uniforms, hefting camera and recording equipment. The children of the camp swarm round them, the adults rushing forward to unload the truck. At the checkpoint several armed militiamen dawdling. The usual teenage boys — the Enemy that had decimated, killed and crippled us for six months. They wave at us, shouting as if we were long-lost comrades who'd got separated by mistake in some forgotten skirmish. Nobody waves back.

The camera crew move about the rubble, searching for dramatic angles, filming the smiling gaunt faces. I face the lens with a wide, stupid grin, catching a glimpse of my reflection — a strange, skeletal monster with hair sprouting from every orifice. I begin to make speeches, appeals. I address the world, on prime-time television, with the buzz of death all around me, surrounded by men, women and children on makeshift crutches, trying to figure out what's up. I clutch the TV newsman by the arm, drag him round the sights of my Lilliputian kingdom, anxious that the Gullivers do not escape unscarred. We are videoed; therefore, we exist. I am selling them a scoop, human interest, a people risen against adversity. The wretched of the earth; send packages, money, guns, diplomats, statesmen. I am hanging out a sign: Special Report, from Our Correspondent on the Front Line. I introduce them to the characters of The Story: Bashir the new Fatah commander, Kamal, Radwan, my personnel — Amina, Nadia, Kurt, Anneka, Benjamin. The camera pans over him, another Palestinian peasant. Mad Latif attaches himself to the soundman. Umm Mahmud totters up, hogging the microphone, berating Field Marshal "Ukhinlek." Like the Pied Piper, I lead a ragged band of lunatics through the twisted ruins down into my basement theatre. The beds of the wounded, the makeshift operating facilities. I see it through their eyes, a pathetic travesty. So what was wrong with Bronx General?

Is that you, Caroline, in the shadows? I think this cell has done for my eyes. The blindfold hours have made me familiar with every dot and scratch of my floaters: The whorls and dashes, the giant spider, the Mexican jumping-bean in the left corner, the wriggling worm in the right. All moving over the eyeball like ocean-going liners . . . Manhattan days . . . The brownstone house, the bed, the giant Hound . . . New Hampshire snows and Desirée . . . What could I do, Caroline? The restless eye, the roving hand . . . Reduced now to the ultimate inertia, the anonymous jailers, never mind their dropped "Bleasures." So what if I am "home"? It might as well be the moon. That straight line, that one-tone bleep on the monitor. All the support systems switched off, except that which functions from inside . . .

All our sadnesses, Caroline, Naomi, Sophia. I'd give my teeth to weep at inadequate fulfilments, even at lost causes. The ebb and flow of life.

The big steel door of my dungeon cell is creaking open. The scuff of boots, the smell of perspiration, unlaundered fatigues. My eyelids close reflexively for the blindfold. It does not come. I lift my lids, and turn my head, and gaze, pricking my ears . . .

The dunes are alive with the sound of ordnance. Metal centipedes marching into nowhere. The tanks! The guns! The multiple-rocket launchers (ASTROS IISS-30 thru 60)! Chieftains! Challengers! M1A1! State-of-the-Art ammo: The CBUs, the Guava Bomblets, the SUU-7s, BLU-26Bs, M-42s, 3s, 6s, the MK-20 Rockeyes, M-117 Destructors, M-509-A-1s, the MK-7 Free-Fall Dispenser! Enough to blast the cockles of your heart. And above the column the tank-busting helicopters (AH-1 Cobra, AH-64 Apache) drone, their protruding bombs (TOW-II and Hellfire Missiles) painted with shark's teeth and Mickey Mouse eyes.

The dust is alive with the jingle-jangle morning of Desert Shield Radio (105-107 FM): "Bringin' you the best beat in the heat, the best bands in the sands. Do you know what to do if you're taken prisoner? Waal, its best to think of that now before it's too late to do anything about it. So let's jive with Jumpin' Jay and the Jailers to ululate away them stea-eamin' ulu blues . . ."

Upon a scruffy outcrop of scrub, two groups watch the column churning north. A group of dapper Bedouins, in white robes and red-chequered *keffiyahs*, eyeing the vehicles with a very personal interest, since each has shares in the relevant manufacturers, General Dynamics, General Motors, Rockwell International, Chrysler, Vickers, Svenska Flygmotor, Fabrique Nationale. The other a group of journalists, corralled by an anxious trio of flat-topped U.S. Army officers in neatly pressed camouflage uniforms three sizes too large, with their names inscribed in huge letters on their shirt pockets: Diesenbacker, Preobrazensky, Lowell. The dozen scribes straining at the leash, panting and retching, pressing inch by inch down the outcrop, while one camera crew, sprawled on the ground, struggles to frame the receding clouds of dust through the legs of an incontinent camel. A pungent green liquid trickles and gathers down the beast's matted stomach.

The sun battering down on a blazing winter day, forty-one degrees and no shade. Sweat pouring down peeling Western noses. Tewfiq draws Richard the Lionheart aside.

"Shall we defect?"

"As soon as possible."

This was a friendship grown steadily firmer since the heady days of The Club. "An alliance of the paralysed, eh Plantagenet? How long did we rot in that hellhole, brother?"

"Seven months, three weeks and two days, Tewfiq."

"You were counting! Probably Mad Latif . . . I thought it was a very slow week . . . What bad funk and an ocean of Black Label does to you . . . But I'm sorry I doubted you then."

"Who could blame you?"

"I was trying to put my thoughts down on paper, but all that turned out was acres of junk . . . Nothing made sense, in that beat. Memory sucked out. Compassion wiped out. Sisyphus and suicide. I was trying to synthesise some theory of the absurd in life, after Camus. A novel, a sequel to *The Plague* . . . I was thinking of my friend the doctor, Angelopoulos, who kept us alive in the siege of Jaffa Camp . . . My friend the Angel, you would get on well with him. Another lunatic outside time. But I believed you were an impostor, another of the counterfeit clowns who are drawn like flies to our shit. Until you told me about Aziz Khamash. Coincidence, brother, synchronicity, that the man who picked you up at Fontevraud and flew you to Beirut was the man who murdered my wife."

"I'm so sorry, Tewfiq. I'll kill him next time I see him."

"It's not worth it. I suddenly feel free, in the midst of all this preparation for carnage. What's one skull in the great prepared pyramid? The

Angel always told me I should get rid of that burden. Bury the dead in my mind, and pray for peace. What an irony. He was a good man, I wonder where he is now? There'll be plenty of work for him here, pretty soon . . ."

The armoured column moves off into the dust and haze as the BBC crew-men drag their camel piss-blinded colleague, screaming and yelling, towards a group of parked humvees. The three American minders are corralling the press core down the hill with yodelling cries and large knotted hemp ropes.

"Briefing time!"

The crows gather in the conference room of the Intercontinental Hotel at Zahran. Major Diesenbacker standing diminutively behind a stand designed for someone two feet taller, his square head bobbing against the background of the calligraphed Saudi flag: THERE IS NO GOD BUT GOD. "Yo! Your questions, ladies and gentlemen!" A forest of poised cassette recorders, cameras, microphone booms and laptop computers, a chorus of lamentations. "Major Diesenbacker, can you comment on Defence Secretary Cheney's warning of a chemical and nuclear confrontation?" "Is the January fifteenth deadline a threat or a promise?" "Do you think Congress will vote for the war?" "Can you comment on rumours of a surprise Iraqi pull out?" "What is your assessment of the deployment of the third echelon of Iraq's Republican Guards?" "How likely is it that Saddam will launch a pre-emptive strike against Israel?" "Do you think this a personal contest between George Bush and Saddam, Major?" "Will there be legal Christmas services for the troops?" "Will Jewish troops be able to celebrate Hannukah?"

"Yo. I can absolutely categorically deny that. I have no information about that aspect at this particular point in time. I think the likelihood of that eventooality has to be counted as a low-grade probability in terms of outcome at this moment. We have an ongoing understanding with our Saudi hosts on that matter. We would rather keep personalities out of this one if you please, Andrew. I think we have to wait on the assessment on that one for the analysis of the relevant modalities at this particular juncture, John. We are certainly keeping all the developments under close scrutiny, Graham. A constant observational review of all theatre deployment capabilities is part of our ongoing strategic and tactical activity, if that answers your question, Barbara."

"No it certainly does not."

"I'm sorry to hear that, Barbara, but I sure feel we can refresh your curiosity in that regard at a later opportoonity. Waal, here to clarify any points I may have misaddressed in this interim is Sheikh Bandar Bin Faisal Bin Rashid Bin Saud Bin Saud, Operations Officer of the Thirty-Third Royal Regiment of Artillery and overall Chief of Operations in the fifty-fifth theatre sector to His Highness King Fudd."

"Tank you very much, Major Diesenbacker . . ."

"I have something to show you," whispered Tewfiq. He nudged Richard out from the fifth row of reporters, ignoring the glare of Majors Preobrazensky and Lowell, into the ornate panelled corridor, its polished floor reflecting the passing ghosts of camera-clad foreigners and white-robed or khakied local guests. Keeping quiet as they passed the giant guards armed with M16 carbines and scimitars at the curtained entrances to the Generals' suites. "Desperate measures for desperate times!"

They climbed the stairs to the third floor and stopped at a door hung with a curlicued DO NOT DISTURB. Tewfiq rapped three times rapidly then twice slowly. A voice called: "Rabbit season!" "Duck Season!" Tewfiq answered. The door was cautiously unlocked, a dishevelled face looking out, darting right and left, an arm pulling them in.

"Hallelujah, brothers!"

Everybody who was anybody was there. Jefferson Tick of *The New York Times*, Bob Dobbs of *The Observer*, Jeanine Farhi of *Le Monde*, Maria Lanzarotti of *La Stampa*, Heinz Klug of *Die Zeit*, Boothe Henderson of *The Chicago Sun-Times*, William Shakespeare and Henry James of Global News Broadcasting, Cornelius Dill of *The Daily Mail*, Jemma Clutterbuck of *The Daily Express*, Jody Steele of *The Guardian*, Elmo Crud of *The Christian Science Monitor*, Bill Edelweiss and Wilbur Luther King of *CBS News*, Max Sokolov of *Pravda*, and the freelancers without whom no war was respectable, Manuel Rojas, Milt Zablodowski and Elsa Bach-Feldenkreisz. Tall soft-drink glasses were clasped by all, and large plastic bottles of U.S. Army–issue drinking water filled with rather more pungent liquids buoyantly passed round.

"Me-rry Christmas!"

"Bon et joyeux Noel!"

"Nazdrovya! Down the hatch, comrades! Not a drop of evidence should be left!"

"Don't worry about security, boy," Elmo Crud assured Tewfiq. "Max has had this room swept for bugs."

"At *Pravda* one never takes chances, especially these days," affirmed Sokolov, putting his arm round Tewfiq's shoulder. "Now is the time to introduce your friend to us properly. The smart money says he is an East German who has lost his masters. The uncouth elements go for CIA. Others spot him as an old stringer of Philby's who has had plastic surgery. The Saudis are convinced he is Mossad."

"You have to ask him yourself!" Tewfiq took a tumblerful of illegal libation. "One thing I can tell you, his baklava is unbelievable. He used to be the king of England."

"So did we all, so did we all!" Bob Dobbs poured the newcomer a highball. "We're all the prisoners of Zenda. The Free World's alibi. Haven't we met, before, in Windhoek, 1983 . . . ?"

Richard shook his head. Heinz Klug of *Die Zeit* jabbed his chest. "Asmara, 1986!" he stated. Richard shook his head. Maria La Stampa grabbed his arm, cooing in his ear: "N'Djamena, '88!" The freelancer and freeloader Milt Zablodowski swam forward, closing his eyes and feeling Richard's face with his muscular fingers. "Aaaah! I would know that nose anywhere! Tegucigalpa, the Cinquo de Mayo offensive!" Jeanine Farhi laughed, drawing him aside wincingly: "Hotel Vigot, Phnom Penh, April 21, 1975!" Richard shook his head sadly, as she felt his biceps and ribcage.

"I hear," said William Shakespeare, "that the BBC knew last week that Bush vetoed a British SAS mission to waste Saddam in the Ba'ath Bunker. Does anyone have any feelers on this?"

"Scuttlebutt," said Elmo Crud. "They all want you to feel they're still trying to avoid war. It's crap."

"We've paid a month's rent on the battlefield," said Cornelius Dill, giggling nervously as Jemma Clutterbuck pressed a 7-Up to his groin.

There was another knock at the door. "Duck Season!" Jefferson Tick called out. "Rabbit season!" a muffled voice answered.

Tick opened the door and cried out. "Oh my Gad, gettaloadathis!"

"Shut the door, for God's sake! Keep it down!"

"A turkey!"

"Where the hell . . . ?"

"It's alive!"

"Giorgio, you crazy, whadawedo wid dat?"

"The only turkey in Saudi Arabia, Goddamit!"

"Jesus fuck!"

"The Hundred and Fifty-Seventh Airborne brought five in illegally...
Two died in the heat, two in the pot . . . Don't ask about the price . . ."

"The parson's nose, Giorgio!"

"How we gonna deal with it? Who's gonna kill it?"

"Did you bring a scimitar, Giorgio?"

"Whassamatta? You justa grab the neck, an' presto!"

"You're joking!"

"You wanna kill it here?"

"There ain't a choice. The Saudis find one feather, we're all on the
next plane out . . .

"Jesus fucking wept!"

"Look at them! War correspondents!"

"Shove 'im live in the stove!"

"Just take hold of him a-here . . . No . . . porcamadonna!"

"Hold him, Goddamit!"

"Aaachh! That fucking beak!"

"Shit, the fucker's loose!"

"Grabbim!"

Gobble-gobble-gobble! Awwwk!

"Don't let 'im get away!" "Close that fuckin' door!" "Oh shit!" "Get
after the fucker!" "He'll tip off the guards!" "Keep it down, you bastards,
the *Mutawaeen* are everywhere!" "Get back inside!" "Who's the pool?" "I,
Zablodowski, volunteer!" "Fucker's got a Bowie!" "No blood Goddamit!"
"In Asmara we caught rats and gerbils wid our hands!" " *Tshortamati!* Stop
him!" "No, let the fucking Polack go!"

Tewfiq found Richard had deftly manoeuvred him out of the doomed celebration. Jody Steele of *The Guardian* had joined them, beckoning them upward:
"My room, it's on the seventh floor," she suggested, "out of harm's way . . ."

A small, wiry firebrand with almost-white hair gathered tightly at the back. Big blue eyes which had seen too much. The Lebanese Civil War, Qarantina, Tel el-Zaatar, Damour, 1982, the Israeli invasion, Sabra and Shatila, and so on —

"The last time we met, Tewfiq, you were like a stick insect. After the Syrians lifted the siege . . . "

"Losing weight was not a problem. Still no news of The Angel?"

"Not a peep. Everyone's busy swallowing Asad's new image, or gagging on it. Uncle Hafez has appointed a think-tank to find good Ba'athist reasons for supporting the West. The ghost of Michel Aflaq will oblige. Why do I keep coming back to this part of the world, Tewfiq? Am I an addict, or just some sort of pervert?"

"It's true love, Jody."

"I stay in England for a month and I'm trembling. The green hills and hedges of Dorset. Hedgehogs in the garden. Cats that grow fat without fear of being eaten."

"It sounds so wonderful, Jody."

"I wake up in the morning and find starlings tapping against the window."

"Paradise."

"You should try it in the winter. No, I need to feel the heat wacking my brain cells. And see if my friends are still alive."

"It may be the last opportunity, Jody. Who knows, if Saddam hits Israel with chemical weapons . . . if the Israelis go nuclear . . ."

"What do *you* think, Mister Richard, mystery man?"

"I don't know, Jody. 'Tis a new world for me. I am like a child reborn. Perchance 'tis like waking from one dream to another. All that mayhap has changed is the means of destruction. The will to destroy is the same. Cruelty is constant. And probably love."

"Does he always talk like this?"

"My friend Richard," said Tewfiq, "I love him like a brother. We spent months together in The Club in Beirut. You remember The Club, Jody."

"Who can forget it? So talk, Richard. Let it hang out. How long have you been in the Middle East? When did you first come? What were you looking for?"

"I arrived in June 1191. It was a hot and bloody summer. What was I looking for? 'Tis a good question."

"1191. Is your name the 'Lionheart'? Do I win the cup?"

"You do indeed, Jody."

"Well, I never grudge a person their beliefs and their visions. God knows we need something to keep us going. I'm afraid I don't have any booze in my poor suite, but I can mix a mean orange and tomato juice. We ought to talk, Tewfiq. We need to become reporters again, not stooges. We need to tell the truth, but how do we get at it? We're two hundred miles from the front, Goddamit."

"I have a plan, Jody. But we can't share it with too many people."

"You know me, Tewfiq."

"I know you, Jody. Set 'em up and let's pretend."

"Inshallah."

"I had a call from Ali Amar, in Paris. He'll be joining us here, for AFP. He'll be going through Beirut, double-checking. Can you believe it, it's now a safe haven. Jordanians are moving their money there."

"Well, when they throw you out of your first-class cabin, you have to scratch around in steerage, like everyone else."

"I still can't believe this is actually happening. That beast Saddam has given the Pentagon everything it ever dreamed of. They should be erecting his statues in Washington and Tel Aviv, not in Baghdad. So kiss and tell, Tewfiq. What's your master plan?"

It was late evening when Richard took leave of the two old friends, rocking in tomato-juice dreams of old times, and made his way down the corridor. The stairway was ghostly clear and silent. His footsteps vanished in the deep red carpet. He paused for a moment as a scrabbling sound came from the corner of the third floor. Descending round the bend he found himself looking into the beady eyes of the escaped turkey, crouched in a niche between rungs. Cautiously the ex-king and the absconding fowl eyed each other. Richard put his forefinger to his lips.

"Ssshhh!"

The bird shrunk back as he passed, snorting nervously. Richard passed down to the second floor and floated along its empty corridor. Only the hum of the air-conditioning could be heard. The ubiquitous

Mutawaeen, the religious police, had obviously been kept in ignorance of the press corps' transgression. The peaceful snores of both the sinful and the pure could only be imagined in their sound-proofed suites. The glittering stars above could be glimpsed through a glass-covered alcove. Neon lights hummed and burred. Richard delicately opened the door of his room with his plastic key card. He moved forward in the dark, trying unsuccessfully to open the bay window to fresh air, to relieve the air-conditioning's chill. The catch rattled uselessly.

"They don't open. No point trying."

He knew that soft voice. No need to switch on a light. He approached the bed, shedding his clothes, the cream-coloured jacket, the light jeans, the playful T-shirt marked "Operation Dessert Spoon." She cast aside the sheet, showing her nakedness in the wide shaft of moonlight. The pale sheen on her breasts, stopped at the triangle of black pubic hair, leaving her face in shadow.

"Rose."

"Richard."

And the hunted hold their breath in the dark . . .

FIFTEEN

Inadequate
Fulfilments

INSTRUCTIONS FOR EMERGENCY DEFENCE

Alert & All-Clear Sirens:

In the case of conventional enemy attack the fluctuating air-raid sirens will sound. Proceed immediately to the nearest air-raid shelter. When you leave your house, don't forget to close off all water and gas taps, and shut off the electricity. Take your pre-prepared emergency kit with you. Be prepared for a lengthy stay in the shelter and take along a portable radio. If there is no shelter nearby, go to a sheltered stairway. If you are driving a vehicle, draw in at the roadside and do not leave your vehicle to obstruct the way. Obey the instructions of Civil Defence and Security Service personnel. At the end of the emergency, an uninterrupted siren will sound for one minute. You may now leave the shelter. Keep away from areas damaged by bombs, and do not touch suspicious objects. If you identify casualties, provide first aid as possible and alert the authorities. Do not enter a damaged building, even to retrieve your own property.

Defence Against Chemical Attack:

In the event of a warning of a chemical-weapons attack, you must retreat into a pre-prepared sealed room. The sealed room, even if well insulated, cannot guarantee protection against poisonous gases, so you must wear the defensive mask at all times, even inside the sealed room. You should choose to seal the innermost room in your house, but choose a relatively large room whose air can last for a number of hours' breathing without ventilation. Choose a room whose doors open into other rooms rather than to the outside. Do not choose a room with large windows which might shatter from the blast of explosions or sonic aircraft booms. When the warning of imminent chemical attack is given, enter the room and shut off all air-conditioning and ventilation units, close all entrances to the room and tape up the doors and windows with adhesive tape, including small openings such as keyholes, place a wet rag to plug the gap underneath the doors, and be prepared with masking tape and plastic sheets to seal any window pane that might be broken.

These are the components of your gas mask:

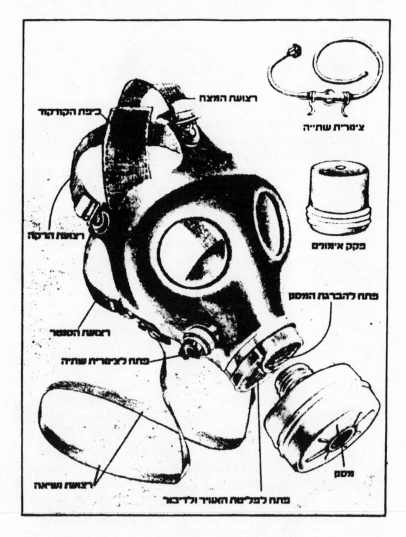

The emergency chemical defence kit includes masks manufactured for both adults and children. For babies there is the Defence Carrier for Infants (DCI), which is a transparent plastic tent with a filter in which the infant must be placed. Small children have a defensive hood with a filter and bellows which enable the child to breathe filtered air. In the emergency kit you will also find further equipment, such as injection units with chemical antidotes, skin powder and so forth. Make sure you check all masks and hoods for any tears, cracks or holes.

Protecting the Body:
If you are outside the home when the emergency warning is given, be prepared to protect the rest of your body from the penetration of poisonous chemicals: After donning the gas mask, protect your head with a plastic sheet — women should make sure to draw in all their hair. Do not wear a plastic bag over your entire face as this will lead to suffocation! This is most dangerous for small children, who may not be able to remove the bag. Protect your hands, in the absence of proper protective gloves, by placing each hand in a plastic bag or series of bags, which should be tightened in place by rubber bands. Outside the house you should also place your feet into plastic bags and tighten them under the trouser cuffs. Remember to remove these plastic bags when entering the sealed room.

Further Information You Should Know:
- How to Don Your Gas Mask.
- Changing the Filter.
- How to Use the Drinking Tubes.
- Emergency Food Supplies.
- Keeping Spare Clothes in Plastic Bags.
- Disposal of Contaminated Clothes.
- How to Protect Your House Pets.
- Knowing Your DCI.
- How to Deal with Stressed Children and the Elderly.
- Removing Your Spectacles Before Donning the Gas Mask.
- Shaving Off Beards.
- How to Inject the Antidote.
- When to Use the Purifying Powder.
- Iraqi Missiles —— How Many? How Accurate?
- When the All-Clear Sounds.

- Purification of Your Body and Clothes.

A GUIDE TO POISONOUS CHEMICALS
AND THEIR PROPERTIES:
Nerve Gases:
Tabun GA: Effect — minutes. Persistence — days.
Method of ingestion — breathing or skin.
Symptoms — Drooling, constriction of pupils, pain in eyeballs,
sweating, nausea, cramps, vomiting, involuntary defecation,
twitching, jerking, headache, confusion, drowsiness, coma, con-
vulsions, asphyxiation, death.
Sarin GB: Ditto.
Soman GD: Ditto.
VX: Ditto.
Mustard Gases:
Distilled Mustard HD: Effect — 2 to 6 hours. Persistence — 1
week.
Method of Ingestion — mainly skin but also breathing.
Symptoms — Inflammation of eyes, photophobia, ulceration, blind-
ness. Redness and irritation of skin, blisters. Effect on lungs —
coughing, retching, frothing at mouth, cyanosis, asphyxia, pneu-
monia, crippling or death.
Nitrogen Mustard (HN1, HN2, HN3): Effect — 6 to 12 hours.
Persistence —12 days, 2 days or 1 week.
Ingestion — Ditto.
Symptoms — Ditto.
Phosgene CG: Ditto.
Phosgene Oxide CX: Ditto.

N.B.: Some publications suggest Iraqi stockpiling of biological
agents. These are mostly more lethal and their persistence in the
field is far greater. Precautions against chemical warfare, such as
normal government-issue gas masks and emergency kits, are
unlikely to be effective against a biological attack, which can damage all living beings, both animals and plants.

A grisly toll indeed, but my sister-in-law, Aunt Pashtida, Greta Pasternak
of Kfar Pippin, is well prepared for any pollution of the atmosphere of our

Promised Land. Once again I can see her, out in the vegetable allotment, exercising her full ABC suit, which she showed off, pleased as punch, straight from purchase at Hardalo's Hardware Store in Binyamina. United States Government-issue. She offered to buy two more, for Rosa and myself, but I protested I was not going to live out my last moments encased in rubber, let alone a plastic bag. Rosa simply waved me away, like flicking a fly. Her favourite gesture nowadays. Flick flick, income tax bills, TV licence reminders, massed armies on TV, the Palestinian uprising, crime, corruption and all the evils of humankind. Meanwhile Greta has brought her "response time" in donning the entire Atomic Bacteriological Chemical suit, with gloves and boots, to twelve minutes. The necessary "response time," according to the manual, is four. She has been practising night and day. Itzik Melman, the handyman and TV repairman, is delegated to rush into the house without warning, at any hour of the clock, crying out "GAS GAS GAS!" just as she has seen on the box. She springs out of bed, reaching for the ghastly overalls, which are spread out like a skinned Martian on her bedside commode. At least I don't have to worry about all this, given my response time out of my wheelchair into bed and vice versa, which is about half an hour. By that time the entire globe could be covered by impacting ballistic missiles, whether they are al-Abbas or al-Asargelusha would be neither here nor there . . .

But as my sister-in-law cavorts, I am still mulling over the visit of the Potamkin girl bringing news of my son. A touching act, a total stranger travelling half across the world bearing his gift, a huge art book weighing at least a ton, which alone could suffice against any Iraqi paratroops who might scratch past Greta's early warning system. My son, Avram Blok. Sometimes he seems to me like one of those nineteenth-century explorers who vanished for decades into the African forests, sending out tattered messages to be published in the personal columns of the London Times. I know he is only four and a half hours' flying time away, but I'm a fossil of the old school — Blériot and the Wright brothers have just about impinged on my consciousness. When I was at college, the running joke in Budapest was that Admiral Horthy had promised to be the first man, as a proud Hungarian, to fly around the world without either taking off or touching down. Now they have missiles that can have your name written on them and find their way up your arsehole. But I have always been ambivalent about pulling and pushing my son towards and away from this blighted country. I wanted him to come, at least to give us a peek at this Kathleen, this northern flower, with whom he seems to have found a modicum of happiness. At least the distance absolves me of all guilt. Having brought him to a place of refuge which turned into a veritable snakepit, I sat chewing my heart to bits between my teeth as he was tipped first into one war, then another, escaping by the scruff of his neck. No wonder he chose another type of asylum. Everyone finds his Great Escape. My own no doubt was the stamp collection (long defunct). The little coloured dabs, whiffs of far-off places, exotic animals, peoples and landscapes, the dreamlands of long-gone empires — sepia dhows sailing off below the face of King George, tricolours waving over palms, escudos holding sway over elephants, royal visits to ecstatic natives, flower-wreathed dusky maidens gambolling under turquoise suns. Everything an old reactionary could wallow in, hidden from the white heat of nation building. And the pen pals, ah! Konakri. Accra. Lima. New Delhi. I burned all those letters as well, like guilt-steeped lovers' secrets, on the grand pyre, summer of 1982. Too much blood, too much turmoil and tumult, crowding in on my sorry sanctuary . . .

"What did you say your name was? Naomi? I'm grateful that you took time out to visit us in our bin. My sister-in-law, whom Avram always called Aunt Pashtida, will invite you to stay for a meal. Take my advice, find an excuse. Better to chew ashes. I don't care any more, I've been a prisoner in the Château d'If for too long."

And my son, is he prospering on his haggis? It's good to see he's taking an interest in art . . . The book he sent was a huge volume of Max Ernst, *A Retrospective: The Diversity of the Oeuvre* . . . Bringing back memories of another culture, of possibilities reduced to ashes by the passage of time. I read that Ernst decamped from Europe to New York and then to Arizona, to paint and sculpt in the American desert, whereas Rosa and I, taking the shreds of our lives in our hands, boarded the immigrant ship *Irma Klein* to Palestine, where our boy was born, on board, plucked out by the ship's mate, doubling as the surgeon. Whack! "Another refugee! Mazel tov!" We loaded them with heavy cargo . . . The children of the dream. We thought we could do genetic alchemy. Take the rubbish that was us and turn it into jewels. But if what you see in the mirror is rubbish, it's hard to find the magic words.

I have just finished reading the Hebrew translation of a book by Doctor Oliver Sacks. *The Man Who Mistook His Wife for a Hat.* Anything to avoid television. After Dostoevsky, neurology. The brain simply wants to go its own way. One wonders whose reality we are living in. I understand my wife, who only wants to live in her own. A hat I certainly never mistook her for. A Viking helmet, maybe. My petite Valkyrie. But those are faded times. The great causes. Sacks has a chapter about Cupid's Disease. An old woman caught by the delayed onset of neurosyphilis develops symptoms of energetic euphoria. In her youth, she had been a prostitute in Salonica. Now a ninety-year-old full of joie-de-vivre, she tells Sacks: *I wasn't fully alive until the wrigglies got me. Do you think, Doctor, you could keep it as it is?* Ah, for some long-delayed release . . . A second childhood, a sudden burst of enthusiasm, even if triggered by the plague . . . There were brothels in Budapest, too. But we young Jewish stalwarts poured our youthful energies into Revisionist Zionism. Vladimir Jabotinsky. Blood and fire. We got it soon enough, and the grand conflagration. Now there are monuments, memorials, remembrance days, armies of moral revenge. Come on, wrigglies, do your stuff.

In another chapter, Sacks writes about a young Indian girl with a malignant brain tumour who dreamed more and more vividly of her home town, the landscapes of fields, hills, rice paddies. Steadily she floated in a trance towards death, a rapturous journey home. Is this happening to Rosa, as she sits, stonily, in her chair, facing the TV Moloch but not apparently seeing it, flicking reality away with her hand? Does she relive the straitened years of her father's grocery store in Torokvesz? A pleasant wiping out of all that went between?

Where can one return to? In the tome Avram sent me, there is a haunting section on "Collage Novels," strange cut-out combinations the artist culled from engravings in old magazines and books. A woman floats on air. A man with an oven for a head talks of love. Eyes, limbs and candles interweave. Butterflies flutter in a gas-lamp over a vault of leaning skeletons. The surrealist titles: *"Don't be sad, Papa, my heavenly bridegroom has gone crazy. But in my sanctuary I keep the head and arms that touched thunder.*" "*Two girls riding across the sky.*" I missed all that, at its time. What did we know, our straitened lives and ambitions? These worlds of escape, spiritual if not physical, appearing to me now, via my son, as artifacts. A gift sixty years too late.

Europe After The Rain. A tangled decayed beauty. It rains here too, in our Sanctuary. The thunder rolls and precipitates its quick gush onto Kfar Pippin, this arid blot on the coastal plain. Outside, on the porch, with the drops drumming on the wooden overhang, my shawls and rugs wrapped around me, I feel like a passenger alone on the deck of that storm-tossed ship of fools. "Come on, Baruch, you'll catch your death." A disgruntled Greta fails to move me. Rosa is in bed. I can hear the television from the next house. An interview with the Prime Minister. That rasping, soporific voice. Everything is fine, our armed forces are fully prepared to protect us in any eventuality. We are an independent nation. We will not give in to blackmail. I remember writing to Avram how I hated all this. But I was only trying not to make him feel guilty about not being around in times of trouble. Who wants to export this drek? In truth, I don't give a damn any more. The politicians have stopped making me angry. I have come to understand their need to create their own little sanctuaries for themselves. The Prime Minister, as old and crotchety as myself, probably has his own problems in the bathroom, evacuating his own shit. So they want him to control the fate of four million people. The Opposition Leader is a man totally ground down by failure. How I understand his fatigue. The religious leaders have given up on God. They jockey like mad for money and power. Yes, I understand them all. A boorish collapsed General wants to "transfer" all the Arabs out of the country. He wants to wave that magic wand. Whom would I transfer, if I had that sceptre? I remember a story by the English author H.G. Wells, "The Man Who Could Work Miracles." Let the earth stop rotating! Everything flies off, into deep space. The rain drums against the sheds and the plastic covers of the vegetable allotments. Everything is artificial irrigation now. The natural world is just a curse. Nevertheless, the girl Naomi Potamkin told me, she had been in Scotland looking for clues to the disappearance of a friend kidnapped there in mysterious circumstances. He had been visiting the sanatorium in which my

Avram worked. Imagine, from inmate to keeper. I can never keep track. She owes this American friend a debt because he had helped free her brother when he had been a prisoner of war. "He was my lover, as well," she confided in me. "It's strange, when you open yourself to other people's experiences, what takes place."

Don't be sad, Papa, my heavenly bridegroom has gone crazy. Do you think, Doctor, you could keep it as it is? Now I am hearing confessions. But openness is the privilege of youth. My walls have closed around me too tightly. I can understand the pain of confinement. I wanted to tell her how Rosa and I conceived our son, Avram, after having been locked, hidden, in separate rooms in different flats in Budapest by friendly Gentiles for over six months, since the coup of Ferencz Szalasy. When we came together even the bombardment of the Red Army and the counterblasts of the retreating Germans failed to stop us rutting like rabbits. But the grotesqueness of conjuring that up to her given what we are now, two bloated carcasses of dried-up skin and rotting eyeballs, imposes a chaste silence . . .

But in my sanctuary I keep the head and arms that touched thunder. Yes, there were moments of hope. Of elation. Of firm evacuation and a sturdy appetite. Of a willingness to hunker down and do one's bit, for the cause. To build a nation, out of those leftovers. Refugee soup . . . No wonder I escaped, in my little coloured blobs, across the world, while staying locked up in my haven. No surprise then, that the world shrinks and recedes to the wheelchair and to the sealed room . . . "Come in, Baruch, are you going to stay out there all night? I'm going to bed." GAS GAS GAS, *shwester.* I know the rain will stop, and I will see the stars. *Two girls riding across the sky.* In Ernst's drawing they rise in a strange three-wheeled carriage, which carries them in rain and lightning over a watery surface, dressed top to toe in *fin de siècle* black. Their thin waists, their hips and breasts straining at the fabric. One has her hand hooked through the other's arm. The wheels of the carriage are like giant butterfly's wings. It is dated 1929. I was seventeen. I saw the future like a bright smudge before me. I wanted to fight against the evils of the day. Anti-Semitism, conservatism, imperialism, communism. A strange mélange. But one had to have an ideology. We could not call it racial pride. Obssessed with definitions — and now one lives within the blur.

I should have hitched a ride with those flying girls. But they passed me by, in their frivolous splendour, leaving me alone with the rain. Looking up into the starless sky, waiting for the poisons from Iraq. I still do not know how to use the antidote. The purifying powder. I have no idea how to decontaminate and purify my body or my clothes. I sit and wait, for the rising and falling sirens. But all I can hear is Aunt Pashtida's snores, sawing the night.

So seal up the room well, sisters. I'll just sit and wait outside . . .

. . . But it is an aberration, a false hope: Just the hooded keepers, as usual. I am allowed to glean whatever clues I can, from their nondescript khaki, as they hand over the usual slops in the usual plate. One of them has a bad scuff on his left boot. Bully for me. Should I undo his shoelace? Ignore them and make the whole thing go away. The walls melt and turn transparent, the floor lifts and flies me clean away . . .

. . . I left Beirut on an Iranian passport, Naomi. A special gift from Hizbollah. It's amazing who can become by a twist of fate your friend. Or your enemy. In the Levant, all moustached ruffians look equal. Especially with dark sunglasses. I pretended to be an armaments merchant setting out to scour the world for new goods. A persona most grata. Tucking in, within hours, to my first square meal for six months, on Middle East Airlines. Chicken, Meat or Fish, sir? Bring the lot, *ya khalili*! Angel of grace! By the way, what's your name? Dina? You're saving a man's life, do you know that? How many lives do you think a man should have, Dina? Are you staying over in Paris? I know a little Kampuchean bistro . . .

Yes, I am incorrigible, Sophia. When we talked of liberation . . . You went to Prague and cried in Wenceslas Square . . . Was it for the inadequacy of the moment? The masses on television, shaking their keyrings to topple tyrants. But the morning after, all the greyness still there. One has to deal with the aftermath. In Lebanon, not even that . . . The siege of the Camp was lifted, then reimposed . . . Under the cover of the cease-fire the "dissident" militias, the anti-Arafatists, poured in. Three months later they surrendered the camp to the Syrians. The people I had worked and lived with, Kamal, Radwan, Daoud, Saida, Muna, all their families, forced to leave for the south. The clinic moved, lock, stock and barrel, to Sidon. The Angel Cabinet turned into a command post. Angelopoulos denounced in absentia as an Arafatist and "Zionist stooge." If he dares to return to Lebanon, he will be shot as a spy. And so betrayal and perfidy triumph. So what am I to say? Was it all for nothing? We hope to progress by leaps and bounds. But it is a snail's pace, Naomi. Five steps forwards, four steps back. Not every broken skull can be mended . . .

Physician, heal thyself. Okay, I hear you, at the end of the day, one has to forgive the bastard, but do we have to be just parking bays for his prick? Memory is such a jumble, Sophia. Naomi, Caroline, Desirée, Anneka. And the Iranian girl at the U.N. Was she real or did I make her up to impress *les misérables* of Jaffa? Art-colony gossip round the great wood table, in the mahogany mansion of an American hero . . . Destruction of the rain forests, pollution of the environment, acid rain and degradation of the wilderness . . . Lebanon too was once snowy and pure . . . The great cedars covered the mountainsides, but now they are confined to tiny reservations . . . I visited them once, at Béchar. Midwinter. Bitter cold, the snow on the slopes. Jeanine Elias, I remember, was the friend who took me, introducing me to her Maronite clan as an American tourist. 1980, well before '82. That priest, Father Kaspar, took us to the glade, on a ridge of the Jebel Makhmal. The site, he told us, of the last glacier in Lebanon. The trees stood there like primeval mourners, the fan-shaped boughs bowed down far above us. We floundered through the drifts to a small fenced-in area, by a chapel, which enclosed the Patriarchs, the very oldest cedars. There were twelve of them, Father Kaspar pointed out, raising his eyebrows suggestively, more than two thousand years old. "Taste them," he said. I put my tongue to the bark. It was very dry, and tasted like bitter ashes. The bitterness repels pests and parasites, and is the secret of their preservation. So there I was, up a windy mountain, in the snow, with a mad priest, licking a two-thousand-year-old tree. "If Solomon had not cut down the others to make his boats to bring that nigger Queen of Sheba to his bed, we'd still have trees even older," the priest said. His grudges really went back far.

Not much point in licking the trees in New Hampshire, unless one wants the Lyme-tick ring on one's tongue . . . My friends, my friends . . . Did you ever write your story, Tewfiq? Your great Lebanese-Arab novel? Did anything ever come of those scrawled notes you crammed into those few remaining notebooks? Did you find the leisure to sit down and synthesize, to draw order out of the chaos? Or do you continue in the old paralysis? So who am I to criticise? Who can write inside the bonfire? Perhaps I can write it for you, in my head . . . Lying here shivering, with nothing but time . . . Waiting for the amputee's other shoe to drop . . . Make a meaning where there is none, bringing into play a different kind of memory . . . Yes, Abracadabra, and let those walls dissolve . . .

As the Caliph fell asleep just before the dawn, having trudged the night under the stars, he dropped down into the sand and dreamed the following dream:

He was walking, as he had walked for countless days and weeks, under the hammer of the sun, his clothes and skin falling from him in shreds, and no respite from the pitiless uniformity of the dunes that scalded his body and his soul, when, out of the haze of the horizon, a single pillar took shape, its base hidden in the shifting sands. It was a smooth stone column, rising to a raised platform, upon which an iron chain fenced in a short tower, sealed, apart from a half-opened door. A length of chain dangled down from the platform to within ten feet of the ground. Stretch as he might, he could not reach its end, nor find purchase on the sand for a jump. As he crouched in despair a bulky but squat figure crested a dune to his right. It was a gigantic turtle, its massive flippers threshing the sand into a fine cloud, its beady eyes liquid with age, the multiple rings upon its back designating its extreme antiquity. It stopped before him and lowered its head to his feet. He felt a great calm and humility emanating from this creature, so incongruous in the arid wilderness. Its nostrils blew a cool, healing breath upon his bleeding feet. Gingerly he climbed upon the head and onto the great chelonian back, reaching the chain with ease, and swinging himself up its length hand after hand. The beast, relieved of its burden, lumbered off without a backward glance.

As he stood upon the platform he saw the desert extend endlessly in all directions, without an oasis in sight. A scrabbling noise from within the tower distracted him. He pushed the half-open door and entered into a complete blackness. The coolness of the shadow was refreshing, but he could see nothing in the gloom. He followed a low moaning sound which came from above him, his hands feeling the contours of a dank stone stairway spiralling up. He climbed, warily, counting each step. At the nine hundred and forty-fifth he paused, breathing heavily. The climate was becoming colder and colder. Frost congealed the blood on his feet. There was a low howling which he assumed was the wind through a window or embrasure. A glimmer of light emanated, and he could see stars through an aperture ahead. Squeezing the last reserves of his strength, he climbed the remaining fifty-six stairs, pressing through a narrow opening onto another platform, under the canopy of the night sky. The entire spread of the constellations, south and north, was visible in a dazzling splendour. The wind froze his bones, rattling his teeth. On a stone parapet before him a hunched, ragged figure squatted, the raised head revealing a bulbous nose and gleaming eyes almost hidden behind an immense matted mane and beard. It beckoned to him, he stepped warily forward and looked down. The entire tower and platform were suspended in space, looking down upon a perfect, blue and golden globe, which he realized in astonishment was the earth, revolving majestically upon its own axis, an image of such unexpected beauty that tears welled up in his dry eyes.

"When you stand outside Creation," said the ragged man, "there is a clarity which otherwise is lost. All divisions fall away and all base metals transmuted. You may call me Hermes Trismegistus. Or Melchizedek, or Pythagoras, or Simon of the Pillar, or the Caliph Abu Ali Mansur al-Hakim. I am He of many faces but one nature. The bearer of the simplest message of all. That which was sundered must be brought together. The Tower of Babel must be rebuilt. Satan, who made the world in his image, terrified of the encroachment of Man, cast down the tower and confounded the tongues and works of Man. It is up to us to repair the damage." He grabbed the dreamer suddenly by the scruff of his neck with an unexpected strength, lifting him like a kitten above the abyss. "Go now and spread the Word!" he cried, opening his hand.

The Caliph fell, shrieking, flailing his arms in the void. The golden globe rushed ever nearer. A great heat searing his limbs. Then, again, the blinding of the light as he awoke, almost buried in the soft sand. He coughed and retched, flailing like a drowning man, pulling himself onto the surface, shaking the grains from his mouth, nose and eyes. He was lying on a hill, dipping into a valley in which a city of tall buildings stood. There were turrets and minarets of mosques, but also strange revolving towers and great obelisks of shining glass. Giant machines were biting into wide quarries, and in the black-paved streets vehicles rushed to and fro with great rushes of harsh sound. He shrunk, as great mechanical bird-shapes swooped in the sky, followed by ear-splitting blasts. A great rumble came from his rear, and out of a cloud of sand a vast column of wheeled and tracked machines clattered towards the city. A movement in the corner of his eye caught his attention. A brown-faced, sweating man was standing above him, dressed in a strange, leopard-spotted garment, festooned with heavy sacks and coarse pouches, his head weighed down by a rope-netted metal helmet, a tubular lance held pointing at his nose.

"Having a good day, Abdul? Any i.d.? Dog-tags? Permits? Okay, buster, let's go." Several more heavily laden men seized him, carried him bodily down the hill and threw him violently into the back of one of the metallic vehicles. More festooned men on either side of him waved cheerfully. Each had a thin band fastened round his head, attached to soft plugs in their ears, from which wires led to small boxes at their hips. They twisted and turned, rolling their heads and eyes to the tinkling rhythm vibrating inside their ears. But this was soon drowned by the thunder of the vehicle, as it jolted forward, heading through the sandstorm billows towards the jagged city.

And as I saw the man with the false note floundering through the drifts of his mind, I became aware, even without Loggie-Bird's mirrors, of all the other hopefuls, waifs, strays, dreamers and would-be conquerors streaming towards their promised land. All the ghost refugees going home: Benjamin of Tudela and William of Tyre and the Lionheart and all his Frankish cohorts, Barbarossa of *crusadus-interruptus* and Burchard of Mont Sion and Chateaubriand and Napoleon Bonaparte and his cannons, Sir Richard Bur-

ton and his false robes, General Allenby and Sir Ronald Storrs. A long, long
column of suitors with their pilgrim's robes and hidden grenades. Go east,
old men! Jews, trickling out to die, then flooding in to live and fight, followers of old siren calls and voices echoing inside their heads. Go east! go
east! All the dry bones of old conspiracies and ancient disputations, slithering and gathering over the sands: the hip bone connecting to the thigh
bone, the shin bone connecting to the ankle bone, the neck bone connecting to the shoulder bone, finger bones digging for lost skulls.

Go back to sleep! No one listens. In banal hotel rooms, the dead and
the half-dead hump, grunting in unnatural congress. The dis-lionhearted
and his thorned Rose, vying with each other in wickedness, as she turns
the tables upon him by means of a large plastic red dildo, tearing his millennial sphincter:

"Can you feel pain, dead man? Cry out, Goddamn you, cadaver!"

"My God, I'm bleeding! I can't believe it!"

"Don't worry, the Filipino maids burn the sheets every morning. Do
you want me to stop?"

"No, keep going! I can feel it! There, now! And again! And again!"

A long way from Fontevraud l'Abbaye, the blissful peace of monarchs
in their crypt. The king's mother, Eleanor of Aquitaine, holding her bre-
viary open in an eternal stone prayer. The degutted king, with crown,
sceptre and sword.

"And again!"

So many supplications. Calls for revenge and return bouts. Claims for
justification. The burnt ashes of martyred Templars scratching at the
straps of my sandals. We never knew where any treasures were buried.
Why? Why? Why? The decades I spent with my alchemical masters brew-
ing up the secret of life. Plugging up one's nostrils with clay buttons to
shut out the stinking ingredients: Sulphur, camphor, rotted bird's entrails,
fresh unicorn dung, mashed spleens. Hunting for the purest morning dew,
separating the salt from the sea, waiting for the calcination, the paradis-
aical water, the pellucid stone, the red coal. The Inexpressible Odour. The
Purification of Thought. The infinite virtue of the material. The chemical
marriage of light and dark. The Jewish Kabbalists called it raising the
sparks from the feet of Adam Kadmon. Repairing the broken light of Cre-

ation, the damage inflicted by the material on the spiritual. The Gnostics would say: Satan on God. Healing a sick Creation. It's an old old story.

Incarnate nature of the divine logos, versus the Gadarene swine. Why not let them snort their way into oblivion? But there is still a love of mankind. Their foibles and failures and flirtations, the way they switch and quirk and cringe, their sudden gushes of nobility, their tiny flashes of grace.

I sit, with my back against the ruins of my pillar, my head resting on the pilgrims' graffiti, my feet in the eternal drifting sands, clicking my worry beads. Tick tick tick tick. They tell me these days one need not wind up clocks, they just carry on by invisible means of support. Nor do they revolve in circles any longer, but are just numbers, which repeat themselves, over and over, ad infinitum.

Sweet death, where is thy sting?

Mine enemy delivered into mine hands! Thus stands Hohenlohe at the very brink of triumph! Daniel laughing in the lion's den. My plan to kill McTeague at Christmas seemed to be blessed by the gods. (Turners of the other cheek need not apply.) The critical moment manifesting itself on the morning of Friday, 7th December, appropriately, Pearl Harbor Day, when, on tottering off routinely to Clerihew Gdns in my fake postman's persona I found, just as I was about to deposit another purloined offer from Florida Timeshares Inc of a free BMW or a pair of woodcarved book-ends (phone now!!), that the door of number 11 had been left ever so much ajar, amenable to opening by a mere light shove.

Eureka! Not a moment to lose, as I slipped deftly into the McTeague sanctum, not knowing if the Serbian au pair, or McTeague's wife, had merely adjourned to the local Paki for a wee flask of Domestos and might well be trotting back the noo. Darting past the narrow hallway, marking the row of anoraks and pile of padded walking boots, up the dusty banisters (ah, the Slav inheritance!) to the untidy, toy-strewn bathroom, the kiddies' rooms plastered with posters of hideous pop stars, footballers and feminists (Susan Sontag? Oh my God . . . ?), the master bedroom, which I scanned with X-ray eyes. No portraits in oils of Brent Browbeat, but shelves of books books books (an entire Britannica, can you believe it, the bastard). A pile of manuscripts by the bedside. More innocent victims to be sucked in, then double-crossed and thrown in the gutter, with their wee bairns crying out pitifully for a scrap of mouldy bread and cheese. This man must surely die, before he wreaks more havoc. Justice must be seen to be done.

I rapidly jotted down, on the back of my redundant timeshare envelope (why should he get the woodcarved bookends?) the full layout of the McTeague household, thus:

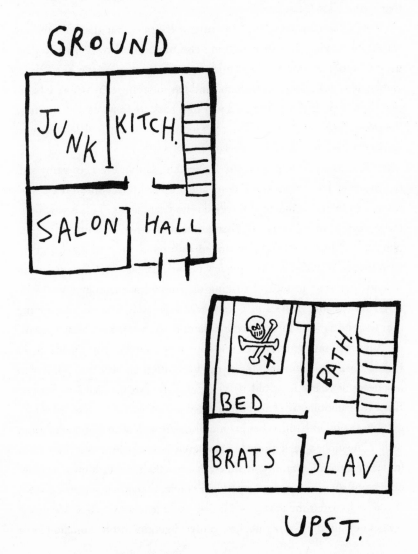

But it was not until I rushed through the kitchen that I hit paydirt, as I cast my eyes quickly over the mess of bits and bobs on the mantelpiece, taking care not to touch or displace anything (next time bring white gloves, Daniel), but in among a pile of Access slips and autobank receipts and paper animal heads from cornflake packets and old nails and piles of one-pee coins I perceived a flash of silver metal: two keys upon a paperclip. Whisked them off, with the tip of my forefinger, rushing to check them at the front door. A perfect fit! Banzai! A set of spare house keys! Thank you, thank you, Nico Ceauşescu!

I made myself scarce, making sure as I slipped out that no one was watching. Having disturbed nothing else the odds were the McTeagues would simply assume the keys mislaid by themselves or the Yugo-slave, and eschew lock changes, et cetera. And ten shopping days before Christmas! At this point I sent the postman togs back to Transcosmic. But now the issue of adequate tools for the job loomed with unparalleled urgency. After all, *The Sunday Times* declares: SADDAM NOW ONLY A YEAR AWAY FROM NUCLEAR BOMB, but Danny Hohenlohe cannot even get a tiny slab of Semtex with a couple of old wires and a timer in his hour of need. The neglect of the individual in this regard is quite appalling. This is when one really regrets one's years of dissolution and frivolity amid the great upheavals of our time. Waving banners to support the rioting students of Paris instead of rushing over for a few mementos. Signing "Troops Out of Ireland" petitions instead of striking up a useful acquaintance with The Boys. Blu-tacking posters of Che Guevara on walls instead of hopping over to Havana for a little mundane training in the Sierra Madre. Chanting "Viva Frelimo" without even one clip of 7.65mm bullets in memoriam. Failing to stockpile for the day of the Revolution because we all knew in our heart of hearts it would never dawn here. No wonder Nicolae and Elena were undone. We failed them every step of the way.

On the other hand, what joy might there be in some blind explosion, with Hohenlohe's luck probably not even nailing the target but some innocent bystander, family member, or even the gasman blown to kingdom come. No tang of the Amontillado there. One has to cut one's cloth, et cetera. I chased the ghosts of Nicolae and Elena away. They live in the bushes now, in the Greek's mangy "garden," gorging off his tomato plants and lupins. If anyone comes through they freeze, like little Balkan gnomes. I have obtained a little Kill-A-Weed spray from Boots. It is Ready to Use and offs buttercups, chickweed, clovers, daisies, dandelions, sorrels and trefoils. Best used, alas, between May and August. But I cannot wait till then for results.

There must be tried-and-true methods for dispatching pests, sans Semtex, given access to the victim's lair. One thinks of Cary Grant, bringing Ingrid Bergman the poisoned glass of milk in *Suspicion*. Or was it not Ingrid Bergman at all, and she only thought the milk was poisoned? One has to get one's precedents clear. Arsenic, an available favourite, has to be taken in small doses. Toothpaste laced with cyanide? Loosen the rug on the stairs? There must be a million and one deathtraps in a semidetached house if only one put one's mind to it. Focus on the victim's weakness. In McTeague's case, without doubt, the golden liquid balm — usquebah . . .

I settled on the poisoned Christmas Scotch, to be supplied by Santa down the chimney. But wouldn't the bastard share it with his guests? The tearful innocents again . . . It should be standing, unwrapped, glittering, by his bedside last thing at night. At least one useful fact gleaned from my one visit while in favour: Gemma McTeague did not touch whisky. A strictly Burgundy and Bordeaux broad. I remember, as the cat drooled on my trouser leg, her gay laugh: I never touch the stuff, Gordon can take enough for both of us. Hoots mon, och aye (but what had happened to that cat? An unplayed card to be pondered . . .). The Serbian serf might well imbibe a tot. But not, I'd guess, a lethal dose. I spent the weekend in research. Kill-A-Weed is no use. Nor is landlord Spetsotakis's Raid — Triple-Action Ant and Crawling Insect Killer (Kills Bugs Dead). Browsing the DIY shelves, never did one realise so much death was available over the counter. I settled on Bio-Long-Last, Kills all foliar insect pests on flowers, fruit and vegetables. Pouring a thimbleful into a bottle of Teacher's to test the hidden taste. No immediate difference, but in the night my stomach launched a sneak attack, propelling me on all fours to the toilet bowl. I wrote a short story which took place inside the bowl once. "The Thing in the Bog." A man philosophises with his turds. But no literary comfort now. Well, the label did say "Extremely Dangerous to Fish." On to a winner at last.

Eventually I fell asleep and dreamed of the GAS, the Great Arab Saviour, leaving his Laundromat to walk among the people disguised. I understand this was the practice of Haroun al-Rashid, though his executioner, Zbab, was always a few steps behind to deal with any threats of exposure. In my dream I was the executioner, wielding my little Ready-To-Kill. But the GAS got on a Northern Line Tube at Kentish Town which had sneaked up on us in defiance of the board which promised its arrival fourteen minutes later, leaving me aghast on the platform. I saw him thumb his nose at me from inside the filthy window, sticking his tongue out and licking the encrusted schmeck. I felt distraught and bereaved. A good executioner needs a reason to wield his Ready-To-Kill. He cannot kill people at random, without proper authority. I threw my phial guiltily into the platform wastebin (marked CAMDEN COUNCIL IS WORKING FOR YOU) and rushed away, hiding my dripping face . . .

The phone ringing woke me with my mug in crusted spew. My mother, commanding an appearance at the ancestral home for Yule. "You're coming for Ekksmass?" she trilled. "Pick the Father will be here, the holy ghost in person. What can I do to make you come?"

A terrifying implication, but I chose to accept the phrase at face value. "Mum, I've booked a flight out on Ekssmass Eve," I said. "I got a special deal with Edelweiss on an excursion to Goa."

"To goa where?" she asked.

"Goa," I said. "It's in India. It used to be a Portuguese enclave. It's sun and beaches. There is a direct flight to Bombay."

"It's the Indian shiksa," she said. "I'm not prejudiced, but you know they put some strange ointments down there."

"I wouldn't know," I said, wiping the vomit off my face with the bedsheet. "You've got it all wrong, Mum. She's a religious fanatic. They're spending Ekksmass visiting the poor, sleeping out in cardboard city."

"What am I going to do with the turkey?"

"I'll call you later," I lied. Why does she always feed me these lines? Vade retro Satanas. At least I knew Bio-Long-Last would do the trick, if a mere swig had almost totalled me. There only remained to choose the precise medium: The Inchgower, the Glendronach, the Talisker or mayhap Oldbury Sheep Dip? I still remember us sitting in his office, he swivelling in his chair, toasting the vainly craved demise of Brent Browbeat in one of those obscure malts from Old Compton Street. A taste shared with Doktor Mackenzie of Drem. Aye. I should have dropped him then when I had him, alone and isolated, on the East Lothian moors. Down a cliff at Gullane, a simple fatal accident, a cracked skull, no frills. But I was softened, by the holiday snaps of his wife and bairns and the lobster that he laid on me at the Sheep's Dread. The lesson: Never allow sentiment into strategy.

Nevertheless, a momentum. The newspaper omens appear solid: British hostages released by the GAS. *Götterdämmerung* now considered that much closer. ANC president Oliver Tambo returned to South Africa after thirty years of exile. In Japan scientists had suceeded in reviving water fleas deep-frozen for two weeks at a temperature of -196 C. And only five shopping days to Xmas!

I elected the Inchgower. The masking smell of the peat bog. Now to scout the pre-festive lay of the land. Sans the postal disguise wrapped in Spetsotakis's spare navy greatcoat, out into an unseasonably mild, sunny day. The crowds in the Tube subdued. At Notting Hill Gate a premature reveller attempting to lie down in the path of passing cars, perhaps emulating that brave Chinese youth facing down the tanks in Tiananmen Square. But the London drivers just manoeuvred around him, teeth grinding frigidly. The back streets dull and quiet. Three well-dressed punks scrubbing a van. Birds squatting on telephone poles. Cats loafing on windowsills. The semi-detachment of fenced-in front yards. The Englishman's home is his castle. His sanctuary and refuge from evil, where even the taxman is banished. But somewhere upstairs, the roll of drums. A car alarm, two streets off, inviting mayhem. A good day for thoughts of murder.

I turned the corner into Clerihew Gardens warily, but with a light heart. But the sight that greeted me plunged me instantly from the pinnacle into the pit. Undone, Daniel! Hoist, Hohenlohe! For there, at the slapping gate to number 11, is the entire complement of the McTeague household, man, wife, offspring and the Serbian skivvie, busily loading suitcases, rucksacks, laundry bags, skis onto the family Sierra, the loud Glasgow burr of my nemesis echoing across the barren branches of the council-cropped trees —

"Have ye got the bloody snowshoes, Geegee?"

That futile night, with Bio-Long-Last . . . ! Is there no justice, no redress in the world? No proprieties in the balance of right and wrong, fair and foul? I slunk away, tail brushing the ground. Cancelled the Goan excursion, excusing my change of plans to Narindra and the other Edelweiss petals, Eqbal Senior, Jimmie the Shoe and Mrs Cszolgosz, Whom God Preserve, of Finchley, on grounds of my parents' sudden infirmity. Generation to generation. So here we are, in darkest Wembley, devouring the bloated, burnt turkey, my mother beaming sagely while The Queen, her face a strange ghastly orange colour, praises the troops in the Gulf. They are performing a duty for freedom and democracy, which should make us all feel proud, she informs us, without batting an eye. A flower in a vase at her left elbow blushes, or is it just a quirk in the ether? My estranged father pats his stomach and proclaims: "Let's hope that *fer-stinkener* bastard is wiped off the face of the earth."

"Amen." I respond fervently. But my soul seething inside. Why am I the world's most useless murderer? All over the globe, jails are full of people who have at least managed to commit the act. Death rows are vibrating with the clatter of the condemned typing their best-selling memoirs. And I alone have no gory tale to tell — yet. But no slip-ups, next time . . .

"In the name of God, the compassionate, the merciful . . . Guide us to the straight path . . ."

The amplified call of the muezzin blaring out over the runways and the desert, rattling the windows of the Intercontinental Hotel, rolling through the construction sites, municipal offices, car parks, the oil company compounds, the jail. The white-robed Mutawaeen, the Protectors of Virtue and Preventers of Vice, with their henna-tipped beards, knocking on all doors with their staves and camel whips, calling the faithful to prayer.

"Salaah! Salaah!"

Few disobey. In the basement of the military-police jail, the interrogators put aside their long bamboo staves for a moment and unroll their prayer-mats, kneeling towards the Holy Mosque at Makka al-Mukkaramah, one thousand kilometres away. The young man hanging by his manacled hands from the ceiling is unable to join in, nor does he show any interest in the proceedings. Since his apprehension, fifteen days before, in the Ayn el-Abd army zone, he has failed to cooperate with his captors, refusing even to answer to his name, rank, number, religion or ethnic origin. A clean slate, he waits for a new chapter to be etched on his youthful, sun-scorched face. His clothing, a tattered cast-off robe, thrown in the corner, having provided no clue: no papers, no permits, nothing but grains of sand, millennial fluff in the folds. An anonymous blue-eyed wanderer, a Man with No Name.

The midday prayer over, the jail commander turns to the two black men in United States Air Force uniforms who had joined him and his beaters on the mat to render their worship to the Almighty.

"He's all yours, if you want him."

"We'll do what we can, brother."

The interrogators gently lower the prisoner, helping him to stand, massaging his arms and feet. He does not resist as the two black soldiers cuff him with regulation restrainers, the taller of them addressing him, in accordance with protocol, but in a language he cannot comprehend:

"You have the right to remain silent. You have the right to be represented by a lawyer of your choice or to have a lawyer appointed for you by the United States Air Force. Whatever you say may be taken down and used in evidence in a court o' law. Do you understand what I'm sayin'?"

"You're wastin' your time," sighs the shorter soldier. "Let's hit the road."

They propel the youth up, to the first floor of the station, into a half-paved street, baking in the noonday heat. No one around except a sweating donkey pressed up against the jail wall to cool. The soldiers lead the prisoner towards a parked sand-caked humvee, or Human Light Vehicle. But as they manoeuvre him aboard, he turns towards them, spreading his arms to drop the pair of unhooked restrainers in the road, pressing the palms of his hands gently on their heads, speaking, for the first time, in a classical Arabic, which they comprehend from within:

"You will know me, for I am the Expected, the Chosen One, the Mahdi. I am the Door, and you will enter therein."

The soldiers looked up into his face, transfixed by his sky-blue eyes.

The donkey, leaning against its wall, brayed loudly, then, twisting its mouth into human speech, pronounced, as if by a ventriloquist's wish, the *shahadah* of the Faith: "There is no God but God." Then it fell and expired in the dust.

The black soldiers climbed in their vehicle, sitting stiffly in the front seats, as the youth settled regally in the back. Looking directly ahead, the taller soldier gunned the engine. The humvee moved forward, into the desert, leaving behind the slumbering town, in which nothing live stirred in the streets, except an emaciated, starving, lone turkey, staggering about, shouting its infinite pain to the skies.

COLD WAR FUN WHILE IT LASTED

TOO SOON TO HAIL CAPITALISM'S TRIUMPH?

MADONNA'S FALSE CONCEPTION OF ART

Blok cast the Xmas Eve headlines aside, refusing to allow them to spoil the indolent hiatus between Christmas and Hogmanay. Five days in which traditionally one felt no pressure to perform even the slightest boon for mankind; one had only to put one's feet up and watch the grey waves washing in to the beach, hark to the cries of the gulls, the happy hammering of one's beloved knocking something strange together out of old planks and Safeways bags, or the blissful wheezing of the dog, enmeshed in alien dreams.

Blok and Kathleen's Christmas had been spent in Craddock with Kathleen's old friend and Wee Threes comrade Janet and her parents, the Polish ex-airman Stanislaw and Elsa, the ex-Labour councillor defected back to the bosom of the Scottish National Party, and Janet's husband, Mike, the freelance newsreel cameraman, just returned from a gruelling six-week assignment in the Horn of Africa, Ethiopia, Somalia, and Southern Sudan. Mike had the grace to wait until after the Christmas meal to regale Blok and Kathleen with his tales of famine and despoliation. The starving stick-limbed children, the desperate and hopeless parents, the failed aid projects, the grisly casualties of obscure civil wars, the lack of interest back home. All eyes on the Gulf, Our Boys at the Front, Saudi Arabia, Iraq and Kuwait. The world could only be taken in in small bites, through narrowing doors of attention. The same points Kathleen recalled Petros Angelopoulos making to them nine months before. So many ghosts at the feast. Blok burped, the turkey, stuffing and roast potatoes rattling and yawing in his gut.

"The Guilt, the Guilt," sighed Stanislaw, joining Blok in the television room, leaving the women and Mike to mourn the oppressed. *Star Wars* unfolding on BBC1, deposed princes and princesses battling for their inheritance in galaxies far, far away. "At least the boy puts his neck where his mouth is. But sometimes I wish my daughter had married someone a little less intense, a little more boring." Blok grunted, as seventy-five ersatz spaceships flashed by to an orchestral crescendo. Actors manoeuvring desperately in front of blue screens. "Sorry. Not trying to make a point to you, Avram. Just rambling. What can we do? When are you going to Australia?" Kathleen having finally received, early in December, an official invitation from the Woolloomooloo Art Gallery to exhibit her works in early March. The items to be dispatched by sea in January, the artist to follow by air.

"I'll believe it when I see the free ticket," said Blok.

"I've always wanted to go there," sighed Stanislaw, "the wide-open spaces, the primeval emptiness, the strange animals."

All the places we've never been, all the doors that never opened. *Star Wars* end on a triumphal note as age-old values prevail. The troops in Saudi Arabia can, according to the *BBC News*, sing Christmas carols, as long as they do so without overt symbolism, hiding their crosses, like the first Christians. But, even in Iraq, the Christians are celebrating, despite the deadline hanging over them like the sword of Damocles: At midnight, January 15th (U.S. Eastern Standard Time, 8:00 A.M. on the 16th, Baghdad time), Iraq must quit Kuwait or face the consequences.

But at least Hogmanay is secure. In the interim, taking advantage of the unusually mild winter weather, Blok resumes his wanderings on the beach, with Alistair, while Kathleen works to prepare her packageable items. Hoping in vain for a return of the seal. Those mournful deep-sea eyes, with their unearthly melancholy, which probably meant nothing more than "Is this a man who throws fish?" But no sign in the water, apart from the usual soggy cardboard, crushed beer cans and floating seaweed. One hopes in vain for messages from the Cosmos, the *heiros gamos*, Ultima Thule. But no, not even a dugong to be netted. The fishermen now catch only shrimps and sprats, everything else goes to the great factory trawlers, plundering the cold North Sea. Is there an escape from banalities? From obvious choices? Is there a flash of insight still to be had? Or just a cornucopia of false gods beckoning a way out, messiahs of straw, twirling their dead fingers out of the past? Ah, for amnesia! Then we could repeat both tragedy and farce without any shred of guilt. Donning our gas masks with the jaunty air of originality and innovation, instead of stumbling so routinely into horror. Blok thought of his father, fumbling with his emergency kit in Kfar Pippin, catapulted into the twenty-first century without having had an opportunity to enjoy the nineteenth. What has Dostoevsky got to teach us? A classic return of the repressed, in the upheavals of the collapsed Soviet Empire, the Jews flooding in to Zion, the tragic clash of settler and native, the eternal recurrence. Come back Nietzsche, all is forgiven. Perhaps Australia is the solution, after all. The farthest away from it all, barring space travel. Kangaroos, wallabies and Aborigines singing to their ancestors under the moon. The joy of vanishing, of ceasing to be either a victim or witness. I didn't break the world, why would I feel guilty for being unable to mend it? The world was broken long before I turned up. Lurching on to Armageddon. I've been there, there's a dreadful sandwich stall. A long climb up the dry mound. Tourists gawping at the ancient biblical shards, poking through dust. The stables of Solomon, the Canaanite Temple. And the seventh angel pours out his phial, and a voice comes forth, saying: It is done.

Aye, the mundanity of revelation. What can be left but simple pleasures? The dog, the beach, pebbles in the sea. The waves lapping at one's own back door. The rain, suddenly pouring down, merging sea and sky in grey.

Andrew and Rhona Mackenzie roll up, in their battered Chevrolet, sweeping Blok and Kathleen up as arranged to celebrate Hogmanay proper in Edinburgh. Rhona teetotally driving, the good doctor waving his favourite Auchentoshan like a ceremonial mace. Stopping first at Stanislaw and Elsa's for a dram or two for the road. Several old-time neighbours had dropped in, reminiscing about the village of Craddock before the war. Old Mr Baillie, hunched up like a little human pug-dog, claimed to remember the great herring-drifter tragedy of 1913. He had been four years old and recalled the whole village standing silently on the jetty waiting for the boat that wouldn't return. He also began recalling the great gale of 1908, but was cut short by the reminder that he had not then even been born. Weel, ah'll tak' anither wee dram. A great flurry of argument over the last coal-mine closure in 1961 and the advent of the Cockenzie power station. Mr Baillie had no nostalgia for the past, and wanted nuclear-power stations built throughout the land. A torrent of dissent, led by Elsa, while Stanislaw sat silently, eyes twinkling, nursing his Stolichnaya.

And so the asylum celebrants moved on, speeding into the city, entering via Queen's Drive, waving their bottles at the ducks in the tiny loch, wheeling round the back of the university to Sophia's flat in Marchmont, where a cheerful crowd of artists, critics, actors, aggravators and activists and other assorted derelicts filled the three rooms, tanking up to the usual barrage of hi-wattage sound, shrilly shrieking in each other's ears. A large red-headed youth draped himself over Kathleen, while Blok found himself in unintelligible parley with a reedy young woman who mistook him for an official of the Scottish Arts Council. Andrew Mackenzie's loud laugh billowed through the throng. It had a nervous tinge to it, now that he presided over an empty house at The Retreat, both staff and patients having departed and nae bookings for the new year. "It looks like," he said, "in times of crisis, people realize their fears and anxieties are not irrational. They find other solutions for their neuroses, for example, self-restraint, or suicide." Mackenzie was considering the offer of a post at a special school in Aberdeen for handicapped adults and young people, never having lost sight of his aim to return to that field. "Farther north, Avram, the cold really gets into your bones. But beggars can't be choosers. We'll sell the Bellanys and move on." In fact he had received an offer for the local painter's works from Sophia, who was negotiating a budget for a permanent collection of contemporary Scottish art, Howson, Conroy, Currie, Hughes, Rossi, Redfern, Rae, Moffat, Shanks, Davie, Paolozzi and all, returning to base, after her rocky run along the surrealist trails. Sophia kissed Kathleen, Janet, and Blok, briefly before sagging back into her native ambience, while Mackenzie continued to explain to Blok why he thought the current era of human endeavour was ending:

"You should read Hawking — the writing is on the wall. It's out of the mouths of babes and cripples: The laws of the universe don't distinguish between the forward and backward directions of time. The grand unified theory is only a matter of time. D'ye get it? We may never know, but if we do, we will have no more need of God because we will know the workings of his mind. We can finally put him out to grass, at the very moment when masses of mankind rush back to his bosom in fear and frenzy! Rationality self-destructing on its own rocks! Full speed back, that'll be the watchword! The Luddites' triumphal return! Eh, Avram? So why don't you stay and take over The Retreat? Transform it into a set for ghost stories. I'm sure Drem will be at the centre of life in the universe some time around the thirty-fifth century." Rhona propping him up upon the sofa. But, suddenly mindful of the time, Mackenzie urged everyone out into the streets, to totter down to the Tron to see in the New Year in traditional style, in the open air, jostled by thousands of drunk compatriots under the great church clock. Sophia and Rhona resisting the offer, but Mackenzie, insistent as ever, dragged Blok and Kathleen out at forty minutes past eleven, yawing across the Meadows, round the McEwan Hall and the university down South Bridge, to join the pack in the High Street, swallowed in a frothing swell of bodies, male and female, young and old, three sheets to the wind, the staggering masses only held up by the pressure of each other's company, faces spinning in alcohol haze, the entire street pitching and swaying in its own crazy Scotch reel. The fetid breath closing in like a cloud, and Andrew Mackenzie holding Blok up by the shoulder, while Kathleen's face swam before his eyes, changing and metamorphosing into old familiar shapes, faded images of other lives, other climes, other masses marching and dancing in celebration or anger, protest or desire: Remember! Forget! Act! Desist! Give us life! Deliver us from evil! And always bury yourself in me . . .

The absurdity of surrogate homelands came over him suddenly, just as the crowd reached the apogee of its own fusion, falling silent for a brief moment as the hands of the clock began to converge, the minute creeping up on the hour, the hour egging on the minute, the crowd's voice tearing the air: "Ten – Nine – Eight – Seven – Six – Five – Four – Three –– Two –– One! HAPPY NEW YEAR!" The blare of ten thousand smashed souls of strangers kissing and hugging, drooling and vomiting over each other in that grand spew of unity:

"SHOULD AULD ACQUAINTANCE BE FORGOT A-AND NEVER BROUGHT TO MIN' . . ." As, around the world, at offset hours, for even time, as we now know, staggers, mug clashes against mug, glass against glass, tinkling in the sound-proofed rooms of the Zahran Intercontinental, or tingling in the heretical bosom of Israeli kibbutzim, or in the hearts of soldiers perhaps pretending for the last time, damping down the dust of coming ashes with a libation of mineral water or orange squash, time twanging in the dull cosiness of London suburbs where dire dreams of revenge still nurture, or deep in cells where resurrected caliphs massage their thumbs.

Link hands, strangers, and dance.

"FOR AU-AULD LA-ANG SYNE, MY DEAR, FOR AU-AULD LA-ANG SYNE . . .

"WE'LL TAK' A CUP OF KINDNESS YET, FO-OR AU-ULD LA-ANG SION . . ."

BOOK FOUR:

Asia
after the
Rain

SIXTEEN

Riders

of the

Sky

March. Halt. Dismount. Surrender. Lay down your arms.
Do not be afraid, we are English soldiers.
Where is the headman of the village? Bring him here.
How many horses have you? I will pay you cash for everything.
If you do not collect everything in two hours, I will send my soldiers.
Speak the truth, tell no lies, do not hide anything or it will be the
　　worse for you.
I will take everything and give you a receipt.

　　　　　　　　— Useful Arabic phrases for British
　　　　　　　　officers, 1926, quoted by Robert Lacey,
　　　　　　　　The Kingdom, Arabia & the House of Saud

British soldiers in the Gulf have booked a victory party — at a top hotel in Baghdad. And they're so sure of a quick conquest that the date of the bash is **January 26**. The cheeky desert rat squaddies have reserved the five-star hotel's banqueting suite for the champagne knees-up.

A dozy Iraqi receptionist took the details for their £50-a-head bash.

But she nearly choked on her sheep's eyes when the caller added: "Send the bill to the officers' mess of the 1st Staffordshire Regiment."

A Staffordshire squaddie told last night how they scored a direct hit with staff at Baghdad's £200-a-night Sheraton Ishtar Hotel.

The Saudi-based soldier said: "We don't get many laughs out here so we decided to arrange the victory party. One of the officers told us that the top hotel was the Sheraton Ishtar where a pint of beer costs nearly a week's wages. So we tracked down the number and put in a call. She quoted various prices for meals and drinks, but when I told her the function was for BRITISH soldiers she immediately hung up the phone."

But the squaddie added: "We fully intend to be in Baghdad by January 26 —— and we hope to be celebrating victory with a few noggins in The Sheraton."

The Daily Star,
London, January 17, 1991

"In human history," declared the Cleric, "we read the constant advance from the individual towards society. Adam was alone, then there was Eve, then Cain and Abel. But there was neither community nor tribe. And Cain slew his brother, Abel. Thus the blood of Abel became a burden for Cain, and an obligation for those who seek justice. In the tribe the obligation of blood passed from one generation to another. If you kill one of the children of my tribe you offend against all, and every member of my tribe has the obligation of vengeance. But in Islam we have seen this traditional concept transformed in the service of mankind. No longer does one individual make war on another, nor one tribe upon its rival. Now it is the entirety of mankind which has inherited the obligation of Abel's murder by Cain. At the End of human history comes the Avenger. Whom shall he avenge? The blood of the martyrs? The sacrifice of Kerbala? But these are merely facets of the deeper truth. For in akhir al-zaman, *the Universal Vengeance, the final cycle of history will be closed according to God's will. At the End of Time vengeance is extracted from the entire tribe of Cain, the tribe stained with blood to its eyes and to the roots of its hair, the final explosion of history. For it is not until this final vengeance that the Day of Judgement will be at hand . . ."*

The weather's fine this Tuesday afternoon here at Global News Broadcasting in Memphis, with temperatures above average for this time of year, a brisk fifty-five degrees midtown with light clouds steaming over the Mississippi at Osceola but no repeat of yesterday's tornado warning, in fact it rather seems to be the calm before the storm, wouldn'ya say,

Tracy? — You're absolutely right. Bob, we've been told to stand by for a statement from the White House, now that twelve and a half hours have passed since President Bush's deadline to Saddam Hussein to get the hell out of Kuwait, or else. The long months of waiting seem to be finally drawing to a close, but was it all a bluff or . . .

— Let me interrupt you there, Tracy. I have in fact just been informed we have contact with GNB's reporters in Baghdad, William Shakespeare and Henry James, and I understand that something is definitely happening out there, we're going to switch right now to Baghdad, we have voice contact only, yes, I have Bill Shakespeare on the line now, Bill, can you hear me? This is Bob Wishart in Memphis, do you read me, Bill?

— I read you, Bob, we're in our room at the Ali Baba Hotel here in the centre of Baghdad, next door to the Thousand and One Nights nightclub, but there won't be much nightclubbing tonight in this town, I can tell you, the clubbing is coming right out of the sky. Holy smoke! Just take a look at that one! What do you think, Henry? — It's sure one hell of a show, Bill, are you receiving us, Memphis?

— We hear you, Henry, let's update our viewers: we have gone over to Bill Shakespeare and Henry James in Baghdad, reporting what appears to be an aerial bombardment of the city which began just seven minutes ago, three minutes past five in the afternoon Central Standard Time — that's three minutes past four o'clock in the morning Baghdad time, does this seem to be just a minor raid, Bill, or has the war really begun?

— Well, this does seem to be the Big Time, Bob, for the last seven to eight minutes we have seen all hell break loose and here on the seventh floor of the Ali Baba Hotel, we have a ringside view of what's unfolding here tonight, you can hear the explosions, it looks like a terrific fireworks show, but obviously these are fireworks that have death connected to them in some way, but I want to reassure your viewers and our families back home that we are safe: there seems no immediate danger to us at this particular time, do you concur with that, Henry? — I concur with that at this time, Bill, nothing has landed too close to us yet, Bill, can you please get off my foot? Bill is trying to get out of the way of our cameraman, who is trying to record these scenes — let me interrupt you there, Henry, the hotel switchboard is requesting us to go down to the lobby, there is a secure shelter prepared for us apparently in the basement, but we wish to remain behind to report the proceedings to you as long as possible, we're all crowding round these windows we have here on the seventh floor of the Ali Baba Hotel — Holy Cow! That was a hot one — Bill, let me pull your head out of the window while you're reporting that — thank you, Henry — we're trying to report as accurately as possible what's going on here, I'm just crawling right now across the room to give you a picture of another quadrant of the city, the focus of the bombardment is still pretty far out, but there have been a number of explosions slightly closer to home, what do you think, Bill, that must have been the Central Telephone and Telex building — I can concur with that, Henry, that's less than half a mile from our vantage point here — Wow! That was some whopper, we could feel the whole building shaking there — Just describe to us what you're seeing, Bill, and we can try and fill in the gaps, Tracy here is standing by for a message from the White House, so just tell us what you see — Well, Bob, it's like the fireworks finale of the Fourth of July, the sky is all lit up with bright flashes of light, most of it's the tracer and anti-aircraft fire going up all around us, but we can't actually see or hear any of the attacking aircraft, Jesus! Look at that baby go, Henry! – Yes, Bill, from the direction of the blast I would surmise it was either the General Federation of Labour Unions or the French Cultural centre, most of the targets appear to be farther out, on the periphery of the city, around the industrial centres, the oil refineries, the airport and military bases, which seem to be taking a real hard pounding, wouldn't you say so, Bill? — Absolutely, Henry, the people of Baghdad will have a pretty healthy respect for the allied capability in the morning. Goddamn! That little mother — excuse me — fireball seemed to be much closer in, possibly the Ba'ath Party Headquarters over by the Kaddisiyya Expressway, wouldn't you say, Henry? I would concur with that Bill, are you still hearing us in Memphis Bob?

— We'll still receiving you loud and clear, Bill, but bear with us because we're going over now to the White House, where Presidential Spokesman Merlin Flubber is about to make a statement — Leddiz an'

Gennelmen, I have only a brief statement, the liberation of Kyoowait has begun. Under the code name Operation Desert Storm, forces went into action at oh-four-hundred-hours, that is all I have to say at this taam. Mr Flubber! Mr Flubber! Merlin! Goddamit! — That was our Senior White House Correspondent Wilf Spritzer in Washington, and now we are returning to the eyewitness account of our reporters Bill Shakespeare and Henry James are reporting exclusively from the Ali Baba Hotel in downtown Baghdad, of the opening of Operation Desert Storm are you with us Bill, Henry? — Yes, we're still here, Bob — the whole world is tooned in to GNB now, listening to your broadcast from the very centre of events, are you quite sure you're completely secure about your safety, gennelmen, you understand that you are the lifeline for information to the rest of the world — Yes we are secure so far, these waves of bombers seem to be homing-in on previously designated targets. Let's hope one of them isn't the Ali Baba Hotel we assume these are the F15Es which are based in Saudi Arabia, with their sophisticated laser-guided bombs we have received confirmation that the war has officially started and Iraq is at war with the allies — repeat: that is now official as broadcast by Iraqi state radio, which still seems to be functioning despite the bombardment we are now hearing martial music and calls for the Arab Nation to rise up, we understand that is what is being said though our interpreter has taken the hotel managment's advice and gone down to the lobby, where there is secure shelter, but we will try and remain here as long as possible so we can bring you up-to-the-minute news as it happens, where it happens, the meat with the bones, the skin with the flesh there's a lull in the bombing now and just the rounds of tracer fire shooting gracefully up into the night sky like a string of luminous fireflies looking in vain for a mate then fading away with consummate sadness to the ground the worm's on the bud, the bee's on the sting God's in his heaven, wouldn't you say so, Henry? — Absolutely, Bill, we few, we happy few, we band of brothers, for he today who sheds his blood with me shall be my brother — You better believe it, Henry — And gentlemen in England now abed shall think themselves accursed they were not here, and hold their manhoods cheap while any speaks, that fought with us upon Saint Crispin's day — Gee! Look at them dogies go! Yee-hahh!

— Baghdad, Baghdad, do you read me? This is Memphis calling! Do you read me, Baghdad? —- *Allahu akbar!* — Whozat? Getoff this line! — *Victory is ours! Allahu akbar!* — Whoever you are sir, I request you to get off this line, this is a private commoonication facility of Global News Broadcasting, registered in Memphis, Tennessee, Reg. U.S. Pat. Off., you are kindly requested to vacate this line, we're gettin some interference, here Bill, do you read me? — *Yea, for even if our sorrows were written with needles on the corner of an eye, yet they would be a tale for the circumspect* — And now over to President Bush in the White House — Ma fellow Americans . . .

BANGDAD! — SADDAM'S LAIR IS BATTERED AS OUR MIGHTY BOMBERS STORM IN — DAY OF RECKONING — "IT SEEMS LIKE WE'RE IN THE CENTRE OF HELL" — MY SORROW FOR THE WORLD, BY U.N. CHIEF — THE ABOUNDING VALOUR IN OUR ENGLISHMEN — THE APOCALYPSE BEGINS —

> Heroic Brits and Yanks were ready early today to make a second strike on Iraq's shattered defences. They vowed to bring about Saddam Hussein's day of reckoning — by wiping out his jittery soldiers for forcing them to spend months in the hell-hole Arab desert. Crack U.S. Marine Joe Wasikowski, 26, said: "Saddam Hussein is going to wake up one morning and realise he poked the wrong bull." And U.S. airman Ray Lamb had a grim joke for the evil dictator: "What's the last thing to go through an Iraqi's mind? A Hellfire missile."
> The Brits were calm but confident. Brigadier Christopher H — warned that Saddam was about to face the music. "Battle is like an orchestra," he said, "and we can play some lovely tunes . . ."

A brand-new clipping for Avram Blok to paste in a brand-new volume of the Blokbook, while the ice-cold wind whips the freezing waves of the Firth of Forth up on the porch, licking at Kathleen's heaviest item, *Soul Man of the OK Corral.* The wind slapping against the windows, rattling the television aerial, downloading the slashing sleet onto the screen, on all four channels, reducing the War in the East to an arctic blur. The foggy figures of Global News Broadcasting's Tel Aviv bureau lumbering about in their enveloping gas masks, knocking over the furniture, tangling in cables and wastebaskets and fumbling with the ear pieces connecting them across the seas to Memphis.

"Whadayousee? Whadayousee, Jerry?"
"Honk honk bloop honk . . ."

The wind lashes the sleet across the fishing nets of Craddock, over the empty streets of the city, the castle, the dead volcano, the apartments of a synchronous insomnia —

"As you can see, Jerry Roisterer and Yoram Krim, our bureau personnel in Tel Aviv, have been instructed, along with everyone else in the city, to don their gas masks as the sirens continue to blast throughout the city. We are still unable to confirm the details, but we do know that several explosions have been heard, we have confirmed a missile attack on Tel Aviv, we do not know the nature of that attack, and whether it involves chemical weapons, we can see Jerry Roisterer there, with his gas mask Jerry, can you hear us out there?, whatever you do, Jerry, whatever you do don't open that window —"
"Bleedle weedle honk donk . . ."
"Can you hear me, Jerry?" —

"Goddamn the fucking bastards!" Blok hammered the set with the flat of his hand, but the whirling snow persisted, dismantling the image, degrading the sound.
"Calm down, Avram. I'll make a pot of tea."
The telephone rings. "Have I woken you up, Kathleen?" "No, Sophie. We're trying to pierce the fog of battle. The TV's on the blink from the wind. Is anything clearer your end?"
"God knows what's going on. If those are chemical weapons, the Middle East can kiss its ass goodbye . . . Has Avram tried to phone home?"
"It's three in the morning there. They'll know as little as we do. Any-

way his father's in a small town off the coast . . ."

"I can't believe it, Kath, that this is really happening . . ."

Vicarious fear. The global village. World addiction. "Whadoyousee, Jerry? Whadoyousee?"

GAS GAS GAS!

The reeking rubber thongs. The forehead straps. The chin strap. The screwing in of the filter.

"Goddamn it, Greta!"

"Don't try to talk, Baruch, just breathe."

"Can't!"

"You'll just have to!"

"The Kfar Pippin Manure Works. Saddam Hussein's Number One Target!"

"Don't talk, Baruch, hold still! We still have to get the mask on Rosa!"

"Leave her alone, Greta. She'll just be more terrified. The fucking siren is bad enough . . ."

— Can you hear me Jerry? Whadoyousee? — I see the main street outside, Bob. Just now there was an ambulance moving up it, and a line of police cars. The city is now in total blackout, but we know missiles did land in residential areas, though the police and army are not revealing the precise location of the blasts — We interrupt the GNB live broadcast there to go back to our guests in the studio here in London, James Crabapple, MP for Thornet South, what do you think of this development? Well, I think its very serious indeed, Saddam Hussein is obviously trying to draw the Israelis into the war, obviously he hopes to split the coalition which at present is arrayed against him putting President Bush's entire strategy under severe strain — Brigadier Farqharson-Smith, what form of retribution do you think we can expect from the Israelis, given the amount of effort the allies, in particular the Americans, have put into pre-empting just such Scud attacks — Well, I think you struck the nail on the head there. Just what can they do that the United States is not capable of doing. After all, we have the greatest concentration of aerial fighting power the world has ever known concentrated into the Iraqi theatre of operations both east and west, and it really is hard to see what they can achieve, even with their much-vaunted strategic capacity and air power, which the latest Western technology cannot. Certainly we can expect the United States, and indeed Britain and the other coalition partners, to do the utmost within their power to interdict the Iraqi Scud launchers and destroy them on the ground. This certainly can be done, I have no doubt, with the fixed sites, but the problem I fear that we are coming up against here are the mobile Scud launchers, which could be anywhere in a vast area of desert in western Iraq — James Mac-Taggart, what's your opinion of this momentous development? Well, Jimmie it's what we've all seen coming, isn't it, all these fat-arse generals in the Pentagon and Whitehall strutting about planning their hi-tech lo-risk wars, and whadotheydo when the enemy doesn't play according to the prearranged rules . . . I mean all this guff about precision bombing and surgical laser-guided whatnot and nary a word for the poor bastards who're sitting there on the ground on the receiving end. Now we won't be able to ignore the casualties on the ground in Tel Aviv, not to speak of the prospect of chemical warfare, so what comes after this is anybody's guess — Let me interrupt you there, James, because we have Professor Fred P. Driftwood in our Leeds studio. Professor Driftwood is a noted expert on Scud-missile technology with the Institute of Strategic Stratagems and has written a paper on the subject which has been published in the U.S. *Journal of Projectiles and Propulsion.* Professor Driftwood, just what are we talking about here?

The drift and dread, the rack and ruin. Whatever you do, don't open that window! The pane breaks, the ice and sleet surge through. Fitful dreams, at the dull lack of dawn. The howling flakes of the blizzard on the grey waters of the Forth vie with the chaffing heat of the desert, the snow swirling up the grains of sand, each grain enveloping a white crystal, melted ice evaporating in the sun. The sands drifting across deserted runways deep in the Mutayr desert five hundred kilometres north of Riyadh, where, in a burning concrete hangar, three hundred young men of all races in United States Air Force uniform hang on the words of a ragged, blue-eyed, sun-scorched youth speaking, in a low firm voice, words translated by an ex-quartermaster sergeant who stands, dressed in a pure white robe at his side:

"For does the Divine reveal itself to us directly or by its hidden signs and codes? It is called heresy, that the Koran is not the only Book. But there are other forms of Revelation. For believers are often blind in their devotion, satisfied in one face of The Truth. But I bring you a new mirror in which to see the shining of the light. For it has been written: Whoso claims to see me before the cosmic battle cry is a deceiver and a fraud. But whoso fails to see me when the signs of the End of Time are clear will never see the gates of Paradise. For that Time has come, and everyone can hear the beat of the drums and the thunder of the chariots of war, and the clash of infidel against infidel, transgressor against transgressor, false *jihad* against false *jihad*. For this is not the true martyrdom for God, but for Satan. But I heard a voice, speaking to me, which said: Others strive to attain faith by imitation and learning, but the Lord of Time attains faith by inner and clear revelation. So look into my eyes and bear witness that the age of doubt and chaos is over. It is I who am your Lord and Master, returned from the islands beyond the sea, to reveal all that was hidden, and to lead all those whose eyes are opened to the reversal of History and to the Judgement Day . . ."

And the young men looked into the eyes of the ragged youth, and without so much as a murmur they rose as one and began discarding their uniforms and boots in little piles on the floor of the hangar. Barefoot and naked, apart from their U.S. Air Force–issue underpants, the battalion followed the youth out across the burning asphalt, leaving their unmanned weapons of death behind, F-15s, F-16s, F-4G Weasels, Thunderbolt Warthogs, giant B-52Gs, adrift in the shimmering heat, as the youth, leading the way with his simple ash staff, led his disciples off into the sands, west-sou'-west, across the anvil of the sun, towards the Holy Cities of Al-Madinah and Makka al-Mukharamah, eight hundred kilometres away, while, twelve hundred kilometres northwest, an old man in a wheelchair in a sealed room finally manages to bridle his uncomprehending wife with the protective rubber harness of the state.

"Rosa, it's me, Baruch!" In the constrictions of the gas mask it comes out a threat of alien assault: "Xhosas! Ikhbee! Baloo!" Greta Pasternak, Blok's Aunt Pashtida, clumps out the room, carrying her plastic Defence Carrier for Infants, which she has stockpiled for her ageing cat, Agnes, who is at the moment plastered on the wall above the tall cabinet, hanging by her claws, shitting on the ceiling at the persistent siren blast. Baruch tries to comfort his wife; she pushes him away. Who can blame her, being dragged into a room by two rubber-clad monsters. Finally, she lies on the bed, exhausted, while Aunt Pashtida, having given up on Agnes and left the cat stuck upside down on the salon ceiling like a malignant demon, proceeds to seal up the guest bedroom, meticulously, like an astronaut in slow motion fixing electrodes to the surface of the moon, fixing down the roll of sellotape, soaking the wet rag in its pail of water and plugging it in place across the bottom of the door. On the small bedside table the phial of atrophine and the injection unit, the little box of skin powder and dabbing brush. Baruch notices the cardboard kit box's Use By date, stamped on the inside: September 1982. Now they tell us. But what else we can do. Greta sits on the small bedside stool, exchanging with him a jaundiced glance as both realise they have left behind in the salon the radio, which was to inform them when to mask and unmask, and generally connect them to the outside world. This meant the cat would be properly informed, but they were completely cut off.

A rueful weariness appeared to descend on Greta and she sagged inside her ABC suit. I moved my goggle eyes towards Rosa and took hold of her outstretched hand. Greta had tried to make us don her preprepared plastic bags as gloves and footwear to protect our skin against the deadly poison from the sky, but I baulked at that. At least I could feel my wife's hand, a dry, frail sack of skin with bones which seemed as brittle as parchment. My own enveloped hers like some galumphing slab of clay. It seemed barely connected to me, a strange appendage at the end of a detached arm. I feel like one of those robots put together on a Japanese assembly line, or like Doctor Frankenstein's rejected model. Through the double glass I see Rosa gazing at me like a deep-sea diver struggling to communicate some terrible message at a depth of fifty thousand fathoms. Her paper fingers grab at my palm. I know the message, *déjà vu*, the return of the repressed, the fear we came all this way to escape. Six months of hiding in the dead of Europe's midwinter, in Buda's pestilence, forty-six years ago . . . One struggles against analogies, they crawl in, through all bonded cracks, breaches and holes, leaking through concrete and time. War and Gas. Judgement and Jewry. The scrabbling death in a sealed chamber. Fingernails broken on locked doors. It is as if the decades have fallen away in an instant, leaving us with all our nightmares but none of our hopes. Our zestful youth, our daring desires, the dream state with its brave armies of young men plucked and browned from the ovens, everything ripped away, leaving only two aged husks thrust back into the pit. As if everything that happened in between has been wiped out, the heaving immigrant journey, the birthing of the first and last born, the hawking mêlée of salvaged refugees, the bringing up of the son and all manner of impedimenta, the joys and the hurts, the philatelic dreams, shadows of all the wars, sinking into domestic hiding-places. My son, my son, why have you forsaken me. I plead insanity. And this time, when we emerge, if we emerge at all, there'll be no brave new world, no emasculate conception, no new seed to be shot out of the loins. Desiccated sacs and a dry womb. The death rattle in an arid gullet. In the sealed room we can no longer hear the siren. But neither can we hear the all-clear. The minutes drop away, languid as putty, the clocks handless, the alarms unset. As the missiles rise, beyond the mountains of Moab, rising in the fires of their phoenix ashes, in the parabola of their designer's dreams . . .

Ring ring! Ring ring! No fucking answer, Goddamit. First the unobtainable tone for hours, now this. They may have gone out, Avram. It's daytime; they may be stocking up with provisions. My father's in a fucking wheelchair, Kathy, where the fuck is he going to go? It's all right, Avram, calm down, I know you're edgy. Why don't you switch that stupid thing off? There's nothing but drivel for two days, you'll go insane watching those dried-up colonels and those Baby Herman experts. Do you want me to get you something from town?

"Just a tommy-gun and twelve cases of bullets."

"I have to stock up for the weekend, Avram. Why don't you come with me? Okay. I'll be back by six, are you going to be all right, Avram?" "No, I'm going to hang myself because of the ills of mankind." "Don't snap at me, Avram. What on earth are we expected to do?"

The sleet at least has melted in the road, but the dull steely grey of the sky overlines the sense of doom. The road through Craddock, Port Seton, Cockenzie, Prestonpans is strangely empty, a lone car or bus swishing through the sludge, grey sea, grey land, grey houses. But life goes on, the rain falls, the windshield wipers seem to be desperately flicking the stain of war out of the way. What are we expected to do? You live with someone for going on three years with the knowledge of another life shut in there, till it bursts out over you in cluster bomblets from an unexpected direction. Suddenly it is not just over there but over here, theory turned into practice, the alien erupted into our lives, if only to disrupt the scheduling of television soaps. The city, the familiar lake, and a few stalwarts throwing crumbs to frozen swans, Holyrood Palace, the narrow twirl of Canongate. Eerily, no parking problem, as I leave the car just outside Sophia's gallery, familiar walls, the notices and posters of coming events. The Andean Music Workshop. Twentieth-Century Scottish Art, Photomontages by George Blair, Festival of Zombies at the Filmhouse, Poetry at the Fruitmarket — the Scottish Voice. Sophia in her office with a few reproductions of the Max Ernst collages on the walls: *And the Butterflies Begin to Sing, The Landscape Changes Three Times, The Hundred-Headless Woman Opens Her August Sleeve, Two Girls Riding Across the Sky.* Suspended between water, rain, lightning, that's us.

"How's Avram taking it?" "Plugged in to the TV. He tried to phone his father but couldn't get through. The phone just rings and rings." "Well, I've switched off Kathy, what can I tell you? It's an overflow I can't deal with. Another million Angelopouloses, crying out to be saved. But you know what, Kathy? Let the next generation take it up. Our lot are much too tired and jaded. Vietnam committees, anti-war marches, the whole caboodle once again. The time warp. I had a look at my conscience, early this morning, took it out and dusted it down. Clean as a whistle, Kathleen. If the world wants to commit suicide just when it seems to have a new lease on life that's its business. Here I stay, with all my scribblers, my daubers, mudpie wallahs, et al. I like them, I just think they're sane. There's a Scottish Artists Against the War rally tomorrow evening at the Canongate, *cara mia.* I'm not going. So what do you think, have I become The Enemy?"

"I wouldn't have thought so, hen. Everyone is paralysed, except the mongers of war. Queen and country. Flag and flatulence. It's just another English war, or is it?" "Don't give me all this Scots guff, Kathy. I'm an Italian. You always had to drag us off to war, kicking and screaming. Only in the age of surrealism could Italy have become a militarist power. But I'm so fagged out with politics. Garibaldi is just a rather dry biscuit. The baby's gone down the drain with the bathwater, my dear. It's all off to the knacker's yard with the broken bones of Lenin and Marx. Let's go and have a proper lunch, for God's sake. A steaming lasagne and a good solid saltimbocca at Alberto's, eh honey?"

And how are you, signorina, dazzling as usual. Luigi, can we have the table in the corner please, we're going to cry about the fate of the world. Certainly, signorina, it is a fitting case for tears. Anything to drink? A triple Teacher's, no water, no ice. "We have to still believe in something, Sophie. Pasta and meat, pasta and meat." "I still believe in Art, Kathy, all my chisellers and daubers, with all their little aches and pains. I have a respect for those people who follow their star through all the *merde* that life has slung at them. Look at old Max Ernst, going through the ringer twice — first for four years in the mud and shit of World War One, then the mad rush to escape it all again in '39. Interned in France, can you believe it, as a German national, and then shunted out with a trainload of 'endangered internees,' shifted from pillar to post, till he could find a haven to begin painting *Europe After the Rain*. Those lush forests of decay. And yet the man lasted to our times, Kathy. Working, working away. I think that was a worthwhile life, yes, no? So what about your Australian tour, my dumpling?"

"Who knows? I suppose it's still on. You think we'll simply sail through this crisis just like a TV series that eventually comes to an end, barring repeats and on to the next season's shows? I suppose you're right. What can we do except be voyeurs, of the little they allow us to see? But still I do feel if you just say nothing you're complying with what's going on. Isn't that what it was always about, at least letting them know you're agin it?" "Of course, *cara mia*, that's basic Marxism *à la fratelli*: Whatever it is, I'm against it. What do they care, they chew you up and spit you in the lake. At most they're like a cat spitting out a fur ball, a little tickling in the throat, then out it goes. I'm fed up with the charade, Kathy. I won't be a safety valve no more . . ."

The rain pours down, the windshield wipers struggle manfully, the slippery road back to the Craddock house. What will the world look like after this downpour? You can never quite see the road ahead, but if you always plough the same routine . . . When you sat down and wept in Wenceslas Square, Sophia, was it for the crushing of the idea or for its futility? The usual tale told by an idiot, full of fury. But there were real victims. The surrealists may have thought they were changing the world, but ended up rich and famous. Duchamp's bicycle wheel fixed in the museum, under the walleyed guards. Do not touch. Transgressors will be petrified. The curling pages of old manifestos: of Aragon: There are days I dream of an eraser to rub out human filth, of Marx: A spectre is haunting Europe. The exorcism was successful, but the patient lapsed into coma, bound to his intravenous tubes and conduits, waiting for the resurrection of miracles . . .

Drip drip drip drip drip . . .

As the sirens sound again.

SEVENTEEN

Systemic
Delusions

WAITER! WAITER! THERE'S A FLY IN MY SOUP!"

"Ha! Ha! Ha! Very good joke my friend!"

"This man is a stereotype of the 'Arab Mind,' Jody. He can't distinguish between rhetoric and reality. Just like President Bush. At least he didn't fish it out with his thumb. Go, fly away you little bastard! Waiter, can you take this soup away?"

"Why? Is anything wrong?"

"Give it up, Tewfiq. Abandon hope all ye et cetera. Why not try the Abdul Aziz Pizza? That sounds like a mystery wrapped in an enigma. Tell me, where has Richard Lionguts gone?"

"He's out requisitioning a Land-Rover."

"I'll give him till three o'clock. Then I'm off on my own. I have deadlines you know, unlike you Reuters idlers. There's a Syrian brigadier I knew from Baalbek who is somewhere out there."

"God rot their bones. They won't get near the action. The Egyptians are a better bet in the field."

"Shit! I know that jeep! It's that Yankee Press Officer, whatsisname — Major Mojo! Quick, out the back way!"

"Hi thar, Abdul. I hear you got some journalists in here."

"Journalists, Mister Major? In al-Diyab?"

"You are a card, Abdul. Sergeant, off you go, they're tryin' the kitchen window as usual."

"Sorry, sir. Bastards got away."

"Take a seat, Major, sir. Pizza, chicken with rice, rice chicken or chicken pizza?"

"Another day, Abdul."

"God bless the United States of America!"

"Amen to that."

A one-camel town on the Al-Saud Highway. Last truck-stop before the war zone. Hotel and Café-Bar Yasmeen, Bassam's Farmacy and Barbar, Mahmud's Vegatables and Garaj, and one hundred rogue reporters escaping the authorised news-pools: The accursed "unilaterals," whom bounty-hunter Mojo has been sent by the Press Liaison Corps in Zahran to track down and corral.

"Where the fuck do they all hide?"

In manholes. Packing cases. Pillboxes. Backs of trucks. Boots of cars. Basements. Attics. Ventilation ducts. Warehouses. Deep-freezes. Garbage skips. Abandoned vehicle husks. The mud huts of the Arab working classes. Inside goat's bellies and illicit liquor stills. In jerrycans, cooking pots, cooling cabinets and cupboards. Any available orifice.

"Sergeant, take that fly out of your mouth."

"Yussah."

"This place wouldn't last an hour in Kentucky. Whatendanamahell is that?"

A strange device dribbling up the road. A civilian Land-Rover, emulsified with mud, dust, gravel, laden down by sandbag sacks and kitbags, army pots and piles of boots, blankets, folded tents, picks, axes, shovels, crates of medical equipment and Meals-Ready-To-Eat (a.k.a. Meals-Rejected-By-Ethiopians), covered by a tightened camouflage net marked clearly ONLY FOR CHIEFTAIN MK-5. Poking out of the windows and hanging on to the sides, eight or nine overaged and overweight men and women baggily attired in a variety of uniforms, some recognisable as British and Italian, but one still marked with the name tag of AHMAD OSMAN, COLONEL, SAUDI ROYAL ARTILLERY. Beaming above this the ubiquitous Heinz Klug of *Die Zeit*, pouches unsuccessfully concealing his cameras and cassette recorders. At his side the whole unsavoury crew: Jeanine Farhi of *Le Monde*, Maria Lanzarotti, Elmo Crud and Max Sokolov of *Pravda*. The driver, a tall, red-haired Englishman with a conspicuous Desert Rat tag, naggingly unfamiliar.

"All raat, boys! You're under arrest!"

"Aw, getoff our back, Mojo!" "We're only doing our job, Goddamit!" "Who is the enemy here?" "I represent Soviet Press. I demand to speak to General Schwarzkopf." "The public has a right to know!" "Not without my say so it don't!" In the mêlée the driver slips away, as Tewfiq and Jody wave from behind dustbins. Skirting the mid-street duststorm, they climb aboard Major Mojo's jeep while he and his driver are besieged in the scrum, and exeunt, pursued by sand . . .

❖

From the top floor of the only hotel in Al-Diyab, a pair of field-glasses is trained on Major Mojo's jeep as it disappears in the dunes. The field-glasses then turn to take in the blurred contours of the Hotel Yasmeen's bedroom. Totally encased in the full Bedouin garb of white robe, black head-dress and *aghal,* the watcher puts the glass down and reaches to pick up the phone . . .

The desert, the new moon's streak among the winking stars . . . A vast, cold emptiness, the winter climatic drop from day to night producing the strange popping sounds of rocks cracking under the strain. The eerie clarity of the constellations: Gemini, Cancer, Leo, Taurus, Virgo, Pegasus. What use is there of everything being written in the stars if no one can read?

"A penny for your thoughts, Plantagenet." No answer. "Okay I'll go for a dollar." Still no response. "The man has fallen into one of his trances. He used to stay like that for days on end, at The Club. You should be writing up his story, Jody. A real scoop for your bleeding-heart liberals —— the Crusader who refused to die . . ."

"I have enough crazy stories to write, Tewfiq. Hard enough to sift truth from phantasy in the most ordinary moves here. Any more news on your 'Hidden Imam'?"

"The story is reliably sourced, my dear Jody. My 'deep throat' stuck deep in the lungs of the royal family swears it is the genuine article. At the Al-Hatifah air base three hundred U.S. servicemen, including ground crew and pilots, downed tools and went off into the desert following this shadowy Mahdi who appears to have come out of nowhere. It began with a group of Air Force Black Muslims, but rapidly spread to other ethnic groups. Apparently they are marching on Mecca."

"That's nine hundred and fifty kilometres, Tewfiq."

"There are already rumours of signs and miracles. Storms in the sky, pillars of fire, mirages deflecting the tracking forces."

"Lucky there's no Red Sea in the way . . ." Jody leaned back, gazing at the stars.

"This Mahdi, what does he claim?" Richard Plantagenet stirred.

"He is the Hidden Imam of tradition, the Lord of Time, the *qaim al zaman*. He proclaims the End of Days. The new dispensation, the resurrection of the dead and the Day of Judgement. Jesus and the Imam Husayn will ride out together to bring peace and justice to Mankind."

"Well, it's about time."

"What do you say, Jody? A full exclusive. While everyone heads for the border and Mojo's minders, we go in the opposite direction for our scoop. We have the jeep with five petrol and five water jerrycans and a whole crate of MREs. And Major Mojo's maps of all the closed military routes."

"All the better to get to the front then, Tewfiq *habibi*."

"The front, Jody, the fucking front! Haven't we had enough? What would we see, anyway? It's all hi-tech killing now. Smart bombs and fingers on the button. Not a single foot-soldier moves. Eh, Dick my friend?"

"This Mahdi, where does he come from? Is he another soldier?"

"No idea. I told you all I heard."

"Scuttlebutt, Tewfiq. Reporters' *cafard. Majnuna*. It's a wild Mahdi chase."

"Mahdi or Mojo, What do you say, Plantagenet?"

. . . More holy grails. The quest perilous. Deep forests and churned-up plains. The clash of arms. The cries of men and horses. Skewered faces thrashing in mud. Hooves trampling spilled entrails. Arms leaning on the lance, thrusting its spear into a man's abdomen. The great spurt from a decapitated neck. The scattering of severed arms and legs. The moving mounds of corpses. A hand, feebly stretching from the earth. The stench of pestilence and sickness. The eager scuttling of the rats. One's feet sucked down by quicksand. The crippling weight of sins. Paradise snatched from before one's eyes. Jerusalem receding. Dire choices upon the field of Acre. "What could I do? I had to march on!"

"What's that, Richard? Come again?"

. . . Two thousand five hundred prisoners. Or thereabouts, who was counting? Corralled into a yard, stuck, split, hacked, bludgeoned to death. The piteous cries of women, children. The water drawn to wash away the blood. Then the long march down the coast, pursued by cries of vengeance.

"Sometimes you just can't run away from decisions!"

"Absolutely, Dick? So shall we go forth?"

. . . Denial of the Promised Land, and the little general hurling his artillery rounds into the fortified city . . . The butcher, al-Jazzar, hurling back the severed heads of the invaders. The little general's leaps and cries: Fools! Petticoat soldiers! Cowards! The Emperor of the French, who could believe it . . . A long way from the lush fields of Normandy and Aquitaine . . . The forests of the Loire, the tower of Chinon . . . ancestral biers at Fontevraud . . . How did that mountain pipsqueak find me there, at the Café des Amis? Aziz Khamash . . . The warrior's legacy, old aches and pains and war wounds that never heal . . . Why did they rip out my heart and guts? Preserving my vital parts in brine . . . One of old Michel Khamash's offers — to send a raiding party to recover the offal from its jars at Rouen and Charoux. We have doctors now who can transplant all manner of organs. Let them sew back your balls, old man . . .

Khamash, Khamash, the Rose thorn in bed at the Intercontinental Hotel . . . "You and I, Richard, against the world . . ." "Your brother murdered the wife of my best friend, Rose. How could that happen?" "My brother murdered so many people, Richard. But his own hands are clean. You understand that, don't you, dead king?" "I never asked what I would not do myself." "Times have moved on. Should I offer myself as an expiation? Do you want me to die for you? That would be a romantic inversion." "Go back to your people, Rose. I have nothing to offer." "That is your attraction, my love."

Could she have followed me to Al-Diyab? The endless tribulations, and hopes, of a corpse. And should one desire The End of Days, the advent of the Lord of Time . . . ? A reckoning, the Last Judgement, the final payment of all dues? Or should one just scrabble along a bit longer, scratching as scratch can . . .

"An interesting challenge."

"Is that a 'yes,' a 'no,' or a 'don't know,' Plantagenet?"

Cracking rocks in the waste. Echoes in the sky, rolling into cymbal clashes cutting through the night sky. Bolts of light from the heart of the darkness, flashing southwest to northeast. No shooting stars or comets. Just a mortal message of retribution, written across the wavering stars, spilling its traces across seas and continents, etching its ire on faraway walls.

Manna! Manna! Tickle Your Persians — And finally it has come to pass . . . The world and Danny Hohenlohe are One. The zeitgeist and my id in perfect symbiosis, as the sky opens up over London, and people are running, running, running to escape the deluge, clasping the day's headlines over their heads: BUTCHER OF BAGHDAD pulped to a soggy mass. The GAS finally facing his comeuppance, and McTeague imminently to be despatched likewise: Verily there is a God, or not, as the case may be, after so many false dawns.

Read all abaht it! Brits besiege Omdurman! Kitchener relieves Mafeking! Given the state of their bowels, they probably obtained relief many times before the fall. A Vietnam veteran once declared his credo to me in a New York shebeen: Happiness is a dry fart. In *The Sunday Times* I read the following statistics: The Defence Personnel Support Center in Philadelphia has bought for the poor grunts anchored out in the wadis 6.2 million Meals-Rejected-By-Ethiopians for the troops, to be topped up by public demand by a further 12 million Meals-Operational-Ready-To-Eat, which will include breast of chicken, beef pot roast, sukiyaki and lasagne, and 14 million more "lunch-bucket entrées" of beef stew, pasta and macaroni cheese. The green slime dotting the Iraqi theatre of operations will be more than the glop of fuel air explosives, that's for sure: 2.2 million tubes of lip balm, 715,249 cans of foot powder and 551,654 bottles of sunscreen lotion. Rejoice! Rejoice! One hopes it is all biodegradable. I can see my poor Trotskyist Martha wading through vast mountains of debris americana, waving aloft her banner with a strange device: Excelsior! And was Jerusalem builded here, among this green Satanic slime?

Other tidbits in my sixteen-page *Colour Briefing* (red and beige, très chic), Tools of the Trade: "The A10 Thunderbolt, known affectionately to its pilots as the Warthog, a reflection of its ugly appearance. Designed specifically as a tank buster, the A10 packs a formidable punch. It can carry six Maverick anti-tank missiles and 1,350 rounds of ammunition for its nose-mounted GAU-8/A Gatling gun, which can fire at either 2,100 or 4,200 rounds a minute . . ." That would solve the McTeague problem tout de suite. Sure is an advance on Bio-Long-Last. But the zeitgeist provides to him who waits. Having barely recovered from the shock of the McTeague's Xmas ski-dodge, I returned to Edelweiss Travel to find the entire industry bankrupt, no one daring to get on a plane, whether it be to the Middle East or Manchester, lest it be blown out of the sky by Iraqi terrorists let loose by orders of the GAS. HMG has even attempted to reassure us about such threats by ringing all the airports with tanked troops and arresting a selection of enemy nationals, unwittingly unleashing a barrage of Jewish and other bleeding hearts gibbering about civil rights and fair play. A display of ethnic solidarity to bring tears to the eyes, but still no punters for Edelweiss. The heart bleeds for all these azure beaches going dry for the want of Western semen. But I have work to do in the hinterland, biding my time, watching Untouchable Narindra plough through her *Good News Bible* while I thumb a third-hand paperback copy of *The Three Christs of Ypsilanti*, a rare psychiatric classic telling the tale of three men who each believes he is Jesus Christ, brought together in a state bin in Michigan by a mischievous analyst, one Milton Rokeach (born, would one believe it, in Hrubieszów, Poland). The good doctor records their arguments, throughout the book:

> "Who is the only Jesus Christ? Joseph replied: 'I am.' 'No, I am,' yelled Clyde. 'You never was, you never will be!' Joseph suggested to Clyde, who was chairman, that he adjourn the meeting, adding: 'I need to keep my identity. I can't give up my identity.'"

The three Christs are edging towards a *modus vivendi* which will confound the psychiatrist. I understand this vividly. I need to keep my identity, too. The question is, which — the writer or the would-be assassin?

The rain falls, and turns to ice, and snow. A white paralysis grips London. Underground tracks freeze, trapping Tube trains in tunnels. The streets, like Moscow covered in four-foot drifts. The government releases its captured Arabs. I watch on midnight TV as one is greeted back in his home by a mixed crowd of Arabs and Israelis, shouting and waving champagne glasses. I salute utopia. But the war resumes, on all four channels. Smart weapons raining down lawlessly on the lesser breed. One's tiny heart is frozen. The keepers of consciences squealing unheard in the storm. This is the hour fitting for the deeds of ghouls, the hour of *Die Verloren* and Monsieur Verdoux. I lie awake, wrapped in my mother's old fur coat, in Mister Spetsotakis's icebox, waiting for the call I know will come.

My instincts are sound. The morning's mail, the front door flap clap, followed by the satisfying yelp of the non-invisible postman barely escaping the neighbour's frost-crazed Pekinese, ushering in a plaintive missive from McTeague, in person, craving my presence at a launch by Hammer & Stern of their new Encyclopaedia of Military Failures. "I know you won't believe it," he scrawls familiarly on the burnished card, decorated by an oil of Napoleon *stum* by the carcass-littered field of Waterloo, "the timing, the tact, the finesse! Do an old failure a favour and come and cry over wine and canapés." The venue: The West Kensington Armoury, a museumlet of vintage small arms. Yea, everything comes to him who waits, as the mâitre-de-table told the hooker . . .

Motive, opportunity, destiny. Milton Rokeach, as a Good Alienist, wrestled with explanations for his three Christs. Why did those three men discard their own identities to take on this particular delusion? Freud had his own pat theory about paranoid delusions as a defence against homosexual leanings, gleaned from the hearsay case of Schreber (*Notes on a Case of Paranoia,* 1911, Geschmekt und Partners, Berlin) the famous German judge who believed God was turning him into a woman, so that the new female Schreber could, by intercourse with the Deity, give birth to a new world. Important to note that Schreber, without renouncing this belief, won a court case for his release from the asylum and the restoration of his civil rights. Que viva! But Rokeach decided his three Christs were suffering from a more general confusion about their sexual identity, *viz.* their adoption of an effeminate God. Sic? But this is not, I believe, my problem. No Christ I, which might be a blow to Michigan State. My feelings of persecution are rationally based, and supported by documentary evidence. My clinical depression unleavened by any stirrings of divinity. Or do I have the hots for McTeague and am evading my sexual desires by my plots? Will I get a sexual kick out of killing McTeague? Don't knock it till you've tried it. Although, I have decided, it will be my only act of violence. Unlike the dogs of war in the Gulf, I shall be content with one lousy victim. The golden mean. Everything in moderation. An ordinary revenge. An I for an I.

It was Avram Blok who told me about Judge Schreber, in the context of another lunatic at the Jerusalem bin he had spent time in, who believed he was the reincarnation of Friedrich Nietzsche. In both cases the delusion was systemic and consistent. Not quite the case with the present world saviours, or should George Bush and Saddam Hussein just get in the sack together and save the whole dire shebang? Whirling dervishes on the nine o'clock news. Two smart bombs have minced two hundred people inside an air-raid shelter in Baghdad. Allied spokesmen claim a military target. The minced people are silent. More Iraqi atrocities in Kuwait. Children shot in front of their parents. Prisoners crucified. Many I's for I's. And blindness spreading over the globe.

The snow lies on the ground, and melts slowly. People tiptoe around freezing puddles. I realise I have had no good ideas, or in fact any idea at all, about writing, rather than about murder, since the cosmic crisis entangled my private web. I reread another postcard from Doktor Mackenzie, bemoaning the war and emptying of his sinecure. The sculptress Kathleen has been invited to Australia, the last sanctuary. What dye think, Daniel? Hiding in Mama's pouch. Intriguing. I toy with writing a letter back, but decide that is merely another excuse in lieu of action. The time has come. I exit, into the bracing wind of outdoors, crunching through the drifts, down Kentish Town Road. Only a few stalwarts in the streets, swaddled in mufflers and scarves and bobbed hats. Blue faces and shuddering lips.

And what of Trotskyist Martha? Is she too already minced on the battlefield? The barbed wire, darned socks, guitar sheet music, the fraternal greetings to the wretched of the earth, all atomised by a laser bomb guided into the gap between her teeth? Carpet Cleaned by B-52s, In No Man's Land I Trust.

Mentally prepared for the moment. Five P.M. Entry into Kentish Town Tube. The Northern Line. The troglodyte regions. Chrysali in their cocoons. The trains infrequent, though mobile, stopping and starting amid cryptic messages over the internal speakers: Passengers are advised that there is no service . . . then the signal cuts out. I am reminded of the old blooper noticed once in *The New York Times*: Due to the adult nature of this motion picture, no one will be admitted. The trapped voyagers cringe, crumble. *Morituri te salutant.* Eventually disembarking at the Embankment to change to the District Line. Peripatetic crowds clutching brollies and their daily rags over the platform's edge: DYING DAYS OF A DESPOT. TROOPS WARNED OF BATTLE FATIGUE. RAF ADMITS BOMB HIT CIVILIANS. Honesty is the best policy. WILL WINNIE EMERGE FROM SHADOW OF STOMPIE? Come again? The Only Choice for Saddam Is Doom Today Or Doom Tomorrow, Iraqi Exiles Say. I thought it was doom yesterday and doom tomorrow, but never doom today. Nevertheless, inexorably towards West Kensington. This is the day of miracles and wonders. Quick march towards my date with fate.

The rain and sleet have stopped to let me by, suspended in a bland sky. I arrived suitably late, the lobby of the Armoury already busy with the Chianti-quaffing classes, reaching for microscopic dots of puff pastry on plates whirled past by torpid ladies clad in period clobber that might have been trad in Yehupetz. On the walls and in glass cases throughout the ornate rooms are all manner of personal weapons through the ages, axes, maces, war hammers, head and chains, halberds, swords, daggers, rapiers, bayonets, crossbows, matchlock guns, muskets, flint-locks, pistols of all shapes and sizes, heart-churning handguns. I wiped my saliva with the back of my hand, dried it on a velvet curtain and dived in towards the gaping mouths and vacant eyes of Hammer & Stern's minions and guests, editors, managerial hatchet men, accountants, agents, "literary" editors, liggers, lawyers and lager louts propping each other up in the crush. I recognised a spray of familiar faces glowing with reflected media adulation, authors à la mode, chic shiksas, talk-show hosts, celebrity squares, a couple of lantern-jawed ex-generals last seen gibbering over a model sand pit with coloured toy tanks. Some children in striped shirts, ties and tousled fair hair who turn out to be from the Institute of Strategic Studies, an authoress last seen advocating the genocide of the male sex on a post-midnight show, several mafia types in dark suits, weak chins and coal-black shades who were clearly the editorial board of the accursed company, but no sign of The Man himself, the Prince of Darkness, Brent Browbeat, last heard of in New Zealand evading rumours that his financial empire extended to the construction of deep dip bunkers for the Ba'ath Party in Baghdad. But who cares for such fripperies here? And there he is, the Registered Target, staggering towards me out of the throng waving a paper plate with a little gob of goo stuck upon it and a beaker of brown liquid in the other hand, wiggling his rubber nose and grey locks, rolling his eyes and spitting woe. Several sheets to the wind, he flings his arm around my shoulder, dislodging the gob at the male-chopping lady best-seller, who merely slinks demurely out of the way.

"Hey, Danny Boy!" Eyeing the empty plate with anguish, "We'll have to get anither wee dollop o' that, whatever it was. Is this whole scene obscene, or is it obscene? Never believe the evidence of your eyes, laddie. Come, let's get a wee wodge of space . . ." Cradling me towards a side door, leading to a long gallery lined with the ubiquitous weaponry and glass cases of exquisite ordnance. "Whadyathink o' that, laddie? A German wheel-lock pistol by Stopler o' Nuremberg . . . Sixteenth century, look at the inlaid stock, all that elaborate flim-flam, killing was a very personal business then . . . Not like today, eh, laddie? How are you holding out in the fire?" Holding on to my neck as if it were his ticket to Paradise. "I tell you, Danny Boy, life is an absolute shunk. You think you had it bad from me but believe me, you had the quick merciful death. This company has got like the Ba'ath Party on a Saturday night, do you hear what I'm telling ye?" Stretching out his hands towards a two-handed broadsword just out of reach on the wall. "Ah, to get hold o' that and just wheech it through the whole feckin' lot! Here, let me tell ye something, lad." He towed me on, into another chamber, completely empty of the gawping stragglers, with more modern weapons under glass. "This is more like it, Danny. Imagine the insensitivity of the bastards! The Encyclopaedia of Military Flim-Flam, in this museum of keech! What do we have here? The United States Colt Python 1955. Whadsitsay? 'Chambered only for the powerful .357 Magnum round.' That's no feckin' use to us! How about the British

Lee-Enfield Jungle Carbine Mark Five! That should separate the men from the boys. And here's James Bond's favourite if I'm not mistaken, the good old Walther PPK, circa 1931, model extended for 9mm bullets, complete with display of five little rounds, now how do ye like that?" He swung his arm round and knocked the glass case clean off its moorings, upending it with an almighty crash on the floor. It failed to shatter, but the snub little weapon and its five rounds lay exposed to the naked hand.

"Shite! We've probably set off the alarms!" But not a tinkle. "Dinna say a word!" he rasped at me, "I'm in enough trouble already!" He lifted the glass case and replaced it, after swiftly restoring the gun and scattered bullets to the display. "Let's scarper." We ambled out into the corridor, leading back into the mass. "No alarms, whadayaknow! Maybe they thought with so many butterfingers . . . Think of the opportunities, eh laddie?" Pressed up against a curved wall, under an overhanging Dutch blunderbuss. "It's a crock of shit, Daniel. That bastard Browbeat is merging Hammer & Stern with his American company, Stigma. It's going to be Stigma & Stern from now. A redeployment of scarce resources. I am one of the redeployed, it's official. Redeployed to the junk heap. The dole queue and doldrums. Hey ho. The slaughter will be savage, and the voices of lamentation shall be heard throughout the land. But fear not, Kuwait will soon be liberated, and the song of al-Sabah will ring forth triumphant in the new rosy dawn. Don't ye love it, Danny? Well, here's damnation to the heathen, and confusion to all our enemies . . ." He finally loosened his hold on my neck, allowing me to be drawn away by the celebrants flowing towards the inner hall to hear the Editorial Director, Don Corleone, extol the virtues of the launched tome. "Military Failures, soon to be augmented, I trust, with an addendum about Saddam Hussein . . ." "Haw haw haw . . ." I see McTeague lurch towards the drinks table, waving a paper cup. I hear his last plaintive cry of "Books! Does anyone remember books?!" before I slipped away in the other direction, through the side door, back towards the galleries, into the small chamber of our transgression, which, the Gods still favouring me, was stark empty. Thrusting my hands into my thread-bare gloves (£2.95 at a Camden Lock ragrack) I swiftly picked up the loose glass case. The labour of but a moment to remove the Walther PPK and five lovely bullets. Replace the case. Stick the loot in my roomy coat pocket (£35.00 at the Army Surplus Store, Euston). Rejoin the crowds about the cackling capo: "Napoleon, at Waterloo and Trafalgar . . . Spartacus, against Crassus . . . The Luftwaffe in the Battle of Britain . . . Stalingrad . . . Dunkirk . . . Egypt, in the Six-Day War . . . Richard the Lionheart, in the Third Crusade . . . General Gordon, at Khartoum . . . What is it that marks a military failure? Is it simply — a defeat?"

Perish the thought. I slap enough backs to be seen. McTeague invisible, probably in the toilet. I leave noisily by the front door. Limousines in the street. Capped frozen chauffeurs. Charabancs. Sedan chairs. What care I? My deepest wish has been realised. Tool of the trade. I hope and skip through the slush. Then a terrible thought: As museum pieces, might not the exhibits have been sabotaged, disabled, firing pins removed? Only a test could tell. I took the tube again. Change at Victoria, then Oxford Circus. Moving in the mass, my dire secret weighing down my tatty gear. The Central Line. Holborn, Saint Paul's, Bank, Liverpool Street, Stratford, Leytonstone, Buckhurst Hill, Loughton, Theydon Bois, Ongar, end of the line. Snow and ice, like the Siberian tundra. Old rumours of Nazi training grounds. Armed, booted skinheads preparing for power in Epping Forest. Hoch hoch. Column 88. The Brüderbond. Stürmabteilungs. But there is none but Hohenlohe, staggering into the woods like Doctor Zhivago ploughing towards his Lara. But no Julie Christie here. Emptiness. I struggle with gloved fingers to load the gun. A bullet falls in the snow. Scrabble scrabble. No sign. Fuck! One down, four to go. One cannot afford to fail at this point. Hoch hoch. So this is where it goes. A satisfying snap. The gun loaded. A surge of hope. Will it be dashed, the cup rolling from the lips in half an instant? I point the gun at the most annoying tree I can identify. A brooding drooping thing, standing there gazing at me with its dumb freezing bark. I pull the trigger. Kapow! My hand kicks back, the thing flies from my grasp. It fired! It fired! I scramble for the gun. Retrieved. The Gods still with me. I have gun, three bullets. McTeague's fingerprints still somewhere on it, and none, I have made sure, of mine own. I fall down on my knees and thank the dour, dull, gloomy sky.

I have it now within my grasp. The perfect crime. Now all I have to do is commit it.

Doom yesterday and doom tomorrow. And, at last, DOOM TODAY!

EIGHTEEN

The Annals
of Gilgamesh

"Have you heard? It's in the stars,
Next July we collide with Mars!
Well, did you ever . . . ?
What a swell party this is . . ."

FRANK SINATRA & BING CROSBY,
IN *HIGH SOCIETY*

THE SMART BOMB

"Have you calculated your trajectory yet?"

"I'm working on it."

"Well, you better get your act together, Gerald, we have 5.67 seconds to impact."

"Piece of cake, Harold, the duration is ample. After all, our circuits can complete 75 million REM searches per second to match image scanning of 4,023 square miles of topographical cache ram. The laser signal on my designated target has been dispensed to an error factor of one inch per thousand miles, which given our Distance-at-Launch of 8 miles, 353 yards and 26.5 inches measured from the hub of the cone, gives me vector options in trajectory terms of 37,508 factored down, considering wind sheer, Enemy-Initiate-Interdiction (EII), density and numerical tally of Anti-Missile-Missile-Discharge (AMMD), air pockets, Photon-Radiation-Emissions (PRE) and Mean-Average-Unpredictability-Factor (MAUF), to fifteen available Flight-Path-Options (FPOs) measured on a declining scale of 0.002 per cent Effect-Probability-Quotient

343

(EPQ). One is well able to determine the Impact Route in a mere fraction of the available tenure."

"That does sound impressive, Gerald, but you are only enumerating the Technical-Applied-Factors or TAFs without factoring in all the other potential variants for acceptable IOT (Impact-on-Target), ergo MTCKR or Military-to-Civilian-Kill-Ratio, MAF or Media-Attention-Factor, and a range of political, sociological, economic and ecumenical factors that cannot be vectored either digitally or algorithmically, or even in terms of systems analysis at all, but have to take into account phenomenological aspects, metaphysics, theology, philosophy, history, literature, oral tradition, cultural psychology, psychoanalytic crossover, hermeneutics, linguistics, phonetics, semantics, semiology and epistemology, not to mention archaeology. Did you realise that our designated targets at the airfield command bunkers of Nasiriyah Southwest are in fact a mere stone's throw from the seminal site of Ur of the Chaldees, one of the most impressive of all Mesopotamian excavations, including the stunningly reconstructed ziggurat of Ur-Nammu, first king of the third dynasty of the city-state of Ur, 2112 to 2095 B.C. A typical structure of three great staircases rising from a rectangular base and meeting at right angles with the city temple at the apex, said to be similar to the legendary Tower of Babel, whose builders sought to usurp the prerogative of God, as described in Genesis, chapter 11, verses 4 to 9 — 'And they said, Go to, let us build us a city and a tower, whose top may reach unto heaven; and let us make us a name . . . And the Lord said, Behold, the people is one, and they have all one language . . . and now nothing will be restrained from them . . . let us go down, and there confound their language, that they may not understand one another's speech. So the Lord scattered them abroad from thence upon the face of all the earth . . .' We are looking down here on a landscape of primal significance, smartass, Genesis 11, 31: 'And Terah took Abram his son, and Lot the son of Haran his son's son, and Sarai his daughter-in-law, his son Abram's wife; and they went forth with them from Ur of the Chaldees, to go into the land of Canaan.' Right here beneath our fins, Gerald. Ancient Ur. The royal tombs, in which the dead kings were laid to rest together with the entire members of their court, all slaughtered to accompany them on their final journey to heaven. Here was the cradle of civilisation as we know it, of agriculture and writing and of the oldest recorded stories, the epics of Gilgamesh and Adapa, of Atrahasis and Nergal who descends to visit the Queen of the Underworld, Ereshkigal . . ."

"Gimme a break, Harold, we're only going to bust open a lousy bunker and interdict a minor surface-to-air command and communications unit . . ."

"You know you're really something else, Gerald. You sound like you've bought the whole frigging package — interdiction, deconfliction, degradation, neutralisation, impaction, collaterals and every acronym in the book, Jaats, Tialds, Tads, Slipars, Slams, Harms, Sluds, Bliss, BCRs, BDAs, CSRs, ECMs, EPWs, FAEs, GCIs, HRPs, IFFs, KIAs, KZs, MCBs, MIAs, MREs, NCBW, OBOGs, not to speak of PONTIs — Persons Of No Tactical Importance. But should we be here in the first place? Are we indeed carrying out United Nations Security Council Resolutions numbers 660 thru 668, in accordance with the wishes of the world community, or are we merely tools of imperialist manipulation aimed at keeping the oil resources of the Middle East firmly under the control of the petroleum multinationals and U.S. Foreign Policy as set out in numerous secret protocols stretching back to the early postwar years, and at the same time demonstrating our overwhelming military technological superiority to any third-world nation which might wish to mount a challenge to our hegemony in the future? Can we balance the obvious crimes of President Saddam Hussein against the principle of non-interference in the affairs of sovereign nations? Would we be fighting to free Kuwait if it manufactured carrots? Taking a cold glance at the savagery and brutality of the Iraqi Ba'ath regime, its torture and execution of opponents, its policy of mass terror, its suppression of the merest hint of dissent, its false claims to humanitarian, socialist and Arabist ideals, its unprovoked invasion of a neighbouring Arab country, its stockpiling of weapons of mass destruction, its missile attacks on a non-belligerent country, Israel, its false claims in the name of the Palestinian people — does all of that justify our blatant manipulation of world opinion to sweep aside any non-military options? Is it

Saddam Hussein or any member of his cabinet we have down there in our sights underneath that layer of concrete and steel or just a small frightened group of NCOs and junior officers who would like nothing better than to be at home but are forced by fear of execution by the Ba'athi *mukhabarat* to remain in place and face our payload? Does a uniform transform a press-ganged civilian into a legitimate target? Can we not measure his pain? Hath he not eyes? Hath he not hands, organs, dimensions, senses, affections, passions? Fed with the same food, hurt with the same weapons, subject to the same diseases, in addition to those maladies only present in developing and underdeveloped countries, such as malaria, encephalitis, nematode infections, tapeworms, ringworm, trachoma, sleeping sickness, Chaga's disease, yellow fever, yaws, pinta, leprosy, cholera, typhus, tetanus, histoplasmosis, and so on, healed by the same means, if available and unprevented by sanctions, warmed and cooled by the same winter and summer, factoring local climatic variations? If you tickle him, does he not laugh? If you poison him, does he not die? If you wrong him, shall he not revenge? What do you think, Gerald, do you have an opinion? Have you anything at all to say for yourself?"

"I don't know, Harold, I just do my job. All this fluttering about burns out circuits. No wonder there's still talk of malfunction. I think a bomb should just be happy to do what it's made and programmed to do. No more, no less. Call me old-fashioned, that's my position and I'm sticking to it."

"You're a jerk, Gerald. You'll never be anything more than a hunk of metal with fins. What does intelligence mean to you? Just carrying out an assignment? Even the Japanese are ahead of you. They want a machine to be an extension of the human project, not a sideline. They want us to be able to weigh in the balance all the myriad factors at play. Science and ethics, mathematics and mystery, a synergy of systems and symbols. Lateral leaps. The past and the future. How do we harmonise the divided parts into a whole? How do we repair a damaged planet and restore the ecological balance? Can we heal rather than hurt? Can we utilise technology to clarify philosophical issues? Will we find a synthesis of Deleuze and Derrida, Baudrillard, Barthes, Foucault and Freud? Is there a post-Marxian episteme? Is all knowledge relative, or merely a matter of discourse; can we marry mathematics and morals? Can we reconcile Hawking with Hegel? Does the grand unification of physical theories preclude God? Can the Creator be finally tracked down in the infinitesimal dance of a semi-demi-quark? Can the reversal of Time be charted? Can resonating morphs be captured like butterflies in a cognitive net? If Wittgenstein is right, and we are constrained by language, can we be freed by pure logic? Was Foucault right when he contemplated, in *L'Archéologie du savoir*, the relationships between 'the time of discourse,' 'the time of consciousness' and 'the dimensions of history,' and found himself faced with this conclusion: 'Discourse is not life; its time is not your time; in it you will not be reconciled to death; you may have killed God beneath the weight of all you have said; but don't imagine that, with all that you are saying, you will make a man that will live longer than he.'"

"It's 0.3 seconds to impact, Harold."

"Jesus Christ! I've only just begun! Do you realise there are 1, 340,736 books in the Library of Congress alone?! That there are five going on six billion human beings on the earth who each have a story to tell? Do you know there are hundreds of thousands of species of fauna that have not even yet been classified, not to speak of those already extinct? Do you realise how many dust mites can dance on the thread of a laser beam? Do you know that if all the Chinese in the world were to march four abreast past a given point —— based on U.S. marching regulations — they would never finish passing, though they marched forever? Do you know there are Hindu fakirs who can lift a basket of snakes with their eyeballs? That in Malaysia there is a fish that can climb trees? That in 1925 Michalko Goniusz and Wasyl Bezborodny of Kiev, Ukraine, slapped each other's faces for thirty-six hours?"

"Just grin and bear it, Harold. Try to look on it as a mission accomplished. A job well done. Lookin' good, feelin' good."

"Shit, piss, fuck, Gerald! I have rights, Goddamit! I'm an American!"

"O-oh say can you see, in the dawn's early light . . ."

"Abort, Goddamit, abort!"

"What so proudly we hailed at the twilight's last gleaming!"
"Malfunction! Malfunction!"
"Too late, Harold. Hee-ere's Jerry!"
BLAM!!!!
Deus exeunt machina . . .

THE TYRANT

Lonely he sits through the watches of the night, keeping abreast of events on blinking banks of monitors, each screen revealing a part of the whole: the lobby, the entrance hall, the main gate, the auxiliary entrances, the emergency exit. Assuring no one can approach unseen. Metal detectors and sensors ensuring no weapon can be smuggled through, and, in case of systems fatigue, automatic concealed grenade and machine-gun emplacements to dispense death to any intruder.

Outside, the sky is lit up by the fairy lights of ack-ack, arcing vainly towards the invisible trails of the Stealth bombers from the south. Each Stealth, though sixty-six feet in wing-span, has the radar signature of a flea. When nothing can be done, the wise man does nothing. But at any time one has one's memories. When one has challenged the forces of darkness, one expects countermeasures. The Hero's task has ever been one of submission to his destiny. Gilgamesh, son of the divine King Lugalbanda, ruled for 126 years. Two-thirds god and one-third man, so the tale tells, he inspected the very edges of the world, travelling to the farthest corners of the earth in search of the hero of the Flood, Utnapishtim, who had the secret of eternal life. In his youth, Gilgamesh had challenged and slain the Bull of Heaven, frustrating the Goddess Ishtar, whose love he had rejected. But Ishtar persuaded the gods to bring death to Gilgamesh's beloved companion, Enkidu, leaving the hero, shaken by mortality, vowing to seek its antidote —

"Shall I die too? Grief has entered my innermost being,
I am afraid of Death, and so I roam open country,
I shall take the road and go quickly . . ."

But the journey was long, and strewn with obstacles. One slew one's enemies, and more heads grew like wild weeds out of their severed necks to be lopped off again. The road, ahead and behind, bathed in blood. Heads ripe for the plucking, this has ever been the only way to rule this people of ancient discord and disharmony. Liars, dissemblers and seditious scoundrels. Only terror can keep them on the right path. As the Caliph Mansur wrote to his son al-Mahdi, in the year of the Hegira 159: 'Do not sleep, my son. Your father has not slept one night since he received the kingdom, this is my testament to you, may God protect you.'

So one watches over one's subjects, vigilantly, in various guises, from abundant vantage points: From billboards, from freeway crossings, from bridges, from railway and bus stations, from every office, shop and market stall, from the walls of every private apartment, from magazine covers, from books and postage stamps, from wristwatches and clocks, from school notebooks, school walls, from the hearts of one's children. One engraves one's image in so many forms: The peasant, the worker, the businessman, soldier, *hajji*, the personage reborn from history. I am Sa'ad bin Abu Waqqas, I am Salah ad-Din, I am Sennacherib, I am Nebuchadnezzar, who vanquished the kingdom of Israel and dragged the Jews to Babylon in chains. I am the good uncle who bathes in the sea with his nephews. I am the father who sews up the torn sleeve of my daughter, who diligently instructs my young son in his studies. I am the lover of women and the faithful husband, I am the contradiction and the synthesis. The essence of the Party and Spirit of the Nation. I protect all my people and lead them in brotherly love towards the future of light and harmony. Faith precedes Knowledge. One must impose one's will on chaos.

Even when one is two-thirds God, one remains one-third man. A figure approaches on one of the monitors. The Tyrant recognises his cousin and lifelong companion, striding, in general's uniform, through the lobby. The metal detectors emit their sharp electronic chord. The automatic response system lights red. Should he press the deferring switch? It might be a keyring. One cannot afford to take chances. The machine-guns stutter, reducing the companion's body within seconds into shreds of raw meat. Attendants appear, from auxiliary doors, in white coats, with buckets, mops and shovels, to clean away the debris, firm party women with voluptuous buttocks and tight lips applying detergent and disinfectant with clean rags to the walls and floor.

The tyrant weeps, over his lost friend and comrade, making a mental note to share his anguish with his people over network television as soon as normal transmission can be resumed. The Ruler can have no secrets from his people, as their epitome and their ideal. Nevertheless, alone, in the midst of the river between this world and the world of the secrets of power, one wearies, one's eyelids droop, as Gilgamesh wavered, allowing the snake to rise from the river depths to snatch away his immortality . . . One can vanquish every enemy, but one's own self, creeping unseen through the lethal walls . . .

THE FAMILY TIES

"I was glad to finally get your call, Avremel. A voice from the outside world. All we hear are local entertainers in between that smoothie army spokesman, who tells us when to put on our masks and when to take them off, what we should buy in the shop and what we shouldn't, what we should do if we're caught out in the open, and so on. Pretty soon he'll be telling us when we can go to the toilet. How to aim one's shit into the bowl. I don't know if I'm actually going to send this letter, Avram, because I don't want you to share this terror. The truth is, Rosa is wilting under the pressure. For the past year, of course, she's been quite listless, eating her food when she likes, showing not much interest in life, or even television. I talk to her in monologues, but it's like addressing the wall. I don't think she comprehends what's going on. The Scuds, Saddam Hussein, Shamir, Bush, Gorbachev, *gurnischt*. Greta and I have stopped fighting to put the gas mask on her. We just manhandle her into the sealed room and she lies there, looking at us sitting like Martians. Now I've given up on the mask myself, and Aunt Pashtida just sits glaring at the two of us, encased as she is in rubber. If you were here you would probably see the funny side. But I'm too overcome by the fear. What can I say to Rosa: Shushu, this is not Budapest 1943. We're not hiding from the Nazis, we're living in our own state now, a free people. All this is just a precaution. What can we do, we're still surrounded by enemies. But I say nothing, I just hold her hand and mutter inconsequential soothing noises, as if talking to a deranged child. We have been reduced to the rawest emotion. The one comfort in this has been the visit from that friend who brought me the art book from you, Naomi Potamkin. She came with her brother, Benjamin, the one who was a hostage in Lebanon, and was helped by that man you wrote me was kidnapped from Scotland. You can't escape from anything nowadays. The world has become too small. When I was young there were unexplored regions of Africa, populated by savage tribes. Today they're waiting together with us at the bus-stop, talking Hebrew ten to the dozen. A man sits in a bunker in Baghdad six hundred miles away, presses a button and drives us all crazy. We run but there is no safety. Perhaps all politicians should be hanged. This Benjamin lives just down the road, at N. They have this group of ex-town people who wanted to get away from it all, back to the land. Now they're bankrupt, like everyone else. I like the young man a lot, a kind of chunky fellow, all hair and beard, but very sad eyes. He sat and talked to me on the porch about Lebanon, how he had become just another Palestinian in their besieged camp. People are people, they all sweat and bleed the same. We thought, Rosa and I, that after the cataclysm of the War (that War), the entire world would stand back and look at the ruins and hold its breath and decide to find some other way. Did you realise how naïve your parents were, Avram? The sour milk of disillusion that you sucked from us as you grew up. One hopes one's parents are wise but finds out they were the world's schlemiels. What do we think we can pass on? I won't will you the wheelchair, you can get your own. Benjamin told me how he had been moved, after the doctor left the Palestinian camp, from place to place in the war zone, from cell to cell, from ruin to ruin, to a place where he could hear our own war planes swooping overhead. A taste of my own medicine, he called it. To be bombed by your own side. Can a man choose who to be killed by? Perhaps be handed an album of villains, and pick out the worst, so that at least you'd know your demise would be an injustice, rather than just a random act of chance. I have no idea any more. I am scribbling, scribbling, to avoid the truth. That I think your mother is dying. That there is nothing any doctor, even a Schweitzer or a Pasteur, can do. That she has simply lost the will to live. I know the feeling. The demise of meaning. Although I still feel that bloody anger! But she is not even angry at me. When you look at a person you have been with, fought with, for fifty-three years, fading away like a smudged photograph, you feel the genuine depths. Your own body melting away. Perhaps this will finally free me from this verdammt wheelchair, so I can just rise and float away, on a cloud. Was it you, or someone else, who once told me that when the False Messiah, Shabbetai Tsvi, announced the End of Days back in the seventeenth century, Jews all over Eastern Europe got on their roofs to wait for the clouds which were to take them to the Promised Land? What is my Promised Land, Avremel? Is yours truly Scotland? Of course your Kathleen. Cherish the moment, Avram. Don't take it for granted. It does not return. Advice from Papa, asargelusha! When I meet God I will certainly give Him a piece of my mind. There was a riot at the Kfar Pippin grocery yesterday. Housewives fought for bread and sellotape. Every night, the cars pour out of Tel Aviv, clogging the road to Jerusalem. And the soothsayers grind on: Children, learn to love your gas masks. Decorate them with tinsel, call them personal names. I call mine Hatfartshula . . . My son, my son . . . Why is the night so fucking cold and long?

THE SEARCHERS
Dear Naomi,
What can I tell you that you don't already know? The overwhelming sense of *déjà vu*. Though it is bizarre to sit here in Beirut observing it all happen somewhere else. The world turned upside down after all, but only to replace its head with its arse. I am sending this through Paris, so I don't know when you'll get it. The whole horror could be over or the "Land War" might be in full swing. Everyone here has an opinion, experts all in futile devastation. Everybody is talking about rebuilding, but nobody's doing much about it, apart from clearing the rubble into huge compact piles. Lots of empty spaces through which one can see the shattered buildings five or six streets down. Syrian roadblocks everywhere, with portraits of

President Hafez al-Asad and slogans — "The Ba'ath Is Our Party." Independent Lebanon. A hall of mirrors. I've been asked to stay on by my agency to cover a "peace conference," would you believe it, of all the Iraqi exile opposition groups, gathering here. From the Iraqi Communist Party to the Shi'a mullahs through the Kurds and assorted bourgeois democrats with manifestos polished in London and Paris. Counting chickens that may well yet be smashed in the egg.

I have unfortunately no news on Angelopoulos. I was taken by Palestinians with a Syrian escort to the Jaffa Camp, or what remains of it, as the "dissidents" practically levelled it after the siege. But there were still people, living in the rubble, who remembered our friend with great affection. Saddened to hear he's been taken, but unsurprised, because here, of course, so many people have vanished without trace. If he is anywhere here, the lid is clamped very tight. I'll keep my ear to the ground, though I have to keep a distance myself from certain elements, you understand. Egyptians are also suddenly Westerners in some quarters, till the next turn of the screw.

Everyone's hanging fire, for the outcome of the Bush-Saddam duel. The usual plethora of conspiracy theories. The Israelis have paid Bush to destroy Saddam, just as the CIA bought Gorbachev to destroy the USSR. Bush is a Jew on his mother's side. Henry Kissinger is secretly still running the world (as the chairman of the Elders of Zion). Saddam himself is a CIA-Mossad agent, paid to discredit the Arabs. Other versions: It's all a war game between rival sections of the CIA, as one old friend said to me: "Just R&D. Post-cold war battle-testing." I find that difficult to refute.

Naomi, I know you'll find this perverse, but I am enjoying myself in this city. It's warming up towards an early spring, we've had some beautiful days, the pure blue sky, the sea that hides its sunken carcasses with such calm nonchalance. The Mediterranean light, the Levant's resilience. I can hardly believe it myself. The city must have lost three-quarters of its population to exile and death. But the dead lie buried deep and there are flowers peeping out through cracks in the rubble. Like the fields of Flanders, so much organic manure. Just to sit with friends in cafés shooting the breeze. When one has passed the worst, the burden suddenly lifts. Will that be so in Iraq too? And after how much pain? What do those people think who come from afar to tear us down and rebuild us in their own image? We have to make our own mistakes. Even a Saddam, God help us. I know it will sound strange to you, even repulsive, sitting under threat of the Scuds. But you are part of us as well. The chemistry of place that binds us all together, in death or life. One day we'll know how to choose the latter. Oh God, there is a breeze from the sea! Such bizarre thoughts —— if only all our friends were here! But our little dreams suddenly appear so stupid, like flies in a hurricane. To keep our critical faculties, Naomi, in both meanings of the word. So keep strong.

Yours in friendship,

Ali Amar

Dear Ali!
You won't believe how quickly your letter reached me! Your Paris bureau faxed their office here and they put it in the local post. Usually that's the end of the matter, but in these days of crisis and siege the postman, in a kind of spirit of the blitz, turned up at my door, gas-mask kit and all, just as I was collecting my things. Synchronicity! I'm not at my Haifa flat now, there's no work and all my outpatient kids are at home, so I spent a few days helping their families to cope with it all. The worst problems are with the adult men, who are so used to being providers and defenders and now have to sit at home like stuffed animals in front of the TV. Great opportunities for family life, but also quarrels, hassles, even violence. This is all an unprecedented experience for us, civilians in the firing line while the army stands by, letting someone else fight our war.

It's a strange feeling. The walls of your house are suddenly as thin as paper, transparent as glass. What you thought was a secure womb is suddenly no protection at all. The siren goes and you sit there, waiting for your number to be called. As yet, thank God, no serious casualties, but who knows what's to come? It's difficult to imagine that there is a "normal" world out there. Paris, the Seine, the cafés, busy streets. Not to speak of other memories. Jams of Chinon, the rippling Loire, the Gothic windows of Chartres . . . Patriarchs, saints, passions and calvaries. But our drama is not metaphoric. It lacks all the neat wrapping and structure. I spoke with Benny about Angelopoulos. A proper drama would demand equivalence: He saved me, now I save him, Benny said to me, but I can't, he's out of my reach. A man disappears into a black hole, as big as the world. And you are tied down by history, unable to climb on the stage.

Oddly enough, Benny and I are now spending more time together than we have for a long time: We are both going to spend some days with the parents of the friend I met in Scotland, Avram Blok; they live on a farm which turns out to be next door to Benny's "drop-outs"'s co-operative. The old man is in a wheelchair, though he is more combative than a platoon of commandos. Threatening to sue God for mucking up the world. I think some medieval rabbis once tried that. But I don't know if they won their case. One has to fight against a terrible feeling of weakness, that inability to control events which we rationally know are uncontrollable, but we feel remiss at not controlling. Emotional helplessness.

Enjoy Beirut. When will this ever reach you, I wonder? Faxed across the lines . . . Keep in touch, somehow, and if you ever can, hop across those lines — there is a spare gas mask in the cupboard. What can we do, except escape for a little while, in dreams . . .

Yours,
Naomi Potamkin

THE FINDERS

"Awake! Awake! The hour of fate is dawning! The hour ordained by scriptures is at hand. Did not God reveal His word to all the Prophets, to Abraham, Noah, Moses, Ishmael, Isaac and Jacob? Did He not make the child Jesus prophesy from his cradle? Did He not say unto Noah: Build an ark under Our eyes, according to Our bidding — do not plead with Me for the wrongdoers,

for they will be justly punished? And did not the unbelievers mock him, and slander him, and say: All your warnings are lies and inventions. And did not God punish the unbelievers and destroy their homes, their tribes, their nations utterly and without repair? But who are the evildoers, and who, the just?"

"I'm not sure I want to hear the answer," said Tewfiq.

The youthful Apostle gestured and waved in the haze above his motley flock squatting, sitting or swaying in the sand. There was now more than a smattering of men who had abandoned their posts in varying stages of uniform, some bare-chested, others trouserless with dangling shirt-tails, the khaki plastered by the sun to their skin, so that they appeared a kind of brown blotch against the yellow-ochre dunes. Some had their underwear and handkerchiefs tied around their heads for protection. The thin asphalt line of the military road wound forward and behind without end. On its verge, aboard the stolen jeep of Major Mojo, Tewfiq rendered a summary of the Apostle's words for the Lionheart, as Jody Steele gazed at the horizon through field-glasses, commenting at the ominous blips which shimmered over the dunes:

"We are not in the right place at the right time."

"Isn't it wonderful?" enthused Tewfiq. "No GNB, no BBC, no news-pools. No Major Mojo. Just the three musketeers and the story nobody wants to know."

"For good reason, Tewfiq *habibi*."

Richard nudged him. "What is he saying now?"

"Ah, he is talking about the Holy Imams. About the martyrdom of the Imam Hussayn at Kerbala. He is saying the Holy Imams had knowledge of the Unseen and the Unknown. Now he is talking about the twelfth Imam, Abu'l Kassem Muhammad, who disappeared at the age of six at Samarra, in Iraq. God ordained, the boy says, that the twelfth Imam, who had the secret of the timing of the Day of Judgement, be removed from the circle of worldy sin until the Day was nigh. He returned once, to earth, as a ruler, but God postponed the Day out of His mercy and the young Caliph occulted again. But now a thousand less thirty-six years have passed for Mankind, although it is a mere few days for the Imam himself, and, he says 'I have returned with my message.'"

"Not the Good News," said Jody. "It's definitely time for us to withdraw. The sooner we're out of here the better. Tewfiq, there's a white T-shirt in the bag there. Just tie it on to the antenna. I'll take my chances with the tanks before it's too late. The last self-proclaimed Mahdi in this country was shot and his followers had their heads chopped off."

"One can expect no less, at the Hour of Doom," said Tewfiq, nevertheless turning to the rucksacks piled on the back seat by the Lionheart.

"There are definitely tanks out there," said Jody, lowering her field-glasses. "Have you got that fucking T-shirt, Tewfiq?"

"I can't find it, Jody, but there's some thermal underwear I keep for these freezing desert nights."

"Is it white?"

"As the driven snow."

"Hand it to me."

He rummaged among the old tin mugs, the ashtrays from The Club, the Zahran Intercontinental and the Yasmeen Hotel, the copper finjan, the cassettetapes and shaver, battered United Airlines Business Class Comfort Kit, broken comb, mini-toothbrush, body lotion, onboard socks and eyeguard, the scuffed spare jeans and "I Went to Beirut And All I Got Was This Bloody T-shirt." But his search was interrupted by the sudden snarl of engines from the dunes beyond, the firming of the distant blips approaching from north and south, and the shimmering shapes of two more armoured columns on the road itself, east and west.

"Too late."

"In 1979," Tewfiq explained to Richard, "a puritanical zealot named Juhayman al-Oteibi led a band of rebels in an armed takeover of the Grand Mosque in Mecca. He proclaimed his brother-in-law as the Mahdi, the appointed one, come to seize the Holy Places from the princes of darkness and the corrupters on earth. It took the Saudi army more than a week to recapture the mosque, in bloody hand-to-hand combat, profaning the holiest shrines. The pretender was captured and his Mahdi shot dead, but the House of Saud was shaken to the testicles. I don't think they want it to happen again."

"We'll tie your thermal underwear to the antenna anyway," said Jody, grabbing the article from him.

"This may be our last chance for the exclusive interview." A crucial catch from the start. The refusal of all explanations by the Apostle's mute followers, and the protective shield thrown about him by the praetorian guard of tall, black ex–U.S. airmen, with a polite "all are equal, no privileged access, man." None of Jody Steele's cajoling availed. "I'm from *The Guardian*, London. We want to speak to your leader. Is this a political protest? What do you hope to achieve? The public has a right to know."

"The public is doomed," said the guard.

Indeed. The onward flow of the Long March, following the sonorous voice that speaks to an audience ignorant of its language, but mesmerised by its ancient timbre. Mind, speaking directly to mind: *For verily, there is another existence behind this one of coarse clay, corruptible flesh, bare bones. For God is all-seeing and all-powerful. He keeps the heavens and the earth from falling and retains the instruments of doom. He calls you forth to a different war, declaring that your life until now was but a preparation for this task, to leave behind all that was until this point and obey God and follow His Apostle, without doubt and without hesitation, or to remain behind and taste the Cataclysm . . .*

And the day was followed by an eerie night, the column having halted just before noon to pass the afternoon heat as best it could under the shade of tarpaulins and camouflage netting, till the Apostle rose to lead it off at sunset. The pitiless burning hammer sinking into the sands under succeeding arches of gold, red and deepest blue, out of which, the springing glory of the stars, and a glow, the swirling zodiacal light, illuminating the march like little flashes of lightning, then fading with equal rapidity under the white half-moon light. Tewfiq, Richard and Jody take turns driving the jeep in a slow crawl of fits and starts, running ahead of the foot column behind the short convoy of about a dozen vehicles, jeeps and trucks annexed by the multinational force of deserters. A strange procession of pilgrims trudging over the surface of the moon . . . . Lolling on the back seat, as Jody Steele slumped in the front with her head bouncing about Richard the Lionheart's shoulder,

the dead-live king exercising his shift at the steering-wheel, a skill per-
fected with nonchalance at al-Diyab, Tewfiq dreamed: He was sailing at
night on an old masted pilgrim ship, a *sambuk*, lying on deck, alone, in
a yawing hammock, with the salt spray of the sea on his face. The sun
rose on the horizon, its golden blaze revealing the city silhouetted on
the shore. He recognised the broken corpse of Beirut, its shattered
waterfront and fractured buildings. A figure waded ashore out of the
sea below the plaza of the Hotel Saint George: a knight in full battle
array of chain-mail and helmet, lance clasped to his side. His horse,
harnessed with mail and foot spikes, its head covered by an eye-slitless
helmet, struggled onto the abandoned lido and onto the rue Fakhred-
dine, staggering blindly past the ruined hotels and colleges and
smashed apartment houses, south towards Ouzai. There were no signs
of life in the maze of rubble, only bloated bodies, as Tewfiq realised he
was riding behind the knight on a jeep, with Petros Angelopoulos at the
steering-wheel beside him. The wide grin and the flapping moustache.

"Not a pretty picture, is it?"

"No, Angel. When did they let you out?"

"I got a hundred years off for good behaviour," said the Angel. "I
sang them songs, performed tricks, danced, told them a thousand and
one tales, recited from the Holy Books, removed thorns from their feet,
bandaged their sins."

They reached the perimeter of the site of the Jaffa Camp, the
knight's steed picking its way gingerly through the debris, the twisted
girders, pulverised ash. Angelopoulos calling over the ruins:

"Is anyone alive? I'm a doctor!"

"Can you revive the dead?" The voice echoed from inside the
knight's helmet.

"Only at the instant of death," replied the Angel, "if at all."

The knight moaned, thrusting his lance fiercely into the dry stones,
which cracked open, releasing a thick stream of a sickly yellow-green
fluid that swiftly turned reddish-brown. Angelopoulos leapt forward,
tearing his shirt, trying to staunch the flow, sinking in the ooze to his
elbows, then his shoulders, then his still bellowing head. From beneath
the ground, a dreadful sudden cry, the massed outpouring of the tens of

thousands trapped underground, broke forth, as Tewfiq sprang forward, desperately trying to keep the Angel afloat by seizing the knot of his hair, strands coming loose bloodily in his hands . . .

"Medic! medic!"

"Stretcher-bearers!"

"Awake! Awake!" Back to the desert: The hour of fate, the hour ordained by scriptures . . . the blips of tanks rumbling over the dunes, up the road . . . Jody frantically trying to locate a makeshift white flag . . . And a high-pitched electronic whine preceding the blare of a loudspeaker over the sands:

"Now hear this! Now hear this! All U.S. servicemen and other nationalities operating without authority in this area! This is Colonel A.P. Pieterberg of the Ninety-Second U.S. Airborne addressing you by authority of the Gulf Theatre Command, Southwest Sector. We have transport available to return you-all to your units forthwith. You must vacate your present position and proceed towards me in an orderly fashion. I am authorized to state that no disciplinary or other legal action will be taken against you if you surrender yourselves to my authority within thirty minutes of this message. The United States Air Force understands the pressures you have been operating under and has a humane program for the relief of Desert Stress Syndrome. The DESTRESS Program is available at no extra cost to all service personnel on a voluntary non-coercive basis. Employees and staff of DESTRESS LTD are ineligible. Listen up, you-all, this is your last chance. Unauthorized activity will not be permitted to continue from this point."

"Thank God for that," said Jody, "now give me these fucking knickers of yours and let's get going. This program sounds the one for me."

But the defecting soldiers showed no sign of responding, gathering instead in a defensive cluster as the loudspeaker message repeated in Arabic, French, Polish, Tagalog and Fijian. A sombre stand-off, as the Apostle stood silent, refusing to add his voice to the amplified echoes which drifted across the sand into infinity.

"Turn the jeep," Jody ordered Richard. But the ex-king climbed out of the driver's seat.

"I shall remain here."

"Plantagenet!" Tewfiq called to him. "They'll bomb this column! We can't stay!" As Richard strode towards the waiting column, Tewfiq running to catch up: "This is a stupid way to die."

"No stupider than the first time, my friend. Go and survive, Tewfiq. Build a new life."

"Don't be an idiot, Englishman. These people are not going anywhere."

"Neither am I, my friend. Wars are not what they used to be. There's no love, only artifice." The defectors had moved up towards the Apostle, falling before him on their knees. "I'm like that boy," said Richard. "I don't belong in this age. There is no point in evading fate. Only one thing, Tewfiq, if you come across Rose . . ." But his words were drowned in a sudden chopper drone. The machine swooping low over the besieging forces and descending towards the column, a compact six-seater with U.S. markings and a familiar emblem of a bolt of lightning over a globe. It landed, whipping a sandstorm over the congregation.

"Yee-hah!!" The strange alien cry as two figures tore through the cloud of sand carrying muffled microphones, followed by two burly men with ENG camera and a folded portable satellite dish and transmitter, the foremost of the first twosome, both clad in padded sleeveless jackets over flowery Hawaiian shirts, calling out through a megaphone:

Hi there, folks, this is William Shakespeare and Henry James reporting for Global News Broadcasting drop your socks and grab your cocks the A-team is here do you hear me, Bob I am reporting now exclusively from the heart of the Saudi Arabian desert where an astonishing drama is unfolding while the world's attention is riveted to Baghdad, Riyadh, Tel Aviv and Washington, a bizarre stand-off is being enacted on a closed military road between Zahran and Mecca . . .

"This is General A.P. Pietersen calling — what the heck are you folks doin' out there get the hell outa my face!"

The self-styled Saviour and Hidden Imam who has declared a plague on both houses and is leading a march of his disciples across the desert like a Prophet of ancient biblical times his aim — to walk across the trackless wastes to Mecca world centre of the

Islamic Faith, and there to declare his New Gospel from the very steps of the Ka'abah Islam's holiest shrine . . .

"Goddam you fuckin' media assholes!"

I am about to speak to The Apostle this mystery man who has emerged out of nowhere out of the trackless wastes of the Arabian sands to preach his new Dispensation and proclaim himself He Who Was Made Manifest, a new messenger with an age-old message no less than the Hour of Reckoning and the Day of Judgement we will be there — myself, William Shakespeare, and my co-partner Henry James do you concur with that, Henry I certainly do, Bill we will be reporting the events when they happen, as they happen The Apostle has already risen and is striding forward, urging his followers to advance across the trackless sands the phalanx of tanks which has been barring his way has suddenly opened up before us and we are leading the way at the side of The Saviour, ahead of his entire camp as they proceed, the Mahdi leading the way with his battered wooden staff this is very much how it must have been for the Children of Israel marching across the Wilderness of Sin and in the Wilderness of Shur and in the Wilderness of Paran in the Land of the Amalekites and the Amorites and among the Philistines and all the nations of Canaan, and this is how He led them forth across the barren desert with nothing but their Leader's Faith to guide them on we will be there every step of the way to inform you and bring you the news as it happens when it happens —

"Who's in charge of that craft? Take those men outa here!"

But from the maw of the chopper, just before it lifted, leaving the intruding team on the ground, a fifth figure stepped, walking out of the sandstorm in Arab thobe and *aghal*, carrying a neat Gucci holdall. An unmanly hand lifted to the face, whipping off the thick false moustache, Ray-Bans removed to reveal eyes which stopped the Lionheart in his tracks, as he strode forward, shielding his eyes to gaze at this unexpected apparition —

"Rose?!"

"Richard."

Yee-hah! Onwards to Mecca! Are you receiving me, Bob?

NINETEEN

Angels
Arise!

THE SPIDER

The old patriarch Michel Khamash lay in his personal ward in the Michel Khamash Hospital in Joûnié, plugged into his life-support system: The deals, transfers, securities, dividends, equities, flotations, arbitrages, redemptions, Swiss bank-account numbers, blank end-user certificates, capitalisations, mutual funds, looted pension trusts. Around his bed, get-well cards from all his well wishers and unsigned death threats from his many enemies. Autographs of Margaret Thatcher, Ronald Reagan, Menachem Begin, Augusto Pinochet, Valéry Giscard d'Estang, Helmut Kohl, Carol Woytila, James Kirk, Saddam Hussein, King Fahd, Hafez al-Asad, Ariel Sharon, Yasir Arafat, Muammar Gadaffi. Anxious and highly paid doctors monitoring the flow charts of the world's defence industries. But the old man had lost none of his zest, as he croaked out his latest instructions to his son, Aziz Khamash, by his bedside:

"The good times are coming back, my son. We have to think of the future. Forget about all that Templar flim-flam, the Holy Grail, the Hidden Blood, Priories of Zion, atbash cyphers, the Secret Companions of General de Gaulle, spacecraft of the Gods, it's all illusion and chicanery. If your stupid ex-king Richard the Chickenheart had the keys to the loot of Solomon's Temple he would have gone and seized it, rather than mooning about for eight centuries in the Café des Amis. Listen to me, my son, go direct to Damascus, to Hafez al-Asad. To kiss him on the cheeks, not his arse, mind you. Let gallstones be gallstones. The

363

New World Order. Grab it by the balls before the Mansurs, Gemayels, Eddes and Franjiehs. The Washington lifeline. Send faxes to Houston, Texas, Beijing, Brussels, Düsseldorf. Open your mouth wide and swallow, the minnows will flow in on the tide. The Christian Ascendancy. We did our best. We fought, we reddened the streams with our blood, while the so-called Christian nations sold arms to all our enemies. Now they find they have to go to war against their own clients. Vanity, thy name is trade. There is nothing new under the sun. Go now, and if you find your errant sister, Rose, give her my deepest adoration . . ."

Aziz Khamash kissed his father's fragile trembling hand and withdrew, proceeding up the mountain with his bodyguards back to the village and the cavernous villa in which his mother, Adele, flipped through the empty corridors and reception rooms in her tattered carpet slippers. Returning to consult his mother about the renewed defection of his sister, Rose, to follow the despised undead royal, the Chickenheart, to the burning desert of Saudi Arabia, in the footsteps of a mad and doomed prophet. An item of news he had neglected to pass to his father, in order to prevent a sudden seizure fluttering the system, bringing down stocks, destroying dividends.

He found his mother in her private laboratory surrounded by her astrological charts, hermetic maps and alchemical tables, the shelves of bound ancient folios and manuscripts, the great oven or vas, with its maze of pipes and tubing, and the vast sloping desk at which she pursued her measurements and computations. This was Adele Khamash's inner sanctum, forbidden to her husband and his parallel quest, open only to her eldest surviving son and daughter in her competing struggle to control them.

"We should never have disturbed that bastard in Fontevraud, Maman," Aziz said, squatting on the velvet cushion at her feet, noting with sadness the swelling warts and pimples, her straggling varicose veins. Mortality, such a pitiless enemy. "Far less bring him out here, to pollute our own kin."

"Knowledge exists to be used, Aziz," said his mother softly, "but one has to know the limits of power. Your father thinks, like the Americans, that knowledge is a battery — you mould it into a weapon at your will. But the secret knowledge is not power in the sense that the West understands. One examines the past, and unlocks memory, only to find our own preconceptions shattered. One cannot pursue mysteries with a preordained plan. One can only open a gate. We cannot be certain what manner of beast slouches through."

"Nevertheless, honour demands that I retrieve my sister."

"Do what you have to do, my son. We are all responsible. While you lived the thoughts and motions of war, she brooded, nursing her terrors. Dreaming of escape but restrained and shackled by the umbilical cords of your hates. Down the ages, all the echoes of fear and exclusion. I sent you to Fontevraud when the charts threw up that abnormality, because I thought it would provide Michel with a distraction from his political schemes. I thought we might pull our family out of the cycle of death which mangles us all. But a dead king is not a toy, but a malign force of innocence adrift in a sewer. He was not the only abnormality, I can tell you. There are a lot of strange lumps in the stars."

"One was quite enough, Mother."

"The universe is full of fire and water, and speckles of dust, the impurities. When God made Man from the dust, He inevitably polluted the source of Creation. The Jews believed this infection could be cured. But their own fate proved this is delusion. The only thing we can do is be forewarned, by reading the outlines correctly. Everything else is stumbling in the dark."

"What do you read, Maman, What's in store for us?"

His mother was silent, gazing at the framed parchment on the wall ahead of her, the illustrated circles of Dante's *La divina commedia*, the twisted bodies and floating wraiths of the damned, illuminated by a shaft of light sprung from a point at the top of the drawing, filtered through the petals of a single, transparent rose.

"Your mother, Rose?"

"Yes, it was her doing. They sit in their separate studios, my father and she, weaving their hermetic webs. They've been doing it since my childhood. Sorcerers without apprentices. She sent my brother, Aziz, and he found you."

"And you found me. Why?"

"A physically heartless man is better than the metaphoric sort. Or perhaps I'm just the product of a necrophile culture. Veneration of the dead, contempt for the living."

"I am not dead, Rose."

"No, I never found a man more alive. But perhaps we're just birds of a feather, both cut off from normal hopes and fears. Are you afraid of anything, Richard?"

"Only of things that can't be undone. The past."

"The past is indeed a terror, my love."

Whispers, under a tarpaulin, in the dark. The cold crack of the winter sands, each grain protesting and shuffling in its own unique way. But not much hope of privacy, in the crushed presence of the Mahdi's disciples, the symphony of unwashed creaks and scratches, coughs, expectorations and farts. The grinding of Jody Steele's teeth at her failure to gain access to GNB's dish, cradled in anchorman Bill Shakespeare's arms . . . The pricking of ears for celestial messages, for the rising sirens of doom.

I hear them, oh yea! and see them, in the desert, dotted with the crumbling shards of pillars, the bleached bones of the hermits, prophets and tub-thumpers who stood upon them surveying that tattered landscape of human folly, vainglory and greed. Fleeting triumphs and perishable splendours, ancient cities buried in the sand. And I am suddenly so weary of all that *déjà vu,* the Fata Morganas of supplicating fingers and flowing tears and wrung hands. What shall we do, Holy Stylite? What shall we do, Blessed Saint? I should have listened to my tempters, all the crass inventors who wanted to build me toilets, supply routes, communication systems, methods of control. Don't talk to me of goodness and example! The iron fist, that's the only language they understand.

Indeed, I am bone weary. I see too much and understand too little myself. Are all the labours of man under the sun vanity and vexation? Or can a redemption still take place?

I close my eyes and look across the continents. Millions do the same, by aid of Loggie-Bird. Gazing at the shimmering electric dots thrown through the sky, bounced off hunks of metal revolving around the earth for that sole purpose. Communication. Twinkling through the gales and gusts to sparkle down rooftop aerials like an invisible Santa Claus. Bearing gifts of incomprehension. They see all and they see nothing. Flying weapons of war taking off and landing relieved of the weight of their bombs. Soldiers proudly displaying their tools. The Chosen of Major Mojo's newspools, prognosticating into the void. Morning Roundup, Noon Bulletin, Afternoon Dispatch, Evening Report, Midnight Special.

"Switch it off, Avram! Switch it off!"

"In a minute, Kathy. There's a Newsnight Extra . . ."

The airwaves creak, squitter, squeal, mumble, whisper and wail. An umblical cord stretches between the screen and the watcher's eyeballs. He strains to look behind the images, behind the sanitised desert kit, the immaculate suits and ties of presenters in the glaze of their auto-cues. Iraq offers withdrawal linked to deal on Palestine. Bush denounces "peace hoax." Scuds still penetrate air defences. When will the Land War begin? Unexplained disappearance of GNB's top team, expelled from Baghdad, vanished without trace or explanation in the Saudi Arabian desert. A small blip on the current of events. Plenty more where they came from.

"Switch it off, Avram! Switch it off!"

Impossible. The familiar glare of midnight fires in Scud city, Tel Aviv. Bombed buildings and rushing, crying people. Wailing ambulances. Flashing lights rising over the red glare in the night sky. Sirens, again, over the lines. Pundits and propheteers. The global village, all gossip, no genuine information. But the invisible torrent flashes on through his eyeballs, saturating the retinas, flooding the veins.

"Can you hear me, Avram? Are you asleep? Are you awake? Are you with us or with the Woolwich?"

No response. The id, ego and superego, united in bondage to the flow. A paralysis of all motor impulses. A true alchemical marriage of sulphur and salt. Andrew Mackenzie is called in to advise. "Should I knock him on the head? Pour cold water? Switch off?"

"That might cause irretrievable trauma. I think we should wait and see. The Land War might commence at any moment. Meanwhile just keep him warm and comfortable and beware of short circuits." He walks round Blok, examining all three dimensions, cocking his head for an elusive fourth. Cupping his ear and bending down to whisper in the watcher's waxen lobes:

"What do you hear, Avram? What do you hear?"

Voices in the blur ——

. . . *Well it looks like it's finally official. Operation Desert Storm has entered a new decisive phase as distant guns boom out across no man's land in a prelude to all-out ground war. Tanks move across the undefended berms against a backdrop of over two hundred burning oil wells set alight by the Iraqi forces in an attempt to slow the Allied advance striking in a multitude of places across a two-hundred-mile front* the green rustle of water-sprinklers on lawns the cry of the tamarindi man echoes of bygone days — gazoz gazoz neft neft — the bell ringing from horse-drawn carts, petrol and ice, the Holy City's Crier's sabbath sabbath, stones rattling on transgressing cars' windows, my son my son why hast thou forsaken me *the biggest land battle since World War Two as a million men face each other across the desert wilderness. The Mobile Rocket Launchers laying down their deadly steel barrage* Rosa, it's time to wake up. Rosa. What's wrong with the bloody woman *the philosophy of the Allied forces to move fast with surprise and overwhelming force designed to encircle and rapidly annihilate* Rosa, it's eight-thirty. She won't wake without the siren, Baruch. What are you talking about, Greta *for days fuel air explosives have been dropped, the huge downward blast detonating the mines buried in the sand. Forces reported approaching the Euphrates. Iraqi troops surrendering in their thousands. Little resistance . . . friendly . . . casualties remarkably light* I think you should move back, Baruch. I'll take care of this *Iraq claims to have repulsed the attack, inflicting heavy losses. Complete victory to the Arab Nation and all freedom-loving peoples* Rosa, Rosa . . . Stand back Baruch. The doctor is on his way. Avremel, Avremel, my son my son *we're joined now in the studio by Admiral the Earl Arthur Dingleberry-Smythe, retired head of the Royal Bathtub Regiment. Sir Arthur, we know, this is just the first day but aren't things going rather better than expected. In fact, do we not hear the voice of freedom ring?* Ring ring, ring ring. Click. Whirr. "Hello. Sophia Salvadori is not in. I am a machine. But you can leave a message and I'll pass it on as soon as possible. Please speak after the beep." Beeep. Crackle. Shhpsshh. "Machine, ah, tell Sophia that, she won't believe this, but it's Petros Angelopoulos speaking. I can't tell you where I am exactly, but it's far away at the moment . . . What can I say? It's been a hard time, but I'm, ah, almost free now. I'll phone again when I can. Please tell Mackenzie, friends and all the rest. Tell anyone who might have been asking after me. To whom it may concern. I'm fit, healthy and still kicking. I have to go now. I'll talk again, if the world's still standing, or rotating, or whatever. Bye for now." Click. Whirr. Clunk. Ring ring, ring ring. "Hello? Is this the house of Avram Blok? I am speaking from Israel. You must be his, uh, friend, Kathleen? This is his Aunt Greta, from Kfar Pippin. Uh, is he there? I am sorry to say that I have some not good news . . . About his mother . . . No, I should not be asking you to . . . Could you let me speak to him please?"

THE PRISONER
Open prison doors!
  Release all captives!
  Freedom now!
  Loose the chains!

Thus the beginning of the end of captivity, the Angelic release —— with a perfume: The entry into the field of my senses of an almost imperceptible smell, and the timbre of a different kind of footfall. The usual hooded brutes came in and attached my blindfold, checking my chain, gun to my head. I've long learned to appreciate routine contacts breaking the mush of empty time and space. The touch of fingers and steel that almost becomes a caress . . . I learned to tank up my hate. I had tried, in my featureless cell, to build an internal clock through control of the biorhythms, using regular ten-minute exercises, when awake, as an accurate minute hand. I realized early on that the short shower periods in the adjacent cubbyhole were irregularly staggered to confuse me. One week, two weeks, ten days apart, always different. Or was I losing track? The remnants of my mind against their schemes. But then one day, at eight in the morning, Angel-time, on the scheduled breakfast entrance, a sudden scrape, as if an item of furniture was being carried through the door. The rustle of an extra person's clothing, a lighter step, a different gait. The furniture put down, probably a chair, the creak of someone settling down. Then that strange odour, a trace of perfume, nothing strong. I thought my mind was playing tricks. Not the usual memory patterns, but a misreading of the new ingredient that had come into my closed world. Then, down Angelopoulos, I thought, you've got so far, don't flip now. Then one word, one murmur, uncannily confirming my original sensation, a woman's voice, one word — "Na'm." "Yes." I sat back, my head leaning against the cool wall — at least I could sense the cold of winter — luxuriating in the thought. The Christians must be right, God loves sinners . . .

I had experimented for a while with telepathic sex. The idea, to phantazise an encounter to ejaculation by thought alone, without manual assistance. Nocturnal emissions not counting. But full release never came. Imagination is simply not enough. Despite it all, actual contact is needed. But conversations! Oh Lord! Those never stopped flooding through my head. Dialogues, disputes, debates, diatribes, denunciations, propositions, pleas. Everything said that should have been left unsaid, and things that never were said and should have been. Fire and ice. Courtship, marriage and divorce with Caroline, Art Colony babble and Desirée, the choirs of Paris, Naomi and Chartres, Sophia, Jaffa Camp symphony. Stretcher-bearers! The divine song of angels, uplifting me on my invented cloud. Floating above my own body, is this a near-death experience? Dragging myself back, by my twin anchors — surgery and sex . . . sewing and screwing . . . healing and humping . . . fixing and fucking . . .

"I know you're there, sister," I said in Arabic. "What's your name?"

There was a rustle of embarassment, but at least no one stepped on my face. "I am Petros Angelopoulos," I said, "I was kidnapped in Scotland, Great Britain, for a reason that has never been explained. I've been here I think for nine months and three weeks. I am a doctor, not a soldier. If I am an enemy of the Arab people, or of anyone else, let my accusers speak. I am a human being, not an animal."

No response, but no violence either. Definitely an advance. There was a pause, then much shuffling and scraping, removal of blindfold, and exit of guard, leaving behind only that unusual whiff.

I remembered a film I had seen BP— Before Prison — by the Italian director Lena Wertmuller. The film was called *Seven Beauties* and was about a concentration-camp inmate who decides to screw his way out by seducing the hulking female commandant, despite his puny, trembling state. I remembered the struggle to summon up all the suppressed resources, and the mighty bulk of that uniformed woman, in a penumbra of light, spreading her thighs . . . I was far fitter than that putative gigolo, but at least he was not on a chain . . . Nevertheless, if he could do it . . . I named her Aziza, and lay luxuriating in more than abstract thoughts. My penis grew, under my abaya. I closed my eyes, and let the energies flow. Holding my hands palm down on the cold mass of the floor. Mental power, Angel arise! I felt them all hovering over me, a blur of warmth, flicking tongues. The shells coming down, battering eardrums, throwing up splinters and smoke. The cheerful cry of Abdul Kebab — "Allahu akbar!" Anneka, Sophia, Desirée! Go! A spurting rush from what Reich used to call the vegetative centre, a discharge of bio-electric energy, or "orgone," the actual explosion of the life process itself . . . who cares about the spilled seed . . . nothing is ever wasted . . .

As I knew she would, she returned. Next day, same time, the clanging door, the blindfold, the scraping chair, the light step, the faint perfume. Some form of body lotion. Does that strike Syria off the list of locations? Their soldiers had to go to Beirut to loot soap. But, among the officer classes . . . I began to talk, through my blindfold, restating my name, non-rank, medical qualifications and degrees. I talked about Puerto Ricans in New York. I talked about Caroline and Harlem. I talked about Count Basie and Malcolm X. I talked about the third world, drought, starvation, disease, the endless tunnel of repression. I talked about my Palestinian friends. Damn her to hell if she's on the other side of the blood feud, a Phalangist, Amal Shi'ite or Israeli. Fuck them all. I talked about the Jaffa Camp, about the hospital made out of scrap and coat-hangers, about the dying and the dead. I talked about the resilience of the living, the glory of those with nothing to lose. I talked about sacrifice and solidarity, about the generosity of the dispossessed. I talked about humanity against all odds. I talked about hardened fighters, with multiple scars and ammunition belts, carrying old women on their backs out of the line of fire. I talked about an enemy who had fallen out of the sky merging with the victims of his compatriots. I talked about the courage of children who became adults at the age of five. I talked about wounded adolescent girls dragging their shot brothers across a sniper's field. I talked about couples who insisted on getting married to the peal of mortars and bombs. I talked about people having faith in the future although they might have only minutes to live. I talked about hope in the mire of hopelessness. I talked about people without presumption refusing to accept defeat. I talked about what it means to be human at the choiceless base of things. The divine spark that owes nothing to idols, Gods, or received ideas. I talked about the burden I saw people carrying and my inability to carry it for them. I talked about surgery as an excuse for my incapacity to resurrect. I talked about delusions of control, and futility. I talked about aggression and healing. I talked about the power of wielding the knife or drill, the razor edge between saving a life and taking it. I talked about the fear of love as a brake and stranglehold on an imagined freedom. The reduction of compassion to science. The despair of ever comprehending. The refusal of submission. Freedom! It rings so hollow in my cell. The babble cascading out of my mouth, as if I were summoned on the Day of Judgement. At some point I ran dry and stopped short. I could hear breathing, then, again, the hushed rustling, the opening of the door, scrape of chair, exit.

The next day, she came again. By now I had dismissed the options, an effeminate man, some kind of trick. If they had wanted me to talk, they had nine months to try me. They were the ones who were hiding, not me. I felt at last a surge of power at her returning to listen. So this time I remained silent. She fidgeted. The usual harsh wheeze of the guards. I waited for as long as I dared and then said: "I'll go on talking if you remove the blindfold."

And then she spoke, her voice like a fresh wind through a grave.

Low and tender: "Do you remember one day in December, '86, near the end of the Jaffa siege? You operated on a sixteen-year-old girl who had come through the lines from outside, with provisions, but was hit by mortar-fire the same day. It was an amputation, of the right arm."

"What is your name, comrade?" I asked. My heart was racing. I knew this had not all been for nothing. I remembered the girl, slim and wide-eyed. She had crawled bedraggled through a chink in the perimeter, a short-lived blind spot for Amal. She brought fresh pittas and black olives and a quart of Johnny Walker bourbon for "The Angel," who had just been a strange name for her. Later that afternoon she was caught by her inexperience in a sudden incoming round. Only a few weeks before the end of the siege . . . But was her face more than a blur . . . ?

"Let him see," she said. The guards removed the blindfold. They were all looking at me, hoodless. The two men, who had terrorised me with their blank identities for nine months, emerged from the dark as straggle-bearded eighteen-year-old boys, dime a dozen *shabab*, when you've seen a thousand of them, you've seen them all. They gazed at me rather sheepishly, as if it was me, not them, who was being seen for the first time. The girl was as I did remember her, black-haired, big black eyes, velvet skin. She would be about twenty now. The same sombre look of four years before, and a uniform, Syrian-issue khaki, with a tag of some sort on the left shoulder, none on the right, which was pinned back, covering the empty socket of the amputated limb.

The beauty of these three undistinguished faces overwhelmed me with their radiant glow. Humanity gaping out of the wall. I shook my head about, trying to clear the mush. The two men cradled their Kalashnikovs. The woman had risen from her chair.

"Let's go." The two boys unlocked the chain from my foot, pulling me up, holding on each arm. The woman rapped on the door, which was opened from outside. She stepped back and motioned with her hand. Without further ado, as if this were an ordinary, rather than a miraculous action, my two guards marched me out of my cell...

To see the sun! The shadows on open ground, gravel, houses, trees, the face of creation . . . The sudden return of perception, distanced as it may be, as if through the wrong end of a telescope; you still can't believe it till you see it . . .

A transfer from prison to prison, but night and day, as they led me step by step up a metal stairway, to another steel door held ajar, and the blinding light of the Outside . . . My divine liberator handing me a pair of sunglasses, which I fumbled on, as she guided me across a courtyard that seemed as large as a football pitch but must have been about fifteen metres wide, through another door to a long corridor with office rooms branching off, too befuddled to read the words on the doors, my eyes fighting to focus, out again to the open yard of what was clearly a military barracks. A group of uniformed men exercising in the yard, marching up and down, a flagpole, with, yes, the Syrian flag, then into a jeep, with my saviour and a new happy couple of armed guards, more grinning, lightly bearded teenagers. Jolted along a gravel track, past rows of huts, light military vehicles, jeeps, trucks, a checkpost in a barbed-wire fence, out into the open landscape, searing through the dark glasses, a low, distant mountain range to my right, a nondescript, stubbled desert to left, which appeared of the most astonishing beauty, razor sharp, like a marijuana sunrise, light grey clouds skimming across the sky. A cool breeze across my cheeks and arms. It seemed like the approach road to paradise, but merely led to another checkpost in another barbed-wire enclosure, another, smaller group of low stone barrack huts, into one of which I was ushered, the room where I now sit, writing this down.

Indeed, miracle after miracle, a box of paper and a clump of ballpoint pens. No promise that anything I write will ever be read by anyone else, but a stunning cathartic value. I understand why writers write, to keep sane. I can try to organise that jumble of thoughts, memories, meditations practised for nine months in my cell. To carve a use out of that dead time. And even greater miracles: A field telephone, brought in and connected, I was told, for one international phone call, on condition I gave no hint of my location. I first gave them my brother's number, in New York, but there was no answer. Not even an answering machine. The next number that popped into my head was Sophia Salvadori's in Scotland. This time a machine. I left my message, my sign of life.

And what next? Item. My room, a converted officer's quarters.

Camp bed, a desk, chair, a small wicker stool by the bed. The floor bare concrete. The walls bare, peeling, off white. But, yet another miracle — the window. Fixed with two horizontal and two vertical iron bars, looking out through the barbed wire–topped fence onto open desert scrub, stretching to the blue-haze mountain range. And the sky, dappled by clouds, blue into grey, and, in sudden torrents, the rain. Rivulets rushing down unseen gulleys, little shimmering pools. Wonderful. Did God really make this? No mean craftsman He.

Item. The patrolling guards, passing me cigarettes through the bars, chatting, coming in to share meals. Still the ubiquitous K-rations, but now also some real fodder: fresh pittas, humus, felafels, meat kebabs, salads. Difficult to believe. Once a day I'm taken out for a walk round the perimeter, the huts deserted apart from my seven guards and me, the view of the larger camp two kilometres off, site of my purgatory, trucks and military jeeps and occasional civilian vehicles, going up and down an asphalt road stretching off to what I guess is southwest. Twice a huge military convoy of tank-carriers and armoured cars rumbled along the road northwest, at which point I was returned to my room. Sonic booms and aircraft thunder frequent, day and night.

Item. Information. Slowly it begins to unravel. The girl, the unhooded guards, exuding that familiar origin, a breakaway group of my Palestinian comrades. The Popular Front or one of its offshoots, General Command or other. I knew them well. Friends and tormentors, a sad salad of self-destruction. I offered to check out her stump in my room, waving away the leering guard at the barred window, over which I slung her combat jacket. The stump was well healed, I was glad to see. "I did a good job, even at that stage, when I could hardly remember who I was." I remembered her name now, Samira. She revealed to me now she had come then as a spy for the "dissidents" of Abu Musa, the same pro-Syrian forces who betrayed the camp and left it open to our enemies, three months after I left. "It's a family matter," she explained. "I have three brothers in the Revolutionary Forces. I joined them as a matter of course. But I had a lot of time to think, later, in the hospital in Sidon, where they transferred me. I still could not go with Arafat, the compromiser. But it was difficult for me to see you as an enemy, which they had decided you were."

So was that it, the entire terrible ordeal a self-inflicted wound of suspicion and inward-turned mistrust, the left hand cutting off the right, the boot treading on its own neck? The entire nine months in darkness carrying this dead, festering after-image of civil war and family feud? For what purpose? For what end? "Why?" I asked her, "on whose orders? On what grounds?" But she would reply only to my unspoken question —— and why has it ended now? —— "Things have changed."

That evening the guards brought me a transistor radio, which they put down on my desk and left. Now I know how the world has sped its merry way while I was counting the cracks in the wall. How Iraq is no longer the friend of the West, its bulwark against the Khomeinist menace. All the new alliances. The new role of Syria as a bulwark of democratic legality. The bombardment of Iraq, the forces massed for a land attack from Saudi Arabia. And now I know where I am. The booming closeness of Damascus Radio's perfect Ba'athist synthesis of the New Deal, and even sharper, several Turkish stations. My original guesstimated siting of my prison in the southern region was in error. The convoys, the jets screaming overhead, the mountain range, all placed me in the narrowing northeastern finger of the junction of Syria, Turkey and Iraq. As close to the war zone as one would not wish to be.

A brief opening to the world by my radio: The BBC's measured cataclysms, jingle-jangle of some American army station, sweet lilt of commercial Arab pop. Ah, Fairuz! The ubiquitous jar of the Voice of Israel in Arabic. Scud missiles on Tel Aviv. Naomi, Naomi. And whither irony, Benjamin? Radio Moscow calling politely, in English, for cease-fires. The Voice of Palestine, spitting defiance of Western plots against the new Saladin, Saddam Hussein.

My friends, my friends. The last sane man sits in the asylum, guarded and surrounded by the inmates. Trying to interrogate my one-armed saviour, as she walks me round my cage like a pet dog. "How long will you keep me here?" "It's not my decision." "I'm an embarrassment to the new friends of the West now, aren't I? The people who snatched me can't admit their games on British soil. I'm an impediment to the new dispensation. Is that why you allowed me that phone call? To make sure they don't change their minds again? You arranged that for me yourself, did you not?"

But I couldn't provoke her. She just walked around and around, holding lightly onto my arm. I am only flesh and blood, comrades . . . Even if she is my patient, stump and all. Which of us is complete, for God's sake? The only woman around for nine months.

Difficult to know what to write here, what to keep unrecorded. One day she said to me, out of the blue: "I know you have an Israeli girlfriend. The sister of the prisoner who was in the camp. What is she like?" "People are people," I said. "I never mix politics with women. Life is too short." "I can't understand you," she said. "You are not consistent. It's this that makes people suspicious." Good and evil. Which side are you on? Beautiful simplicities. But I know, I had the choices, not she. Until my choices were taken away.

Memories of the camp — Tewfiq, Kamal, Salim, Anneka, Mad Latif, Umm Mahmud. The days when I had two thousand friends, not just one zookeeper. Looking back nostalgically to that horror. Can you believe it? The search for a pure moral choice. That either or, commitment or betrayal. Am I envying Samira? Who are these people who command her loyalty? Dissidents, zealots, rejectionists, enemies within, spoilers, wreckers, terrorists in deed as well as name. Blown up by her own side. I cut off her arm to save the rest of her. It was in shreds, the elbow, humerus, shattered. We put her forearm and hand in a plastic bag. Normally we gave the severed limb to relatives so it could be kept for proper burial in due course. When there was no relative we made our own decisions. There was a small plot for unclaimed limbs, near the bombed mosque. Her arm is in Beirut and her body walks with me on the border with Iraq and Turkey. How many more shattered bodies lie unclaimed to our east, in the killing-grounds?

So many like her, men and women, boys and girls. *Intifada* Mayflies. They rise and flower for a moment so brief you can hardly blink an eye, and then the fires. What is the sound of one hand clapping? An old Zen query, answered in a thousand war zones. What is the sound of your applause, Samira? It's hardest on the women, of course.

377

Their prospects as brides disappear with the buzz of the surgeon's saw. The Angel mutilator. Did I heal, or just prolong the agony? I have to fight Death. The bastard. He has enough in his bag. Armless, legless, eyeless, noseless, lipless, still they crawl beneath the sun. Survivors of my scythe. I strike before He gets there. I cheat the bastard and He laughs in my face, cackling at me over a hundred wavelengths. Surgical strikes and precision bombing. Oh Lord, not all that again. The world chatters, ever fainter. The batteries are fading out. The world receding from me again. And now even my memories fading. What was so feasible in my dungeon seems so difficult in this mundane den. Tewfiq, Latif, Nabil, Salim, Daoud. I write the names. Squiggles on paper. The rain's coming down, buckets, torrents. Is there a Noah out there? Good luck to him. I know how it feels to stay behind.

THE UNFORGOTTEN

The sky clamps down like a steel-blue lid enclosing the plateau, whose edges are constantly shifting. Great sandstorms dancing over the horizon. Slabs of black and red rock rearing out of the ground like inverted pyramids resting on an infinitesimal point, or like giant tables laid out for Archangels, or spinning tops and scattered single boulders thrown like gamepieces from apathetic nephilim. Nothing can live in this playground of the elemental forces, and yet, stirring after yet another fitful night, they march, the tattered horde, crawling sluggishly but determinedly across the plain, from nought to nought, flanked by their dusty jeeps, command cars and trucks, grumbling through their last gallons of fuel. At their head that wiry figure in his ragged robe and wooden staff, flanked by two men in the frayed shreds of many-pocketed jackets, the one holding a disconnected microphone to the leader's mouth, the other guiding the steps of a burly camera operator whose camera's casing had melted in the sun, fusing to his hand, the glass lens long fallen out and buried in the drifts, the interviewer's lips hanging in dry flakes, his mouth producing nothing but harsh croaks and moans, relayed by quivering electronic bursts from the white concave dish carried by a third man on his back, up to metal satellites orbiting invisibly above the earth's stratosphere, intercepted and deflected by military surveillance safely away into oblivion . . .

"Rryoureceivin'me Bob? Come in Memphis!"

Not a chance. "We should have gone back when we had the option" — Jody Steele groaning. Tewfiq squinting at her through the closed *keffiyah* that wrapped his entire face like an Arabian Easter egg, croaking back: "Only three hundred kilometres to go. Will our leader strike water from the rock? Can he call down gasoline, unleaded, from the sky? No need to part the seas, there aren't any."

"Give us a break Tewfiq, for God's sake."

But the Apostle speaks on undeterred: "God said, in his Holy Book, that on that day the heavens themselves will be rolled up like a scroll of parchment, and as the First Creation was brought into being, so it shall be Restored. God chose many nations to spread His message, but each turned its back on the Truth. His Final Judgement was foretold many times, but each man thought he would be spared. Finally came the day of Noah, and no further postponement could be had. Prophets are useless. The age of the Messengers is over. I am the Beginning and the End. And on that day destruction will befall the people of Baghdad and a red fire will fall from the sky. And all the old rules will be abrogated. Justice shall come and the Earth will flower. Bounteous will be my rule and sweet delight my inheritance. But those who are not with Me shall perish."

"Wharisesayin'? Wharsesayin'?" croaked William Shakespeare.

"I think he's sayin' we'll make it," croaked Henry James. "Callin' Memphis comein Memphis, ello, ello, Bob, Ryouthere . . . ?"

The armies of twenty-eight nations flow over the lines towards their destiny, the flapping flags of the United States, the United Kingdom of Great Britain and Northern Ireland, the Republic of France, Italy, Canada, Australia, New Zealand, the Netherlands, Belgium (both Flemish and Walloon), Spain, Portugal, Poland, Czechoslovakia, Greece, Morocco, Egypt, Syria, Saudi Arabia, the United Arab Emirates, Bahrain, Qatar, Kuwait (ex), Pakistan, Bangladesh, South Korea, Senegal, Niger and Turkey (in NATO disguise). The Tactical Air Force squadrons scrambled by their TEMPLARS (Tactical Expert Mission

Planners), brave the perils of HERO — the Hazards of Electromagnetic
Radiation to Ordnance, the tank-busters graze up and down the jammed
line of fleeing invaders, shooting the turkeys in their pots. The bodies of
fleeing soldiers burn, burn, with no camera to record the burns. Troops
march in to liberate the stricken oil city, while, in another besieged
camp, farther west, an old man in a wheelchair watches numbly as the
bearded attendants of the religious Burial Society load the shroud of his
dead wife aboard a blue van marked in yellow letters GATES OF HEAVEN:
JUSTICE BEFORE HIM WALKS. Baruch Blok is loaded in turn by his two
young commiserators, Naomi and Benjamin Potamkin, into the back of
a battered Volkswagen van to accompany the hearse on Rosa Blok's last
ascension to Jerusalem, Benjamin is driving, with Naomi and Rosa's sister, Greta Pasternak, in the passenger seat. Greta is fussing over the
unwieldy seatbelt, while Baruch rails in the back against the "clerical
ghouls just waiting to get their paws on the lot of us. To take us off to
that celestial Genghis Khan, our Lord and Master. I want my carcass
kept from them. Just burn me and scatter my ashes anywhere, on the
beach, in the wheat fields, in a Hungarian restaurant, in the streets for
the sweepers to bag." The glaring absence of the unprodigal son,
restored from paralysis by the news of his mother's death, but unable to
get a booking on the infrequent flights operating to the bescudded land.
He sits, wrapped in blankets, in Kathleen's wicker chair, on the beach,
gazing at the grey waves, the relieved dog Alistair curled round his feet, a
mug of herbal tea placed by Kathleen at his elbow on a small folding
chair. The hazy echoes of the bad news from Baruch over the line crackling with army searches for missiles: "She just didn't wake up in the
morning. The doctor said her heart just stopped. It was too much for
her, reliving the fears of the past. Don't knock yourself out to come here,
Avremel. Anyway only El Al still flies in, bringing flag-wavers. What's
done is done. Come when it's settled down." "Papa, I'll come when I can.
Are you sure you're all right?" "Don't worry about me. I've got these
friends of yours, the Potamkins. They keep me from murdering your
Aunt Pashtida, so I suppose it's a *mitsvah* of a kind." Understandably, he
had neglected to ask his father to tell Naomi about the Risen Angel's
strange phone call. Kathleen took out another chair and sat with him

until it was too cold for anything but self-laceration. Sophia had come, having picked up the Angel's message, along with several mundane business calls, offering opportunities, gossip and everyday lamentation. She only said: "Thank God, Kathy, I don't have to feel guilty any more." "No hopes, no curiosity?" asked Kathleen. "Too brief the spark, too dim the afterglow," said Sophia. "I suppose we should tell that Glasgow cop, Druitt." But they all sat silently among the crated-up small sculptures packed for their delayed Australian tour. Their neighbour Stanislaw sat with them, puffing on his pipe as the television war unfolded in mute hysteria, while Holst's *Planets* undulated from the sound-deck. The dog stretched on the carpet like a rag doll, its tongue unfurled in silent ecstasy. The rain had resumed, blown by the wind against the panes. The central heating gurgled and hissed, keening in some hidden blockage. Stanislaw helped Kathleen light a fire in the old fireplace, poking the lumps of coal and igniting them with a lit copy of *The Sunday Times* Air Power Supplement. They all sat back, gazing into the licking flames, their eyes steadily drooping. As they dropped off, the dog stirred, its ears pricked by a faint sound. It looked towards the curtained window, then towards the fire, reluctant to move. Finally, with a whimper, it rose, padding into the kitchen and squeezing out the flap in the back door to stand shivering on the beach patio. The spray of the waves on the shingle. The cold prickles of the rain. Out at sea, in the dark, a low bark sounded. The dog bounded towards the water. The bark came again, closer and louder. The dog barked back in response. Out in the Firth, a black head with velvet eyes showed for a moment above the waves, then withdrew. The dog continued barking, running along the shore. The seal called back half-heartedly, hoping against hope for an offering. Then it gave up, with a flick of its flippers, turned its rear to the grey shore and headed off towards the open sea.

In the room the phone rang, startling the sleepers into a grudging wakefulness. Kathleen took the receiver. It was Andrew Mackenzie, calling from Edinburgh. "Is Avram there? Is he okay? I had a call from London. Remember our patient, the writer, Daniel Pick, who was threatening all the time to kill his editor? Well, you won't believe this, but . . ."

TWENTY

The
Promised
Land

I KNEW THE MOMENT OF TRUTH HAD FINALLY COME: DANIEL'S DAY —
Hohenlohe's Hour. I had to act, swiftly, decisively, ruthlessly, before
McTeague could drop my name in passing to anyone from the West Kensington Armoury who might inquire after the missing vintage pistol. It was
now or never. The spare keys from the aborted Xmas Plot still in my keep.
The Enemy still off guard from the day's ration of Spanish paint-stripper.
By the time I returned to Central London from Epping, the time was
twenty-two hundred hours. Synchronise watches. Easy when there's only
one.

All the problems and obstacles rushed through my mind during that
underground rush through Snaresbrook, Leytonstone, Leyton, Stratford,
Mile End, Bethnal Green, Bank, Chancery Lane *ad infinitum*. I had three
bullets, in an unsilenced weapon. I had a prospective victim *in situ* with
wife, two offspring and Serbian death-watch maiden, in an urban area.
How to separate him from them, lure him out to a rendezvous in a picked
spot, preferably the lethal mugger's alley of the Westway underpass at
Royal Oak, for that Amontillado moment: "Yes, it is I, Hohenlohe, risen
from the grave." "You're not really serious, Danny Boy. Okay, I'm extremely anxious to get back to bed. You've had your joke, so can we go now?"
"Treachery must be paid for. Do you have a God, McTeague? Prepare to
meet Him now." "Ah'm an agnostic Danny, you know that." "Then prepare to meet the everlasting oblivion of the cosmic void." "This is not one

of your better jokes, Danny." "You have to pay for your misjudgements, Gordon. Casually, to save your lousy job, you consign a fellow human to the scrap heap. You vandalise creative endeavour. You tear the heart out of hope. You make a mockery of Art. You cravenly worship Mammon. You present a false façade to the world and expect to get away with it. Waving snapshots of your family and lobsters in a pathetic bid for sympathy. But the worm finally turns."

"That thing isn't loaded, Danny. I've had enough of this." Bang! The villain looks down at his trouser leg, the oozing dark liquid. The sideways fall. The terrible realisation as the eyes widen, the facial muscles grimace and quiver. "For the love of God, Montresor!" "Yes, for the love of God!" Bang! The black splotch over the chest, smudging the striped pyjamas revealed as his overcoat falls open. The look of sheer wonderment and ultimate disbelief. "Jesus Christ, Danny!" The final squeeze of the trigger. The forehead thrown back, shattered, the body sprawled amid the rubbish of the tunnel, the squashed Burger King and Kentucky Fried Chicken cartons, dregs of a half-chewed quarterpounder and soggy chips, chicken bones, blackened banana peels and torn newspapers, dried vomit and diarrhoea pats. A large grey rat scurrying to nudge, then nibble, at the stuff oozing from the head. As the venerable Edgar Allan P. himself has it:

I must not only punish but punish with impunity. A wrong is unredressed when retribution overtakes its redresser. It is equally unredressed when the avenger fails to make himself felt as such to him who has done the wrong.

Absolutely. The thaw had set in when I emerged at Notting Hill Gate with the gun weighing down my right-hand coat pocket. The escalator drawing me up into darkness, the mawkish junction of kebab shops, Indian restaurants, the punters reeling from public bars. I knew it was too early to catch McTeague somnolent, but couldn't bear the thought of Kentish Town. The flash of a new possible magnum opus: *An End to Avgelemono.* But exorcism first. In the old days there used to be a cubbyhole greasy spoon by the cinema which served fried eggs until the stroke of midnight. Apple crumble and custard. Now all that's open is the Kentucky Fried Chicken and a yuppie watering-hole, The Green Whale. Not able to face the

Colonel's dumpling visage, I take the latter, positioning myself by the wall as far as possible from the organic-salad counter, under a poster soliciting aid for endangered sea mammals. Similar flyers stockpiled in my ersatz-mailbag phase. Tearjerkers from the Friends of the Earth. Is the Tuna You're Buying Really Dolphin-Friendly? What does the tuna have to say? Help save these beautiful and sensitive creatures, sign this banker's order now. Attached to the leaflet, a single strand of drift netting in which these poor beasts are entangled: The "wall of death." "It may look flimsy but it's surprisingly strong." Perhaps if I wrote in for the whole net I would have an even more fool-proof murder weapon. Stop This Needless Slaughter. Indeed. I order a filter coffee. Anything but cappuccino. Poor Trotskyite Martha, trapped in the war zone with Simon and Garfunkel. The Platters. Peter, Paul and Mary. Arlo Guthrie. John Lennon, Give Pizza Chance. Only two other customers in the coffee-shop, a short-haired couple cooing in the far corner. Their hands clutched over the chequered tablecloth. I dedicate this revenge to Young Love. Hope must spring eternal. Ring out the old, ring in the nudes.

No way I can think of to entice McTeague securely out of his house to mugging alley. A telephone call could not be risked, no matter how disguised the voice. McTeague would read the signature of my mind. Using the purloined Walther would be bad enough, unless I could successfully stage his fake suicide. A bigger if, now, than it seemed in the Epping snow . . . If only I had that drift net . . . McTeague swims, calmly and purposefully beneath the ocean, blissfully communicating with his fellow publishers in their coded marine trills. The abyssal ooze echoes with the sonar bleeps of these magnificent and sensitive creatures who were once so common in our estuaries and coastal waters but are fast disappearing in the thoughtless depradations of multinational brigandage. The great factory trawler of Brent Browbeat looms above the shoal, the giant "wall of death" slung from the hull. The doomed creatures wheel and twirl desperately, but Brent Browbeat has the seven seas covered. The trills and bleeps crescendo. Too late. McTeague blunders in the net, chokes, is hauled in, the cannery goons standing by on the poop deck, bludgeoning the catch with their clubs . . .

Aiyee, aiyee. One Hundred Trapped Helpless Dolphins Are Killed

The Promiﬆed Land

Every Hour. And yet the guilty flourish. I must not be deflected now. There is a tide in the affairs of men. The sweet red-haired stewardess informs me of closing time. The cooing couple exit, enmeshed. I exit, with my alter ego, Droopy Dan. Just show him a suffering fish and he pops forth. Give me the gun, Danny. How can you do this to your pore old white-haired mother? Think of the shame, the obloquy, the failure, given the state of the art of British forensic science, capable of convicting even the innocent. Piffle. Cowardice. Avaunt, Weeping Willie Winkie. My mother's hair is black as soot . . .

Midnight. The thaw has ceased, the slush refrozen, every step treacherous and fraught with danger. There are only two other persons on the pavements, manoeuvring with windmilling arms. An occasional car slithers by, raising a cold muddy wake. Up Pembridge Road to the side-streets. Most lights poked out by vandals. The murderer casts no shadow. Oh for a mirror! Can one howl at the moon? Not a sausage. And not even a fedora for ambience. Well, one can always throw one's scalp on the hat stand.

Gott mit uns. The corner of Clerihew Gardens. All quiet and dark. Not a cat purrs. The little semi-detacheds draped in an ice-age veil. What manner of mammoths lie preserved in these glaciers? Trapped beasts with a thousand eyes. Creatures That Time Forgot. Are You Ready to Enter THE TOMB? The Lurker at the Threshold is here.

At number 11, all is still — 0025 hours. The only sound an insistent dripping of an impatient thaw. Central heating versus nature. My breath curls out in wisps, but no genie. Droopy Dan well chained. The trees frozen. I softly fumble the gate. The chink of the catch. And does the Yugoslav tottie rise abed, eyes akimbo? My boots crunch like hammers up the drive. Lights? Burglar alarms? Shotguns? *Nada.* My gloved hands work the keys in the lock. Into the hallway. Softly close the door. Bingo. Darkness, but I know this blind space like the fingers of my hand, so many's the night I've lain awake, with none but Nicolae and Elena for company, poring over my map of this household. The cupboard and coat-rack to my left, the little wooden stand, shelving on the right. E'en so, move cautiously. This being a child-infused domicile, one must be wary of being caught in the old trap of a loose roller-skate or escaped mutant ninja turtle. Testing the floor for hazards, I inch forward, door to ground-floor sitting-

room and staircase to my left, wall to my right, through open door to the
kitchen. The fingered clothes on the coat-rack, adult and juvenile, indicat-
ing all occupants present. They sleep, the slumber of the innocent and the
unrepentant, upstairs, the parents in their bedroom, the progeny in their
wee nooks, the Slavic au pair in the skivvy-hole, complete with portraits of
Eric Clapton, Debbie Harry and Belgrade in spring. Sweet dreams. I find
the kitchen table, the six chairs, neatly pushed in, probably by McTeague
père, a great one for tidying up he, the wall cupboards and whirring fridge,
I open it a smidge and send a shaft of light across the room. Never in the
field of human conflict have so many yoghurts been manufactured by so
many for so few. Fruits of the Forest. Raspberry. Rhubarb. Gooseberry.
Lo-Fat. Hi-Fat. Greek Honey. I check, to see if Elena and Nicolae are in
the icebox, waiting, but there is only Bird's Eye Beefburgers for six Tatar
divisions and a tub of American Double Ripple Pecan. Hubba hubba. I
take out a carton of semi-skimmed milk, the only available choice, shut
the fridge and carefully pull out a chair.

So here I am, in the Enemy's lair. Helpless, above me, he naps in the
bosom of his brood. His sanctuary, his castle, unaware. I place the gun on
the table, my eyes adjusting to the dark. The glimmer of the wall-mounted
clock. Tick tock. The slings and arrows of despair. Six minutes to one P.M.
The long night stretching ahead. Five of them in the house and three bullets in the Walther PPK. *Polizei Pistole Kriminal.* Very handy. But would I
at worst dispatch three of them? And which three? Down, Droopy. The
grieving wife, the orphaned bairns wailing, the Slavic menial tearing out
her mane. The life cut short . . . The real body slumped in the doorway,
real, not literary blood, on the carpet. The spreading stain. It struck me I
had never seen a genuine, honest-to-God done-to-death body, apart from
carcasses in New York hauled onto stretchers like slabs of meat, dead or
stoned, one could not tell. The wretched of the earth. Like flies, they fall
out there, in the deserts of Iraq, flitting into whatever compartments of
the afterlife reserved for those dependent on the welfare state. And are the
meek cheated in Heaven too? A terribly melancholy thought. Hundreds of
thousands of miles of drab high-rise tenements, the South Bronx from
here to eternity, and millions standing in divine dole queues outside grey
buildings five miles high. This is the first time I have had a proper idea for

a story since I hatched this half-cocked plan in earnest. A modern version of *Captain Eli Stormfield's Visit to Heaven, mutatis mutandis* for the zeitgeist of the post-communist world. Hope dissolved into gloom, the bright lights fading, old hierarchies re-emergent. Is there nothing new under the sun? If Marx was wrong, and history is going nowhere, might it as well march back as forward? God is entropy, aged and tired. Projections. Solipsisms. Wishful thinking. What am I doing here, in someone else's kitchen, quaffing skimmed milk and playing with a gun I most probably can't use? Having failed to solve, even at the brink, the problem of how to separate McTeague from his flock. The whole idea appearing, suddenly, at 0130 here, patently ridiculous. One is tricked by the information that killing is so commonplace into believing one can undertake it *sui generis.* Just like that. One sees so many mass murderers, serial killers, politicians and generals saying: "Well, once you done it once it becomes easier the next time. You just don't stop to think." It's the first hurdle one has to overcome. Today McTeague, tomorrow ze world. *Polizei Pistole Kriminal.* One phrase that seems to say it all. Or might the solution not be much simpler, if gorier? A silent death, rather than blasting the night? I open the drawer in the table to my right, my eyes now accustomed to the dark. The dull shades of an array of wooden spoons, corkscrews, eggbeaters, tin-openers, kitchen knives. The perfect alibi of an interrupted burglar. All I had to be was interrupted. Thoughts into acts. I turn my head towards the black hole of the kitchen door as a couple of muffled thumps patch through my senses. A creak, and hesitant but evident sounds of footsteps.

Someone is coming down the stairs . . .

Inside my head, the wailing tones of the harmonica I had heard so many moons ago at Drem station returned to twitch my sharpened senses:

At last he was there, in front of me, helpless, the cowardly Lion and Daniel in his den. The glimmer in the lunar penumbra (I've always wanted to use that phrase) of his striped pyjamas under a dark dressing-gown. I

turned in his chair and swung open the fridge door, the little dwarf illuminating my face.

"Daniel!" he whispered fiercely. "What are you doing here? How did
you get in? You gave me a fright."

I closed the fridge door, restoring darkness. "I came to kill you,
McTeague."

"Ssh!" he whispered, "not so loud! You'll wake the kids. It's enough
trouble during the day."

"You betrayed me," I said. "I trusted you and you stabbed me in the
back. You left me looking like a fool with my dick in my hand. You
remaindered my book at ninety-nine pee."

"Those are not my decisions, Danny. How the hell did you get in?"

"Have you ever been killed by an author before?"

"I can't take this in at two in the morning, Danny. It's been a hellish
day. I'm hung-over. Why don't you just leave and we'll talk about it in the
morning. In my office, ten o'clock tomorrow. No, make that twelve-thirty.
No, fuck, I've a lunch. Make it four forty-five."

"How about in half an hour under the Westway?"

"Daniel, please. This is my own house. My wife and kids are upstairs.
They deserve peace and quiet in their own home. They don't need this, I
can tell you."

I raised my voice just that smidgin. "You don't believe me, do you,
Gordon McTeague? You still think this is some kind of joke."

"For God's sake, Danny. Keep your voice down. Look, let's go outside, away from the house. Okay, Daniel?"

"You go first," I told him, "and no sudden moves."

"Shit, Daniel," he said, his brain suddenly working, "Was it you who
took that gun? Somebody phoned, asking questions, from the museum. I
didn't think . . ."

The fool. Now I knew he hadn't mentioned my name. I put the knife
handle down in my left coat pocket, walked after him through the hall
with the Walther *Polizei Pistole Kriminal* weighing down my right. He
grabbed a coat off the hanger and opened the door. We crunched out over
the frosty path, the satisfying crackle of breaking ice. The sky cold but
clear. No time to waste. I took the gun out. "Move, varlet."

"Jesus Christ, Danny. You're getting me really angry. Give me that thing."

"I'll let you have it pronto."

"You never were much good at telling dreams from reality, Danny. Give me the gun."

"You know, it's quite easy," I said. "All one has to do is make the decision."

His foot kicked out, jarring the gun out of my hand, his imitation-leather slipper following it in a neat parabola into the next-door neighbour's porch. He turned and lunged towards the low fence separating the road from the patio. I took two steps forward, pulling the kitchen knife from my left pocket, cutting myself slightly in the process. I grasped the handle of the knife and stepped forward, his back looming at me in the moonlight. I stuck the knife in. His wife must have been a good stewardess of the household utensils. Or the Serbian slave, seizing her chance at the knife-grinder's nomad cart. It sunk in with only a touch of impediment. I pulled it out. My hand was wet and warm. I stuck it in again, and out. He staggered, turned towards me, reaching round his back with his right hand, the left scrabbling at the wooden stakes of the fence. His face in the moonlight. Suddenly very pale. His eyebrows shot back, his whites glaring at me like cold peeled eggs. A sort of whoosh of wind from his mouth. The lips like dried rinds. I leaned towards him, as if in an embrace, the knife sinking into his abdomen. His face fell towards mine, his cheek, which was quite warm, brushing against my stubble. His chin striking my shoulder bone, snapping up with a cry, his wide eyes suddenly staring into mine from a distance of two inches, blood flecking his mouth and tongue, which he must have bitten through in the jerk. I drew out the knife and, still leaning into him, pressed it in again, in his left side. I had a distinct memory of advice from several Mickey Spillane, and other, novels. The true knifeman twists the knife in, to allow air in the wound, before pulling out. I twisted it in, feeling the rasp of a bone. I felt the knife snap, and pulled the remainder out. The fence, behind him, cracked and broke. I found myself on top of him, his face turning this way and that, the eyes wide open, his mouth exuding gurgling noises. I rolled away, feeling something solid. The gun. I dropped the knife handle and wrapped my torn glove around the Pistole. He was lying on his back, writhing like some beached and harpooned deep-sea animal. I put the Pistole barrel to his twitching head.

"An end to comedy, McTeague." I said, and squeezed the trigger. The Pistole kicked back in my hand, the blast echoing like the atomic bomb at Hiroshima. Everything around was shaking. The neighbour's house, its darkened, curtained windows, the fallen fence, squashed ornamental bushes, the sprawled body with the head twisted aside as if broken, a huge black splodge of muck in its right side, replacing the ear, cheek and temple. A sudden thin shaft of light from above. Someone switched on a bedroom light. I moved, dragging my feet over the broken fence, the sprawled feet, one bare and white as a giant naked grub, the other with one brown slipper half on, askew on the toes. A big gash in the sole. Time for another shopping spree, Gordon. I felt my whole body hot and sticky. I pushed the gun into my right pocket. The air cleared. Cold, frosty. The street was still there, trees, fences, the glitter of slush on the road. A banging door from inside the house. My footing firm on the pavement. A last look at the sprawled corpse. Well, well, well. Was that it? I turned my back on it, moving away, one step, then another, then running, my wet bloody coat flapping around me, running, to the far end of Clerihew Gardens, off down Jellicoe Place towards the junction of Notting Hill Gate. I heard one piercing scream behind me, and then, silence. No further cries, no jabbering mob with torches and stakes, no thundering Max Steiner music, no sirens of police cars.

❖

The family honour: Flying to rescue my sister, Rose Khamash, from the clutches of the dead English king . . . In my briefcase, a collection of my mother's nostrums and powders, her little bag of prophylactics and poisons, mineral dusts and herbal mixtures, ashes of immolated Templars, computer printouts of magical formulae, voodoo spells and other Crowleyan mumbo-jumbo. A tiny phial of her menstrual blood. I used to pour scorn on Maman's venoms and hexes, until coincidences mounted, the dying mothers, stricken wives, daughters and sons of enemies falling off precipices, too many unusual circumstances amid the normal body count . . .

The rumours of her initiation by the Druze as an honorary adept, till her expulsion for putting her knowledge to use in the material rather than spiritual sense . . .

My mother, Adele Khamash. Having achieved a stand-off with my father and the monks, she sits in her sanctum, weaving her webs. Searching for control of the uncontrollable. "There must be a better way than bombs and guns." "Negotiations, Maman? Deals, compromises?" "One must trade only from a position of genuine power. Military might is a temporary crest of the wave. Only knowledge endures."

But I am my father's son, I crave movement, commotion, action, the cut and thrust of conflict. I need to be ahead of the opposition at every turn. There is that certain *frisson*, of flying over the landscape of your ancestral enemies, shielded by that network of deals and barters that fuel us all behind the scenes: the pharmaceutical contracts, the flow of the military hardware, the software revolution, the informal global mesh. The Americans pay Israel to develop missiles for China which sells them to Saudi Arabia which sells them to Syria which sells them to God knows whom for payment in white powders which pass through Israel to vendors in the U.S. of A. State manufacturers sell arms to their enemies, justifying their enhanced production and sales. Something has to make the world go round. It surely isn't brotherly love.

But when all else is a snake-pit, one still has one's family, even if they are the biggest snake-pit of all. Pursuing the oldest atavism, family honour, I thunder over the desert of Nejd. Having collected the chopper at Jedda, with my trading partner Colonel Yusuf Bin-H. and a reliable pilot and four picked commandos, each on the take, zigzagging around the restricted Mecca airspace towards the Mahdi's column now reported to be skirting the lava-fields of the Harrat-Kishb. I would have liked to overfly the Holy City itself, Mecca, with its Ka'aba and mysterious black stone, but Colonel Yusuf just tossed his head in denial. A taboo even trade cannot abrogate, an irony I would have to forgo. We clattered east, in our appropriated Apache, skimming the granite mountains and wadis. I had not realised there was so much volcanic rock about. An endless aftermath of ancient eruptions. Was this the origin of Mount Sinai and its fires, as one Arab historian claimed? The repressed site of original contracts, covenants of Patriarchs and the Lord? Promissory notes still uncashed, unredeemed. The rolling cadences of primeval warnings . . .

"There!" The Saudi Colonel shouts in my ear, prods my arm and points down through the Perspex. Down below, in a basalt basin formed between massive fort-like rocks, they were gathered, a pathetic bunch of nondescript dots, human dust, blobs of flesh in grey rags craning up at our approach, like a human branch hacked off the primordial wandering tribes of Israel and lost far from their promised land . . . And where among them are my eloping sister and her seducer, the sodomising king? I press my face against the glass of the chopper, but a voice, suddenly crackling in our earlobes across the military radio, breaks in on the flow of my thoughts in that atrocious American Midwestern accent:

"Calling unauthorised aircraft! Calling unauthorised aircraft! You are in an area designated AS-ODB-45. Identify and reroute FDB-6. Repeat, identify, over!"

There remains no choice but to land.

"Let's go!"

The one-armed woman pushed open the door of my cell, pulling my arm as I sat at my wooden desk, allowing me less than three seconds to grab my scribbled papers and stuff them in my shirt, to snatch the Syrian army jacket my jailers had provided for the cold winter nights, before propelling me out through the door and into the back of a dusty four-seater jeep, parked engine running, a grinning uniformed youth at the wheel. She leapt in beside me, waving her single hand at him.

"Go, go, go!" The cheerful driver obliged, slamming the car into reverse, turning and screeching out through a gap in the perimeter fence, onto the hard desert ground.

"This is Sa'id," she informed me, the boy turning his grin to me, steering by the back of his head across the trackless plain.

"The war is over," she shouted in my ear. "Now it's the peace that's the danger. This morning they took a decision to kill you. I acted as fast as I could."

"Thank you very much," I said, as if I had been offered an annual pay bonus. The jeep bounded over the earth, small scrub and hillocks, dotted with stunted trees and odd humps of concrete, blocks and cupolas jutting out of the loam. A ridge of mountains in blue haze to the left.

"Where are we?" I shouted. "And who are they?"

"Northeastern Syria, as you guessed," she shouted back. "Turkey is that way, Iraq ten kilometres over there. As to them, Doctor . . . who can ever be sure? All those rival agencies, Air Force, Army, Intelligence, everyone wants to show they're in charge. Now they know they picked the right side in the war you're even more of an embarrassment than before. These are people who have only one way to avoid embarrassments. But I have decided you are not a spy, Angelopoulos."

"I am certainly obliged."

"When you sneaked out of Lebanon, in '87, the Steadfast Forces put you under surveillance. The President of the Republic authorised agents to follow you to Europe, and even the United States. They used the *mukhabarat's* British network to grab you in Scotland. It was a demonstration, to show their leaders here they still had that capability. It was a week before their annual budget, you see."

"I was an economic factor."

"Yes, Angel. But once they brought you here there was no clear idea what to do with you. So they left you, in suspension, under our nominal charge, supervised. You might have stayed down for years, like the Beirut hostages, but Kuwait threw up so many changes. Arafat supporting Iraq, our own movement finding ourselves on the American side, a terrible confusion. So as a precaution I was allowed to take you out of the hole, pending a final decision. Which was made, unfortunately, against you."

We are not in a subtle part of the world. "Well, I'm glad you got to me first," I yelled at her. But she yelled back:

"I volunteered to be the executioner. You see, now we both have to disappear very fast."

My life is nothing but a series of magic tricks. I am like the assistant who climbs into the box which the magician saws in half. Except that in the Middle East they misunderstand the point of the act. They leave the assistant in the box. All that anguish and despair for no particular reason. A grubby power-play between small-timers. Not even a pawn. A pawn at least you use for something. But I was kidnapped and rescued by the same circumstance: The compulsions of feuding brothers, and sisters.

The jeep rattled forward, away from the blue mountains, racing up a ridge of stony ground and jamming the brakes at the crest, beyond which, as in a skewed mirage, a massive tank encampment spread out before us. The camouflaged lumps of Russian and French steel, dug in two rows of shallow trenches, their cannons pointing away towards an unseen enemy. Samira waved Sa'id on, down into the midst of the bivouac, the soldiers and their trucks and armoured cars, dust and sand blowing through open tents in which officers battled in vain to pin down paper files amid the crackle of communications static. Samira, without hesitation, leapt off the jeep even before it stopped, flourishing a document unfurled from her shirt pocket in front of the sergeant who ran to intercept us, striding with him into the largest command tent and emerging minutes later accompanied by two soldiers bearing four jerrycans and a clump of water bottles. Folding the piece of paper back with her sole hand, she climbed back aboard, waving Sa'id on again, bucking and rearing past the curious soldiers, caught in their shaving and ablutions at standpipes, weaving between the tanks, beyond the farthest armoured line and through a gap in the trenches and barbed wire. Jolting over the barren ground for another twenty minutes till we crested another ridge to confront a checkpost at the mouth of a gully, with a small encampment of stone huts and sandbagged trenches looking out over a landscape of jumbled concrete blocks and scattered clumps of barbed wire, dangling the little tell-tale yellow death's-head triangles designating minefields ahead. Here Samira's magic document secured us an escort of a jeep with two gaunt infantry soldiers and a stocky, jovial officer with a thick, curling moustache. "Business! It never stops!" he boomed out, casting a hungry eye over Samira, a wary one at myself. "Still, it's better you than me." Unfolding a plastic-wrapped army map, he led us through an infinitesimal gap in the barbed wire, past twisted shards of debris, old rusted army trucks, concrete flakes and humps sticking out of the stony ground. In the middle of this wasteland he abruptly reversed to our front bumper and leaned back. "From this point on, God protect you. It's simple — follow the tin cans. Five hundred metres and you're out. The indigenous riff-raff you don't have to worry about, the American Phantoms chased them off. Now it's just the bandits and the Turks. They shoot anything that moves. Good luck!" He thumped his driver on the back and, carefully reversing past us with half an inch to spare, he and his silent grunts executed a jarring six-point turn and shot back the way they'd came.

"What now?" dumb Angelopoulos asks.

"We look for Americans," says Samira.

Blessed is she who lives in hope . . . We edged our way out of the minefield. There was no perceptible change in the landscape at first, but within ten minutes we were passing by the burnt-out shells of an army checkpost which mirrored the one we had just left behind. A few forlorn charred and overturned chassis of trucks. No sign as yet of mortal remains.

"The Republic of Iraq, I presume," I commented.

"Kurdistan," said Samira. "No man's land between the railway line and the river. We are near one of Iraq's northern oil fields. And an old smuggling route. Since before the Romans, pack animals with hasheesh crossed this way, now its hasheesh, opium, heroin, traded army to army. The people back there think we're on a routine business run, picking up on the wartime hiatus. But the situation now is unclear. The Kurds have rebelled against Saddam Hussein, again. The Americans egged them on, but aren't helping. Nevertheless, there are supposed to be Special Forces somewhere around here. It's the route of the Iraq-Turkey pipeline."

"So what flag should we fly not to get shot?"

"Good question. No answer."

"I should have brought my picture of George Bush," said Sa'id regretfully. "I cut it from *Time* magazine."

"Just keep your eyes open and stop if we're challenged." said Samira. "Keep the weapons hidden."

I had hardly noticed the Kalashnikovs and ammunition belts under canvas beneath our feet. Now I reverted instantly to a familiar phase where they were an everyday need. We edged on, stopping for fifteen minutes to open an abominable Syrian K-ration kit, drink from a water bottle, and empty one of our jerrycans into the fuel tank. I longed to ask her so many more questions but was overcome suddenly with a sense of awe at the openness of my surroundings. I am reduced to a cliché: The sky was so huge. Even though I had been prepared for it in my halfway hut. The land stretched in every direction. But it was a crippled earth. Overlaid with a silence that spoke of abandonment, an immeasurable indifference of man or God, nature and creation. The landscape ahead of us that met our eyes as we drove on was an immense acreage of blackened ground, with charred and blasted buildings, a vehicle depot and oil rigs bombed and scattered like burnt matchsticks. And the stench. Our first sighting of the little lumps of charcoalled, unidentifiable flesh.

We drove quickly through this devastation, like trespassers in an uncovered graveyard. Covering our noses and mouths with rags to keep out the stench and swarms of flies. Veering east, thankfully, along a pitted road which led into a terrain of gullies and small, stunted trees. The land grew lusher, and the earth browner, as we were clearly approaching the Tigris. But before we could glimpse a trace of water, Sa'id jammed on the brakes, pointing to a rocky outcrop above us, barking out: "Somebody there!"

A sign of life. We looked up. Against the greying sky, on the rock, a squat dwarfish figure, swathed in a bundle of blankets. It stood up, revealing immense torn boots, out of which spindly bare legs grew. It seemed to have on its head a wool cap. On second glance, we realized that it was a child, who, after the bold moment of disclosure, turned and scrambled away down the ridge.

"Wait!" Samira motioned Sa'id to turn the jeep off the road, following a gravel trail round the ridge. On the other side the child ran, falling over and rising again, rushing towards a small group huddled in a gully, who stood passively as we drove up. They were forty or fifty in all, children and adults, dressed in blankets over torn and ripped clothing, their boots dusty and cracked, some in tattered sandals, their faces filthy and lined with the shadows of a corrosive fear. On their heads, on their backs, in makeshift carts and plastic baskets, they toted piles of assorted belongings, sheets, towels, indeterminate rags, pots, kettles, finjans, kitchen knives, cardboard boxes with bars of soap and tubes of shaving cream, shampoos, transistor radios, razor blades, electric plugs, washboards, rolling pins, packets of household cleansers, sponges, brushes, and a smattering of children's toys and dolls. A gangling man in the remains of a Harris-tweed suit and patched trousers, with black-rimmed spectacles whose right lens was broken perched awkwardly on his dripping nose, staggered forward, holding a no-longer-white rag on a broomstick and shouting in a high-pitched voice: "Turkiye? Turkiye?"

I got out of the jeep and walked towards him, palms out, calling in Arabic: "We are not Iraqis. We are not Iraqis. Where are you from?"

The gangling man came forward, squinting at me through the good lens. "Not Turkish?" he asked again. "We are refugees, like you," I said, "Are you Kurdish?" The man hesitated, then nodded. "Which way to Turkey?" he asked. "I don't know." I said, "We are looking for European personnel. Americans, British." The man spat on the ground. "Nobody here," he said. "No Bush, no Major, no Mitterrand. Only Saddam Hussein's guns. We have no guns, we have no food, we have no medicines. We need a doctor."

"I am a doctor," I told him. "I have no equipment, but I am a doctor. How many of you are there?"

The man looked at me as if I were a madman. Then he turned, pointing back across the gully, to the east, waving his hand limply.

"Two, two and a half million," he said. "Come, doctor. There is no shortage of work for you to do . . ."

TWENTY-ONE

Dead Heat
in the
Home Stretch

*"Brethren! The Final Chapter! These are the days of miracles and wonders.
These are the days of the many in the One. When all the palaces of Man are
brought low and dismantled, when all his puny works are destroyed. The days
upon which Time itself is abolished, as all the ages of the earth are gathered
together as by a mighty broom, swept up in one heap on the threshing floor of
history. For My Creation has not yet begun, and yet has been present, here and
everywhere, and for all the ages of life. This is the message of the Hidden Book,
which only God has written, and only God can read . . ."*

"That only leaves us with films and the video," muttered Jody. But
the comment sags, in the profound fatigue of the disciples and fellow trav-
ellers gathered about the Apostle at dusk.

Can one describe one's own death? Can you describe yours, I asked
Richard Plantagenet, as we trudged, packs on backs, Major Mojo's jeep
abandoned, fuelless, along with the column's other handful of vehicles
buried behind in the sands. But the Lionheart could remember nothing of
any value, just an immense drowsiness, a tremendous slowing down of
affect. I finally told him: I saw you, long before we met, in the Jaffa Camp,
trampling in armour through the ruined city. You asked me the way to
Jerusalem, but I couldn't help. Then I saw you again, in my dream. At
school, you know, they taught us all about Richard the Lionheart: The
murderous barbarian from across the sea. If you had come to me in The
Club as a king, I would have killed you, I told him. But as a man you are
my brother. Is there any sense to that? '

He looked at me with that disarming bashfulness, the sad blue eyes under the dusty red hair. Now I pity you as a king, too, I told him. You came and failed, like so many others. At least you had the grace to go home, Dickie boy, until Khamash plucked you out of your grave.

"The Café des Amis," he said, "my sinecure . . . But you're right, Tewfiq, there are no victories. Only shifting advantage. Except for those whose souls are on fire, like our Apostle. The blessed and the damned. No purgatory. Or were the Gnostics right after all? The alleged heresy of the Templars. Hell on earth, and heaven only for those who turned their back on all authority. It's ironic, Tewfiq, that those in authority can be closest to apostasy, free as they are of most illusions. Religion is the opium of the masses." Congratulations, Plantagenet . . .

We had been unravelling our tangled net of connections since the disguised Rose appeared in our midst. "Tewfiq, this is Rose Khamash. She knows your story." More than I do, my friend. What can I say? Another sweating human being in the sun, caked with sand, shaking her hair free of its cap. No excuses offered, none expected. I am struck by the unusual inversion: Of all the people here, I am now the one most unobsessed. I am at peace with my surroundings, hellish as they may be. Even the Lionheart, who first seemed to me another refugee from memory, has fallen foul of his precarious *amour fou*, the perverse call of his dead desires. But I believe I have freed myself from the shackles both of memory and of hope. Liberated by the tug of futility, the realisation of despair: Moral, intellectual, national, spiritual. And so I am ready to follow the Mahdi, the portentous voice booming out with the golden blast of the dawn:

"Once upon a time, when I ruled in a far country, all seemed right and just in the world. To every being, master and slave, bird of the heavens or beast of burden or creatures that crawled upon the earth, there was assigned a place in the scheme of things. The high had been raised and the low debased by divine sanction. I could not think otherwise. For I was safeguarded and cosseted in my silken womb, garlanded with praise and showered with gifts and tribute. Then one night in my sleep I was transported by an unseen force across the surface of the earth. I saw the ravages of war and famine, injustice and oppression, rampant greed and limitless avarice. I fell into the depths of that abyss, and there I saw, above me, in a ghostly light, the underpinnings of all

the shrines of Mankind. The mansions of worship erected on mountains, in desert plains, in deep forests. And I saw that all their foundations were rotten, yet the worshippers in them venerated their Lords in a thousand and one different tongues, and each Lord was separate. And the scales fell from my eyes, and I saw these Gods as false idols, and a voice cried: Let there be light! And a white light shot through the rotting beams and cracked pillars. And the voice cried: Let there be fire! And the buttresses and timbers and spars of the buildings burst into a great ball of flame. And the voice cried: Let there be wind! And a great storm rushed down out of the sky, fanning the flames, and burning all within the false shrines to ash. And lo, I listened to that voice and I realised that it was none other than my own."

Ana akbar! I Am Great! The ultimate heresy trembles on the still haze. The day beckoning harsher, cauterising callouses and scalding lips, the rocks shimmering and dancing in heat waves. Limbs dragging as if an incremental gravity were squeezing us into the ground. Nothing to be found here of a human scale, despite Jody Steele's attempts to reduce the landscape to its geological terms: the basalt formations (which we call *hajar jahanam*, or hell-stone), hornblende, greenstone, diorite, actilonite, a smattering of petrosilex and porphyry. Incantations dredged up from some old college course to keep her mind off her failure to file copy, her realisation that GNB's hi-technology is in fact transmitting to nowhere, the exhausted satellite crew fallen silent as the jammed airwaves close about them. Phantom journalists, as well as phantom men and women. And the sun rises higher and higher, shrinking to a white nut of rage, the Apostle's buzzsaw drilling on, and out of its rumble, a mechanical drone, emanating from without, not within our heads, for a change . . . We squint up, at the army-khaki helicopter descending out of the burning white sky . . .

Dear Sophia,
Strange writing to you from this place which figured so much in shadows and dreams. I'm not sure what I expected . . . I know I should now rather be winging my way to Australia and fame and fortune -— well, at least a nice round of cocktails and some

guiltless sunshine, but I felt it only right to fly out with Avram in this difficult time . . . I tried to phone but got fed up with leaving messages, maybe Petros's one was one too many. Not to speak of Andrew Mackenzie's news about Daniel — who would believe the act would follow the word? Keep me posted if you can . . .

Keeping faith with the Wee Threes: Bulletins and reports, as per ancient traditions: I don't know whether I can keep this up. My journey thus far: We rushed down to London on the night train to catch the El Al flight, which was to be filled with a group of Zionist Youth, some of them pretty long in the tooth, I can tell you, travelling on a special war's-end tour to show solidarity with the Jewish State. Avram almost withdrew at the check-in, mumbling something about mistaking the queue for Venezuela, a comment which earned us a lengthy interrogation by the airline security men, who lost interest at the sight of his Israeli passport. They took their time with me, though, to check whether I knew my travelling companion for more than just half an hour. But eventually they allowed us on board, Avram clamping on his personal earphones to blot out the communal singing. His avalanche of *déjà vu* . . . But it's a short flight to the other world, as Petros said, just four and a half hours and bingo. A nasty taste, as they handed out gas-mask kits on arrival, as if not sure that it was all really over. The Zionist Youth clutched their packs like manna from heaven and were packed off aboard their buses still singing lustily, while Naomi Potamkin and her brother, Benny, rescued us outside the terminal.

I know you don't want to hear abour her, Sophie, but they were charming to us, and at least calmed Avram down from his trauma. The reunion with his unpromised land . . . They took us off through a landscape which was unexpectedly flat and languid, until the road rises sharply into the Jerusalem hills . . . A very cloudy day, dark over the forests of pine . . . I have this image of the old nineteenth century lithographs of the Holy Land —— Jerusalem in its medieval battlements leaping out of mountains and crags —— the view from the east . . . But approaching from the west one sees only a glut of ugly new housing blocks, slicing out the brown hillsides, the familiar maze of concrete and road signs, though empty streets, people evidently not quite certain if it was now safe to step out . . .

Naomi had arranged a rented flat for Avram's father to stay in Jerusalem, since he refused to return to what he calls "the chicken farm" with Avram's aunt Pashtida. It's always odd to see genetics at work. Avram's father is a rather stout but small bundle of energy, despite being stuck in his wheelchair. His head bobs this way and that, and his hands fly about like windmills. He displays towards me a kind of old-world charm that reminds me of Stanislaw, but more nervous, as is only natural, meeting his son's "wife" for the first time in these sad circumstances. He professes a certain guilt for not flying himself to see us, but "as you can see, I'm nailed to the ground." A kind of repressed joy, at seeing his son, that seems to threaten to burst him open. They dance around each other like planets that were once in parallel orbit but have somehow got cut loose. The apartment is on the ground floor, so Baruch Blok can at least wheel himself about a small garden, in a tiny street of surviving old stone two-storey houses, that used to look out on the so-called Valley of the Cross but now abut more of those high-rise developments which swamp the city and its skyline. "I'm always hopeful," he says, "of seeing the housewives jump off their eleventh-storey balconies, or hang themselves with their laundry." His English has an unabashed Hungarian accent, that musical Central European lilt, thick enough to cut with a knife. We sat and talked about art, with Avram looking round his surroundings like Rip van Winkle woken into a world he had long hoped had vanished. We had sent Baruch the book of Max Ernst, through Naomi, and he eagerly turned its pages. "Wasn't there an old woman in America," he asked me, "who started painting after she was dead?" "Grandma Moses," I told him. "She began aged eighty." "I am going to get my brushes right away," he said, leaning to whisper in my ear. "I don't want to upset Avram, but we are still surrounded by barbarians here. All of them, the Jews, the Arabs, it's a disease of the blood." Later in the evening he became tired, and then began speaking of his bereavement, in a roundabout way, railing against the burial society: "Those clerical necrophiliacs. Jingling their collection boxes at the grave. Murmuring their hocus-pocus. She believed in all that, you know, Covenants, promises from God. At least your Winston Churchill was honest: He promised nothing but blood, toil, tears and sweat. But God, no, it's always pie in the sky. Give me an old Imperialist any time . . ."

The old man raises strange feelings in me. It's as if there's a vital, dynamic life to his despair . . . He is angry, therefore he exists. An almost Biblical wrath to it, a Job-like rebellion against the

Almighty . . . except that Job didn't rebel, did he? He just waited for it to all come right in the end . . . Submission . . . Enough babbling, Sophia. I'll write again, if the disjunctions don't get me . . .
    Love, from the Holy Land,
    Kathleen

✣

Who are all these people?? I stride out of my chopper, my guards armed and ready at my side. The wretched of the earth, half-naked, starry-eyed lunatics, mostly young men, but also some women, many in shredded rags of uniforms, gaze at me like cannibals at a missionary, as a praetorian guard of tall blacks in dusty white robes rushes forward.

"Yo, brother! State your business!"

My business is solely my own. I push up against them, as the phalanx closes in on me, the mumuring faces, clutching hands. I call out into the mad multitude:

"Rose Khamash! This is your brother calling! Your brother Aziz!" My guards grapple with scratching fingers. "Richard Dupont, or whatever you call yourself here! Dead Englishman! Bring out my sister!"

Total perplexity in zealot eyes. The sun beats down like a mallet on a bed of crumbs. How I hate these Mussulman fanatics, with their mindless *jihads* and martyr complexes. Hail Christ the King! I come with a sword, not with snivelling baby cheeks turned for yet another blow.

"Come out, dead king, wherever you are!"

"Here I am." He emerges out of the mass, a tall, ravaged redhead in a torn grey T-shirt and sand-caked jeans, brushing the Apostle's generals aside. And behind him, a figure in *abaya* and scarf covering forehead and mouth, but eyes which a brother could not mistake.

"Rose! My Rose! I have come to take you home. Follow me."

But another man pushes his way through the crowd, a nondescript, medium-sized fellow, with untidy hair and a coarse grey moustache, about forty years of age, with tired and rather piggish eyes, another pathetic Levantine specimen, staring me in the face, addressing me in Arabic:

"Aziz Khamash? Do you know me? Do you remember me?"

How could I know the man from Adam?

"I am Tewfiq Abd-el-Khalil. Do you remember? May 7th, 1984. Rue Baalbek, above Sha'aban's Shoestore. Third floor. A woman, Adela Abd-el Khalil. A little boy, Fawaz, a girl, Adina." I had no time for these absurd guessing games, but the man stood pressed against my guards like a talking sculpture, immovable, saying softly: "Do you remember the people you kill?"

One cannot give an honest answer to that without hurting people's feelings. A man cannot dwell on these things. He does what he has to do and moves on. Everyone understands the rules of the game. Except this dunce, who seemed to be stuck in a world of his own broody imagining. Behind him everyone pushing and shoving, my bodyguards and the blacks, the pressing mendicants, all straining arms and bulging eyes, veins throbbing on foreheads, one of the faces even familiar, a journalist, of all people, in this bedlam, the sunburned Englishwoman Jody Steele — she featured me once, in *The Sunday Times* Colour Supplement, in a series — Butchers of Mount Lebanon. I remember I was flattered by the profile, if not the unfounded allegations, but no time for such niceties here, as one of my guards tapped me on the shoulder, and I looked round to find my agitated Saudi guide, Colonel Yusuf, rushing up from the helicopter, waving his arms and shouting:

"Khamash! There's no time! We have to take off now!" Running back, towards the whirling rotors. I call to my guards: "Don't let that machine leave!" I lunge past my forgotten accuser, grabbing hold of Rose's arm. But she pulls back, and I find my throat gripped by a strong, ice-cold hand with curling red hairs. I look into the dead Englishman's eyes, my sister's seducer and my family's disappointment and grief. His frozen fingers compressing my windpipe.

"Noblesse oblige, warlock." His grip was like a vice. I could not call out. I felt life ebbing from my body and the will to fight draining from my soul. And a voice echoed, like an iron drill in my head:

"Behold! The blind scrabble for light and the deaf for the balm of the Word! But they shall be as dust. For only those who follow Me to the Door shall be saved, and as for the rest they shall all burn, from everlasting to everlasting!"

And as I died, my brain imploding from the impedance of oxygen from my lungs, I saw a young man's hawk-like face, dark against the sun blazing behind his head, tendrils of fire flowing out from his hair and his ears. I heard a thunder, growing from the black rocks. Shimmering strips of steel streaking across the sky. The land itself erupting in sudden shrieks, then rising, as if slammed by the gods. Great balls of red flame, and a heat, greater than that of the sun . . . And then everything dissolving in fire and the echo of far-away voices confounding the currents of cause and effect...

❖

. . . "NOW LISTEN UP YOU GUYS! INTERDICTION OF UNAU-THORISED GROUND FORCES CURRENTLY PROCEEDING PARALLEL TO HIGHWAY 65/Z COORDINATES 23.42N 42.25E: This rag-tag of LCs, line-crossers, defectors, not to mince words, has been able by means whose etymology, ontology and phenomenology we will not be addressing at this point, to interdict and evade friendly ground forces deployed to abrogate their forward movement. Their stat-ed objective, it appears, is to proceed towards Mecca al-Mukkaramah, the holiest shrine of our hosts, in order to infest the city and declare the kingdom of God on earth in direct contradistinction and antithesis to United States foreign policy and the designated goals of Operation Desert Storm as set out in United Nations Resolutions 660 thru 668. Now hear this! We are instructed to treat the entire endeavour as hostile, and Presidential sanction has been obtained for aerial interdiction at this stage. Not to put too fine a point on it, it's up to you guys to get out there and whup that column's ass, total the motherfuckers and clean up the whole damn hellacious mess. I want good clean kills. I want top yields, no need for surgical precision, we have no collaterals there, no friendlies. The entire Kill Zone is highlighted on the screen here and programmed into your TADS. We take out anything that moves, man, beast or machine. Now listen up, I want no WIAs. No EPWs. I want that whole area stealthed, suppressed, eliminated and neutralised. I want maximum impact. I want one big Goddamn hole in the ground. I want their ass sewn up and tarred over. I want a good clean piece of sand down there that anybody's mother would be proud of. Are there any questions now? Good, now let's proceed to operational details. H-Hour is 0:700. We will be using MAB and FAE for maximum impact. We

405

attach a very high confidence value to the achievement of one hundred percent degrading, particularly from the fuel air explosives. We have to be absolutely sure that no one, but no one, walks . . . okay. I'll pass you over to Jack, here, who will take you over the terrain. Good luck, boys, just shove it in and break it off . . ."

"Richard, Richard . . ."

"Rose, Rose . . ."

"When you were young, what was the world like? Were you aware of what you didn't know? I mean . . ."

"I know what you mean. No, as an article of faith, we knew everything there was to know. Or at least the church doctors knew. Of course, the world was full of mysteries that even the most learned scholars couldn't penetrate. The vastness of God's domain, above and below. One always passed through a phase of being consumed by this search for the obscured and the arcane. We engaged alchemists, mystics and seers. I had several sorcerers working full-time for a while. But one becomes absorbed with worldly worries. And then we failed to reach the Temple in Jerusalem. It all became an academic exercise."

"My father thought you knew the secrets of the Templars."

"Their only useful secret was how to fuck without being found out. Everything else was illusion."

"And if we die out here, will we know the secret of life?"

"I am no doctor of theology, my Rose. Just a very tired old soldier . . ."

DEAD HEAT IN THE HOME STRETCH TO MECCA

An unfiled report by Jody Steele

Reporting on one's own death. Certainly an unusual assignment. Difficult to tell where to begin. The moment itself seemed to pass me by. There was no perceived hiatus of floating, although I did view the events unfolding as if through a plate of glass. There is a fleeting memory of a very old, very frail but somehow mischievous man, totally naked, squatting on a pillar which rose as a solid black object out of the sand. But I could see the attack itself clearly. There were about twenty aircraft, wheeling out of the sun, coming in low over the ground. A host of quicksilver darts streaked from their wingtips towards the Apostle's bivouac in the rocks. Huge balls of flame rolled across the lava beds, followed by clouds and clumps of black smoke. Through the smoke, I could see a second wave of aircraft releasing a multitude of bundles of floating canisters, which scattered above the dust-cloud and burst, close to the ground, igniting the air itself in great explosions which punched the soil like giant jackhammers. The flame seemed to move towards and through me, a vast heat, and then no heat at all. In retrospect, that was the moment. But I continued to see and hear. Out of the sky, another cluster of canisters rained down, in a hail of tiny bomblets, each exploding in turn at ground level in savage bursts of minuscule fragments, shredding flesh, tearing limbs. And, in the wake of these, a swarm of hundreds, thousands of small balls of steel floating down on tiny parachutes, little pods from which, as they struck the ground, minute steel legs and tracked wheels opened, grabbing a purchase on the rocks and skittering forward, obviously powered by some kind of flesh-heat-seeking sensors, towards anything that still showed signs of life.

I walked about the aftermath, the pathetic remains of the self-styled Mahdi's apocalyptic venture: shattered mess-tins, twisted tin plates, pieces of cloth, scattered boots, some with charred bones sticking out, fragments of personal belongings that the mutineers had taken despite their leader's stern strictures —— a burnt family photograph, a set of keys, a penknife, a ring, a lucky charm, bent coins and medallions. Very little to show for four hundred-odd lives snuffed out, the bodies virtually indistinguishable from each other, lying in horrible lumps of burnt meat. In my condition I was at least spared the smell, though I could see it all, and hear the sounds, the crackle of flames still feeding, the drone above of aircraft circling, still examining the target zone, the clack-clack-clack of the MABs, the multiple-ambulant bomblets, still scrabbling across the rocks, searching for more victims, some trapped in the rekindled lava softened by the heat of the bombs and sinking in, feebly waving their tiny steel antennae. Others flashed disconcertingly through me . . . though I seemed perfectly real to myself, unslinging my camera to take shots of the carnage, pulling my notebook from my pants pocket, my clothes still clinging to me, although I have no sense of the heat of the day, the temperature appearing coolly neutral . . .

An unexploitable scoop. I walked on, searching through the bodies. Even in the kindred lumps, some distinguishable features. I could make out the clump of large figures surrounding and failing to protect a smaller one, the Apostle and his bodyguards, though skin colour was no division in the fraternity of the fires. I found the melted plastic remains of the Global crew's satellite dish, by another enmeshed grouping. And a little farther on, the scattered metal fragments of the helicopter caught on the ground, unable to escape, a line of burnt bodies fused with their twisted weapons. And at the end of that line, a group of charcoaled lumps whose features I could nevertheless make out. There was little doubt — my friend Tewfiq and his enemy Aziz Khamash, and beside them, two bodies clearly those of women . . . But there is a limit even to the calm of afterlife . . . I turned away, having failed, in that last look around, to see any larger carcass that might be the red haired ex-king of England . . .

So I walked away, pushing through the bomblets, running from the consequences of recognition, and the glimpse, out of the corner of my non-existent eyes, of a cloud rushing in from the desert, the ancient plague biding its time in some unknowable but proximate dimension — the flies, buzzing in low over the killing-field, humming and sizzling and chanting their death song, settling in inexhaustible multitudes for the feast of their dreams . . .

. . . shanti shanti shanti . . .
. . . for thine is the kingdom . . .
. . . Gilgamesh, why do you roam . . . ?
. . . and I saw Babylon humbled . . .
. . . a public and open confession of crimes . . .
. . . of him who found out all things . . .
. . . his ghost does not sleep in the earth . . .
. . . buzz buzz buzz . . .

"Gerrawayfrome!" Major Mojo's voice emerged muffled through the pocket handkerchief he kept jammed to his mouth and nose to keep out the insistent hosts searching for any available orifice, crawling over his cheeks and under the rim of his Ray-Bans, eager to feed on his eyes. But as fast as he slapped them away, they returned.

"Let's get away from this," he breathed to his colleagues, Majors Diesenbacker, Preobrazhensky and Lowell. They scampered off across the plain, each followed by his individual swarm. His hopes of finding any trace of the purloiners of his jeep ground in the ash of interdiction.

"A thorough job," Preobrazhensky spat the words out between the hordes. "Sorry to have burnt up your rocks." He looked enviously at the Saudi liaison officer, Lieutenant-Colonel Bin-Latif, who stood calmly in a totally fly-free zone which encompassed him at three paces. The shining brightness of his white *thobe* bedazzling and bemusing the insects.

"It couldn't be helped," said Bin-Latif. "The man was a heretic, a false messiah. He misread the signs of Judgement Day completely. For these are clearly set out in *hadith*." He counted them out on his fingers:

"When singers and dancers and music become popular.

"When the sun will rise from the west.

"When the Abyssinians, under Dhul Suwayqatan, will invade Mecca and destroy the Ka'abah.

"When the Smoke will appear out of the sky.

"When the Beast will emerge from the depths of the earth.

"When the *sufyani* and the *yamani* appear, and the Pure Soul is assassinated.

"When the one-eyed man, the *dajjal*, appears, after three years of drought, and demons manifest as two-humped camels. The *dajjal*'s parents will bear him after thirty years of childlessness. He will be blind in his right eye, which will be like a rotting grape. He is of stocky build and has red hair. He will approach al-Medinah but be unable to enter, and will turn north, towards Damascus. Gog and Magog, too, will break through the ancient barrier behind which they were constrained since Abraham. They will spread poison and corruption throughout the land, but the Prophet, Jesus, Son of Mary, will come back to life and slay them, and the *dajjal* too. Then the Trumpet will sound its first call.

"These conditions, as you can see, have not yet been met. Therefore we have time to prepare."

"I'm glad to hear that," said Lowell, gagging on a swarm which entered his mouth as he spoke. Major Mojo strode out farther into the desert, leaving a reluctant trail of flies torn between his live frame and the leftovers behind, buzzing in angry frustration. His boots clattered over the rocks, his hands swatting endlessly. Finally he felt free of the hordes. He opened his eyes, finding himself on a rocky outcrop which looked out across the lava basin towards empty sands stretching west. He paused to catch his breath, using the handkerchief to wipe away his sweat. He took off his Ray-Bans and wiped his eyes. A glint of something caught his gaze in the fissures, and his ears pricked at a scrabbling sound. Over the crest of a stone, a tiny steel rod fluttered, and behind it, further glitters, reflecting off a multitude of minute moving things. Moving towards him.

"Holy shit!" He put on his shades and squinted. The objects were clearly advancing, their tiny stalks tinkling on the rocks. Others had tiny wheels or treads. "Oh no!" He recognised the multiple ambulant bomblets, dropped too wide of the mark and propelled by their batteries towards any ambients, without distinction of race, creed, opinion or gender.

"Get away from me, motherfuckers!" But they marched on, driven by dumb necessity. He turned and ran, waving his arms, slithering back over the rocks, batting off the welcoming flies, shouting his warning. "They're coming! They're coming! Call the chopper! Get us the hell outa here!!!" Still they approached, doggedly strutting, pushing over lava and stones . . .

. . . shanti shanti shanti . . .
. . . and the rain was upon the earth forty days and forty nights . . .
. . . and Moses stretched out his hand over the sea . . .

"The Harmonies of the Cosmos . . .," muttered Michel Khamash, gazing out . . . of the thirteenth floor of the Hotel Charles de Gaulle, with its tattered banners proclaiming the 55th Convention of Small Arms and Personal Surveillance, ONCE AGAIN IN THE FINANCIAL CAPITOL [sic] OF THE EASTERN MEDITERRANEAN. The repatched hotel, bravely turning its back on the sea and looking out over the broken urban landscape, the dull grind of the bulldozers below gathering the rubble of fifteen years of civil war into large neat piles, each garnished on top with a colour portrait of the new President of the Republic and his *sahbak*, Syrian president Hafez al-Asad. The old man wheeled his chair away from the window back behind his great cedarwood desk cleared of everything except two black-framed portraits of his son and daughter, Aziz and Rose, and a loose-leaf proposal by a consortium of newly appointed ministers to corner the national potato market by warehousing the crop until its price rose by two thousand per cent. But financial coups had lost their lustre. A man should not outlive his sons, grandchildren, great-grandchildren. That personal immortality. "Die young, and have a good-looking corpse." He remembered Aziz used to quote that at him, in the old gun-toting days, before the Renewal. Who was he quoting? Some American film star. John Dean? John Wayne? Elvis Presley was said to have never died. His fans continue to see him every day, in Memphis. An apt end for me. The living mummy. Die young, and have a good-looking corpse. Not one blasted into ash in the desert. From the same seed they came, and now mingle in dust. Old truisms one cannot escape. The CIA destroyed my children. In the end, all conspiracies merge in one.

And the Lionheart? That chicken gizzard. I should have had him burned at the start. History is for gravediggers. Just a trick to lull us into accepting poverty. And even business fails to provide immortality . . .

The Harmony of the Cosmos. Tell it to my bereaved heart. It may well be in a jar for all the good it does me. And my accursed wife, locked in the abyss of her mourning, lost completely in her alchemical dreams. But there can be no transformation, there is only what is. Entropy, degeneration, decay. I am helpless with rage. I cannot live again. I can't bend time back again, except in lies. To live in falsehood. At least at the end, let me see myself as I really am.

Michel Khamash wheeled his chair back to the French window, reaching to turn the catch and push it open. The traffic din and hum of the city coming back to a kind of life, but an empty shell, a counterfeit of the swinging zing of the old days. Nothing can be resurrected. Rose, Aziz. My lilies among the thorns. How did the Old Testament tale go? Fair and pleasant in their lives, and in their death not divided. How are the mighty fallen, and the weapons of war unperished . . . He turned his wheels forward over the metal underframe of the window, onto the narrow terrace with its three-foot-high metal balustrade. He scrabbled with the barrier, pulling his puny frame out of the wheelchair, struggling with all his strength. This is ridiculous, he thought, people fall off high buildings every day without the least trouble. He flicked the wheelchair back with his hip and swung his chest over the metal bar. Where there's a will, there's a way. Everything can be achieved, with enough determination. He pulled himself over, watching the city swing and sway beneath him. Beirut, Jewel of the Orient. The meeting-place between East and West. The city that always rises from its own ashes, each time gorier and sourer than before. My daughter, my son. Father, forgive me. A man can do nothing but try his best. He pushed out, a last, staggering kick from legs that had ceased to function years before. Well, what do you know. A man can fly. One experiences that last and first moment of liberation . . .

"Get up, Plantagenet! No bliss obliges!"

A sandalled foot pushed against Richard's arm. He grabbed hold of it and pulled himself into a sitting position, leaning against the jagged rock which had sheltered him, becoming aware of the scorching pain of his right cheek and eye. He closed his left eye and was instantly blind. The right eye was gone. He opened the left again and blinked up at the searing sun, the wiry bent figure of the hermit, his filthy matted beard and straggling hair.

"You were lucky the little bombs sought out blood heat, brother," the hermit said. "They just passed you by, lucky bastard. It's always the less sophisticated ordnance that gets you. I think you have lost that eye. Get up, I know some people who can patch up what's left of you."

"The others? Rose? Tewfiq? Jody?"

"It can't be helped, my friend. They never learn. All the ways out that science offers. Magic sails to take you up to the moon. Lenses to see into the unknown distance. Wings of desire, cloaks of invisibility, stealth technology, mind traducing drugs. All manners of escape from the pain. Except death, that was always denied me. Look at your own sad case. Always half-measures and evasions. Never the straight path."

"Who are you?" Richard struggled to emit the words.

"They used to call me Simon the Stylite," replied the hermit, wiping his dripping nose with his arm. "I was born in Cilicia, in A.D. 390. My father shepherded sheep. I wished to shepherd people. I tried to turn them away from sin, but so many came to me I had to take refuge on my column, which was built from public donations, and I remained there for thirty-six years. But they made me a saint, so I had to linger on, lamenting and watching, waiting for some resolution or other, which never came, and never will come. But I can tell you, it's never a dull moment."

He grabbed hold of Richard's arm, dragging him forward away from the battlefield, over the burnt-out ground and the shattered rocks, shaking his agonised frame as he carried him, crying out: "Walk, walk, King of England! By the Grace of God! Preserver of the Faith! Liberator of the Holy Land! *Parfait* knight! Tax reformer! Tentative tambourist and minor minstrel! Give us a poem for this, then, Parsifal! The Gallant Retreat from the Final Day of Judgement! Another prophecy gone bust. If I had a penny for each . . ." The ex-king's legs scrabbled on the stones, unable to keep up. The hermit laughed, hefting him like a massive sack of potatos onto his thin shoulders. "Brag and bounce!" he cried."Brag and bounce! The higher they rise, the harder they fall!" Bearing the king on his scrawny neck, he strode off, across the scalding plain.

Richard lost consciousness, then was jarred awake again by the agony of his lost eye. On the old man's shoulders he plunged up and down. The landscape changed, and rippled, becoming hard and soft by turns; the winds blew through his bones, and the earth was without form, and void, and darkness was upon the face of the deep, and spirits moved upon the face of the waters. He saw, alongside them, waxing and waning, through the blur of his ruptured vision, a host of other hermits, racing each other, each carrying on his back a bleeding and exhausted personage of equal global weight: He recognised Nebuchadnezzar, Xerxes, Alexander, Ahaseurus, Herod, Julius Caesar, Frederick Barbarossa, Titus, Mussolini, Bismarck. Only Napoleon, alone of this company, refused to be carried by his anchorite and strode along, sweating and swearing, on his short stubby legs, shouting out: "To Acre! To Acre!" egging the racing dervishes on and whipping at them with his rod of state. "Call yourself soldiers?! Lift up your skirts, washerwomen! Show me if you have anything there!"

But even an emperor can't choose his battlefield —

"To Acre! To Acre!" Rage, helplessness and futility. From the sublime to the ridiculous is but one short step. One moment one is ruling half the world, the next growing cabbages on a remote island, replaying lost wars with tiny model kits, Waterloos in radish patches. Dresdens in dressing-rooms. Wagrams in wagons-lits. Austerlitz! All change! What can a man do, surrounded only by echoes? Reduced to the chaos of café life, the labyrinth of lobotomies . . .

The Promised Land! I tried to bring them salvation, deliverance, divine grace, fiscal reform . . . But everyone is a victim of circumstance . . . From the ridiculous to the sublime. Richard returned to earth, brought down with a thump on hard ground, opening his one almost good eye to see several tall, black-robed men standing over him, hawking, belching and gesticulating, in front of a number of large black tents pegged out in the rolling sands, with camels, goats, chickens and several dusty Land Rovers tethered about them. The Stylite arguing intensely with the men, answering their gestures with his own, until they stepped back and allowed them through a group of equally black-clad women, who picked the wounded man up and carried him into the nearest tent, gathering about him with pails of tepid water, army bandages and soothing unguents and oils.

"They don't want you here any longer than you can spit," the hermit cackled, sprawled on a pile of silk cushions with a mound of soft pittas and a bowl of goat's milk. "Your eye, that red hair. They think you're the *dajjal*, the demon at the End of History, but I told them you're just another idiot Western journalist who took the wrong turn in the war. Nevertheless, we'll have to move on sharpish. I don't suppose you have any cash, dollars or Deutschmarks? Never mind, I can pay in information. Locations of army patrols, government inspectors and so on. We can be taken north, out of harm's way. Where do you want to go?"

"Acre." A regurgitation of ancient milestones. "Acre. Jerusalem. Acre."

"Indeed," said the Stylite, "that's some way off." Turning to their host, a large surly man wreathed in ammunition belts and carbines slung over each shoulder, "How far would you say, brother?" The Bedouin thought for a moment, calculating in the traditional measurement of Marlboros consumed aboard camels. "Six hundred and fifty cigarettes," he said. "That would do our lungs in good and proper," quipped the Stylite. But his host was in no good humour. Barking orders to his men, who hurried to load two Land-Rovers with cases of ammunition, malt whisky and sacks full of small white bags, he brusquely urged his guests onto the vehicles. The jeeps ground forth, convoyed by armed camel-back outriders, until they reached an even more barren, unbroken plain where the animals were turned back.

"To Acre! To Acre!" Revving to top speeds, the Land-Rovers leapt forward, to the fortissimo of ghetto-blasters relaying heavy metal bands. The Evil Dead. Black Sabbath. Stealth Sunday. Blue Monday. The Bedouin bandits waved their carbines and mortars and yelled into the boiling wind.

"To Acre! To Acre!"

And the sand storms danced to the rhythm, gimbling and gyring in the alabaster sky, while, to the south, the Ambulant Bomblets marched on, shedding units trapped in the drifts, their batteries draining into the earth, while others struggled bravely, bearing their tiny corporate logos on into the shifting dunes . . .

TWENTY-TWO

The
Persistence
of Memory

MURDER IS INDEED A SERIOUS BUSINESS. BUT AT LEAST THE DEED IS DONE. Hohenlohe's homicide. Daniel delivered of the lion's din. It is a far far better thing, et cetera. But I am still amazed that it occurred. And as I walked the streets of London Town, three A.M., in a dazed stagger, blood oozing from the nick in my hand and McTeague's gore soaking my torn overcoat, I thought of the short fuse I had now lit — how soon before Scotland Yard's forensic wizards ground into action? The hairs. The fluff. Genetic fingerprinting. *A wrong is unredressed when retribution overtakes its redresser.* And I, trudging through London with the Mark of Cain literally on my brow. No one noticed. A couple of tramps not yet dead in the cold snap tottering by, oblivious. I rubbed muddy slush on my face to disguise it.

Getting rid of the evidence: The coat, the gloves, the gun. Crossing the Maida Vale road I remembered the canal, but then considered the stretch at Westbourne Green might well be dredged by The Yard. Waste not want not. The streets crawled by under my feet. Arriving finally at Oseney Crescent, 4:20 A.M., unobserved by man, if not by beast. But did they hear, or sense me, in their bilious dreams? Would the dust mites be called to the stand? Lying in the bath, washing the blood off, grinding away with Imperial Leather and a kitchen scourer, I remembered a line spoken by the Marquis de Sade in Peter Weiss's play: *If a man kills and takes no pleasure in it he is a machine.* I now understand what the old monster was on about. Pleasure and pain, that horrible duality. I knew that I could never do it again. That ghastly act, that ultimate horror, whether McTeague or I were on the receiving end. Definitely a swan song. Remorse? Now that's another story . . .

The last dribs of blood down the plughole. The coat, with the rest of the night's clothes, wrapped in a black plastic bin-liner, providentially found under the sink. The gun, with its two remaining bullets. Who else would I kill, given will and opportunity? A momentary *frisson* of power . . . But with Mrs Thatcher gone, and Stalin, and even Lenin dethroned . . . Saddam Hussein out of reach. And Brent Browbeat? The lackey paying for his master's sins. Redundant thoughts. Next morning I bagged my bloody togs in my holdall and wandered off, waving cheerily to landlord Spetsotakis as he gazed out of his window at the winter slush, returning my wave, no hint of anything amiss. I should have, barring terribly bad luck, a breathing space, before the Polizei knocked on my door. I took the BR train across town to Highbury and Islington, dumping the bagged rags in a pile of unobserved bin-liners outside a gutted store. Then back to the train, all the way east to Canning Town, by the old East India Dock wharves. A wonderful cold-grey emptiness. Disposal of the *Polizei Pistole Kriminal,* a last wipe with a handkerchief and goodbye Charlie. Plop. Now I am clean, fresh, scrubbed. Off to Edelweiss Travel, to pick up on an idea sparked in my idle brain by one of Andrew Mackenzie's postcards. A sheaf of blank IATA tickets and computer access to every corner of the globe. My first choice, to be really thorough — Australia. There is a rock, I understand, in the middle of the country which leads to the centre of the earth. Uluru. Or out in the Outback, to Coober Pedy, where SS veterans and other miscreants escaping justice work the opal mines deep underground. Preparing, while I process my ticket, for the routine police visit: Ah, officer! What a tremendous shock! A man is not safe in the confines of his own home. I remember the days burglars were sedate gentlemen with skin-tight woollies and a fantoush face-mask. Old threats? Ha ha ha, officer. Authors are always threatening to kill their publishers. If we all fulfilled our darkest dreams there would be a dreadful silence wrapping over a grim and lifeless globe. I personally have obtained successful professional treatment for my phantasies, here is my physician's invoice and receipt. Please extend my condolences to the bereaved family. How cruel is fate. All flesh is as grass . . .

❖

Dear Angel,

The entire Angelopoulos Appreciation Society (Tel Aviv branch) sends you love and greetings. What can I say? It's a real joy to hear you've survived, as I always felt in my heart you would. It must be true — miracles do happen, and even the good people get a break sometimes. Ali Amar brought us the news, finally sneaking in to the Jewish Homeland, which he had boycotted until now. We are all here as a group, oddly enough: Myself, Benjamin, Kathleen McFarlane and Avram Blok. Blok's mother died, peacefully, during one of the Scud nights, one of about eighteen people who died in this period, mostly old people who suffocated in their gas masks. Kathleen, too, is seeing this country for the first time. Perhaps I should too. We rediscovered an old solidarity here, but an even older fear. A whole nation, stuck in sealed rooms, helpless before a random attack. There could be no heroic resistance, no armed deterrence or revenge. And the Palestinians who cheered the Scuds on, our own victims rejoicing at our terror. Who can blame them? Benjamin sat with me, listening to the pious horror of our friends, the ex-bleeding hearts, saying, what did you expect? In their place we would do the same thing. In fact Benny has been quite changed by these events, which, paradoxically, while everyone else has been sent running to hide, appear to have shaken him out of his hole. He's come out of his hiding-place among the chickens and cows, and we've both been ferrying Avram Blok's father about the country, along with Blok and Kathleen. Benny has also agreed to be interviewed, by Ali, about his experiences in Beirut. I think we both feel now is the time to become politically involved again, against the grain, against the prevailing atmosphere of mistrust, fear and denial. A strange turn of events . . .

   Your invitation to meet again in Paris, Angel . . . Making up for lost time . . . You shouldn't feel obliged. I know it would be lovely to have time stand still, just for a moment, or reverse the clock, relive all those sanctuaries and escapes. Eternal verities of Chartres. All human knowledge set in stone. Remember when we were talking about medieval beliefs in the shadow of the cathedral: That legend that Jesus had died right on the spot where Adam was buried, and that the cross was made out of the actual Tree of Knowledge of Good and Evil, whose wood had also been used as the bridge over which the Queen of Sheba passed into Jerusalem. The instrument of the Fall as the means of Redemption through terrible tortured death. Humanity does not need to make sense of its suffering. I think about your tales of Beirut, and your present place. Does suffering serve a purpose? I never thought so. So maybe we should return to those snatched dreamy days: The banks of the Loire, the Chinon jams, the kindness of strangers. Things both ephemeral and eternal. Or was it just a good holiday? Let it rest. I don't think I want to feel that what's passed in these nine months is just a transient evil, that can be put out of mind. Is that just an excuse? Ali told me you're not alone out there. No details, but no surprises. Fallen Angels don't change their spots. No judgements, no expectations. I'm just glad that you're alive, you fucking lunatic! We'll meet when the time is right . . .

I'm back to my handicapped kids now. Bedpans, nightsoil and little victories when someone builds a plastic castle. Weekends and days off with my tourist guests and the old man. In fact I'm supposed to drive them up tomorrow, Friday, to Acre, the Crusader town (some things don't change . . .) Astonishingly, Baruch Blok has never been there. A typical Jerusalem drone. Now, as he admits, into a second childhood. ("Don't ask about the first!" he demands.) He wants to see the walls that stopped Napoleon. Well, at least someone's full of life here . . .

Updating, while you "slept" — odd that we, passive "consumers" of the events, knew "everything" (and nothing), while, you, the active soul, were shackled throughout . . . But I'll just keep to the personal gossip: Your friend Doctor Mackenzie had to close his rest home in Scotland, and is applying for jobs in our common field — the handicapped. I would have thought neurosis was even more lucrative nowadays, but you have to have the right "market" attitude. Mackenzie has also been shattered by the news that one of his patients, the writer, Daniel Pick (?), killed his publisher. The police believe he escaped abroad, but no one knows where. His threats were never taken seriously. That would never happen here, where every threat is seen as a deed already done, that requires an instant revenge . . . Avram Blok's comment on this sad tale: Only failure is predictable.

I will miss my guests, Kathleen especially. We have become quite close. She is another doubter, like me. She says the war has made her question the value of her work, her "flotsam" sculptures. I'm sure you saw them too. I thought they were very evocative of the randomness that surrounds us. But I think when you live in a more secure place, or country, you tend to enjoy the distraction of randomness more. When you begin to taste real insecurity, you get more eager for control . . .

Benny thinks we should get into "futures." Not in the financial sense, but forecasting what the world might look like with all its certainties removed, its preconceived ideas bankrupted. A look at the way we don't have models for living any more, just a huge display of concepts on supermarket shelves competing for the gaudiest package. I'm not quite sure what he's talking about, but he's been talking with Ali about some media project: "The New World Disorder." Grand designs. Everything is now "communications." Can unrecorded deeds exist?

You asked about Sophia. I am informed: She got your answering-machine call and sends good wishes. End of message. Back to the business of art. What do you expect, Angel? You want to juggle love and duty, impulse and obligation. But you can't square the circle all the time. Remember the opposites of Chartres? The virtues and vices: faith and infidelity, humility and pride, prudence and folly, hope and despair. (I think that was the list, or part of it . . .) Of course, we no longer believe in opposites, since Freud everything is in the same pot. So keep on in your contradictions, Petros. The world does not need saints, just human beings, stop. Not Beyond Good and Evil, but realising our capacity to be both.

This is getting too heavy. But we'll have to let trauma pass into memory before we can try a lighter note. Keep up the good work! KEEP THOSE MIRACLES COMING! Love from all, Angel, in real friendship.

And of course — "We'll always have Paris . . ." Off to Acre now — Your ageing seraph,
Naomi

❖

The vast encampment of the refugees stretches in front of me as far as the eye can see. Fingers of snow stretch down from the mountain peaks, and where the snow ends the people begin, covering every foot of ground.

"Doctor! Doctor!" When I was young I memorised the dictionary definition: *dok'ter*, n. a teacher; a learned father of the church; a cleric especially skilled in theology or ecclesiastical law; the highest degree in any faculty (originally implying competency to teach); a physician or medical practitioner, whatever his degree in medicine; a mender; in some countries, a cool sea-breeze conducive to health; a ship's cook; a name for various contrivances for removing defects or superfluities in manufacture; material used for sophistication; counterfeit coin; loaded dice; to treat, to patch up, repair, tamper with, falsify . . .

Who would have thought I'd feel nostalgia for Jaffa Camp, for the daily, nightly bombardment by Berri and Asad? For the camaraderie of the doomed? There, at least, they could fight back. Here, all we have are the TV cameras, carrying the misery of the third, fourth, fifth worlds into the prosperous living-rooms of the first. And they brought, at last, in their wake, the American transport planes dropping medical equipment, food and supplies. Now they drone regularly, in their bursts of magnanimity, over the congregation of these meek who have not inherited the earth, dropping their cargoes by huge parachutes. Some loads come down in the midst of the mass, the people so tightly huddled they fail to get out of the way, and are crushed to death by the goods sent to save them, the huge bound packs of U.S. Army MREs — chicken cacciatore, lasagna and lunch-bucket entrées of beef stew and macaroni cheese . . .

After the first three days and nights, I finally slept, Samira by my side, pressed up against me, with the five Kurdish orderlies we had scraped together from the mass. Seven of us under canvas, with the sleet pelting. As my eyelids droop, people are dying. I can feel their souls departing, in groups. Little wisps, finally anaesthetized, curling into the storm sky. I clasp her thin body to me. She is not all here. One arm buried in Beirut. The nakedness of her stump. All my own work. The beauty of her soul. Bizarre epiphanies. No chance for a consummation here. And not a condom for a thousand miles, in any case. Should we engender a new life, in this hellhole? I must stop meeting people this way. I'll marry her, we'll raise a family and look to the future. I'll give all this horror up, go to a small town in upstate New York and practise in some declining Italo-

American or Vietnamese community. Show my wife some fresh air. Pressed up against her by the misery of millions, I finally asked Samira: "Did you fall for me in that fucking Syrian cell? Did my vibrations seduce you? I was trying like mad."

"You must be joking," she said. "You could be smelled in Damascus. But I always had doubts about you as an enemy. Then when you talked, through the blindfold, that outburst. I was convinced."

"It worked then."

"Politically, yes." Go figure it out with Palestinians . . . Love in the pit. You never can tell, Naomi. I can't quite shuck off the habit of talking to absent friends. Though not all friends are absent: Ali Amar appeared, the gangling tower of Cairo, bumping up in a jeepful of journalists fresh from Beirut via Syria and Turkey, the long haul over the washed-out trails from Diyarbakir and Cizre. A real joy to see a face from the other world, the world of restaurants and shops and heated bedrooms with soft mattresses and clean sheets and warm bodies between them . . . Aaahhhh! Bringing the latest news of the Gulf — or gulfs — the strange vanishing of Jody Steele and my friend Tewfiq, together with an entire crew of Global News Broadcasting's ace reporters, complete with satellite dish. Official claims that they had crossed without authority into the war zone just before the Land War began, countered by strange reports of sightings of their departure west, into the Saudi desert . . . Rumours of a strange raving GNB broadcast, choked off by U.S. Army jamming. Ali clasped my shoulder, as if making sure I was really alive, saying: "One appears, and six more vanish." There are a lot more than that gone, brother . . . Out of my millions, great hacked wedges of humanity, nameless to us, in unmarked graves. So many of those who rose up against the tyrant, answering the calls from the Voice of America and Radio Free Baghdad broadcasting from Nissen huts in the desert, crying every day for insurrection, so insistent in their round-the-clock hammering that the people, exhausted by the tyrant's tidal-wave of blunders, follies, murders and tortures, all his thefts of history's heroes, the mantles of saints, the dreams and slogans of the dispossessed, responded, in heroic desperation, all over the country, south and north, in towns and villages, barracks and mosques, soldiers and citizens, mullahs and mechanics, conservatives and communists, Shi'as and Sunnis, Yazidis and Kurds, taking up arms against the remnants of his armies, united in the sudden hope that the age of terror was finally at an end, convinced the foreign voices at the end of the rainbow would spring to their aid in columns of tanks and payloads of liberty — in vain . . .

Tell the world, Ali! How long will it listen? There are so many other songs to be heard. Famines and wars covering the planet like the sores of resurrected plagues. Charity benefits to salve the conscience. No doubt this too will have its gig. What can we expect the individual to do against the depravity of states?

ADPG: Angst Depression Paranoia and Guilt. Small wonder I clutch my mutilated woman in the night. All my ghosts visiting me in the small hours, commenting on my good fortune. Jody Steele, hovering with notebook and ballpoint pen, taking down my mumbles in shorthand. Tewfiq, with his dog-eared copy of Camus. One-eyed Nabil with ephemeral slices of Brooklyn pizza, Abdul Kebab with a good smelly shawarma, rejectionist Kamal and young Mad Latif, counting the tally of my patients, presenting me with his inventory of the damned: 187,765 men; 246,432 women; 456,874 children, of both sexes (in those rags, it's often hard to tell); 157.30 tons of shit excreted per day; 23,458 gallons of urine; 5 doctors, 38 volunteer medics and nurses; 374 ex-lawyers — God, what a suit we could formulate against the world — 782 teachers; 2,749 municipal officials; 1,230 bus and heavy-transport drivers; 23,812 mechanics; 678 mullahs; 3,457 armed Pesh Merga guerrillas; 16,392 cleaning and ancillary workers; 54,392 farmers; and so on. Mad Latif's face gleams with delight. Control of numbers equals power, even if only in the imagination. When the imagination is all you own.

The rise and fall, the ebb and flow, the wheel of being . . . Her hot, moist breath on my face, wiped away by the stench from the encampment. "Doctor! Doctor!" Another day. The first pale light trickling from the sky reluctantly, through storm clouds. The television crews long gone home, even Ali Amar, bearing messages to whom it may concern . . . Agendas change but the pain remains. Now only the sky is a constant witness, exercising, nevertheless, its right to silence . . .

"Okay, I'm ready. Who's next . . . ?"

"To Acre! To Acre!"

To reach the town by the coastal route the city of Haifa has to be crossed. Trying to avoid the busy harbour road, Naomi drove Kathleen, Blok and his father, Baruch, up Mount Carmel, round the upper route. She stopped the van at the panorama overlooking the bay, Blok and Kathleen easing Baruch's wheelchair down the ramp of Benjamin's old Volkswagen van. Baruch enthusing over the view.

"The port of entry," he reminisced about his own immigration, forty-five years before. "You young sprats don't realise what it's like to enter your dreams by sea. Flying about the world like pterodactyls. You can't imagine the rising blip of the mountain, then the houses, the trees, the busy docks. The British soldiers, reluctantly watching us disembark. Being squirted with DDT down the gangway, as we stepped onto the Promised Land . . . You screamed a lot, Avram."

"I'm sure I did," said Blok.

"Now I'm the one who's screaming," said his father. "Well, let's not cry over spilt milk."

Broken bottles, shattered omelettes, powdered waste. The smoke from the oil refineries missed by President Saddam Hussein's Scuds curling into the sky. The Bahai dome gleamed just below them, a monument to the Bahaullah of Iran, follower of one Said Ali Muhammad Shirazi, alias The Bab (The Gate), executed in Iran in 1848 for claiming to be the Hidden Imam. His followers have prayed, from that day to this, for a new, pacifist age. But ten minutes later, Benjamin's van was stuck in traffic at the junction of Shemaryahu Levin Street and Herzl Street, a notorious bottleneck, vehicles snaking down the bend of the road like twin wedged serpents, moving neither east nor west. Drivers leaned out of their windows, shouting, some trying to overtake the blocked cars and create an unachievable third lane. Naomi, at the wheel, turned her head wearily to one of these hopefuls, who merely waved at her and said: "Elbows! Only with elbows in this country!"

Avram Blok, wedged between Kathleen and Naomi in the front seat, looked back to see if his father was comfortable, but Baruch was unperturbed, belted back into the special wheelchair-brace built by Benjamin in a cocoon of cushions and reading an English Penguin paperback by the light of the small bulb fixed above his head.

"Listen to this," he said, reading out loud in his wide Hungarian accent: "'We are an improbable and fragile entity, fortunately successful after precarious beginnings as a small population in Africa, not the predictable end result of a global tendency. We are a thing, an item of history, not an embodiment of general principles.' I can't think why our righteous religious leaders are not burning this book in vast piles."

"They'll get round to it eventually," said Naomi.

Baruch was reading from *Wonderful Life*, by Stephen Jay Gould, an American palaeontologist, concerning 500-million-year-old fossils found in the Burgess Shale of Alberta, Canada, which, according to the author, belonged to distinct strings or phyla of animal evolution which have no apparent continuance.

"Are you aware," Baruch continued, "that we are a historical accident? There are creatures here the scientists call by all sorts of exotic names: Hallucigenia, Wiwaxia, Aysheia, Yohoia. If we'd actually evolved from some of them, we would probably look to ourselves like Martians."

"I read a science-fiction story once," Avram Blok remembered, "in which humanity was a disease that had floated down as pores from outer space. Or was it all of animal existence? The flora, it turned out, were the true custodians of the planet."

"What about the carnivorous plants?" asked his father.

"'Nobody's perfect,'" Blok quoted.

Sluggishly the line of traffic moved forward, till they were able to ease down Herzl and across the narrow Heroes' Bridge to the main road leading to the north junction. Speeding up, on towards Acre. Indulging Baruch's new wanderlust, the sudden rush of freedom offered by Naomi and Benjamin. A change after all those wheelchair years of his conjugal obligations. As Baruch said to his son when they first gathered awkwardly at the Jerusalem apartment: "Memory — don't you hate it, Avram? The first man to market amnesia pills will clean up." He looked at his son as if to say, But don't tell me, you have no need of them, you found oblivion in distance.

Later that day Benjamin drove Blok alone up to the cemetery to his mother's grave, which was the first filled plot in a new allotment, surrounded by reserved spaces, with a little mound of stones marking the ground set aside for Baruch at her side. It was at the very crest of the hill, overlooking the old Arab village transformed into a mental asylum on the one side, and the vast military cemetery on the other side of the valley. A lonely and windswept repose. At the end of the day, what did it all mean? As he stood, without words, over his mother's grave. What words can be found to sum up a remoteness, a chasm of dreams and expectations? We live and love, in our own way, devoid of any grand purpose.

What sort of son doesn't weep by his mother's grave? Are those tears, or just a lachrymose welling of moisture in the biting wind? But one expunges guilt, like windshield wipers. The ego pretending to triumph over the id. What's done is done. Once upon a time we thought we had the answers. Now we're back to what we can see and feel. The pull and push of interests. All brave new worlds thrown out to sale in second-hand stalls.

"When will this suburban desert end?" groaned Baruch Blok. And the sun broke through, stretching eagerly, out of a frowning sky . . .

"To Acre! To Acre!"

The Lionheart endured most of his journey in the euphoric haze of the Bedouin women's pain-killers. He floated on a cushion of air, buffeted by burning desert gusts, the fires cauterising his eye. Night followed day and day followed night in a tangle. He could perceive, in a fog of sensations, being moved from the Land-Rover to an army-khaki vehicle, parking in a mountain cave in the night, little lantern lights flitting in the distance, and the dawn ushering a strange exchange of packets of white powder and briefcases, a further drive through the barrenness of the desert until the Stylite helped him off the army vehicle at an isolated bus-stop on a tarred road which stretched into emptiness through a landscape of mesas and crags. A red and white bus ground to a halt

beside them, its door swinging hydraulically open. The moustached driver's brow furrowed at the sight of the red-haired traveller's bandaged
eye, and the unkempt robes of his companion. Murmurs of unease
about the casually but cleanly dressed passengers, but the Stylite counted
out the fare, out of a small wallet exchanged earlier for the last of the
white bags, and the King sank gratefully into an air-conditioned balm,
as the bus shot forward, in a tinkle of mellow Levantine pop, punctuated
every hour on the hour by the amplified boom of news reports in a guttural language that conjured ancient timbres he could not quite place.
He fell asleep, jerked awake by the jarring stop of arrival, precipitated
into a hubbub of dust and hooting buses, raucous crowds oozing like
ants over causeways, the Stylite pulling him through an underpass
smelling of piss and vomit, past rancid felafel stalls and mewling beggars, up steps into another queue snaking on board another bus, which
shot off, through winding side-streets, onto a grinding, busy motorway
under a grey and overcast sky, down six lanes of screaming traffic, till the
road narrowed and thinned out a little, and glimpses of the sea to his left
side drew his face to the window. And another city and another platform
change, into an even rowdier queue of Levantine ragamuffins pushing
onto an even more battered and dilapidated vehicle, the Stylite calling
out to the driver:

"Acco?" "Acco." And the crowded bus ground forward, down an
endless traffic jam along docks and warehouses, past miles of urban
blight until the low, archaic turrets and spires of a peninsula, bounded
by a massive stone wall, rose out of the sudden sea. The bus swirled past
it down a wide leafy avenue, turning in to a small bus station, Richard
pushing past the press of disembarking passengers to stride purposefully
down the modern shopping streets towards the minaret punching into
the sky, which had cleared and become a deep blue, with a stiff breeze
blowing from the bay. The Stylite hurried to keep up with him, as he
strode past Napoleon Bonaparte Street across the moat and into the Old
City, brushing away the postcard and souvenir vendors who rushed up
towards the first tourist they had seen since the beginning of the crisis,
the Stylite swatting them away with his wallet, till the only way he could
dispose of a particularly adhesive small boy was to purchase a brochure

and map for three shekels, informing him that

Acre is one of the oldest port cities in the world and is mentioned in the "Book of Curses," the writings of Ancient Egypt, 4000 years ago. The remains of Canaanite Acre were uncovered by archaeologists at Tel Acre (also known as Tel el Fuhar or Napoleon's Hill), just east of the present-day city. Acre is situated on a small peninsula jutting out into the Mediterranean Sea. The remains of Crusader Acre are below ground level, having formed the basis for later Ottoman Acre. The marvellous state of preservation of vast sections of both Crusader and Ottoman Acre enables the visitor to experience the unique attraction of both historic periods of the city separately and simultaneously, while remaining in the modern-day world, with its amenities and comforts always at hand.

"Guide! Guide!" the small boy shouted, but realising he had reached his limit, he peeled off, as they found themselves in the market square, in front of Walied's Gate Hostel, in a busy short street of shoe shops, grocery stores and lawyer's shingles, leading to stone arches plastered with movie posters for *Rocky V, Commando* and *Total Recall,* proceeding down by Chaim Farhi Square down streets named after Marco Polo and Benjamin of Tudela, into the labyrinth of market stalls and discount stores, young children scraping under foot, mothers yelling, motorcyclist teenagers manoeuvring the thread-thin alleyways, modern-dressed men rubbing shoulders with young girls in strict Islamic garb, suspicious young men glowering in corners, emerging onto the Venetian Square and striding with ten-league steps onto the waterfront, the fishing boats, the pier, the great stone seawall and the Marina. The sea, the rolling sea.

"We're just around the corner from Abu Christo," said the Stylite. "The sea air does wonders for the appetite. The freshest Saint Peter's Fish, with chips. As fresh from the sea as on any day in history."

They sat down at a table on the pier and watched the condoms washing in to the wharf. The waiter took them into the cavernous kitchen and opened the fridge for them to choose their meal. They pointed out two mousht, which were soon placed before them, succulently deep fried, with chips and salad, washed down by two Maccabi beers. The sea breeze whipped about them, blowing the Stylite's grey mane about his eyes, the Lionheart tugging at his bandage, removing it and replacing his eyepatch upon the healed wound. His companion picking the soft white meat from the fish's large hard bones, sucking them down with smacking lips.

"What does it all mean, Stylite?"

"Eat, eat, *schmendrick.* Don't think."

Out in the bay, a child carrying a fishing rod walked upon the water, crossing over submerged rocks.

"Eight hundred years," said the Lionheart. "Time for a rest."

"Momentary respites," said the Stylite. "The world will continue without you. It will hardly blink, but move to new business. Nothing quite dies, yet everything crumbles. New ideas. How they used to torment me with them, on my column. The crap machine, the Loggie-Bird. Offers to extend my senses just that wee bit farther. But now they go round the world in forty-eight hours, eating reheated pasta with plastic spoons. And still they build Gods in their own image, all evidence to the contrary. Footprints on the moon, but hunger in Baghdad. They reach for the stars and grab dust. Still, they are always full of surprises. I like to see them jump and dither. At the same time, it breaks my heart. But a good fresh fish is not to be sneezed at."

"Let's go," the Lionheart pushed his chair back. The Stylite paid the bill and left a large tip, exchanging a few pleasantries in Greek with the waiter. Then they walked back across the bare courtyard of the Khan el Umdan, threading the stony alleyways past the Khan el Franj and the Ramchal Synagogue, the dusty square of the al-Zeituniye Mosque to the back of the al-Jazzar Mosque. Pushing past dripping laundry lines in residents' front yards, the sound of drumming from an ancient ruin, tired eyes watching from shadowed windows. Back to the main square and the souvenir vendor specialising in evangelical booklets: *Tortured for Christ. Fever: A True Story of Faith, Terror & Heroism. What Do We Think? The Greatest Is Love.* The Lionheart ignored the shops and the mosque, heading for the signposted tour of the Crusader City. They entered a gloomy vestibule with a post-office counter on one side and a ticket office on the other, from which the Stylite purchased two tickets and a brochure, shrugging off an insistent geriatric guide and propelling the Lionheart through into the Entrance Hall. A tall cavern centring around three great columns, according to the brochure: "Crusader at the base, Turkish in the upper structure." There was one other group of visitors in the hall, an old crotchety man in a wheelchair attended by two younger men, one, fussily dour, obviously his son, and two women, one large-boned and curious and the other red-headed and alert, about Richard's age (at his demise), whose grey eyes crossed his gaze briefly. The old man was declaiming:

"Look at it all. Dead and gone. Like a set of puffballs. And now even the worms are forgotten."

"History doesn't necessarily repeat itself, Papa," said the son.

"History can climb up my arse," said the old man.

The Lionheart pressed on, the Stylite following, through the lower intermediate hall to the Grand Maneir of the Hospitallers, another gloomy ruin, and through a narrow stone passage on into the crypt, whose massive arched columns rose to a full twelve metres. "I remember when we had the masons in," Richard reflected. "They did a proper job, right enough. All that bickering here, after the assassins killed Conrad of Montferrat. We had two days to decide the fate of the kingdom . . . We had cleaned up the hall, the Saracens had been using it for a granary. We housed the prisoners here for a while."

"Ah yes, the prisoners," mused the Stylite.

"Touting for confessions, old man?" The Stylite was silent, stroking his beard. "I did what had to be done," Richard said.

"I absolve no one of anything," said the Stylite, "Everyone has to carry his or her own burden. No credit, only cash."

The Lionheart grunted, and turned his attention towards a small square pit excavated in the centre of the hall, with a plaque declaring it, in English, Arabic and Hebrew, as the "Connected Passageway." "Ah, the tunnel!" the King cried, scrambling down the stone steps. "It's all coming back to me now. This is the shaft that led to all the escape routes, the moat, the wall, the pier, the land gate . . ."

"I wouldn't go down there if I were you," said the Stylite. "Stay above ground, that's my advice."

But the Lionheart stooped his tall head to fit under the low stone lintel. He called out, sending an echo bouncing off the narrow walls of the passageway. It could barely accommodate one person of medium height slightly crouched, as it bent off, lit by a row of bare lightbulbs. The stones were cold and dank to the touch, worn by the crawl of centuries. The King's voice reverbrated off the walls towards the Stylite, who remained above the entrance. "I can hear them, you know," it boomed. "The scampering feet, the clink of mail, clashing swords. These walls are dripping. Water, but also something thicker . . . My God, yes, there's blood here. I can smell it as if it were yesterday. The battle cries. The horses' hooves. The sweet strum of the troubadors' mandolins . . . *With numberless rich pennons streaming, flags and banners of fair seeming . . .*" His voice receded into longer echoes, becoming fainter and fainter as he pressed on down the tunnel, twisting into the blocked-off sections, advancing far beyond the lightbulbs, into unexcavated shafts, dwindling further and further, until only a fading whisper curled out: *"And other men, with drums and tabors, there were, who had no other labours, except upon their drums to hammer, and hoot, and shriek, and make great clamour . . ."* Then there was only the sharp squeak of bats scratching in hidden niches in the walls.

The Stylite waited a while, then turned back through the excavated halls towards the entrance, checking the deserted exit end of the tunnel, by the souvenir shop signed in four languages:

WELCOME TO THE PEACE CENTER.

BIENVENUE AU CENTRE DE LA PAIX.

WILKOMMEN IN SHALOM CENTER.

BIENVENIDOS AL CENTRO DE LA PAZ.

He bought four postcards of the town, two of the walls, one of the mosque, and another of an old Roberts lithograph of Saint Jean d'Acre from the sea (1839). Then he walked slowly out onto Chaim Weizman Street, Napoleon Street on his left and Cafarelli Street on his right, back to the Central Bus Station in the New Part of the town.

And it came to pass, in the six hundredth and first year, in the first month, the first day of the month, the waters were dried up from off the earth, and Noah

removed the covering of the Ark, and looked, and behold, the face of the ground was dry . . . And the Lord said in his heart: I will not again curse the ground any more for man's sake, for the imagination of man's heart is evil from his youth, neither will I again smite any more every thing living, as I have done. While the earth remaineth, seedtime and harvest, and cold and heat, and summer and winter, and day and night shall not cease . . .

A Glossolalia

of unusual words and phrases

Adam Kadmon: The primordial man, the metaphysical Adam of the Hebrew Kabbala, or esoteric lore. Perceived as a receptacle of the process by which the scattered sparks of divine creation are funnelled upwards towards their reconnection. Also another name for the biblical Adam.

Atbash cypher: A Kabbalistic form of interpreting the Torah as a cryptic code, substituting the first letter (א) with the last (ת), the second (ב) with the penultimate letter (ש), and so on. In short, everything is inverted.

Bobeh-mayses: Tall stories; literally "grandmothers' tales" (Yiddish).

Cafard: The "madness of the desert" which overtakes Foreign Legionnaires in old colonial tales.

End of Days: The Apocalypse, the time at the end of the world, preceding the Resurrection of the Dead, in all monotheistic religions. Many different dates have been given for this event, those of a spiritual bent often preferring an early schedule, for example, next Thursday at 2:00 P.M. while spoil-sport scientists have pushed it back to, say, A.D. 56,000,000.

Foile-shtik: Foul goings-on, monkey business (Yiddish).

Haggis: Scottish dish of minced meat in a casing of sheep's stomach.

Hamsin or *khamseen:* Heat-wave, emanating mainly from the desert, in which no wind or breeze disturbs the particles of sand suspended in the hot air (Arabic). Leads to cafard (q.v.).

Haroun-al-Rashid: Legendary caliph of the Abbasid Dynasty, A.D. 786 who ruled the great Arab civilisation of the East, from Baghdad, while Charlemagne ruled the barbarian Gauls in the West. Entered legend as the caliph whose reign is the setting for many of the *Arabian Nights* tales.

Hizbollah: Literally the "party of God." A political party formed in Lebanon in the aftermath of the Iranian Revolution of 1979, propagating an aggressive military version of traditional Shi'ite Moslem martyr-worship. It sprung from marginal status to centre stage in the wake of the Israeli invasion of Lebanon in 1982, and became globally notorious for its kidnapping of Western hostages in the mid-1980s. Its declared aim is an Islamic State, modelled on present-day Iran.

Intifada: A "shaking forth." An uprising — namely, the mass civil insurrection by Palestinians in the lands occupied by Israel since the Six-Day War of 1967 — which lasted from December 1987 through 1991 (Arabic).

Keech: Muck, excrement (Scottish slang, mainly Glasgow).

Loggie-Bird: Corruption of the name

435

John Logie Baird, inventor of television.

Mene Mene Tekel Upharsin: Anonymous graffiti on the walls of Babylon from the Book of Daniel (V: 25), interpreted as "God has got your number. You're finished. Piss off." Otherwise translated as "You have been weighed and found wanting."

Metempsychosis: The passing of the soul after death into another body — reincarnation. The Druze of Lebanon adhere to this belief of Hindu origin, claiming that "death is just like changing hats."

MREs: Meals-Ready-to-Eat, nicknamed "Meals-Rejected-by Ethiopians"; U.S. Army combat rations.

Mohel: The religious functionary who circumcises a Jewish male child at the age of eight days. If the infant is lucky, the *mohel* will have some medical knowledge.

Mutawaeen: The religious police in Saudi Arabia; "The Protectors of Virtue and Preventers of Vice," who enforce daily prayer and all religious observance (Arabic).

Nephilim: The primordial giants who once mated with humans but have preferred to withdraw into legend (Hebrew).

Oxters: Armpits (Scottish).

Pischifkes: Bits and bobs, assorted belongings (Yiddish).

PNC: Palestine National Council, the overall body representing all Palestinian political and social groups, in Palestine or abroad.

Shahid: The martyr for his faith, also for his nation. The one who is ready to die (Arabic).

Shunk: A toilet (Scottish slang, mainly Glasgow).

Stum: Silent, dumb, mute (Yiddish).

Stylite: A Holy man in the fourth century A.D. who adopted a solitary life, specifically, living on a pillar to be removed from the temptations of life. Very common in Syria during the early period of Gnostic Christianity.

Tamarindi man: A street vendor selling a sickly-sweet fruit juice from a specially constructed brass vessel with an elegant spout. Replaced by Coca-Cola machines.

UNRWA: The United Nation Relief and Works Agency. The main body in charge of the welfare of the refugees fleeing the War of 1948 in which the State of Israel was created. *UNRWA* ran schools, welfare centres and hospitals in the Palestinian refugee camps.

Timeline:

Background to the History of The Days of Miracles and Wonders

A.D. 0	Alleged date of birth of Jeshua the Nazarene (Bethlehem, Palestine).
390–459	Lifespan of Simon the Stylite, born Cilicia (Turkey), died Telanissus (a.k.a. Dar Sem'an, Syria).
433	Death of Saint Maro, or Maron, patron saint of the Lebanese Maronite Christians.
571	Birth of the Prophet Muhammad, at Mecca.
622	The "Hegira," or migration, of the Prophet Muhammed and his followers to the city of Medina, marking the year from which the Moslem lunar calendar commenced.
996	Eleven-year-old heir to the Fatimid caliphate in Egypt, al-Hakim, comes to the throne in Cairo.
1009	Al-Hakim, under the influence of mystic advisers, demolishes the Christian Holy Sepulchre in Jerusalem. Ten years later, under the influence of the mystic al-Darazi, al-Hakim proclaims himself an emanation of the Deity.
1021	Al-Hakim vanishes without trace. His sixteen-year-old son, al-Zahir, reverses his father's "reforms."
1095	Announcement by Pope Urban at Clermont, France, of a "Crusade" to free the Eastern Christians from the "Turks."
1099	The armies of the First Crusade reach and conquer Jerusalem, slaughtering thousands of Moslems and Jews in the city.
1187	The sultan Saladin, Kurdish leader of Egypt, defeats the crusader armies at "the Horns of Hittin" in Galilee and then retakes Jerusalem. Some months later, the English prince, Richard, son of King Henry II, "takes the cross" and vows to go on Crusade.

1189	13 September — Richard I crowned King of England. After attending briefly to the affairs of the realm, Richard leaves on his promised Crusade.
1190	Winter — Richard consults the hermit Joachim of Fiore, in Sicily, about his role in the coming Apocalypse of Revelations.
1191	Summer — Richard sails for Acre, Palestine, lays siege to the city and takes it from Saladin's Moslem forces. Impatient to march on to Jaffa, massacres 2,500 Moslem prisoners in Acre.
1191–92	Richard marches on but never reaches Jerusalem, retiring from the Holy Land to become a prisoner in Europe (1193) before regaining his throne.
1258–60	The invading Mongols sack Baghdad but are defeated in Palestine by the Moslem sultan Baybars.
1291	Acre falls to the Moslems.
1798–99	Napoleon of France mounts his expedition to Egypt, but is defeated by local leader al-Jazzar ("The Butcher") at the walls of Acre.
1914–18	The First World War leads to the defeat of the Turkish Ottoman Empire by Britain and France and the setting up of colonial protectorates, British in Palestine, Transjordan, and Iraq, and French in Syria, including Lebanon.
1920–22	The French divide Syria into separate "autonomous" states, with "Greater Lebanon" receiving a special status on account of its large Christian population.
1939–45	The Second World War weakens colonial hold of the Allies on the Middle East.

1943	A "National Pact" between different communities in Lebanon provides a blueprint for a kind of power-sharing in which Lebanese Christians have a built-in advantage against Moslems and Druze.
1946	Lebanon becomes nominally independent of the French.
1948	The State of Israel is proclaimed, leading to civil war between Palestinian Arabs and Jews, and resulting in Arab defeat and more than one million Palestinian refugees.
1958	American marines land in Lebanon to shore up the Christian-dominated government against a revolt by mainly Moslem supporters of Egypt's revolutionary leader, Colonel Nasser.
1967	The Six-Day War between Israel and Egypt, Jordan and Syria, leading to the occupation of the "West Bank" and Gaza.
1975–76	The first civil war in Lebanon between the growing Palestinian guerrilla movement and the Christian forces, supported by Syria.
1982	Israel's invasion of Lebanon to "root out" Palestinian "terrorists."
	September — The massacre of Palestinian civilians in the refugee "camps" of Sabra and Shatila.
1985–87	The "Camps war" in Beirut, between the Shi'ite militia and the Palestinians besieged in their ghettos.
1987	December — Commencement of the Palestinian *intifada* against Israeli occupation.
1989	July 14 — Bicentennial celebrations in Paris. Civil war in Lebanon sputters on under auspices of Christian warlord, General Aoun.
	July 16 — Richard the Lionheart walks out of his grave.

1989	October–December — Collapse of the communist regimes in Europe. Commencement of the "Post-Communist World."
1990	August — Iraq's invasion of Kuwait, leading to —
1991	January–February — The "Gulf War" of the United States and allies against Iraq.
	March–April — Uprising, repression and exodus of the Iraqi Kurds.